2-

LIAR'S MOON

LIAR'S MOON

MOON

ELIZABETH C. BUNCE

ARTHUR A. LEVINE BOOKS

An Imprint of Scholastic Inc.

Library of Congress Cataloging-in-Publication Data

Bunce, Elizabeth C.
    Liar's moon / Elizabeth C. Bunce. — 1st ed.
       p. cm.
    Sequel to: StarCrossed.
    Summary: In a quest to prove her friend, Lord Durrel Decath, innocent of the murder
of his wife, pickpocket Digger stumbles into a conspiracy with far-reaching consequences
for the civil war raging in Llyvraneth, while also finding herself falling in love.
    ISBN 978-0-545-13608-2 (hardback : alk. paper)   [1. Fantasy. 2. Murder — Fiction.
3. Fugitives from justice — Fiction. 4. Magic — Fiction. 5. Robbers and outlaws —
Fiction. 6. Social classes — Fiction. 7. Mystery and detective stories.] I. Title.
    PZ7.B91505Li 2011
    [Fic] — dc22

                                                                      2011005071

Map art by Mike Schley copyright © 2011 by Stephanie Elizabeth Bunce
Book design by Phil Falco

10 9 8 7 6 5 4 3 2   12 13 14 15

Printed in the U.S.A.   23
First edition, November 2011

TABLE OF CONTENTS

Gerse

Oss Gate

Charicaux

High Gate

Stantin

Hobin

River Oss

Koya

Nob Circle

High St.

Harvest "Green" Gate

Warehouses

Third Circle

N
W   E
S

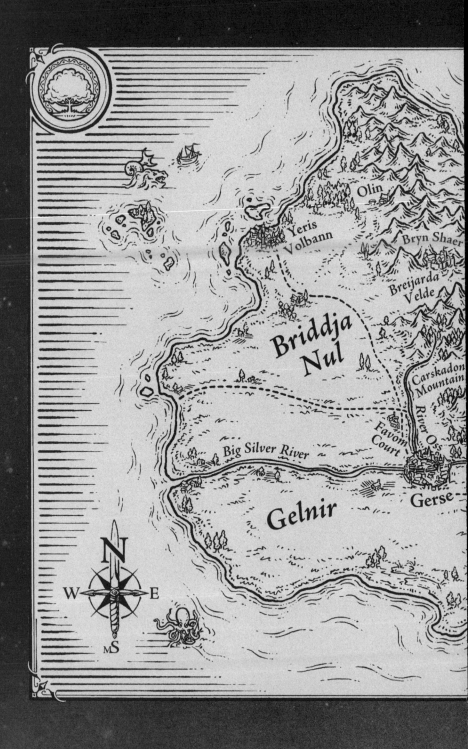

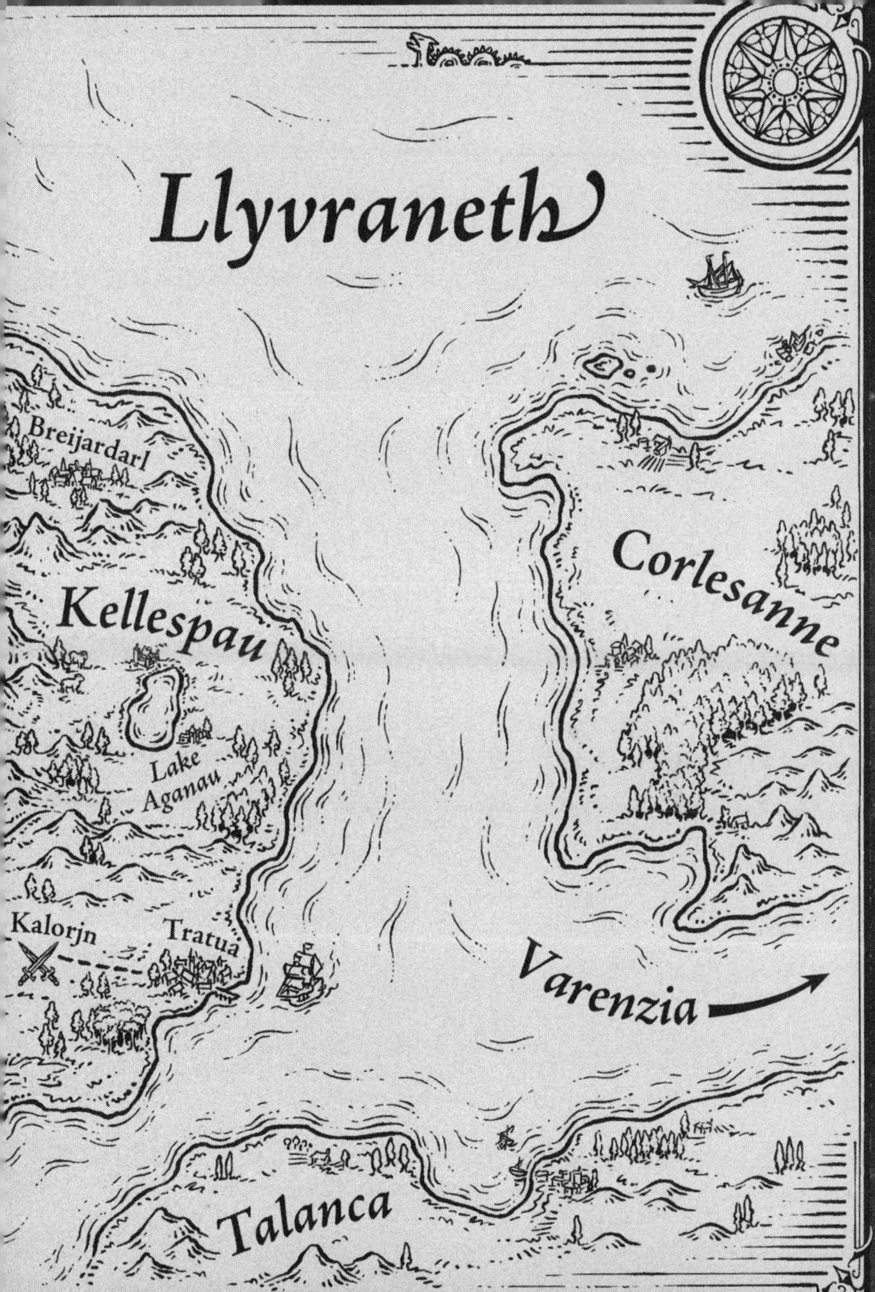

Llyvraneth
Breijardarl
Kellespau
Lake
Aganau
Kalorjn
Tratua
Corlesanne
Varenzia
Talanca

PART I

KEEP YOUR
HEAD DOWN

CHAPTER ONE

I'd have gotten away if that little guard hadn't cracked me in the eye. His elbow hit me sharp against my cheekbone and sent me reeling. I stumbled backward, blinded, straight into the waiting arms of his partner. The captain.

An arm clamped around my neck and I couldn't pull away. Squirming in his grip, I kicked out and promptly had my legs seized by the little one and a third man, who hoisted me high between them. One of them whipped out a rope and had my feet tied together before I had a chance to struggle. I opened my mouth to scream, and the captain shoved a filthy rag in my mouth. I gagged, and the men laughed.

"Got her. Easy night's work. Let's get our goods delivered and get home to our wives." The captain twisted hard on my arms until my whole body shrieked with pain. All I could see was his leering face, swimming above me as he swung me easily over his shoulder. I fought back nausea as we bounced along; the last thing I needed was to choke to death on my own vomit before I managed to learn what was happening to me.

It had been a normal night, more or less. I'd dodged the curfew and set up my patch on the riverfront, near some of the seedier taverns belching out their night's clientele of drunken merchants' sons and slumming nobs. Their purses were emptier this late at night, but pickings were easier with them well lubricated. Nobody would get rich off scrum like that, but I couldn't afford to be picky these days.

Shadows gathered beneath the unlit flamboys; the city had stopped paying to light our less prosperous neighborhoods. I was settling into the darkness when three dark figures melted out of the alley and strolled past me, the wrong direction to have come from one of the bars.

I heard a voice say, "That's her," and didn't even think to be nervous.

Until the blackjack hit me squarely in the back and sent me facedown into the gutter. For a moment I was too stunned to move, just lay there, breathless, the voice echoing in my brain, all wrong. *That's her.* That's *her.* Not *him* — and I was dressed in men's clothes, filthy trunk hose with a ridiculous codpiece, my hair tucked up in an oversized cap. There was nothing feminine about me. Oh, hells.

I scrambled to my feet and spun around. Three of them, in red uniforms. This was not a fight I could win. Still, I dodged and swung out hard, catching the middle guy in the gut. I shoved him into the biggest one, the one with the gold badge on his chest and the blackjack swinging casually from his meaty fist. I turned to run — and that's when the little one came out of nowhere and clipped me in the eye.

We trotted along at a pretty good pace, but I couldn't track our location, not with the world lurching past upside down. Gray cobbles, dark pinkish cobbles, gray again — oh, very useful. I craned my neck to see if I could recognize the footings of any buildings and nearly passed out from dizziness.

"Keep your head down, thief." And as if I needed help with that, a stinking hand shoved me hard in the face.

"Easy there. We don't get paid extra for bruises."

For some reason, that sounded notable, but the blood rushing through my brain made it hard to focus. How had they found me? Why? I thought I'd been careful, but maybe they'd finally tracked me down, linked me to the rebels.

But the Night Watch didn't bother Sarists and magic users. Even through the roar of blood in my head, something about this didn't make sense.

The captain came to an abrupt stop, swinging me partly around as he turned. I caught a glimpse of pale stone wall, nearly white in the waning moonlight, and an impossibly tidy flagstone walkway, and I felt every aching muscle in my body tighten.

This wasn't the Cages, the city gaol. And, of all the stupidity — these weren't Watchmen. Red-and-gold livery meant *royal* guards, and the high white wall topped with its iron spikes and shattered glass was the Keep. The king's prisons.

"Mmmph!" I struggled then, flailing at the captain with my feet and bound hands.

"That's enough of that," one of the others said, and clapped me hard on the side of the head. The captain shucked me off his shoulder and plucked out the gag, and I stood, wavering, just inside the ironbound gatehouse of the Keep. A bristly, one-eyed guard pawed at me, turning my head to look under my chin, patting at my legs and chest. For weapons, I hoped. His grimy fingers lingered too long against my throat, and I slapped his hands away with my bound ones.

"Boy's a fighter, then," the guard said. "He'll be popular with them nobs."

Well, at least my disguise had worked on *somebody*.

"What is this?" I demanded. "Why are you arresting me?" Though *kidnapping* might have been more accurate.

The guard shrugged and flipped through a battered ledger book. "Take it up with the magistrate at your trial date."

"No!" My voice verged on panic. "Let me go — I haven't done anything!"

But the guard had turned away to the rear of the gatehouse, where he now worked a massive hand-crank set into the stone wall. From above came an ungodly screech and clank of metal on wood; at our feet, the splash and ripple of ink-dark water. The Keep sat on an island in the middle of the Llyd Tsairn, the Big Silver river, a bowshot from the king's royal palace. The only access was by way of a drawbridge mounted on the opposite bank and operated from the guardhouse. Or on the coroner's barge, sailing out from the executioner's block.

The red guards who'd nabbed me lingered outside the gatehouse, as the captain emptied out a purse among his fellows. I frowned, but the bridge slammed down with a shudder that shook the whole gatehouse and drew my attention elsewhere. The maw of the Keep doorway across the river gaped black in the distance as two more guards in royal livery stepped onto the bridge, an iron chain swinging between them. Smoky torches made long shadows on the narrow wooden planks. The gate-keeper hauled up the gate and gave me a little nudge toward the landing.

"Get on, then, boy," he said. "No way out now but over." The iron bars crashed down behind me once again. I felt cold all through. Everyone knew the trial was a fairy tale; people thrown to the Keep waited months or years for a magistrate's appearance that might never come. The guards crossed over the river in practiced, easy strides, and just when I'd more or less decided to take my chances with the Big Silver — not that I could swim with my hands bound — they shoved me before them onto the narrow, railing-less bridge.

I cast one last glance at the water behind me as they pulled me through the prison gates.

"That's two marks," the guard at the gate said to me. They charged for *everything* in the gaols, including, it seemed, the privilege to be dragged off to your cell.

I lifted my chin and glared at him. "Bite me," I said, and another heavy fist clapped into my head.

They led me through a twisting knot of noisy corridors obviously designed to upset one's sense of direction. But I kept my eyes open, counting the turns and staircases and committing them to memory. After a long, spiral stair winding up the core of the tower, the guards let me out onto the top floor of the Keep. Sallow torchlight flickered wanly, illuminating a long, gloomy passage lined with sturdy, ironbound doors, one tiny, barred window set high in the wall at the very end letting in the ghost of the moonslight.

My guard stopped before a cell and banged on the door. "Your *lord-ship*," he called, and I could hear the sneer in his voice, "someone's sent you a present. Quite a pretty lad this time." A finger stroked along my ear, and it took all my restraint not to bite him. He heaved the door open, and I stumbled forward, pitching headlong into the cell and landing hard on my knees. The door clanged shut behind me. Scuffling through the filthy rushes, I got my back against a wall and set about trying to wriggle out of my bonds.

"Damn it." I heard a soft voice from the dark recesses of the cell. "This stopped being amusing several days ago." Another sound — quick and light, a flint striking — and the cell wavered into a faint, sickly glow. I blinked and reached instinctively for any weapon, but they'd taken my knife and there wasn't anything else at hand.

"Stop right there," I said, but I didn't sound terribly convincing.

"Look, I'm not going to hurt you," said a tired voice, and my cell mate stepped forward, bending low over me. "They'll get tired of the game eventually and move you down a level, so you'd better enjoy your-self while you're up here. There's fresh water — well, relatively fresh, anyway — on the table."

I stayed where I was, my thoughts tumbling. My companion — *your lordship*, my guard had called him; a nob, maybe? — crouched before me. He didn't look much like a nob, in his torn shirt and no doublet, with unshaven cheeks and a fading bruise under one eye, but he held out his hand.

My head pounded brutally, and I felt disoriented. In my confusion, my cell mate looked almost familiar.

"That's a nasty gash," he said, reaching for my face. I knocked his grubby hand away. "Easy," he said. "I won't hurt you, but you need to relax so I can see what they've done to you. You must have put up quite a fight; they don't usually come in quite so . . . used up. Here, sit up into the light."

Warily I let him draw me forward to a plain frame table and benches in the middle of the cell. Something about the smooth curve of his jaw, the bend of his neck as he leaned over me . . . I winced, trying to shake my head.

"What's your name?" he said.

I paused, considering. Who should I be this time? Maybe I could play this — and my wealthy cell mate — to my advantage. Boy or girl? Would tears help? I sat forward and pulled off my hat, letting my braided hair, coiled round my head, show I was a girl.

"I don't believe it." My companion held up the candle. "Am I delirious?"

"Not unless we both are," I said. Because I was looking into the haunted eyes of Durrel Decath, a young man who'd once saved my life.

CHAPTER TWO

"Celyn?" Durrel sounded tentative, incredulous. He'd known me only by that name, a silly last-minute alias I'd concocted on the spot (and then had to live with) last fall, when he'd whisked me aboard a boatload of his nob friends and gotten me out of the city after I'd run afoul of Greenmen during a robbery that had ended badly. A friend had died on that job — more than a friend — and I was still making up for it, months later.

I hadn't thought to meet the scion of the House of Decath ever again. Certainly not under such circumstances. Though given the twisted humor of the gods, why was I surprised?

"Milord," I said, cautious. He'd changed since I'd seen him last, grown thin and ragged and almost unrecognizable. "What's going on? What are you doing here?"

"I don't know," Durrel said. "This is very odd. You're injured." I touched my face, which was streaked with blood from the cut under my eye. "Let's get you cleaned up, at least."

"I don't —"

"Hist." He helped me untie the ropes on my wrists and ankles, then dabbed at my cheek with a rag dipped in water, wincing as he looked at me. "This should have stitches," he said.

"Stop. Will you *explain*? Why are you in prison? Why am I in your cell?" The rising weirdness put me on edge. The guard saying, "That's her," the money changing hands at the prison gates, getting dumped in a cell with a nobleman I almost knew . . . Fickle Tiboran, god of thieves and liars, might love coincidence, but I was suspicious.

Durrel dropped the rag on the table. He looked older than I remembered; he was twenty-one, but there had been something boyish about him that was gone now. "Unfortunately I'm afraid I can't answer the last question. I'm just as perplexed to see you." He held my gaze steady. "But in regard to your other question, they think I murdered my wife."

I sat back, stunned. When I'd left him last fall, he was heading off to be wed, in an arranged marriage to one Talth Ceid, a woman much older than he was. The Ceid had been ruthless in their conquest of Gerse's waterfronts a hundred years before, while the Decath were nothing if not respectable. Durrel's marriage linked one of the city's most powerful merchant families with one of its oldest noble houses, and it had all seemed like a completely sensible match for rich folk.

Still, I'd known Durrel wasn't exactly happy about it; he had, in fact, fled the betrothal ceremony in a drunken escapade, sailing out of the city with his cousin and two other nobs. It was that debauched party I had blundered into, those sauced-up young nobles who'd given me refuge. A few months later, I'd heard the marriage had gone through, and though it was clearly never going to be a love match, it hadn't seemed likely to end in *murder*.

Durrel saw the expression on my face and gave an attempt at a wan smile. "It surprised me too." He wrung out the rag and wet it again in cleaner water.

"Let me do that," I said impatiently, tugging it out of his hands. "You just talk." I held the cloth hard against my throbbing cheekbone.

He stood up and paced into the shadows, disappearing for a moment. "It's difficult to explain," he said. "Even now I hardly believe it's happening. One moment I'm a married man, and the next I'm in here, a murderer."

"Tell me what happened," I said gently, because there was something wrong here beyond the obvious.

"She was poisoned. A — a fortnight ago, I think. What day is it?" He pushed his unkempt hair from his forehead. "It seemed like suicide, at first, but I didn't believe it. I found her, the next morning —" He faltered, taking a swig of his water like he wished it was something else. "It wasn't pretty. I didn't know what to do. I sent for my father and the surgeon, but it was too late. The coroner identified the poison as something called Tincture of the Moon."

"I've heard of that," I said. "It's rare. Expensive. Hard to distill, harder still to get hold of." They said you went numb and cold, bit by bit, until the poison reached your heart — unable to speak, unable to move, until you drowned in your own blood. Hours of silent agony. "It wouldn't be anybody's first choice for suicide." That was only half the story, though. "But why *you*? How could anyone think you'd killed somebody?"

"Isn't it always the husband?" A twisted smile tried to form itself on his lips, but died prematurely. "They found a vial of the tincture in my rooms. But it wasn't mine —" He turned back. "They're going to execute me, Celyn."

A chill washed through me. My knowledge of nob murder trials was only sketchy; commoners were liable to be summarily executed as soon as the Watch reviewed the evidence. More than one bar fight had ended when the instigators were strung up on makeshift gibbets outside the tavern door. But for someone of Lord Durrel's stature, and a victim as important as a member of the House of Ceid, they'd probably be a little more careful. Noblemen accused of crimes were tried before the king, in royal courts — but the king was ill, maybe dying, and all royal courts had been suspended because of the war.

Still, the biggest risk I could see came not from the king's justice, but the Ceid's. Everyone in Gerse knew what they were capable of, though nobs and officials turned blind eyes. Foe, friend, family — it didn't matter, if you crossed the Ceid. A blade in the back, a pistol shot to that downy head; Durrel looked scared, and he had reason to be.

"I didn't do it," Durrel said.

I glanced up into his shadowed face. "Of course you didn't," I said. "You couldn't have killed anybody. I don't believe it."

Durrel looked hard at me for a moment, then everything in him seemed to slump. "Thank you," he breathed. "I don't think I realized how badly I needed to hear that."

"You can spare your gratitude." I tried to say it lightly. "Your cell mate's word probably doesn't carry a lot of weight."

"It does with me," he said, and there was something low and urgent and desperate in his expression. I pulled away and left the table, crossing the cell and peering into corners, tapping at the edges of the door, kicking aside the filthy rushes with my toe.

"Keep talking," I said, giving the lock on the door my attention. Of all the idiotic times to leave my lock picks at home. "Why did you have the poison?"

"I *didn't*. I don't know why they found it in my quarters. I have no idea how it got there. What are you doing?"

"Looking for a way out." The lock on the door was solid and huge, but that just meant the tumblers inside were bigger and easier to reach. Of course, that left the problem of what to do once the cell door was open.

"We're locked in a cell at Bryn Tsairn Prison. There's no way out."

"Ha," I said. "You've never been locked up with me before." Although, strictly speaking, I'd never actually *escaped* from a prison cell; the two previous times I'd been arrested, my business associates had bailed me out. I grabbed the bars on the cell door's little window and hauled myself up to peer into the hallway. One lonely torch burned out of sight, splashing ominous shadows on the walls and ceiling.

"Hey." Durrel's voice came gently through the stifling darkness. I dropped back to the ground and gave the locked door one last tug. "Easy, Celyn. We're not going anywhere, at least until morning. And you need to rest, with those injuries. Come back to the fire and sit down."

"The fire?" I tried to scowl, but my face hurt too much.

"The candle, then." He held out his hand, creased with prison dirt though it was, and I let him lead me back to the table. I sat obediently, but my mind was still turning over the problem of the lock and an escape.

"Talk to me," he said. "Tell me what you've been doing since I saw you last. I thought you were going to stay out of trouble."

That startled a laugh out of me. "I *try*, milord. Can I help it if trouble has other plans? And besides, who sent me into the nest of Sarist rebels?"

"Ouch!" Durrel's hand flew to his tattered shirt, as if I'd wounded him. "How was I to know my aunt was going to start a war? And from what I hear, *you* were not wholly blameless in that affair. I looked for you," he added, sobering. "Meri told me you came back to the city, but I didn't know how to find you."

"I —" I faltered. I never knew what to say about last winter, about the Nemair, the family who took me in and sheltered me from the Inquisition; about witnessing the start of the civil war that now spread through Llyvraneth like flames through a library; about Prince Wierolf, and Meri, and all the others. About not *wanting* to be found again. "I don't know what you heard, but —"

"You were a hero," he said. "You saved Meri's life. You saved the *prince*." He leaned closer, and there was a strange, earnest spark in his eyes. "Is that why you're in here? Something to do with — *the rebellion*?"

Durrel mouthed those last words, and I scowled, considering. Was it possible? I'd been on the wrong side at the Siege of Bryn Shaer; perhaps the king was rounding up everyone with any tenuous Sarist connections, as he'd done before. And mine were rather more than tenuous, or at least they had been.

"I thought so, but it doesn't feel right," I said. "They grabbed me off the street in the middle of the night. Traitors to the Crown are usually arrested with a little more ceremony, so everyone can quake in fear of the king's wrath. This feels more like Greenmen — but these guys weren't Greenmen."

"And even if you were arrested for your ties to the rebels, it's highly improbable for you to end up in here with me. We're not so overcrowded at Bryn Tsairn that we need to double up on accommodations."

He was right. There was something else here, something lower and stranger than royal politics. "Somebody apparently paid a fair coin for the privilege of sending you a thief," I said. "The question is who, and why? That guard said somebody sent you a present. What did he mean?"

"I just assumed he was playing with me; 'Bait the Nob' is a grand sport here at the Keep." Durrel spoke slowly, as if turning a thought over to examine it. "You think he might have been serious; someone — *sent* you to me? To what end? That doesn't make any sense."

"Oh,. milord," I said. "I've learned it's easier if you stop expecting things to make sense." I rose slowly and leaned back against the wood. "It would appear we have a common enemy. Who have you pissed off?"

He eyed me evenly. "You mean besides Talth's family?"

"Well, that's no good. I've had no dealings with them at all. Is that it? No dark secrets in Durrel Decath's past or present?" My voice was as light as I could make it, and Durrel shook his head. I frowned. My own list was definitely longer — dissatisfied clients and frustrated assassins, disgruntled former rebels, jealous nobs. Inquisitors. The standard assortment. "There must be someone else. Could it have anything to do with the war?" Even now, magic-tolerant Sarists commanded by Prince Wierolf were advancing on the city, pressing with surprising success against Prince Astilan's royal troops. "Where do the Decath stand?"

"Where they've always stood, off to the side where they can't get into trouble. Waiting for the pieces to fall so they can still be everyone's friends when it's over." I thought I heard an edge of bitterness in his voice. "But what about you? I seem to recall there was rather more about you than you originally let on."

That was no surprise; my relation to the High Inquisitor had become a more or less public secret in the last few months. "But no one knows I'm back in the city," I said — which wasn't *strictly* true — "and even if they did, they'd be looking for a waiting gentlewoman, not —"

"A ragtag, street-brawling urchin?"

I had to grin. "Something like that."

Durrel gave my stained and rumpled men's clothes a critical eye. "I think I preferred your last disguise."

"Runaway nun?"

"More romantic, definitely."

"Well, that's what I was going for." This conversation was ridiculous, but I couldn't help it. Lord Durrel was too easy to talk to.

"This is probably not the time to mention that you should maybe have stayed out of the city," he said, a quirk to his lip.

I shook my head. "I had to come back. I had friends here, and —"

"No, I get it," he said. "It's home."

Home. I wasn't even sure what that meant anymore. I leaned my head against the curving stone wall of the cell. It was late and surreal, and the bumps on my head were taking their toll.

After a silent moment, Durrel straddled the bench and poured out another cup of the stale water. "Maybe we're looking at this the wrong way," he said. "Maybe we're not looking for a mutual enemy, but a friend."

I choked on my water. "I thought I'd gotten past the sorts of friends who have you arrested."

Though we ran through our tiny circle of shared acquaintances once more — many of them his cousin's family, who'd taken me in for the winter, and all their friends and allies — we had no better luck. I couldn't fathom any of the Nemair or their fellow Sarists having me arrested.

"We're left with a puzzle," Durrel said, and there was a lively spark to his voice that seemed all out of place.

"Pox," I said. "I hate puzzles."

"Surely we'll know more come morning," he said. "Our — friend — must have some plan."

"I hate waiting too," I said, and personally didn't care to stick around to learn the plans of people who randomly had their acquaintances arrested. But it seemed I didn't have a choice about that, so I plied the rest of Durrel's story from him.

It seemed their marriage, however promising on paper, was troubled from the beginning. Talth, generally accounted a respectable widow, turned out to be cold and controlling, unaffectionate but to her four children, and kept Durrel on a tight leash, like a prize dog she'd bought to show off to her rich friends. By the time his tale wound round to the night of the murder, a dark picture had emerged. An overheard quarrel, a witness who saw Durrel leaving his wife's bedchamber, the empty poison bottle in his rooms.

"But I didn't do it," he insisted. "Her maid is lying. I left Talth's rooms at midnight; she can't have seen me there two hours later."

"And no one can confirm your story? That you were alone in your own quarters all night?"

"*I* can barely confirm my story," he said. "I don't remember much about that night. I — I was angry, and there was . . . rather a lot of wine involved." He gave a mirthless laugh. "One thing she wasn't stingy with was her wine cellar."

"What was the fight about?"

He shrugged. "Money, Koya, who knows. Nothing, anything. I barely *knew* the woman, Celyn, but apparently she'd decided to hate me almost as soon as we were married."

"So in a drunken rage, angry over money, you broke into her rooms in the middle of the night and poisoned her."

"I know it looks bad. Her family is convinced I'm guilty, and —" He faltered and stared up at the ceiling. "And so's mine."

"I don't believe that," I said. I had met his parents, Lord Ragn Decath, his genial, good-natured father, and a sweet, soft-spoken stepmother, Amalle. They'd been kind to me, when their son thought I was an errant Aspirant on the run from convent school. I had liked them.

But I'd touched a nerve. Durrel's expression grew closed. He shook his head. "Amalle has left the city, and my father won't see me. He hasn't come or even sent word since I was arrested." He rose and crossed the cell, looked out the high, barred window at the fading sky. "We've talked the moons down. The guards will be back on duty soon."

"And then what?" I said. Bludgeon the one who brought breakfast and steal his keys? Not a *terrible* plan, the more I thought about it.

He sat beside me. "It seems the gods keep throwing us in each other's paths, Celyn Contrare," he said. "I say we see what they have in store."

He sounded so patently silly that I had to laugh. This entire situation was completely cracked, but it was almost worth it, to see Lord Durrel again. "That sounds like one of your friend Raffin's lines," I said. Raffin Taradyce had been the engineer of Durrel's escape (and mine) from Gerse last year.

He did grin then, but sobered quickly. "Speaking of, I have news you won't like. Raffin's joined the Guard."

I felt my eyes narrow. "City or royal?"

"Ah, no . . ." Durrel was shaking his head, almost wincing. "Acolyte."

I shouldn't have gone cold all over, but I couldn't help it. Durrel Decath's best friend was now a Greenman, one of the brutal henchmen of the Inquisition who tore children from their beds and tortured their victims in secret dungeons all over the city in their ruthless quest for magic users and heretics. All in the name of Celys, our great Mother Goddess. I clutched at my bare wrist, where I'd once worn a silver bracelet given to me by Meri Nemair. It was too dangerous to wear silver in the city now; the slightest glint of the metal would condemn you as a magic user. "His father's idea?"

"Who else?"

I sighed. "Remind me to tell you how I met Lord Taradyce sometime."

"Hist," Durrel said. Outside in the hall, we heard footsteps, then a loud bang on the door, and a guard threw it open with a godless crash.

"You there, girl," he said. "You've made bail. You're out of here."

I scrambled to my feet, Durrel behind me. "Who?" I demanded. "How?"

The guard shrugged. "You want out of here or not?"

I turned back to Durrel, feeling suddenly helpless.

"Go," he urged.

"I don't want to leave you."

"It's not so bad," he said. "The most surprising people pop in to see me."

The guard was glaring at me in brutish impatience, and as he edged me toward the door, Durrel called my name. I hung back. "Can you get a message to my father?"

"I'll try. What do you want me to say?" The guard had hold of me now and was pulling me into the hallway. Durrel looked flustered, perplexed. "Think on it," I said. "And tell me next time."

"You can't come back here! It's too dangerous."

"There are visiting days every week," I said. "I'll come then."

The guard slammed the door hard between us, but I watched over my shoulder as pale fingers curled through the bars in the tiny window.

CHAPTER THREE

Outside the gates, across the drawbridge, a lanky young man in a ridiculous powder blue satin suit leaned casually against a rain barrel.

"Rat?" I raised my arm against the piercing sunlight. "What are you doing here?"

"I believe that's *my* line. Gods!" Rat jumped as I lowered my arm from my face. "Marau's balls, Digger. I hope somebody's bleeding in the street somewhere thanks to you."

"How did you find me?"

"Were you expecting someone else? It hurts just to *look* at you." Rat winced, leaning in to inspect my bruised eye and gashed cheek. "I have a boat, thank the gods. If they'll even let you on. You smell like —"

"I know what I smell like." A hired river launch bobbed nearby, and I hobbled toward it. "How did you know where I was?" I repeated, lowering myself into the boat — without any help from Rat, I'll note. He hopped down after me and told the boatman where to take us.

Rat, properly Halcot Granthin, my roommate, produced a slip of paper from his doublet. "They sent a note." I unfolded the page, a crisp sheet of stationery so white it was almost too bright to look at directly. *Your lodger has been arrested. Fifty marks bond to release her from the Keep.* "Aunt Grea found it under the bakery door this morning. By all the hells, what were you *doing*?"

"Working. Red guards pinched me in Markettown."

"Entertaining," he said, obviously waiting for more.

"You do it next time." There was nothing on the paper to give up its origins.

"Recognize the handwriting?"

"No." It was neat and featureless schoolroom calligraphy, carefully anonymous. And unsigned, of course. "Thank you," I added belatedly. "I owe you fifty marks." Not that I had any idea where it was going to come from.

"Lucky again. They sent the money too. But you *do* owe me new trunk hose. You've ruined my favorite pair." He leaned in distastefully and plucked at the stained fabric near my knee.

"Oh, they weren't either. I pulled these out of the fireplace."

"Evidently."

The pier where we were moored was crowded, mostly with Watch craft unloading prisoners. I seemed to be the only one getting *out* of the Keep this morning. In among the city boats were two long, gilded vessels packed with soldiers in green livery — more of the king's army being shipped into the city to remind us all to stay in line. Above the horizon of buildings on the opposite shore, a sliver of green glass dome colored the sky: the Celystra, visible from nearly every point in the city.

Tensions in Gerse had always been high, but now that we were finally, openly, at civil war, it was even worse. Soldiers patrolled the streets and waterways, and the city had closed down most of the markets, lest we citizens gather and start a riot. There was hardly anything to buy now, anyway, with the troops outside Gerse diverting most of the food and goods from the farms of Gelnir for their own use. Neighbors kept their doors and windows closed fast, and nobody met each other's eyes. Everyone was afraid of glancing up and recognizing enemy sympathies in people they'd lived and worked beside all their lives. As the summer days grew hot and long, the king's grip on the city grew so tight we could barely breathe.

The boat slipped into the current, and I settled back into the cramped seat, reaching to pull my cap over my eyes. My fingers closed on air; I must have forgotten it in Durrel's cell. I couldn't shake that final image of him watching me, one hand reaching out as I walked away. What had happened to him? It was hard to reconcile the hopeless young man I'd just left with the gallant, good-humored nob who'd plucked me from the riverbank and swept me to safety last fall.

Rat was watching me. "What?" I said crossly.

"Just making sure you weren't going to career out of the boat," he said. "You're about to tip over, you know."

I hunched lower. "Have you heard anything about the murder of a nobleman's wife recently — a Talth Ceid?"

The expression on Rat's face was immeasurable, and even the boatman turned to stare at me. "Where have *you* been, then?" the sailor asked, then reddened under his sun-weathered skin, the shadow of the Keep still darkening the water before us. "Oh."

Rat wasn't so polite. "Honestly, don't you pay attention to anything? Lord Durrel killing Talth Ceid is the only thing anyone's talked about for the last two weeks!"

"Just fill me in," I said. "My head hurts."

"I should think so," he said. "Well, it's brewing into quite the scandal. It seems that things behind closed doors at the Ceid household were not so dignified after all."

"What kind of scandal?"

"Talth's daughter, to start," Rat said in a low voice. "They're saying there might have been more than paternal affection between Talth's oldest and her stepfather."

"What?" It took a moment for my sluggish brain to work through that. "You mean, Durrel and —?"

"Koya," Rat supplied. "And it's not quite as seedy as it sounds. She must be well into her third age by now, and Lord Durrel's only just a man. Or so I've heard."

"And that's why he supposedly killed her? For this Koya?"

"Or for the money. You can pick your motive — no, really, odds makers on Bonelicker Way are taking wagers for it — but apparently the Decath got the marriage settlement back *and* the house on Garrison Street when his lordship's wife was so conveniently dispatched. Not that any of them will do him much good where he's at now. The Ceid are screaming for Lord Durrel's blood, and the way things look, I think they'll get it." Rat's gaze had gone narrow. "Why all these questions?"

I scratched at the back of my head, gingerly probing one of the bruises. "Apparently I've just spent the night in a cell with the city's most celebrated murder suspect."

Rat's expression was carefully neutral. "*That's* what this is about? How do these things happen to you?"

"I know him," I said. "Oh, don't give me that look. You've heard that story a dozen times."

"I didn't realize he was *that* Durrel Decath."

I turned the anonymous note over in my hands. "I don't think he did it," I said.

"He should find that encouraging, since you're obviously an expert on the case."

"Maybe I am," I said, fingering the ink on the paper. Maybe whoever'd had me arrested really was trying to give Durrel a gift — the gift of a light-fingered sneak thief all too adept at digging up nobs' secrets. "Can you find out where this paper came from?" I handed the letter back to Rat. He was the son of a cloth merchant, but he had a talent for procuring any number of oddments — contraband wine, rare imported tobacco, more exotic entertainments — at below-market prices, without ever technically stealing any of it. If I wanted expensive white notepaper, or information about it, Rat could get it for me.

"Isn't that your area of expertise?" he said. "Very well. And if I find your mysterious stationer, then what?"

"We figure out who wrote this note." And had me arrested, and be one step closer to unraveling the tangle that Durrel and I were both in.

The boat finally pulled up alongside the Bargewater Street landing, and Rat helped me up to the street in front of his aunt's bakery. The hot, yeasty scent wafting from the ovens was sour with the acrid tinge of old smoke.

"Another burning?"

Rat nodded toward the alley, his face grim. "That family with the twins. Nobody's seen them in about a week, and last night the Guard came and emptied their house into the street."

Down the side street a blackened heap still smoldered on the cobbles. "Was anyone —?"

"No," he said quickly. "It's just their belongings. What was left of them, anyway. Crockery, bedding. Books. Apparently they were running quite a trade in seditious literature. We're lucky they didn't burn the whole block. Bardolph must be feeling lenient these days."

I breathed through my mouth to quench the smoke smell, but couldn't draw my eyes away from the dying bonfire. Just last week I'd seen those twin boys tussling in the street. It had taken me a shocked moment to realize they were playing at Sarists. One boy raised his hands against his brother, who clutched at his chest and cried out, "Magic, magic!" before falling dramatically to the cobbles. Their mother, a small, tired-looking woman with nervous eyes, had been swift to round them up and usher them back inside — but someone must have seen them anyway.

"Are we sure they got away?"

Rat just looked at me, silence the only possible answer.

The bakery was busy at this hour of the morning, packed with its typical Seventh Circle trade of harried fishwives, out-of-work dock-hands, and night girls fetching supper before sashaying off to their beds. Rat, sensing my desire to avoid their company, steered me down the alley and through the bakery's kitchen door. He grabbed a hot loaf from the counter and gave me a gentle shove toward the stairs. An orange tabby descended from the landing, tail erect, scolding us loudly.

"Talk to her," Rat told it. "She's the one who was gone all night."

Upstairs, I found a bottle of wine and leaned against the table. There was a stool, but I was too tired to move the cat. Rat fished a bowl from the shelf and tore the bread into chunks, pouring wine over them. "Milk would be better, but I know you worshippers of Tiboran."

"Not even you can find milk these days," I said. As a flatmate, I liked Rat just fine. His room, the top floor of an old bakery in the Seventh Circle, was big enough for two, out of the way, and always warm. The window dropped onto a clay roof with quick access to the buildings next door, so it was easy enough to go to work and, usually, come back again unnoticed. I couldn't complain.

Especially because lodgings hadn't been that quick to come by when I got back to the city. Strangely enough, saving a nob family from the Inquisition doesn't endear you to many Seventh Circle underground types. When Rat took me in — in return for my assistance in a little scrape involving him, two Temple Street boys, and a cartload of imported Vareni tobacco of debatable ownership — I was just grateful for the walls and roof. Our arrangement was simple: I paid my share of the rent on time, he provided the food, and we didn't ask each other too many questions.

"I recognize that look," Rat said. "You're planning something."

I stirred the sodden bread with my spoon. "They're going to execute Durrel." Rat was silent. "He didn't do it."

"I hate to quibble, but I'm not sure the evidence agrees with you, and the Ceid certainly don't share your faith in him."

"Lots of unhappily married people don't kill their wives. And why would he need money? Wouldn't it be easier to stay married to his rich wife than kill her and have the cash flow dry up?" Even to my ears, that sounded weak.

"What are you going to do?"

I looked up, rubbing the back of my neck. "How do I get in to see the Ceid?"

"You *don't*," Rat said. "They're untouchable. It would be like walking up to the Celystra and demanding to see the Matriarch. Fair enough, bad example." He leaned against the table, looking thoughtful. "Well, I suppose you might try the daughter; she's just odd enough to grant you an audience. But why in the world would you want to?"

I made a noncommittal grunt, and Rat pulled my bowl away. "Look at yourself," he said. "You ignore the curfew, come home bloodied and battered from a night in jail, and you're *still* looking for ways to get into trouble."

"That's not it," I said. "I just want to help him, if I can. Maybe I can find out what really happened."

"And if you find out he really killed her?" Rat's voice was gentle. "Never mind. How are you planning to do it?"

I sighed. "I have no idea."

He gave me a little grin and patted me on the arm. "Well, that's never stopped you yet." He plucked my spoon from the bowl and licked it clean. "I'm off to the baths."

As Rat strolled to the door, I glanced over his blue satin doublet and matching breeches. Topaz-pale, they set off his fair hair and bright eyes. "Are you seeing Hobin tonight?"

"And tomorrow, if things go right." He blew me a kiss. "Don't wait up."

"You never bring your friends home," I said. "It's me, isn't it? I embarrass you." I struck a defiant pose, sticking out my bloody chin.

"Careful. I am this close to getting milord to spring for a new apartment. Don't make it so tempting."

"See if he has any word about the war, will you?"

Rat paused, his hand on the doorknob. "Word about the war. Right."

"Don't start."

He came a few steps back into the room. "You should have joined up, Digger. Why are you hanging around the city, when it's so obvious there's somewhere else you want to be?"

"And there's such a big call in the prince's army for short, ugly young women with missing fingers and a limp." I pulled away from the table. "I'm no camp follower."

"Don't be so hard on yourself," Rat said. "The limp is barely noticeable."

After that, I fell into bed and slept all the way through till night, waking cramped and knotted in more places than I could even identify. I pushed open the shutters. The night air still smelled of smoke, and the moons of

Zet and Sar shined down through the haze. Royalty and magic, a good omen for Prince Wierolf's campaign. I curled into the corner of the window, wondering where they were now. I'd had one sweet letter from Meri, now a mage in the prince's army, before the fighting started, and then nothing. News came in snatches, and we clutched at it: The prince had found unexpected allies in the north, where distance — both physical and ideological — had bred less devotion to the king, and several noble houses had either capitulated without struggle or pledged outright support. The fighting was now concentrated on the plains of Gelnir, where wealthier houses with more to lose by a change in regime had made treaties with Astilan's forces and now stood in defense of the routes toward Gerse and the throne.

The only thing I knew for certain was that Wierolf still lived; any report of his orange banner falling would make swift course to Gerse. But of the Nemair I had heard nothing, of Wierolf's infamous army of wizards only rumors; that they rode before him like an unseen apocalypse, laying waste to the countryside and bewitching innocents in their homes. Those were Royalist claims, to strike terror into Bardolph's subjects and drive us harder to the king's side.

I'd come back to Gerse ready and eager, I thought, to do — something. Storm through the streets leading a battalion of my underworld cronies on secret Sarist missions to undermine the king and the Inquisition? Well, not that exactly, maybe. But *something*.

Instead I'd returned to a city I could barely recognize, and I couldn't find my place again. I'd tried, gone poking around in likely places, looking for Sarists. I'd thought they'd be easy to find for someone like me; I could see their magic, track them to their hidden lairs, offer my services as thief-for-hire. But it hadn't happened. The problem with the likely places was that Bardolph's men had gotten there already, long since cleaned them out and burned them to the ground, and the stale smoke and ashes left such a bitter taste in my mouth that eventually I'd stopped looking.

Below me, the city was silent. It was past suppertime, and the streets should have been noisy with traffic, people gathered at fountain and tavern, children playing along the river. Thieves lurking in the shadows. A lot had changed while I'd been gone. And not just me. Everything changed, when Tegen died.

I should have expected what happened. I was Tegen's — Tegen's girl, Tegen's partner, Tegen's — *whatever* — and with Tegen gone, his work went with him. Though I saw plenty of sympathy in the eyes of the old friends who'd seen me back, I knew what they were thinking. I was bad luck. My partner had died on a job with me, and nobody wanted that kind of fortune rubbing off on them.

Plus I'd come back with the taint of nobs all over me, like a scent the others could pick up from blocks away. It was one thing to sneak into their bedrooms and lift a necklace or a letter or a bottle of wine you could never afford to buy. It was quite another to move in, cozy up to their children, and play their pet. Nobody knew who I was anymore. And I didn't blame them. I wasn't exactly sure myself.

Although apparently I'd landed another job saving noblemen. It seemed I just couldn't keep from sticking my fingers into their business. What had really happened to Durrel's wife? Was he just an unlucky suspect, or was he being framed? Besides the question of who wanted *me* involved, which I could hardly ignore, there was Durrel himself. He wouldn't kill anybody. I had nothing to support that but a core of certainty in my gut, but I felt it, somehow. I knew it. I didn't care what the evidence said; somebody was lying, somebody was *wrong*. That lost, anguished face hadn't hidden the cold iron of a killer. And he was more than just a nob who'd been nice to me; he was Meri's kin. I hadn't had a lot of people to turn to in my life, and I knew what it was like to be in danger and have somebody step up out of nowhere and say, *You'll be safe now; I won't let anything happen to you.* I was bound to help him, if I could.

The Keep was a far cry from the Inquisitor's dungeons where Tegen had died, lost and alone, and there was nothing of Tegen in Durrel, but my stinging heart couldn't help drawing the connection. I wasn't going to leave a man I cared about behind in prison, ever again.

I peeled myself from the window. Nursing misery by moonlight wasn't remotely productive; I'd be in a puddle of it by morning if I didn't get out and *do* something. Since it seemed I had plenty of room in my taxing schedule of fomenting rebellion, I gave my abused limbs a creaky stretch and set out into the evening to hunt up what I could about Durrel's dead wife.

Grea — Rat's aunt, the baker, and our landlady — caught me the instant I stepped off the stairs. "You're not off again?" She planted herself between me and the door. "You're barely *in*." She was a tall, wiry woman with arms like a stevedore; there was no way I was getting past her by force or stealth.

"Just to look for a healer for my eye," I hazarded, hoping Grea wasn't hiding an apothecary in the kitchen. The common room was nearly empty, just one of the regulars, an old soldier sent back from the front, drinking sleepily by the cold fireplace. "I'll be home by curfew." Grea was legally liable for her tenants; if I was caught — again — she could be fined. Or worse.

She gave me a narrow-eyed stare, then stepped aside. "If you come back without stitches, there will be hells to pay."

Nodding, I waved her off, silently vowing to help roll out dough when I got back. My hip was still sore, so I hired a boat, and by the time we slipped into the moonlit water, I was almost cheerful. Movement soothed me. A locked door and a bottle marked POISON were practically a holiday. Nosing around a murder might turn out to be entertaining.

It beat the hells out of what I'd been doing the last couple of months, at least.

Durrel and his wife had lived far across the city, at an ugly old lump of stone called Bal Marse, and I wanted a look at the place — the murder scene — before I decided my next move. I took the boat as far as I could, then took to the streets by foot, easily finding my way by Bal Marse's watchtower, which loomed over the rest of the neighborhood. I clung to the shadows, but couldn't help glancing over my shoulder at every imagined sound behind me. I had a knife *and* my lock picks this time, and I wasn't taking any chances, but I was still skittish from last night.

Bal Marse meant "well defended," and that wasn't a euphemism. Clearly the Ceid thought it was more important to look powerful than beautiful. Kings had once garrisoned soldiers there, and the tower looked straight at the royal residence. A flag of alarm over Hanivard Palace would be clearly seen, armies quickly dispatched. The house itself was a plain-faced, blocky affair, long and low with few windows, the square watchtower like a striking snake protecting the estate. But the windows were dark, the torches in the courtyard cold and unlit. Was the property abandoned? A high wall edged an empty alleyway, only the blank back-side of a warehouse for a neighbor. I flexed my hands and shook out my neck. Scaling that wall should have been as easy as trotting up a flight of stairs, but my sore hip screamed at me with every step.

Finally I got lucky. Someone had left a gate unlocked. I said my thanks to Tiboran, and braced myself for a dog or four to come barreling at me from around the house, but the yard had a lonely, empty feel, like nobody alive was anywhere nearby. Even without its mistress and master, a grand house like Bal Marse should still be occupied with servants and staff and other family members. Hadn't Durrel told me Talth had four children? Where was everyone?

I looked over the flat stone walls, down across the dusty courtyard, along the perimeter wall. Talth's maid had seen somebody leaving her mistress's rooms in the small hours of the night, and Durrel swore it wasn't him. Could it have been an intruder? The more I looked at the building, the more unlikely that seemed. Even if security was a little stiffer when the house was occupied, there were no windows big enough to climb through on the first two stories, and it would take even a skilled climber a good effort to scale one of those smooth stone walls. So maybe Talth's murderer had been welcome here, known to the household. A visitor, if not a member of the family or staff.

Whoever had left the gate unlocked was just as careless with the kitchen door, which swung easily on well-oiled hinges. Why would anyone leave a *well-defended* house open to the elements and intruders?

It didn't take long to see. The house was empty, just a stone shell with no furnishings to speak of, as if thieves or debt collectors had swept through and taken away anything that wasn't bolted down. In fact, it was so picked over it was hard to tell what some of the rooms had been used for. At the center of the ground floor was a huge, round court, pillars soaring to a colonnaded gallery. Whether it had once been a reception or dining hall, or something else entirely, I couldn't decide. The only decoration was the family seal, a sigil of intertwining initials set into the stone floor.

It was eerie walking through the crust of a building where someone had been murdered. I shook off a shiver and found a set of stairs leading to the private spaces upstairs. Without furniture to guide me, I thought it would be hard to find Talth's bedrooms, but one entire wing of the second story had been converted to apartments, and though all the hangings and case goods and rugs had vanished, the way the rooms unfolded into one another, plus the new fireplace with its massive carvings of Mend-kaal in the stonework, plainly announced that someone important had called these rooms home.

I wandered through them, but only the outermost chamber had windows, and the rest of the rooms barely received any of the filtered moonlight. It didn't matter; it was obvious that any evidence that might have been in this room was long gone. Whoever had stripped these rooms had done away with any clues as well. I wondered which chamber Talth had died in, lying in her sweat and horror, waiting for Marau to finally stop the beating of her heart. A stain on the floor to give up her position, maybe? A shaft of moonlight to show me the cold flagstones? But there was nothing. She could have died here two weeks ago, or twenty years, and it wouldn't have made a difference. With a grim sigh, I went back downstairs.

Yet as I crossed back through the empty court, something that *wasn't* moonslight flashed in the corner of my vision. Swearing silently, I spun slowly back around, my eyes squeezed closed until the last moment. I hadn't imagined it. There, by an arched doorway, in a streak like the mark left on the floor from heavy furniture, was the faintest trace of something that should not have been there. I knelt on the floor beside the mark and cautiously dipped my fingers toward the flagstones, tapping the floor just lightly enough that a stream of silvery mist spread out from my touch like the radiating arms of a star, flooding the floor with glittering light.

There was *magic* at Bal Marse.

Of course there was.

CHAPTER FOUR

I scowled at the ceiling. "I'm sure you find this amusing," I said, address-
ing the gods directly, Sar and Tiboran in particular. All over the country,
the Inquisitor and his Confessors were desperate to expose magic — real
or imagined — wherever it lurked, and they had devised the most cruel
and elaborate methods for seeking it out. And here I, the Inquisitor's
wayward, gutter-rat sister, could *see* magic, plain as moonslight, could
wake it up with a touch — and I'd developed the most ridiculous knack
for stumbling over it everywhere I went.

I drew my finger in a wary arc against the stone floor, silvery dust
sparkling in my wake. This certainly put the murder in a new light. Was
Talth a Sarist? Was she magical? That would give almost anybody in our
nervous city motive enough to kill her, although most people would just
call down the Greenmen to do the Goddess's dirty work. Unfortunately
one sweep of glitter on Talth's Round Court floor couldn't tell me much.
But it was more to go on than I'd had that morning. I crisscrossed the
court, trying to see a pattern to the magic, but it was too confusing.
There was a large sort of blot near a back entrance, like someone had
spilled a bunch of it, and there was a wide swath sweeping along the
floor. Here and there throughout the room were small random scratches,
as if magical mice had been milling about, searching for crumbs.

From outside, I could hear the temple bells clanging the hour. Pox.
I'd forgotten about the blasted curfew again. I hurried back toward the
river. If I didn't get to a water landing soon, I was going to have to walk
back to the bakery, and risk being picked up *again*. And that would try
even Rat's patience.

I was awake late that night, my bruises throbbing and my mind
bumping uselessly against the mystery of Bal Marse's magical stains. I'd
ask Durrel if he knew what it meant, but I'd hoped to collect some useful
information for him before I went back to the Keep. Maybe I could learn

more from someone else who was intimate with the inside of Talth Ceid's home. Rat had told me the Ceid were untouchable — but he'd also said I might convince Durrel's stepdaughter to speak to me. Besides, I was more than a little curious about this infamous woman who'd gotten Durrel Decath in so much trouble.

The next morning, Grea called to me as I sneaked through the bakery kitchens. It was late; I'd slept through the breakfast rush, and she was tidying up. "Don't hie away so fast," she said. "You've had another letter."

I turned back. "Anonymous?"

She looked affronted at the suggestion that she would read my mail, but she shook her head. "Not this one." I felt a flash of hope; maybe Meri had figured out a way to get another message through from the front. But Grea tugged a square of folded green parchment from her apron.

"Ah," I said. I plucked the note from her hands and dropped it, unopened, into one of the great bakery ovens as I went past, not even staying to watch it curl satisfactorily into cinders.

"Lass! Don't you want to know what it says, then?"

I halted at the common room door. "I know what it says," I said. "The same thing as all the others." Letters — four of them now — from Werne. My estranged brother, depending on the day you asked him, and the Goddess's ordained High Inquisitor. I still didn't know how he'd found me; I'd moved three times since coming back to the city, and that was tracking that could put *me* to shame. But as long as he limited his contact to mawkish letters begging me to return to the bosom of Mother Church, I could handle it.

Although I hoped not to be questioned too closely as to the precise definition of "handling it."

Grea clucked disapprovingly as the letter went up in flames. I couldn't blame her; five months wasn't a terribly long time to get used to the idea of ignoring a letter from the Inquisitor, particularly when His Grace's men were burning your neighbors out of their homes. "You don't need my kind of trouble here," I said. "I should move on."

Grea leaned low on her elbows. "Now where would we be if everyone in this city moved house whenever the Bloodletter said 'boo'? Nay, I knew who you were when you took the room, and besides, you're the only tenant I've had who can put up with that nephew of mine. You stay put."

I nodded gratefully and left her to her flour-strewn work boards. Outside, I headed uptown toward the Third Circle, a more respectable neighborhood than mine. The hired boats gathered here were nicer, their boatmen less inclined to nick your purse when your back was turned. I wasn't exactly sure where I wanted to go, but I wagered one of these sailors could steer me in the right direction. I waved down a vessel.

"Take me to see Koya Ceid," I said in my best imperious lady-in-waiting voice. I almost looked the part today, in the nicer of my dresses, a gold brooch pinned to the bodice. I'd found it a couple months back, working the Spiral, and just hadn't gotten around to selling it yet.

The boatman looked confused. "Mistress Koyuz, you mean?"

Did I? I realized I didn't know anything about this Koya, except the scant rumors Rat had shared.

"Not too many ask for her by name," the boatman went on. "Most people just name the house over in Nob Circle."

That sounded promising, so I nodded and paid my fare. As the boat skimmed across the city, a buzz of mosquitoes in the humid air, I thought over what I knew of the Ceid. The family hailed from Tratua, their Gerse branch just an outflung arm, but they'd been fixtures in the city almost since its founding. Gerse was too much the royal capital for merchant-class families to seize control of the city government the way they had in Tratua and Yeris Volbann, but wealthy gentry like the Ceid had made inroads in shipping, trade, and banking, amassing local fortunes, allies, and power along the way. It was hard to imagine Durrel tied up with a family like that, but I reminded myself that he was a nob, every bit as used to wielding power as any clan of rich gentry.

I'd heard that in Tratua, the Ceid had so many guards and retainers that they amounted to a standing army, and though they weren't quite so powerful in Gerse, they were still people you didn't cross if you could help it. More than one rival — business, political, or personal — had disappeared over the years. And the Ceid made sure the world knew who was responsible, so no one would mistake the disappearances for the work of the Inquisition.

It occurred to me that perhaps I ought to have thought this errand through a little further.

We pulled up before a modest riverside *teriza*, all pink marble and cultivated topiary, white banners flying from the pillars and balconies. Belatedly I recalled that this would be a house in mourning; Koya had lost her mother only a fortnight or so ago. Would she even be receiving callers yet? Before I could give the bellpull a tug to find out, the terrace doors flew open, and three huge sighthounds burst through, followed by a tall young woman in blue velvet, cut low about her neck and shoulders.

"Pol! Fana! Kusht! Do not go *near* that water —" She saw me and broke off yelling. "I don't know *you*," she said, leaning forward to take me in. "Do I?"

"No," I said hastily, as the dogs snuffled hungrily around me. I pulled my arms in tight to my body. "I —" Pox. I hadn't even come up with a cover. "I'm Celyn Contrare. I've come to — pay my condolences."

"Oh." She looked oddly disappointed, but snapped her fingers, and the dogs fell back. "I suppose you can come inside." She turned in a swirl of blue train and cascading golden hair, and led me into a room with high ceilings and spindly, gilded furniture. "I'm Koya, and my brother Barris is skulking about here somewhere. Did you know my mother well?"

So this was the notorious Koya, for whom Durrel might have killed his wife. It now seemed altogether believable; there was something striking about her, the warm flush of her cheeks, the fair hair, the dogs — she looked like a statue of Zet, goddess of the hunt, come to life. She was watching me expectantly.

"No," I said without thinking, then added, "I'm a friend of her husband." Who might have killed her, and whose name was surely not welcome in this house these days. Brilliant.

"Lord Durrel? How marvelous!" Koya said, and I blinked at her. "Come in, come in. Such tales we hear these days. Apparently he's quite despicable. Oh, do I shock you?" She gave a gay laugh. "I shock everyone."

"Yes, she delights in it," said a dull voice. I turned my head to see a gentleman a few years older than Koya descend a curved staircase. "Have you forgotten that this is a house of mourning?"

"With you haunting about like a figure from a funeral masque? Hardly. Celyn Contrare, my brother Barris Ceid." He strode into the room to greet me. I saw that his neat, dark beard was just starting to fill in, and he wore white armbands on his pale gray doublet — the very picture of respectable mourning.

"You're acquainted with our stepfather?" His voice was cool, restrained.

"I — yes."

"And yet you felt it appropriate to come to this house. Why?"

I was spared the need to answer when Koya guessed it, somehow. "Oh! I remember who *you* are," she said. "Celyn! Of course. Lord Durrel spoke of you many times. Are you looking into my stepfather's case, then? Can you find out who did it?" There was a sudden urgency to her melodic voice. Who was this person? But her question was interesting: *My stepfather's case.* Not *my mother's death.*

"Koya, don't be an idiot. We *know* who did it. This ridiculous farce can only satisfy your own curiosity and boredom."

"Shut up, Barris." The musical voice lost almost nothing of its tenor. "Durrel didn't kill Mother. You only wish he had."

My eyes swung from sister to brother. There was tension here, but without more information, I couldn't be certain of its source. Or its significance.

"Do let's sit and discuss this like civilized people." Koya led me to a delicate, carved bench and settled beside me, but Barris lingered at the fringes of the room, like a suspicious dog that didn't want to let me out of view. "Can I offer you some refreshment? Vrena, precious, bring us some wine," she called to an out-of-sight servant.

"No — really, I'm fine." I hadn't forgotten that one member of this family had already been felled by poison, and the suspects were still at large.

Koya looked at me oddly for a moment. "I'm sure you have questions. And we have *nothing to hide,*" she added pointedly, looking at her brother.

I glanced from sibling to sibling, realizing just how out of my depth I was. I had no experience *investigating* crimes; committing them, yes, but never reconstructing them, piece by piece, backward in time. The thing I really wanted to ask was who had had me arrested, but I kept that tidbit close. It might be more telling to see what they did if I *didn't* mention it. Instead I seized on the first thing I thought of. "I thought there were four children."

"The twins live with the family in Tratua," Koya said. "Leys and Reton. They're thirteen, and Mother felt it time to expand their horizons."

"She wanted them out of the way of her and her new plaything, you mean." Barris had moved from glowering to pacing, and he practically pounced on Vrena and the wine when they appeared.

"You didn't approve of the match with Lord Durrel?" I said.

"As if Mother ever courted anyone's approval. Here —" He gestured for me to follow, and, curious, I stood and trailed after him out of the room, Koya and the dogs behind us. Barris led us to an open breezeway, where a massive portrait of a woman and her young son stared out onto the water.

"It's a Fioretta," Koya said at the same moment Barris said, "Does that look like a woman who cared what other people thought?"

I studied the woman in the portrait, a thick, proud figure in a stiff clay-colored gown, with blond hair drawn severely back, and startling pale eyes glaring out from the canvas. The boy — Barris, probably — looked just as defiant. Koya had much of her mother's stature, and the unnerving direct gaze, but she was more delicately built.

"Why did she marry Lord Durrel?" I couldn't imagine what that clay woman could have seen in a boy her children's age.

"To be Lady Decath, of course," Koya said. "A noble title, not to mention a noble heir, was the one thing Mother didn't have."

Since we were being so candid, I forged ahead with my next indelicate question. "And where were you both when she died?"

"I was dining with my grandfather," Koya said promptly. "It's exactly an hour's sail between Grandfather's house and Bal Marse, and I assure you at least a dozen witnesses can place me there all evening."

I knew a thing or two about alibis. The more precise and elaborate one was, the less likely it was to be true. "At two o'clock in the morning?"

Barris frowned. "What?" His voice was gruff.

"Your mother was killed in the middle of the night. Her maid saw someone leaving her rooms at that hour."

"The dinner ran late," Koya said simply. "We had . . . family matters to discuss."

"What about the curfew?"

She gave a broad smile. "We're Ceid. The curfew doesn't apply to us."

Of course it didn't. "And you, Master Ceid?"

Barris set down his glass. "Unlike my sister, I don't find your questions entertaining, and I have no intention of continuing this conversation."

Koya sighed daintily. "Unfortunately," she said, "despite his efforts to suggest otherwise, my brother is entirely innocent. He was at home in Tratua when Mother died."

"Wait. You don't live in Gerse? Do you keep a house in the city?" The Ceid owned properties from the Seventh Circle to Nob Circle. Maybe edgy Barris's quarters would be worth checking out.

Barris gave me a chilling look. "I *did*," he said. "The Decath own it now."

I realized he meant Bal Marse. "Lord Durrel got your family home in the marriage settlement? Why?" What reason would a family as cozy and rich as Durrel's have to lust after an ugly, hulking lump of stone like Bal Marse?

"My mother's house," he said. "She owned it outright. And you would have to ask the Decath, since she's no longer able to explain it."

"And you're convinced that Dur — Lord Durrel is guilty?"

"Well, who else? It was common knowledge Decath was only after her money. He was the last person seen with her before she died, and they'd been arguing."

Koya turned to me. "Anyone could see my mother and Durrel were a *dismal* match. Oh, the theory was sound, but once they were actually pinned together in the same house, well . . . it doesn't always work out like the strategists plan."

"Do you mean to parade all this family's shames before a stranger?" Barris said savagely. "Very well then, let's talk about your own failed marriage."

"Hardly failed," Koya said brightly. "Celyn, my husband is Stantin Koyuz. Perhaps you've heard of him."

Oh. That *was* an interesting development, and I should have known it. Wealthy merchant Stantin Koyuz, who had to be decades Koya's senior, was infamous for breaking the hearts of younger sons of noble families. But marriage was mandated by Celys's law, and it was difficult for a man to advance in Gersin society without a wife — at least in name. Looking up, I saw Koya regarding me, the same placid smile still on her face. I suddenly had the very uncomfortable feeling that she knew every thought inside my head. I didn't like it. I dropped my gaze.

"I can assure you, Celyn, that my marriage has nothing whatsoever to do with what happened to my mother."

"Of course," I mumbled, changing the subject. "Who do you think is responsible for your mother's death?"

"My mother," she said simply.

"Then you think it *was* suicide?"

Barris barked out a laugh, absolutely mirthless.

"Certainly not," Koya said smoothly. "I only meant, it must have been something she was involved in. My mother was a very skilled woman. And one thing she did particularly well was make people unhappy. Now, I wouldn't call them *enemies*, exactly —"

"Enemies?" That was a strange choice of words.

"I'll make a list." Koya fluttered off to fetch paper and quill. She returned and spread the paper across her lap, writing with a swift, swooping hand. "This first name is my grandfather, Mother's father. He was opposed to the marriage —"

"Because he thought Decath was too young," Barris broke in. "Koya, what are you doing?"

"He was opposed to the marriage," Koya continued as if her brother hadn't spoken. "But I doubt he'd kill anybody. Although . . ." She paused thoughtfully, then wrote another name. "You should look into her business associates. Durrel was always trying to become involved in Mother's interests somehow, but I'm afraid he didn't really understand how things work in this family. Now, she was intimate with the Corsour family, although Emmis Corsour was no match for Mother, and she'd been seeing rather a lot of an Alech Karst recently —"

"Koya, enough!" Barris crossed the room in long, determined strides and whipped the paper from her hands. Ink splattered her hands and gown, but she just regarded him with the same patient, composed expression. "My sister is a bored, unhappy girl, just looking for some amusement," he said to me. And with that, he tore Koya's list into pieces, which he dropped, one by one, into the pooling candle flame.

"Why, brother, whatever's the matter with you?"

"I believe this meeting is over. Mistress Contrare," he added with icy politeness, "please allow us to offer our personal barge to return you to your . . . home."

I hadn't managed to ask what they knew about the magic I had seen at Bal Marse, but it no longer seemed like such a simple question, and my ability to detect it was hardly the sort of thing I went about boasting of to total strangers. And certainly not to these two, who were about as strange as they come. Not even waiting for me, Barris stalked toward the open doors to the terrace landing. I lingered only long enough to see Koya watching him, a tiny furrow between her brows. She rose eventually, barely brushing down her skirts before leaning in to kiss me on the cheek.

"Thank you for coming," she said quietly. "Please don't think too much of him. He's highly strung. Like Mother was." She studied my face for a moment, her wide, blue eyes dark and probing. "You'll help Durrel," she said, and there was a note of pleading insistence in her voice.

"I'm trying."

"I'm scared for him, Celyn. I don't believe he truly understands what a force this family is. Mother was but *one* of us. I don't know how long they'll be willing to wait for justice."

I was taken aback that her concern should be for Durrel, when it was her own mother who'd been killed, but I nodded. Finally she led me toward the terrace, pausing in the doorway.

"There was nothing between us," she said abruptly, her skirts whispering to a stop around her feet. "Except a foolish girl's infatuation with an attractive man she couldn't have, and the harmless warmth of a gentleman too kind to give her the boot in the face she deserved." Koya gave me one last smile, this one tinged, I thought, with sadness, before turning back to the house and disappearing in a sweep of silk.

Down at the landing, Barris paced the deck, where an elegantly painted skiff waited, clear blue water lapping its glossy sides. One of the sighthounds had followed him, and stood panting nervously in the humid air, its sides quivering.

"I'm sorry for that scene," Barris said. "Koya can be . . . difficult, and I'm afraid she's always known just the right places to rub me raw." He paused a moment, looking me over. "You are thinking something, and I would know what that was before I send you off."

"Only that you're too old to be Talth's son," I said.

He nodded evenly. "I'm her stepson. She married Grensl Ceid when I was but a child. She is the only mother I ever knew," he added. "Such as she was."

I made a guess. "You're responsible for her business affairs now."

"I am. Both here and in Tratua. Those I managed to keep from his lordship's grasp. But that's little change from how things had been these past two years, if you're thinking I had some motive to murder my mother."

"Stepmother."

He ignored that, which said something. What, precisely, I wasn't sure. He wasn't easily rattled, though. That part was Ceid, through and through. I was beginning to get a sense of these people; if they were going to kill someone, they'd do it thoughtfully and stolidly. As he handed me into the boat, I asked one last question.

"What position did your mother take in the war?"

"The same position she always took. Whatever was best for Talth Ceid." He looked out over the water briefly, then turned back to me. "We're not a subtle family, Mistress Celyn. We make our enmity plain, and we welcome your investigation, since it can only confirm what we know. We are aware of his lordship's history, and we know who murdered our mother. Reasonably soon, you will too. Good day."

CHAPTER FIVE

I wasn't at all sure what to make of the family Ceid, and mulled over the bizarre way they related to each other as the boatman steered me across the Oss. Quibbling brothers and sisters were entertaining and familiar enough, but I hadn't learned much that was particularly useful, aside from Koya's vague references to her mother's enemies, and her own confession about her marriage and her relationship with Durrel. Her brother had called her bored and unhappy; unhappy enough to strike back at the powerful mother who'd yoked her to a wholly unsuitable husband? It would be more practical to kill the inconvenient husband and escape the marriage altogether. Even if Koya had wanted Durrel for herself, killing her mother didn't seem to accomplish much.

Unsettled after that meeting, I convinced the boatman to let me off in Nob Circle so I could walk the rest of the way home. Charicaux, the Decath family home, was nearby, and I had promised to try to see Durrel's father. I found the house easily from Meri's wistful description of the place last winter. It sat a few streets off the river, in the shadow of the Celystra's green dome, a pretty, older building of white stucco and flower boxes in the windows. A tidy tile courtyard separated it neatly from the street, giving the family within the opportunity to prove how wealthy they were, by way of ornamental fences and cultivated fruit trees. True to the Decath's neutral reputation, Charicaux flew no colored banners from its towers.

But there was one small detail Meri had omitted from her description of her uncle's home: the guards. I stopped behind a flower stall across the street to get a better look. Two men patrolled the front courtyard, heavily armed and making no effort to hide the fact. This was a curious development; these guys looked like ordinary street heavies, not the kind of neat, trained guards commonly employed by nob households.

They also weren't the kind of people likely to welcome a caller off the street, and when I crossed over and rapped on the gate, a heavyset guard with a pockmarked face and a clunky gait sent me away without ceremony. Assertions that I knew Lord Decath were met with sneers and a curt, "He ain't in." I gave the guard my best dazzling servant smile and promised to come back.

I pondered this curious development as I made my way back across town. With the war edging closer, life in Gerse was getting more tense every day, and I supposed it was conceivable that a man who'd just lost a daughter-in-law to murder might be nervous of his — and his wife's — safety. But I had visited one of the Decath properties before, Favom Court, a day's sail outside the city, and I'd had complete freedom of movement while there. I didn't remember any guards, or even so much as an armed retainer. Lord Ragn and Lady Amalle had opened their arms and their doors to me without a question. Yet here was their city house, fortified with armed muscle.

Well, people changed, I supposed. And a change like that was different and interesting — certainly worth investigating further.

I made a last stop on the way home, at a rag shop on Bonelicker Way, a tiny, cluttered storefront hidden between an unlicensed tobacconist and a cheap bawdy house. With no sign out front, and a tattered rug for a door, it was easy to miss, which was exactly how Grillig, its proprietor, liked things. I pushed aside the rug, wary of fleas, and stepped into the lamplit shop. Another customer was already inside, a hard-looking fellow with a pistol in his belt, leaning over the counter and studying something with great intent. It was technically illegal for the common citizens of Gerse to walk about the streets wearing firearms — but the residents of this neighborhood didn't generally subscribe to what was technically legal.

"We're closed," announced a raspy voice from behind the counter, and a squat man about my height waddled out of the back room.

"Well met, Grillig," I said, and the storekeeper gave me a frantic look and waved a stubby hand to silence me.

"I said, we're *closed.*" Grillig shrugged when I gave the other customer a pointed look. "We're closed to nonpaying customers."

"I can pay," I said, and came farther into the shop, sidestepping the fellow with the gun. The shop was cluttered with all manner of goods — books, knives, tapestries, clothing — all of it secondhand, and most of it stolen. Grillig was the best fence this side of the Oss, or at least the cheapest. I'd been a good customer here, welcome, once. I'd often come by with Tegen to sell our spoils, and one night he'd bade me pick out a treasure to buy from among Grillig's shelves and cases. He'd meant a gem, maybe, or a blue silk petticoat like the night girls wore — something pretty and feminine. But I'd chosen a book, bound in red calfskin, full of drawings of fanciful beasts. He'd teased me for that, long after, but would lie in my arms, turning the gilded pages and tracing his slender fingers along the colored images, as I read the words aloud to him. I wondered where that book was now. Had it burned with the rest of Tegen's belongings when he was arrested?

The man with the gun lost interest in the item he was examining, and left the shop without a word. Grillig glared at me. "Never mind," he said. "What do you want?"

Information, was what I wanted to say — but asking for it outright would spook him. So I poked through the heaps of rags and dishware until I unearthed something worth buying.

"That's three marks," he said when I plopped the shirt on the counter, and "Three *silver* marks," when I laid the copper coins beside it. It was an outrageous price, but it might be worth it, if he could tell me anything useful.

"Fine." I dug the coins from my bodice. "How's business?"

"As if you'd care," he said sourly. "We don't hear from you for *months.* You're doing trade with that nip on Tower Street now, aren't you? Gotten too fancy for us Seventh Circle folk."

"The Tower Street fence?" I said. "That stings. You know if I had business, I'd bring it to you."

His furtive eyes darted past me as he gathered up the coins. "I wish you wouldn't," he said. "We don't need your trouble here. I'm running an *honest* business now, and —"

I looked in the direction his previous customer had gone. "I see that," I said.

Grillig leaned toward me. "My son's in the war."

"Not Orrin," I said. "What — happened?" I'd been about to say, *What side?* But that was a stupid question. Nobody admitted to having sons fighting with Prince Wierolf.

The shopkeeper made a face. "Conscripted. To pay my bond after I got arrested last spring, thanks to people like you mucking about where they've no call!"

That did sting. It wasn't like I'd personally, single-handedly *started* the war. "I'm sorry to hear it," I said truthfully. Grillig was slippery, but nobody deserved to have his children sent to battle to pay for his sins.

Grillig cast a hand in a dismissive gesture. "You didn't come here to buy a shirt."

"No," I said. "I was wondering what you'd heard about the murder of a nobleman's wife recently."

"That Ceid thing? Bad business. You want to know about the poison." That was the Grillig I remembered. "It didn't come from around here," he said. "There might be a handful of potioners in Gerse who deal in stuff like that. Freitag up in Sixth, or maybe Ver — nay, he's gone to the gallows. Anyway, with the restrictions and the embargoes, nobody wants to take that kind of risk these days."

"So you wouldn't happen to have any."

Grillig made the sign against Marau. "Like I said, we don't need that kind of trouble. My son —"

I nodded. Strange days, if the gods had figured out a way for a man like Grillig to go honest. "Thanks all the same," I said. "If you hear anything about that poison . . . ?" I slid another silver mark into the pile of coins for the shirt. Grillig scowled, but swept them all into his broad hand, nodding. I gathered up the secondhand shirt and headed for the door.

The next morning I surveyed myself before Rat's mirror. In a blue linen kirtle and a lighter blue wool overgown with matching sleeves, my hair tucked up inside a linen cap that mostly shielded my cut cheek, I could do a fair turn as the servant of a decent family with an unfortunate member in the Keep. The only problem would be if one of the guards on duty recognized me from my first visit. Which seemed unlikely, dressed as a girl and with much less blood on my face this time. There was just one more thing I needed: a visitor's pass. And I didn't have time to wait for approval from the king.

I crossed the city on foot, trotting up Bargewater Street toward the First Circle, the district mostly taken up by Hanivard Palace and the Celystra. The Keep stood just on the edge of First, where the Big Silver river circled the royal palace. When I got to the harborside landing, a few other people milled around, waiting to cross over to see their loved ones detained at His Majesty's convenience. I studied my companions in the crowd, a handful of people dressed like servants, here for masters or family? A wildly overdressed young nob couple, the girl sobbing hysterically into her lad's velvet shoulder. A fat gentleman dressed in the gray robes of a lawyer and doing a poor job balancing a document case, a mug of beer, and a meat pie. He'd have a pass for sure. I was just aiming myself for a carefully timed collision with the fellow so I could knock his papers from his hands, when I heard a cough from behind me.

I turned slowly — and found myself a scarce inch from a Greenman.

I lost all my breath. I couldn't help it. He was facing away from me, but the grass-bright livery of his uniform loomed before me, tunic and hood and nightstick. And the gleaming golden tree, silhouetted against the full moon of Celys. I edged aside carefully, trying to look anonymous, invisible, nonexistent. I was nobody, just a servant in a crowd, waiting to visit somebody in the gaol.

The Greenman turned and saw me. "Sweetling! Fancy meeting you here. Come to visit our boy?" Raffin Taradyce, Acolyte Guardsman, took two easy steps toward me, everyone else melting out of his way from habit, and lifted me bodily from the street.

"Put me down, you oaf!" I struggled in his grip, then surveyed his uniform. "That suits you, I guess." His fair coloring and easy height made him look like one of the Goddess's own.

"I think there's an insult in there somewhere," he said cheerfully.

"Not at all," I said. "I have nothing but respect for the Guard." And Tiboran praised liars. "Drag any old ladies from their beds lately?"

He gave a shrug and looked over my head. "It's a living."

Raffin hadn't answered my question, but every once in a while I knew when to leave well enough alone. "What about Durrel, then? What have you heard?"

He looked grim. "Not much more than you, I'll wager. He's in a bad way, though. The Ceid don't care he's noble; they'll shove this thing through the courts like a merchant's son with a two-mark hus —" He caught my eye and gave a cough. "Right. And thanks to his father being so damned neutral, the Decath can't rely on support from Court or Council. He's on his own in there." That was more or less what Durrel had told me. His family was famous for not taking sides during any political conflict. In peacetime, it made everyone their friends. But now?

"Durrel said his father won't see him, thinks he's guilty."

That drew a pause. "You'd have to ask them about that. Did you meet the family?"

It took me a moment to catch up. "You mean the Ceid? Just the two children, Barris and Koya."

"Entertaining, aren't they?"

"That's one way of putting it." I looked up at him, shielding my eyes with my hand. "What's the story with Durrel and Koya?"

A slow grin spread over his face. "Our boy caught himself a bodice full of trouble this time, I'll tell you that."

"If there's a point, you'd better get to it. They're about to open the gates." Across the landing, a bell was clanging, heralding the lowering of the drawbridge. And the lawyer was long gone now. I'd missed my best chance for nicking a pass. A pox on Greenmen.

"Listen, peach, I'm going to be late for muster," Raffin was saying. "Wouldn't want them to take away my baton, now, would I?" He bent low, as if to kiss me on the cheek, and whispered, "We're not to touch you, you know. Lord High's orders."

"What?" I pulled back to stare at him. "Why?"

"I don't know. But word came down that you are not to be disturbed by the Acolyte Guard, at least until His Worship decides what he wants to do about you. Looks like you have a free pass in this city, greensleeves."

A hands-off order from the Lord High Inquisitor? What was my brother up to? "Not from everyone," I said. "I was arrested the other night."

"Were you? And yet here you stand. Might as well enjoy it. You know how His Grace is, sun one day, shadow the next. But if anything changes, I'll warn you."

I was suspicious. "Why? What do you want in return?"

He edged a little closer than was comfortable. "Just take care of our boy. Something's off about this whole affair. Do the job you've been engaged for."

"Wait — *what*? What do you know?" I asked, my voice cold. "Did you have anything to do with this, with getting me pinched?"

"My, my, such self-absorption!" he cried. "As it happens, I've been far too busy dragging old women from their beds."

"You're hilarious."

"And you're not listening." Raffin pulled me closer, and his grip on my arm was exactly what I remembered of Greenmen. "*Something* is going on here, and Durrel is trapped in the middle of it. You are in a unique position among all his acquaintances to look into it."

"That's ridiculous. You're a Greenman; that has to be more useful than some petty street thief. Why don't *you* look into it?"

"I am trying," he said, his voice uncharacteristically serious. "But I'm just two months on this job, and my father paid twenty thousand crowns for my commission. There is no way I can go poking around asking questions, *particularly* of other guards."

The pieces were starting to click together, with Raffin Taradyce holding the purse strings to this whole situation. "Whoever paid to have me arrested also put up my bond. Fifty marks."

That wolfish grin again. "Extraordinary! Be flattered, peach. I don't normally shell out nearly that much money on a woman. You can pay me back later." He finished the kiss he'd started and, still bent close to my cheek, whispered, "Help him. You *know* he's innocent."

And he passed me something before he ducked away, whistling and swinging his nightstick, and clearing crowds as he went.

It was a rolled-up parchment, thickly inked, with a royal seal stamped in its center, right above the words *Admit the named bearer, CELYN CONTRARE, into the presence of His Majesty's gaolers at Bryn Tsairn Prison. Good for three months from the date of issuance, and Signed by the Left Hand of His Exalted Majesty, Bardolph the Pious.*

A visitor's pass. Made out to me. I glanced up to see Raffin across the landing, still watching me, a blot of green against the brown sunlit docks. He gave me a brisk salute before turning away into the morning.

CHAPTER SIX

It was only a little different visiting the Keep as a free woman with a pass. I looked considerably more respectable than I had on my last visit, but the guards on duty still sneered at me, grabbed my basket and pawed through it, and made lewd comments as I pushed my way past them. I flinched from the stench and the roar of the other prisoners, banging on their bars or wooden doors as I climbed up through the prison's ranked tiers to Queen's Level, where Durrel's cell was located. The royal prisons were divided into three levels of worsening conditions, having nothing to do with the severity of the prisoners' crimes, and everything to do with their ability to pay for their lodging at His Majesty's convenience. The cells on the highest floors were reserved for nobs and gentry with wealthy friends who could bring them bribe money. Accommodations were said to be relatively pleasant — emphasis on *relative* — a private cell with a window, furniture, books and wine if you could afford them. Folk with more modest means were kept down a level on the Mongery, three or four to a cell, with meat once or twice a week and maybe a clean chamber pot, if someone paid for it. And deeper still was the Rathole, little more than sewers where Queen's and Mongery prisoners were dumped once they'd exhausted their funds, left to rot in the sunless dungeon and kill each other over crumbs. How long a prisoner lasted on each level depended directly on his ability to keep up the bribes.

Queen's Level seemed curiously empty today, as if the weekly bribes had come due and the other prisoners had fallen short of their rents. At that thought, my belly tightened and I hastened down the narrow corridor, toward the cell I remembered. Trotting down the row of cells, darting glances from barred door to barred door, I spied a pocked, pale face against the tiny, grilled window of the cell across from Durrel's. Bony fingers curled around the bars, and a muddy brown eye tracked me down the hall.

"Milord's got a visitor, he does!" cried out a shrill voice from the cell. "She looks good enough to share!" I turned and made a rude gesture at him. A mistake; something foul flew toward me and splatted into my sleeve. I jumped, swearing, but it seemed to be rotten vegetables, and not . . . something worse. He was lucky I was in a good mood today.

I brushed my fingers against Durrel's cell door as his neighbor's taunts continued. "Milord," I called softly. "Are you still in there?"

I had to stand on tiptoe to see inside. Someone had cleared away the filthy rushes, but the smell of a chamber pot that had needed changing days ago made me gag, even from outside the cell. Durrel was folded up on the bed, staring at the ceiling, but at the sound of my voice, he propelled himself from the bed to the door.

"Celyn!" His voice, cracked and thin, was filled with so much hope and fear it *hurt*, like an ache in my throat. His fingers reached through the little window. I hesitated, but found my hand gripped in his. He held on so tightly I used the force of his grasp to pull myself closer to him.

"You look like hells," slipped out of my mouth. There were dark smudges under his eyes, and his scraggly beard showed up every contour of his boyish face. In the daylight now, I could see how much weight he'd lost.

"You shouldn't be here," he said. "It's too dangerous."

"Oh, but I have a pass." I flashed it at him.

"Do I want to know where you got that?" he said.

"I should be offended," I said, forcing cheer into my voice. "It's *completely* legitimate!" As if anything from the hands of a Greenman could really be called legitimate. "It answers one question, though. I think we can credit Lord Raffin for our little rendezvous the other night."

"Damn. I'm sorry, Celyn. I had no idea. What the hells is he thinking?"

"He's thinking his friend is in trouble and nobody seems to be helping!" Durrel didn't answer, and I didn't know what else to say, so we stood there, with the door between us, a long, stupid moment. Durrel finally broke the silence, moving back to where I could see him. "I see you've met my neighbor, Temus," he said, gesturing at the stain on my arm.

"He has good aim. He should talk to the guards about being released for the wars."

Durrel smiled faintly. "What's that?" He nodded toward my basket, where I had the shirt I'd bought from Grillig.

"Oh. It's — here." I handed it up, and watched as he shook out the now-wrinkled linen, took in the mended patch in the sleeve and the slightly worn hemline.

"I was going to bring you one of Rat's, but he only has nice things," I said. "This one, well, I thought it would be less of a shame if it got —"

"Befouled?"

"Something like that."

Without hesitation, Durrel stripped off his own filthy shirt and shook the clean one over his head. I could see the lines of his ribs, the points of his narrow shoulders, a taut belly that barely held his trunk hose on — he looked like he'd been a prisoner here longer than a fortnight. Weren't they feeding him *at all*? Or was it life with Talth that had wasted him?

"Who's Rat?" he said, coming up for air. The new shirt was far too large; I had guessed him at a bigger man.

"My, uh, roommate," I said, and, for something to say, so I didn't keep staring at his too-thin body, I explained about Rat's skills at acquiring the exotic and rare.

"Sounds like a useful fellow," he said. His voice was warming up, a cheerfulness creeping into it now that seemed all wrong, somehow. He leaned his head back and took in a deep breath of stagnant, stinking air, as if it were fresh and breezy as a spring meadow. "You're a miracle," he said. "You have no idea how good it feels to get into something *clean*."

And why was *I* the one bringing it, and not his father? "I should have brought you a razor," I said instead.

He gave a mirthless laugh, so harsh and quick it startled me. "I'm supposed to have a beard, aren't I?" he said, his voice bitter. "I'm mourning my dead wife." He dropped his hands and turned from me, pacing away from the door.

"I went to Bal Marse," I said, and he halted, turning back.

"Bal Marse! But why?"

"I want to help you. I thought I might find something."

His drawn face turned curious. "And did you?"

"It's been stripped bare." I explained about the missing furniture, the empty rooms, the open gates and door. "The place is abandoned."

"I don't understand," he said. "Why —"

"Barris said the property came to you on Talth's death. Is that true?"

"Wait — you talked to Barris?" He sounded alarmed. "Celyn, hold on. What are you up to?" I looked at him impatiently, until he finally sighed. "Fine. Yes, technically I did inherit Talth's house in the city. But since I've been in *here* since she died, I really have no idea what's going on with it. Her family probably came in and took away anything that wasn't strapped down. That would be like them." He resumed pacing. The ceiling was so low in places he had to stoop. "And there was *nothing* there? No files, no ledgers or records?" When I shook my head, he continued. "I've been thinking maybe the murder had something to do with her business dealings, but that's probably just the captivity talking."

"No, it seems likely," I said. "What kind of business are we talking about?"

"Well, the Ceid shipping business, primarily, but Talth also owned some properties in the city. Houses to let, or something. I really wouldn't know. She wasn't that . . . receptive to the idea of my participation in her work. She liked to say I was just —" He stopped abruptly, his face clouded. "Just the *studhorse*."

I winced. The implication was obvious; the Decath were famous for their horse farm, and the comment gave ugly credence to Koya's claim that her mother was interested only in the title and heirs that marriage to Durrel would provide. "That's horrible," I said, but he just shrugged.

"Sometimes she'd have callers, late at night, and she'd entertain them downstairs, but she always sent me up to my rooms, like a naughty child."

"And you don't know what they might have been involved in?" Durrel shook his head, one curt flick that was barely noticeable. I wanted to press him for details, but it was obvious he didn't want to talk about his marriage.

"There's something else." I pulled myself closer to the door, and spoke as quietly as I could. "I found magic at Bal Marse. Do you know anything about that?"

"Magic? Are you certain? Of course you're certain." Durrel knew about my odd affinity for Sar's touch; it had been one of the reasons he'd saved me. I explained what I had seen at the Round Court at his house.

"Did Talth have magic?" I said.

"No. Definitely not. I'd have known about it." I believed him; Durrel had spent years living with a magical cousin, always keeping an eye out to make sure she was protected, her secret safely concealed. He didn't have my ability to spot the Breath of Sar on somebody, but he had a knack I trusted. "Do you think it has to do with her murder?"

"It might not." But I wouldn't put money on it.

Durrel was silent a long time. Finally he spoke up again. "Celyn, this is too dangerous. I'm sorry I got you involved. You should go home and forget about me."

Fat chance there. "*You* didn't get me involved, remember? And besides, I want to help. I owe you."

"Owe me?" He stood close to the window again, looking down, a curious expression on his scruffy face. "How do you mean?"

"You saved my life," I said. "Perhaps you've forgotten?"

"That wasn't the same thing," he said. "This is *dangerous*."

"You don't think what you did for me was dangerous?" I might have laughed, if the memory of that awful day we met, when Tegen died, didn't still make me sick with dread. "You smuggled a fugitive — a *magical* fugitive — out of the city, lied to Greenmen to do it, and harbored her in your family home. And then you *armed* her!" I added, recalling his gift of an expensive House of Decath dagger when we'd parted.

Durrel watched me evenly for a moment. "In my defense, I was drunk at the time," he finally said, and there was a note of mirth in his voice.

"You were sober enough," I said drily. "Durrel — milord — what are you so concerned about?" I watched him, suspicious. "You know something, don't you?"

He shook his head, but there was more evasion than denial in the gesture.

"Tell me! I have *nothing* to go on but a smear of magic in an empty house. If we can't find out who really killed your wife —" I stopped myself. Durrel knew the stakes, and my yelling wouldn't help. "Please, if you know something —"

"I don't *know* anything. Just that Talth did business with a lot of dangerous people."

"Like who? Inquisition?"

"I don't know," he said again. "Criminals, maybe."

"Well, that's all right," I said, trying to sound bright. "I'm good with criminals."

"Celyn —"

"Digger," I said.

"What? Oh, right. Sorry — I keep forgetting."

I actually liked the way his voice sounded when he called me Celyn, but I had a point to make. "No, I just mean, they call me that for a reason. I'm good at what I do. I can help you, if you let me."

There was silence as he stared down at the cell floor. His mouse-colored hair was shaggy and tousled, as if he'd been dragging his hands through it. Finally he looked up and nodded. "All right," he said. "I trust you. But be *careful*."

I gave a half smile. *Careful* wasn't my usual approach, but why press the point?

"Celyn? I mean — Digger?" He looked up at me, and his face was open and vulnerable. "You met Barris. Did you also see —"

"Koya?"

Whatever passed across his face at the name was gone so fast I couldn't identify it. He nodded. "How is she?"

How to answer *that* question? Interesting? Incomprehensible? "Bearing up well, under the circumstances?" Whatever those circumstances actually were.

Durrel gave a slight sigh. "Thank you. This can't be easy on her."

"Or you," I said pointedly. "You know what people are saying? About you and your stepdaughter."

He made a face, just a small wince of distaste. "It's just gossip. Sometimes I think Talth courted it. She had a cruel streak, particularly when it came to her daughter."

"Could Koya have killed her?"

There was that odd little fog to his expression again. "Of course not."

"Are you sure? You sound a little —"

"Completely." The weight of that one word killed *that* conversation.

I frowned, trying to dredge up another question. "All right, didn't you tell me it was a maid's word that had you arrested? She claimed to see you leaving Talth's room before the body was discovered?"

Nodding slowly, he said, "Geirt. Her chambermaid. But I told you, she had to be mistaken."

"Or lying," I said. "If we could talk to her, figure out what she really saw, or why she'd lie about it —"

It was like a shaft of light had broken through the gloom of the cell. "Celyn, that's brilliant. But the servants are long gone, it sounds like." And just like that, the shadows fell again.

"Maybe Koya knows what happened to her. I'll see what I can find out." Below us, the ugly bell clanged out the hour. The visiting period was ending. "Pox. I have to go. Do you need anything?"

"I need to see my father."

"I'm working on it. He's not so easy to reach, these days." I explained about the guards at Charicaux, but Durrel only looked more confused.

"No, you must have been mistaken. We — my father doesn't have any retainers like that."

The pistol carried by the guard at the gate had seemed pretty conclusive, but I let it pass. "Don't get discouraged. We'll figure this out." I forced more confidence into my voice than I felt.

He reached a hand out the small window, and my fingers brushed his. "Thank you," he said faintly, but I heard him.

Behind me, Wet Onions had awakened again. "Lift your skirts up a little more, girl. I can't see much from here."

I was tempted to give him a taste of what I kept under those skirts — a three-inch steel blade that I was getting pretty good at throwing — but I just gave him a tart look as I passed by. "Watch your fingers," I said. "Someone might come by and bite them off."

He gave a cackling laugh, but it was Durrel's small chuckle I heard, all the way down the stairs and across the bridge.

CHAPTER SEVEN

As I walked away from the Keep, a pall seemed to fall over the afternoon. I wasn't making much progress. The only real lead I had was the magical residue I'd found at Bal Marse, plus the name of a maid I may or may not be able to track down, and I had to admit that neither of those might amount to anything in the end.

One problem was that merely *seeing* magic wasn't terribly useful. I couldn't determine anything about the trace of power I'd discovered — how old it was, how it got there, where it came from, or how to track it back to its source. The presence of magic at Bal Marse intrigued me, but without more information, it was just another tantalizing mystery. Durrel needed *answers*.

I stopped at the storehouse adjacent to the bakery, squeezed into a nook out of view from the street, and pulled myself up onto the low roof. There was a loose tile near one of the chimneys, a good little spot to stash things. I pried the hot tile aside with my fingernails, leaving a line of red dust beneath it. Inside I kept the few small treasures of my life: a pair of black leather gloves; a silver bracelet; a single gold sovereign I could never bring myself to spend; and a tiny, fragile book hardly bigger than my small hand. I slipped the little book into my bodice, where it felt warm against my breastbone, and I carried it back inside, climbing gracelessly over Rat, asleep in the bed beneath the open window.

"Uf! Gerroffme —" I dodged flailing limbs and bedclothes to land neatly on the shabby rug. Rat propped himself up on his elbows to glare at me. "I am *not* taking that to the laundry this time."

I bit my thumb at him, then peeled off the stained sleeve and flung it at his head.

"Cabbage," he said judiciously, pulling it away from his face. "Nice."

As Rat wrangled himself into something akin to respectability, I perched on the cheese barrel in the kitchen and pulled the little book from my bodice. It was warmer than ever now, and the worn velvet of the cover flickered briefly when I stroked the plush fibers. It contained a somewhat fanciful history of magic in Llyvraneth, from the days long before Sar's power had faded from our land — myths, songs, drawings, and legends set down by various authors through the years. I had been given this book by the only person I knew who could truly be called a mage, Master Tnor Reynart, one of the Sarists — in the truest sense of the word, followers of Sar — I had encountered at Bryn Shaer. When I met him, he had been Meri Nemair's secret tutor in magic, and the leader of a band of refugees camping in the Carskadon Mountains, but now he was the commander of Prince Wierolf's magical army, a small company of magic users made up primarily of those selfsame refugees, now better dressed and fed and legitimized. I had seen a taste of what Reynart's troops could do in battle, with Meri's powerful magical support to fuel them, and it was awe inspiring. But they were only a handful, and they weren't nearly as powerful or well trained as the rumors claimed, and the Sarist forces were far outnumbered, even with allies from Corlesanne and Varenzia fighting alongside them.

With a sigh, I flipped through the pages of the little magic book, seeing if it said anything to explain the stains and scratches on the Bal Marse floor. It would be helpful to have someone like Reynart here now, but as far as I knew, there *weren't* any other people like Master Reynart — or if there were, somehow, knowledgeable magic users hiding in Gerse, I certainly didn't know how to find them.

I had tried when I first got back to town, armed with Reynart's book. I had studied its pages — the ones in languages I could read — thirsty for the knowledge within, veiled lessons well hidden in stories and verse, and hopeful that it could tell me something about myself, about those like me and how to find them. *Magic settles in the low places*, the chorus of a song had told me, and so I had sought out sewers and river basins and basements in abandoned homes, never coming any closer than one crude, seven-pointed star scratched into a lintel. The charm was so old and worn, my touch could barely coax its magical light from the wood, and when I tried, it left me feeling cold and sick, my skin prickling uncomfortably at the idea of hunting down Sarists. Gerse already *had* people to do that, equipped with green uniforms, nightsticks, lodestones, and scalding silver irons to force magic to show itself. Whether it was the thought of leading the Inquisition straight to a magic user's doorstep or the fear of coming too close to my brother's work that stopped me, it amounted to the same thing. I wouldn't do it.

"What's that?" Rat said, sitting across from me at the table. He had dressed and shaved, and set about slicing an apple into wedges, half of which he piled before me.

"I'm not hungry," I said, pushing them aside. Someone had let the orange cat in, and it hopped onto the table beside me, stalking my apple with its slow, amber gaze.

"You're *always* hungry. Still trying to figure out your Bal Marse mystery?"

I snapped the book shut. Rat was good about the whole magic issue, and I'd mentioned my curious discovery at Talth's house — but this was one area where I didn't push the boundaries of trust. What he didn't know couldn't hurt either one of us.

"Fair enough," he said equably. "I've solved your other one."

I looked at him blankly. He'd solved . . . the murder?

"Your anonymous letter?" He whipped it from his doublet. "It was sent by —"

"Raffin Taradyce," I said, feeling only a little bad for interrupting.

"Well, you certainly know how to spoil a surprise. Still, it wasn't wholly a waste of time. You may thank the grocer's next to the stationer for your breakfast, mistress. Since you're unlikely to thank me."

I met his gaze solemnly. "Thank you. May Mend-kaal of the hearth praise your everlasting generosity."

"See? Was that so —"

"I need a favor."

"What a surprise." Rat plucked the cat from the table and settled it in his lap, waiting.

"I need to see Lord Decath," I said. "Can you arrange that?"

"You mean, can *Hobin* arrange that? Why don't you just go visit Decath? I thought he knew you."

"I tried. I couldn't get in to see him at home, and I don't know where else to find him. But it needs to be discreet."

"Digger, love, you do realize *discreet* and Lord Hobin don't belong in the same sentence, right? I'm sure he'll do it. But you won't like it."

"What does that mean?"

Rat grinned evilly across the green rind of his apple. "He wants you to come for dinner."

Lord Hobin's *teriza* sat just a few piers down from the house where I'd met the Ceid family. Rat took me there by boat the next evening, just as the moons were rising over the water and the heat from the day was starting to lift. Together, we looked the part for dinner with nobs. Rat wore his powder blue suit, and I wore a heavy gown of coppery red satin that Rat had produced out of thin air, perfectly tailored to my small frame.

"And you're sure Decath will be there," I pressed for the thousandth time.

"Stop fidgeting." Rat leaned over the edge of the boat to trail his fingers in the water. "This is Celyn Contrare's debut into Gerse society. Try not to ruin it for her."

Lord Hobin was an official in the Ministry of War, not a high-ranking noble but comfortable enough. As if anyone could really be comfortable in that position in this climate, with word spreading of border skirmishes and pitched battles that drew closer to Gerse by the day. If Wierolf really was gaining ground, as some of the more optimistic rumors claimed, Hobin's job, and along with it his favor at court, had to be in jeopardy. As we neared the *teriza*, I took in the ivory brick façade, the green banners listless in the airless evening, the guests already gathering on the terrace, and told myself I'd survived worse. *This is for Durrel.*

When we mounted the travertine steps to Hobin's back terrace, a dozen pairs of eyes swung my way, curious, measuring, predatory. Nobody actually whispered anything, but they might as well have. Their thoughts were as loud as any gossip: *There goes the Inquisitor's sister. Oh, is she the one? Funny, not much to look at, is she? I can't decide — does she look like a Sarist?*

"You must be Digger," said a robust voice behind me. "Halcot talks about you endlessly."

I turned to see a trim man in his fourth age, graying at the temples and softening at the waist, but still handsome. "Lord Hobin," I said. "Thank you for your hospitality." I gave him my very best curtsy, learned backstage at tavern theaters and perfected at the court of Bryn Shaer.

"Think nothing of it," he said. "I've been dying to meet you, but Halcot said you'd never come. I must say, you're not nearly so shocking as he described you."

I had to laugh at that. "Oh, wait. It's early. I'm sure there's still plenty of time for me to disrupt your evening."

"Digger," he said confidentially, hooking his arm through mine and leading me across the terrace, "look around you. You would have to make a very concerted effort to overset this society. Oh, look, here's Koya. Do you know Davinna Koyuz?"

The same Mistress Koyuz was at that moment springing lightly up the terrace steps, trailing yards of pearl gray beaded silk behind her. Her color was high, and she waved at Hobin.

"Koya! My treasure." Hobin bowed low and kissed Koya's outstretched hand. "I was so hoping we'd see your husband this evening."

"Don't be silly, you know he and Claas never go anywhere." She rose from her curtsy and gave him a glittering smile. "They'd love it if you visited them, though."

"Here, darling, why don't you take Celyn," Hobin said with careful emphasis on the name. "I think she'd feel more comfortable with you.

You're the only person here more notorious than she is." With a completely wicked smile, he kissed us each and strolled off into the tangle of his guests.

As Koya dragged me about, introducing me to people as if she and I were lifelong friends, I realized that Hobin was right. My presence here tonight no doubt deflected attention from her mother's murder and her relationship with Durrel. I saw Lord Ragn across the court and tried to move in his direction, but Koya was steering me toward the banquet table.

"Rat looks good," she said, giving the neckline of her bodice a tug. I didn't blame her; it was getting warm in here.

"You know Rat?"

"Everyone knows Rat," Koya replied. "His parents are wealthy, you know. Growing up, whenever the Granthin and the Ceid gathered, the children got thrown together by default. He's a nice boy." She sounded almost sad when she said that.

Suspicious, I probed gently. "And Hobin?"

"Hobin's Hobin," she said inconclusively, ending the conversation with a smile. "And look, here's our dinner. He'll want you to sit with him."

Hobin's food was good — rich, expensive, much of it imported or heavily taxed, tiny slices of some pink citrus fruit from Talanca, the sweet, blue mussels harvested from the Oss at low tide (I'd heard about them all my life but never eaten them before; after my first bite I decided I'd never eat anything *else*), goblets of sparkling Grisel from Corlesanne. "The last in the city, my good gentles, so drink up and enjoy it!" Corles wine had been banned a few months earlier, when that nation openly pledged its support for the Sarists.

Conversation swung easily from topic to topic, but only skirted the surface of any but the lightest of subjects. No one mentioned the war, the succession, the Inquisition, or the Green Army spreading through our streets like a summer plague. It was exactly what I would have expected from a dinner party held by someone Rat was involved with. But by the time they served us a frothy confection of strawberries and some kind of flaming sauce (fire! And dessert!), talk shifted to more serious matters.

"What do your sources tell of the war, milord?" a plump woman in pink asked Hobin.

"What do yours say?" he replied, to general laughter.

"Only that the front will reach Gerse by the end of the summer," she said. "Do you think that's true?"

"Nonsense. There hasn't been fighting in the city in a hundred years," one of the male guests said. "Even the last uprising never came near our gates."

"This is more than an uprising," someone said. It was not until I felt everyone's eyes on me that I realized it was *me*.

"Mistress Celyn has it right, as she must surely know," Lord Ragn said. "We must be careful not to discount Prince Wierolf's army as a band of disgruntled rebels. With support from Corlesanne and Varenzia, and more *popular* support than anyone wants to admit, they won't be as easy to defeat this time."

"Spoken like a true Sarist," said the lady in pink.

"Not I," Lord Ragn said.

"Then you're for Astilan," said the young man beside me, but Lord Ragn only smiled.

"And why *haven't* you made your allegiance plain, milord?" Lord Hobin said.

"You mistake me," said Lord Ragn. "I've never made a secret of my politics. But when this conflict is over, people in Llyvraneth are going to have to go back to living and working *together*. Someone needs to be here to help make that happen. People neither side hates."

"Or people both sides hate equally," I said.

Lord Ragn lifted his glass. "Spoken like a true courtier."

"Come now, Lord Ragn, there's no call to insult the girl," said Koya, making everyone laugh.

As we ate, one of the diners mentioned some story about a Greenman who'd been found dead a few days earlier, up in the Fifth Circle. He'd been discovered in an abandoned house, not a mark on his body. "But a handprint on the wall behind him — in purple paint."

My attention had wandered, but it snapped to at that. "What? Where was this?"

The pink lady glared at me, but her companion said, "Out near the city wall, where they're building that new armory. I only heard about it because my housemaid comes from that neighborhood."

"Do you think it was Sarists?" asked the eager young courtier to my side.

"Hardly," Lord Hobin put in. "Assuming it happened at all, assuming this wasn't the hysterical fancy of an excitable servant, I'm sure it was nothing more than some poor vagrant who expired from hunger. Plenty of that these days, anyway."

"If rumor spreads, we'll be seeing purple handprints all over the city," the older gentleman said wearily, as if he were predicting an outbreak of fleas. Nobody mentioned the obvious: Such a rumor was likely to whip the Greenmen into a terror, more devoted than ever to scouring the city of magic users. I kept my eyes on my plate, but I still felt more than one stare boring into me.

The meal broke up shortly after that, and as everyone rose and milled about, I approached Lord Ragn, who held his arms out to me for an embrace. "Celyn, my dear! What a joy it is to see you again. Our stray cat has finally found her way to the bowl of milk, I see."

"If you feed them, they'll never leave."

He gave a warm, rolling laugh; it was the line Lord Ragn had given when Durrel presented me to his family. "Well, we don't feed you enough, apparently. You're looking thin. Come stay at Favom, and Morva will fatten you right up."

"I'd like that." My last visit to the Decath country holding had been rushed and confusing, and my memories of the fine old house and grounds were clouded with grief and panic. "Milord, I bring news of your son."

His face shadowed over, and he nodded. "Come. I'm sure our host won't mind if we speak privately in here." He led me to a set of glass doors I had assumed opened onto another terrace, but which admitted us into a small, comfortably furnished office, its wide windows open to admit the night breeze. And any common thief skulking about in the bushes outside; Hobin had papers (not to mention more tangible valuables like candlesticks and inkwells) lying about everywhere. I quite fancied that inkwell, actually — scarlet Tratuan glass, traced with gold — I wondered if Hobin would miss it. No wonder Tegen had liked Nob Circle so much.

Lord Ragn settled himself in an ornately carved chair, drawing it close to a small bench by the window. "You've seen Durrel? Please — tell me, how is he?"

"Not well," I said bluntly. "Milord, have you been there?"

"No, I —" He shook his head. "He doesn't want to see me."

"That isn't true." But I stopped, wondering. Maybe Lord Ragn was right. Durrel was in a bad way up there, and he was proud. "You should go anyway."

"I know," he said. "It's just . . . I don't want to make things worse for him."

"Worse?" I said. "I don't understand."

Ragn looked grim, and he didn't answer for a long moment. "Things can go very rough for nobles in prison. If I call attention to his presence there, I'm afraid it will make him a target. For thievery, or violence, or —" He faltered. "Besides, the Ceid have effectively blocked my applications for a visitor's pass."

"Can they do that? You're a lord!"

Something twisted in Lord Ragn's expression. "The Ceid have the royal shipping contracts for goods in and out of the city, and the supply lines to the troops at the front. That's powerful leverage right now for the king. And I have —" He spread his hands, encompassing nothing. "They're hoping to break him by keeping us apart."

I leaned closer to Durrel's father. "I can get you a pass," I said, willing meaning into every word. Thanks to Raffin, I had everything I needed for a flawless forgery. Lord Ragn looked confused for a moment, and then alarmed.

"No! Celyn, that is a *hanging* offense if you were to be discovered! I couldn't possibly allow you to take that risk." He rose and paced to the cold fireplace. I wanted to follow, but something in his manner held me back. "Gods," he said under his breath. "I can't believe this is happening again."

"Milord?" I said. "What do you mean?" Barris had said something strange about Durrel's history, but it hadn't meant anything to me at the time.

"There was an . . . incident. In Tratua. A few years ago when Durrel was studying there. A girl was hurt. It was a horrible time, and he'd only just begun to move on from it. This time, I'm afraid I won't be able to help him."

"*I* can help." I explained how someone (I didn't say who) had sprung for my arrest and bond, just to get me inside the Keep to talk to Durrel, but Lord Ragn only looked more worried.

"Be careful," he said. "This situation is far more delicate than you realize, and you've already put yourself in too much danger. Perhaps it's best if we let things take their course. We must have faith that the truth will come out in due time."

"Take their course? If things keep taking their course, they'll be cutting Durrel's head off by the end of this month!"

"No!" Lord Ragn turned back, his face set. "By all the gods, my son is not a murderer!" He took a steadying breath, a hand to his strained forehead. "I know you know that. Forgive me. You've been a very good friend to this family, Celyn. Durrel is lucky to have you. Can you tell me how he is? Does he have everything he needs?"

"He needs *you*," I said, but I told him what I could of Durrel's condition, his state of mind. "Maybe if you just sent word, a little money? They can't stop that."

"Of course," he said, his expression just slightly relieved. "And what about you? Do you have everything you need?" He drew a purse from his belt, loosening the drawstrings. "Money? Safe lodgings? I know my niece's family was concerned when you left them. I should like to report that Gerse has not forgotten you, that we did not merely abandon you to the wolves upon your return."

My heart caught a little in my chest, and I nodded. "Yes, milord."

"Will you let me give you a little something? It can't be easy, being on your own."

"Milord, it isn't necessary," I began, but he looked so stricken that I didn't protest further, and let him drop a handful of gold coins into my hands.

"Nonsense. You're practically family." Lord Ragn put a hand on my shoulder. "It was good to see you," he said sadly, and I realized with a start that he was ending the conversation.

"Wait, milord — Durrel thought Talth might have been killed over some business she was involved in," I said in a rush, before he could slip away from me.

He frowned. "I assure you that her son Barris was questioned closely by the Watch, and if they had discovered anything to exonerate Durrel, surely we would have heard."

"He also asked about his wife's chambermaid, the one who claims she saw him."

"Celyn." Lord Ragn's voice was gentle. "I know you want to help, but truly, the best thing you can do for Durrel right now is be his friend. Good night." He brushed the top of my head with one light hand, as if I really were his kin. I wanted to tell him I could save Durrel, but he was gone before I could form the lie on my lips and will it to become true. *The truth will come out in due time*, he'd said. But in my experience, the truth was bashful; it tended to stay hidden until somebody *made* it come out.

I lingered in the little office for some time after that exchange, frustrated and weary and in no mood to don my Celyn Contrare mask once more for the benefit of the assembled audience. With a sigh, I rose and walked to the window. The moons shone brightly on Hobin's desk, and I couldn't help glancing down at his papers. Maps showing troop movements, quartermasters' reports . . . I turned one of the maps into the light. Where was Wierolf? Did he have enough men, did he have enough food? Was someone there to remind him to eat, to watch his right side when he struck a blow from above?

"There you are," said a mellow voice. I glanced up guiltily and saw Lord Hobin advancing on me. "Halcot said you'd be getting restless, and that somebody ought to check on you before —"

I smiled and held up my — empty — hands. "Have no fear, your lordship. I was only looking for my own benefit."

"Ah." He came up beside me. "And what did you hope to learn from — Lieutenant Scalda's report on malaria in the swamps outside Tratua?"

"That the prince doesn't have malaria." Somehow I said that out loud.

Hobin sat on the edge of the desk, loosening a couple of the clasps on his doublet. "The prince does not, as far as I have heard, have malaria. Neither prince," he amended — not quite swiftly enough, had anyone been there to overhear. "Your prince is in the west, with the troops advancing on the Spirau Plain. Reports have him in good health and high spirits. He fights well, and he has good advisors."

I nodded, relieved, but wondered why he would tell me this. He was Bardolph's man, according to the signature on his payment orders.

He was watching me, keen eyes bright in the dim room. "Not everyone in the current government is entirely satisfied by the way His Majesty has chosen to conduct his affairs in this war. It's despicable, really — holding his own armies close to Gerse, while Astilan and Wierolf battle it out among themselves? Damnable way to choose a successor."

"And if it's Astilan, Bardolph will open the city gates and hand over the crown?"

Hobin shrugged. "I suppose that's what everyone's expecting. Wierolf's army will be tired and spent, and the royal troops at Gerse will be fresh. It keeps the king from risking too much, of course, but I can't think much of it." He shuffled the papers into new order. "And if Astilan falls during a battle somewhere? What will His Majesty do then, I wonder."

"I thought Astilan was being kept away from the fighting." That's what rumor said, anyway.

"He was," Hobin said. "Until the Sarists won a few key battles in the north the last couple of months, then he insisted on taking an active generalship. Nobody's happy about it, but they think he's going to be *king*. Who's going to gainsay him?"

"He's trained for it, though." All his life, in his uncle's armies, alongside the best fighters in the world, while Wierolf had spent twenty years in libraries and hunting lodges. I had seen him fight; he was strong and skilled, but he was not a career military man.

"An arrow can strike anyone," Hobin said. "And Zet can deflect a blow, or make a horse stumble. Anything can happen."

Somehow, that didn't make me feel any better.

CHAPTER EIGHT

Lord Hobin led me from his study through the balcony and down wide, curving stairs to the moonslit terrace below. I heard a scrap of voices, the rustle of skirts carried on the muggy air, and I saw Koya trot up the terrace steps and pause to say something to Lord Ragn. I wasn't sure what to make of my own conversation with Durrel's father, except that it was depressing and unproductive, and once again I had nothing of worth to bring to Durrel. I watched Lord Ragn below me. Koya had gone back into the party, but he remained silhouetted against the torchlight on the terrace, looking out over the water and rubbing the back of his neck.

Sighing, I returned to the house, where guests floated and mingled through the drowsy candlelight. I spotted Rat tucked away in a corner, curled sleepily into a cushioned bench, a wine glass hooked in one hand dangling precarious inches from the marble floor. "Where have you been?" he asked. "You've disappointed everyone tonight, you know. They were hoping you might stab somebody."

"You're drunk," I said. Sometimes it was hard to tell, until he said something stupid.

"Yes," he said. "On the last bottle of sparkling Grisel in Gerse. Care to join me?"

"It's tempting." Fortunately, if that was even the right word, at that moment Koya came sweeping by, trailing her gray silken skirts behind her like a spiderweb.

"Celyn!" she cried. "I'm sorry we didn't get to see more of each other tonight, but I must run."

"It's a little early for you, isn't it?" Rat observed. "The moons haven't set yet."

"Alas, yes," she said. "But I have other demands on my company tonight."

Behind her, Lord Ragn had been detained by Lord Hobin, who appeared to be trying to coax him to stay.

"Is Lord Ragn leaving too?" I asked.

"I wouldn't know," she said. "Why?"

"I saw you speaking to him just now," I said, and Koya broke into a wide smile.

"And you think I must have said something scandalous to chase him off! Now I'm almost sorry I didn't."

"Do you often say scandalous things to Lord Ragn?" Rat asked, saving me the trouble.

Koya gave a brief, surprised laugh. "I don't often say *anything* to the man. Why would I? But for Lord Durrel, our paths wouldn't ever have crossed. And, well, what *does* one do with one's — what? — step-grandfather?" She laughed again, then dipped in to kiss me on each cheek. A cloud of exotic scent almost concealed the faint odor of wine. "I must say good night," she said. "But, dear Celyn, come see me again. I have a salon at Cartouche nearly every evening; tell the boys at the door and they'll let you in." With a flutter of her fingers, she danced away.

Rat slinked upward in the chair. "You should go. Her salons are very exclusive. And entertaining."

I wasn't sure what a "salon" was, but I wasn't burning with the desire to spend another evening with these people. Lord Ragn was still at the terrace doors, trying to disentangle himself from conversation with Hobin and the lady in pink. "Why is he leaving so early?" I wondered aloud.

Rat yawned elaborately. "I think he said something about wanting to beat the curfew."

"But he lives only a few minutes from here. We've got a good hour left before curfew. Where's he going?" As I turned the thought over in my head, I decided I wanted to know.

"I don't like the look of *that*," Rat said, sounding abruptly sober. "What are you planning?"

"Don't you know by now I never plan anything?" I said. "Give my regrets to Lord Hobin."

He tilted his head back against the bench. "I would try to stop you, but I can't seem to move. Don't stay out too late."

"Yes, Mother."

Rat was right — this was a bad idea. But I'd had my fill of Lord Hobin's guests, and Lord Ragn's abrupt departure bothered me. It was none of my business and probably had absolutely nothing to do with Durrel's predicament, but I'd seen those strange guards at Charicaux — the ones Durrel hadn't known anything about — and besides, there *was* still an hour to go until curfew. I'd rather be out in the night air, chasing after Lord Ragn, than stuck at the *teriza* trying to make conversation with the lady in pink. I'd come to Hobin's to see him, after all. So see Lord Ragn I would.

He left the *teriza* on foot, which was unusual; most genteel Nob Circle traffic was by water, so the nobs didn't have to break a sweat in the summer heat. I let him get a few dozen paces ahead of me, quickly realizing the impracticality of my impulse; I was *not* dressed for a stealth tracking job. I was, in fact, apparently clad in the loudest garment possible; jester's bells couldn't have made these rustling skirts any noisier. But Lord Ragn's attention was clearly focused on whatever was before him, not who might be behind him.

Out of the grand homes of Nob Circle, under the Oss Bridge, past a public circle patrolled by Green Army soldiers, I followed Lord Ragn doggedly, though the night grew no less sticky the farther away from the water we got. We were headed vaguely uphill, toward the city wall and the Pilgrims' Gate, well away from his own part of town. I imagined he was going somewhere illicit, intriguing — a gambling den, perhaps, or a courtesan's house. But as I recognized the streets and the neighborhood, I slowed down, stumped. What was Lord Ragn doing *here*?

He crossed down one wide, empty, cobbled road, moving with

purpose toward a squat, square building that I recognized. I didn't have to see around the back of that warehouse to know that its neighbor, across a narrow strip of alley and behind a low stone wall with an unlocked gate, was an abandoned house technically owned by Lord Ragn's imprisoned son.

He'd led me to the warehouse behind Bal Marse.

I froze at the mouth of the alleyway and hung back behind the corner as Lord Ragn withdrew a key from his doublet and let himself in through a narrow back door. I scurried down the alley after him, but he'd locked the door behind him, and I didn't dare take the risk that he was standing *just inside*, if I tumbled it.

What was his business here? I supposed it was completely possible he was here for some legitimate purpose — but he'd come alone, by night, with no light, after having an upsetting conversation about his murder-suspect son. I couldn't be *sure* those things were related, of course. But I wouldn't like to wager on it.

I gave the perimeter of the warehouse a good once-over, but it was windowless, the other doors closed fast, nothing at all to give up Lord Ragn's purpose here. I waited a discreet distance away, tucked behind a barrel at the end of the alleyway, but he did not reappear, and eventually my feet went numb in my red silk shoes. If I didn't get home soon, I really would miss the curfew, so I reluctantly gave up my hold on Lord Ragn, and headed back across town to the bakery.

As I walked, I tugged at threads in the scraps of information I'd collected, hoping one might pull loose. Durrel had mentioned Talth's business, and Barris had seemed touchy when I'd asked him about his mother's affairs. And now *Lord Ragn* showed up at one of his dead daughter-in-law's properties, practically in the middle of the night. I needed more information about Mistress Ceid's enterprises. Fortunately I knew just the person to consult.

The next afternoon, after sleeping off Lord Hobin's party, I headed down to the Big Silver, where the Ceid controlled some of the dockyards and shipping houses. I was wearing holes in my good shoes, with all this crosstown running about. Still, it wasn't the Ceid I'd come to see today.

Eptin Cwalo, distinguished merchant and shrewd businessman, was a smallish, unprepossessing fellow who kept an elegant little storefront in the Spiral, that part of the city where lovely, rich streets twisted together in a tight, tidy borough of shops and houses, and neighbors kept a keen eye on one another's safety and turned a blind one to their business. Cwalo & Sons, Importers sold spices and silks, glassware and incense, imported from all over the world; and from his warehouse down on the Big Silver, Cwalo carried out an even more profitable trade in . . . other things. I'd met him at the Nemair's last winter, and he'd taken an unaccountable liking to me, kindly delivering me back to the city when winter was over. After two months traveling the back roads of Llyvraneth with the man, I'd come to share the Nemair's trust in him.

I trotted down the Big Silver as the sun pulsed heavily against the streets. It was getting muggier, and I pulled at my layers of dress, grateful for the slight slip of a breeze I imagined curling around my hot ankles. I crossed from dusty cobbles to rippled boardwalk and passed into the shade of hulking merchant traders, their mooring lines creaking in the humid air. I saw the name on one vessel and had to smile. It was new, Tratuan built, flying neutral flags, and called *Merista*.

Outside a low frame building opposite the docks, a compact, bald man, clad in neat black, spoke with a brace of royal guardsmen. I pulled back, my neck and belly tense, but Cwalo gave one of the guards a friendly thump on the arm. I waited until they walked away, and I noticed one of them carried a distinctive green wine bottle under one arm.

Cwalo's shiny face lit up when he saw me, and he strolled over, arms open. "My dear! I would tell you this is no place for a girl like you, but I think I might be wrong." He pulled me into a quick, firm embrace. I glanced down the road at the departing guardsmen, and Cwalo shook his head. "It takes half my profits maintaining goodwill in this city, but it's worth it, these days."

I cast my eyes around the dockyard. "Is there somewhere we can talk?"

"Always." He led me toward the warehouse's small office room, where he motioned to a chair and perched himself on the desk, rummaging in the drawer behind him for a bronze flask and a set of tiny bejeweled cordial cups. I was lucky to find him back in Gerse; he spent most of his time on the road, and his main family home was in Yeris Volbann, but he made it a point to let me know when he was back in the city — even if I didn't always manage to come see him. "What brings you here? Tell me it's because you've reconsidered my offer!" He grinned as he poured a creamy liquid into the little cups.

"Master Cwalo, you know I love you, but I am not going to marry Garod." Cwalo's overriding ambition was to find brides for his six sons.

He gave a little sigh. "Ah, well. I won't stop asking, you know."

"You have five other sons. Pick me another one. I did like Piral a lot, you know."

"Piral?" Cwalo's face was very serious. "Piral is eleven years old and thinks of nothing but ships and dogs. I think you may be too much woman for him."

I laughed aloud at that. "He popped the lock I gave him on his very first try," I reminded him. "Besides, by the time I'm ready for a husband, he'll be all grown up. Try me again in another ten years."

"My girl, if no one has managed to coax you into becoming respectable by that time, I don't think even Piral will be up for that task. Now. Tell me why you've come."

I sobered and explained about the murder of Talth Ceid. Cwalo had been out of the city for a few months, but it didn't surprise me that he'd heard the news.

"Bad tidings, indeed. Mistress Talth was a formidable influence in so many areas — not an easy woman to like, certainly — but she got things done. I can't imagine young Durrel had any part in this!"

The relief I felt was irrational, but Cwalo had the best nose for cunning I knew, and I was glad to have him confirm my own conviction. Swiftly I told him of Durrel's questions regarding Talth's business dealings, the warehouse near Bal Marse visited by Lord Ragn, the curiously empty home adjacent to it, and the guards now patrolling the Decath grounds.

He frowned at that, leaning forward a little in his seat. "Well, that's not like them at all, I'd say. Ragn Decath's a good man, steady. If he's scared enough to hire a security force . . ." His frown deepened. "I think you're right. It's certainly worth looking into."

I resumed my account, telling him about the encounter I'd had with Talth's children. "The daughter gave me a couple of names. Uh — Emmis somebody?"

"Emmis Corsour?" Cwalo looked incredulous. "The man's got to be eighty, and he never leaves his farm in Wolt. He's obsessed with breeding the perfect hen. I don't think he's your man. Who else?"

"Kurst, I think?"

"That doesn't sound familiar. I can't help you there." He paused a moment, his gaze scrutinizing. "There's a complication you're not telling me."

I hesitated, looking at my fingers spread wide against my skirts. Cwalo knew about me, but the less said about these matters, the better. I nodded.

"Very well, I think I can guess. Go on."

I shifted in my chair; I could see water beneath the floorboards at my feet, and gulls cried loudly outside, their voices eerie in the still air. "I need to know more about Talth's business," I said. "Have you heard that she was involved in anything . . . ?" I trailed off.

Lips pursed, Cwalo rubbed his bald head. "That's a broad question. The answer to the specific question you did not ask me is no, but contrary to your opinion of me, I am not privy to everything that happens on our fair nation's docks. It's entirely possible she was involved in matters that may have caused her path to cross with some of our . . . unique friends."

"Durrel said he thought Talth was involved with criminals. But you're saying she was involved with Sarists?" I kept my voice low.

"No! My girl, you misunderstand me."

"Imagine that. You weren't being oblique *at all*."

Cwalo sighed and tapped his knuckles against the desk, obviously trying to decide whether to tell me something, or how much. I waited, and he finally drew his ringed fingers together in a pyramid before his face. "There are rumors — nothing confirmed, mind you, and no one's approached me directly — but I've heard murmurs of secret shipments in and out of Gerse these last few months."

"Shipments of what?"

Cwalo shook his head. "No word. Could be guns, could be gold — could be oranges from Talanca, for all I know."

"But you don't think so."

He gave an almost imperceptible shrug. "Hard to say. But at a guess, it's not guns. The Ceid openly ship supplies for Bardolph, so there'd be no reason to hide shipments of firearms to the Green Army. And we know where the rebels get *their* weapons."

He meant himself, on that account. "Gold, then?"

"Well, it's more likely, but again —"

"It doesn't explain the magic." I thought back for a moment, recalling everything I'd learned about smuggling while traveling with Cwalo. "You're thinking it's like that woman we met in Wyrst — that widow who sold us her brooch." She'd wanted an outrageous sum for the thing, its value confirmed when it sparked up at my touch, but couldn't say what it actually *did*. I'd poked at it for a fortnight, but never could coax its secrets from it. Still, there were collectors — a black market in rare, magical antiquities that was so secretive even Cwalo didn't usually deal with it.

"I would say that's a distinct possibility. And dangerous enough too. The illicit trade in magical artifacts is risky at the best of times."

"And you think that Talth was involved with these secret shipments?"

"I'm *certain* that the Ceid are involved; nothing happens in this city without their say, but to what extent your friend's departed spouse figured into the equation, I'm afraid I can't speculate. It might not have anything to do with your mystery at all."

"Did you ever do business with her?"

"Some."

"What kind?"

A quirk of a smile. "The *conventional* kind."

"And if it were anything else, you wouldn't tell me." That wasn't a question.

"I would not tell you," he agreed, "but I would be very circumspect in my denials, and I would devise an excuse to slip out of this office and leave you here alone for a few moments. No, my girl, if Mistress Ceid was dealing in anything *unconventional*, she was doing it through other avenues."

"Could you find out?"

"Are you sure? This isn't something to poke at lightly, you know."

"I know," I said. "But it's important. If it can help Durrel —"

"Of course. I don't suppose there's any use telling you to be careful?" When I didn't answer, Cwalo looked resigned. "I understand. Come to dinner? Mirelle would never forgive me for not asking. Besides, Piral can't stop talking about you."

"You brought them to Gerse?"

"My dear, surely you know by now, nobody *brings* Mirelle Cwalo anywhere. She came to see you. Just in case you stopped by. I wish you had stayed," he added.

I felt my heart give a little squeeze. "You know why I left," I said. Werne's first letter had come to Cwalo's house, and I'd gotten new lodgings — well across town — the next day. They had urged me to stay, but I think Mirelle was secretly relieved, no matter what her husband said. She still had children at home, after all, and two boys fighting for Wierolf. She didn't need me adding to her concerns.

Cwalo just gave the ghost of a sigh. "Come up to the house, now. She worries."

"I won't forget."

CHAPTER NINE

Armed with Cwalo's information, I set off on a circuit of the dockside warehouses leased or owned by Talth and her family. It was tricky going; I was ridiculously out of place here, a girl alone, wandering the docks, strolling in and out of warehouses. I ought to have brought Cwalo along, but of course I never think of these things until it's too late. Still, I did my best to look like a servant on business for her masters, straightening my cap and hitching my basket to my shoulder and trying to act imperious.

Also, I had the knife in my boot.

The first warehouse was nearly empty, not a soul in sight and not a dust mote, sparkling or otherwise, out of place. It was all a little *too* clean, in fact — Bal Marse clean, as if someone had gone to great effort to tidy up after . . . something. The few crates stacked in neat rows at the back of the storeroom were empty, their Talancan and Vareni labels plainly announcing their contents and sources, their royal customs and tax stamps frustratingly authentic. I studied the stamps briefly; if it was some kind of smuggling operation, there was no way to tell. That kind of business had too many facets to discern from a quick peek around an empty warehouse. It would require stamps, bribes, falsified manifests and bills of lading, not to mention needing some idea of *what* was being smuggled. I couldn't begin to guess from a handful of empty boxes stacked in a very, very clean Ceid storeroom. But someone was dead, and there was a reason for it.

And there was a reason a perfectly good warehouse stood empty in the middle of the busy shipping season.

Like the gates at Bal Marse, the warehouse office had been left unlocked. Inside, the two neat desks — one tall and angled for writing, the other an ordinary work desk — were likewise bare, as if waiting for their masters to return from a long, foreign holiday. A lamp, an inkwell, a brazier below a window, and nothing else even remotely useful. There was a faint odor of old smoke and ash mingled with the dusty, dry-crate smell of the place, as if someone had had a fire burning in the brazier.

In the height of midsummer.

I slipped my knife from its sheath and poked through the ash in the brazier — people *always* forget to clean out the ash — and was rewarded with a half-burnt scrap of paper, singed and curling at the corners, that had escaped the pyre. I pierced it through and lifted it to the light; it seemed to have been part of a ledger or records book, but it was so badly damaged it was hard to tell. *Light of* something, it said, and elsewhere, something that might have been part of a name — *Caltu* — , or *Catho* — I couldn't make it out. And a list of sums. Fifteen thousand crowns here, another ten thousand on another line. There was a lot of money changing hands here, somewhere. I just couldn't tell over what.

I knew little about business, but a lot about deception and covering up secrets, and it was a safe bet which category *torching your records* fell into. I felt my pulse quicken; here was my first real, *tangible* clue, charred though it was. I gently blew away the blackened edges of the page and tucked it carefully into my basket, below the false bottom I had fitted out for just such an occasion. With nothing more to be found, in or out of the ash, I moved on.

The second warehouse was downriver and across Market Bridge, on a busier dock closer to the castle and the Keep. They were open for business, and looked more like what I'd expected of a Ceid operation, with workers and dockhands bustling about the yard and storehouses, all loaded up with crates and casks and sacks of goods either coming or going. A white stucco building like a small fortress, yellow-and-green House of Ceid flags flying from its mock towers, signaled the heart of the family's business in the city. They evidently weren't accustomed to visitors, however. Down on the docks, workers cut me a wide swath as I passed by, scurrying out of my way as if I had the stench of contagion about me, and when I stopped to ask one closed-faced workman an innocent question (where the master was), he looked first to the office building before deciding not to answer.

This was getting me nowhere. In the hot afternoon sun, I pulled off my cap and let it hang down my back, loosened the button of my smock to let the river air tease my neck. Did one of those tall ships carry some secret cargo that had gotten Talth killed? Or had her business, whatever it was, died with her?

"Oi, there. Can I help you?"

I turned. A dockhand in a work-stained leather jerkin ambled toward me across the docks, a roll of papers under one arm. I held my hand up to block the sun; he had a friendly, open look about him, unlike his fellows. I don't know, maybe he liked short and surly.

"Oranges," I said abruptly.

"How's that?" Dockhand said.

Well, I was in it now. I tugged at my bodice, not that there was anything more to reveal. "My mistress sent me to see what was holding up her oranges. From Talanca? And here you are, and here the *crates* are, but I don't see any oranges." I sounded completely witless. "If you've sold them to someone else —" He eyed me a moment, and I fingered my bruised cheek, for effect.

"Well, let's see here," he said, unrolling his papers. "I've got ships from Talanca, but it don't look like we've had any fruit on 'em." He flipped through the documents, which looked like shipping manifests, listing the goods and the levies, and the ships they came in on and were scheduled to go out on again. Nothing seemed out of the ordinary; typical Ceid bookkeeping that pinned down every last seed and nail to move through this place. "Maybe we can find your oranges inside." And, as if Tiboran himself had delivered this fellow to me as a gift, he turned and led me straight into the Ceid warehouse.

"What a lot of — things," I said as we weaved through the crowded storeroom, looking for my imaginary oranges. "What is it all?"

"This cargo here is all supplies for His Majesty's troops in the field," he said, but confidentially, as if it were a secret. Waving me past a row of grain sacks, he cracked the lid on one crate, showing me the clean, sawdust-cushioned blades of a shipment of swords stamped with

Bardolph's royal crest. I thought it was too bad there wasn't some salt water at hand to dribble onto the blades, so His Majesty's troops would find them rusty and dull when they arrived. Royal approval would make for ideal cover for a shipment of contraband, but my ignorant eyes couldn't see anything out of the ordinary about this merchandise, and nothing unusual happened when I stroked my fingers across the goods. Was there something here worth murdering someone for? I had the sudden, fabulous idea that perhaps there was some magic in these items destined for Bardolph's troops, to give his soldiers the same mystical advantage that Prince Wierolf wielded. That would certainly cause a scandal of Ceid proportions, but when I leaned in to tap the blades of the neatly packed weapons, I was disappointed. The swords were just swords.

"Where does it all come from?" I asked. "You can't get that kind of grain in Gerse." Not lately, anyway.

"All over," the dockhand said. "Gelnir, Yeris. Tratua, a lot of it. Like me." He waved a hand toward the other men working on the docks. "A lot of us boys hail from down there."

Tratua? I looked up sharply from my examination of a barrel labeled GRISSE Á VOLANDE, whatever that was. Why hire dockhands from half the country away when the rivers were swarming with them right here? "Master Ceid must think highly of your work, to bring you all the way out here, then."

A shrug. "I wouldn't know about any Ceid. I was just hired to watch this cargo until the *Belprisa* comes through at the end of the week."

"*Belprisa*?"

"Some Talancan ship. Due in a few days." He fanned the manifests, as if searching for a name.

Standing on tiptoe, I peeked in. "And *they'll* have my oranges?" *And what else*, I wondered.

He snapped the papers shut. "I don't know," Friendly Dockhand said, his voice gone suddenly curt. "Why don't you come back after she's docked?"

"Maybe Master Ceid will know?" I said sweetly, wondering at the abrupt change in tone. "I'm not leaving until —"

"All right! Fine. Maybe they got delivered already. I'll see if I can't get somebody to show you." He turned toward the back of the open storage space, where a woman leaned on a crate, writing something. "Hey, Geirt!"

The girl turned, and I felt a sudden little rush. Geirt! *Talth's* Geirt, the chambermaid who put Durrel with Talth before the murder? As she crossed toward us, details filled in, matching Durrel's description: young, plump, long red hair coiled into braids pinned up on her head.

"Maybe she *can* help me," I said, and slipped away from the dockhand. I met the girl and said, "I have some questions. Can you help?"

"I can try," she said in a bored voice. "What do you need? I heard you say something about oranges? We never have fresh produce here; the masters are too cheap."

"Not about that," I said, my voice low. "About Lord Durrel."

"Durrel!" Her eyes flew wide, and she clamped a hand over her pretty mouth. I'd seen firsthand the effect Lord Durrel had on the female servants in his employ, and I guessed that this Geirt was not immune. "Quick, come over here." She drew me outside, away from the warehouse building. "Who are you?"

"A friend. You told the Night Watch that you saw Lord Durrel leave your mistress's bedroom after midnight. Are you absolutely sure it was him?"

She nodded vigorously. "Oh, aye. I remember specifically, because I thought it was so odd."

"Why odd?"

She leaned in. "Because of the row they'd had earlier that night. I thought my lady — Marau keep her — had finally pushed Lord Durrel too far, and I'd have been less surprised to see him light out for the street, his bags on his back, than to find him in Lady Talth's bedroom again!" She sobered. "I guess I was right about one thing. She must have gone too far that time."

"What was the quarrel about?"

"I couldn't hear. Just a lot of yelling, but louder and longer than usual. My mistress was a hard woman, Marau —"

"Keep her. Right. And you're sure it wasn't anyone else?"

Her eyebrows pulled together. "Who else *could* it have been? It was past midnight. Besides, I've seen milord walk about the house in the dark often enough; I knew him immediately, you know that gray doublet he always wears? I thought —" Her cheeks tinged pink. "I thought he'd gone there to, you know, make up with the mistress?"

I couldn't help cringing. That was a thought that didn't bear imagining. But something about Geirt seemed . . . off, somehow. She was pretty and friendly and she sounded like she believed her own story, so what was wrong?

Standing beside her, I had the strongest urge to *touch* her. Frowning, I stepped closer, laid a hand gently on her arm. "And you're not lying to protect somebody?" I said, looking her in the face but thinking about my hand on her sleeve. "Another servant, perhaps? Or maybe Talth had another gentleman?"

She jerked her hand away. "Why are you asking all these questions?" she said, suddenly sounding defiant. "The Watch *caught* him. He had the poison. What else is there to know?"

Well, to start, I wanted to know why I'd expected Geirt's arm to flash with light when I touched it. But she wore no silver that I could see, no jewelry at all. There was no reason to suspect she might have magic, and she'd passed the only test I knew as emphatically *not* magical, and yet . . . Pox.

"Maybe *you* had a motive?" I suggested, just to see what she did.

Her eyes grew cold. "I was a lady's maid in a fine house in Gerse," she said. "With fine clothes and food and a soft bed to myself. And now I'm working on the *docks*, like some city mudskimmer, thanks to *Milord Durrel*."

"Hey!" I heard a voice like a door banging open, and Geirt started and pulled away from me. Coming out of the wide warehouse doors like a storm rolling in was Barris Ceid. "Geirt! Come away from her. You — what do you want?" He covered the distance between us in a few long strides and grabbed Geirt by the arm. "What did you say to her?" He gave her a brutal shake.

"Nothing!" she cried. "Honestly — she said she was here about oranges!" Tears sprang up in her huge green eyes.

"I don't pay you to gossip. Get back inside." Geirt freed herself and fled back into the warehouse.

"What do you think you're doing here?" Barris demanded.

"You said you welcomed my questions," I said, trying to keep my voice reasonable.

"Yes, into *Durrel Decath*. Not harassing my employees."

"Your employees who don't know anything about you?" I inclined my head toward Dockhand, who lingered curiously at the open front of the warehouse.

Barris's face relaxed some. "Yes, well. Loyalty has always been a trait prized by the Ceid."

"Then you'll be pleased with Geirt," I said. "She didn't have anything to tell me."

"And she won't," Barris said. "Now I'll thank you to leave my property before I call the guards on you."

"Those private guards?" I asked, looking pointedly at a couple of heavies who'd followed Barris out here, now hanging at the warehouse doors and apparently watching him for a signal. "Doesn't the harbormaster provide security here?"

"We have royal cargo. We can't be too careful protecting His Majesty's interests."

"Right," I said. "Did your mother have any dealings in magic?" If I was hoping to surprise him, by saying it quick and random like that, I was disappointed.

"Of course not," Barris said scornfully. "Now remove yourself before I lose my patience."

"I'm gone," I said, turning to leave.

My thoughts were buzzing, full of wool and weapons, Talancan ships, private security (another curiosity shared by the Ceid *and* Lord Ragn), chambermaids, and magic. Pox. Would any of these pieces ever make sense?

At least I had the shipping manifests, I thought, trying to cheer myself on the way home. I'd swiped them from the dockhand when he'd turned to call for Geirt. If there was anything suspicious about the Ceid's cargo or the Ceid's ships, I'd figure it out.

CHAPTER TEN

Rumor skittering through the Seventh Circle had stirred new dirt into the air the next morning. There had been more arrests. A chandler and his grown sons had been harboring Sarist refugees in a crawl space beneath their waxworks. The chandler was dragged into the street where Greenmen had executed him on the spot, but the sons and the half-starved, terrified Sarists — one of them a five-year-old girl, someone said — had been taken. *Taken.* That's all anybody needed to say. We all knew what it meant.

"Where was this?" I asked a customer waiting near the bakery counter.

"Turning Street," he replied, taking his bread and frowning at it. "This looks like it's half rye! Damn grain shortages."

Aunt Grea just smiled and shrugged, and the grumbling customer went on his way.

"They're getting closer," I murmured, not even aware I was speaking.

"Closer to what?" Grea said.

"To me."

"No, Digger-girl, you can't think like that." But I shook my head and pushed through the line of bread buyers. I knew it wasn't rational; arrests were up all over the city, panicking neighbors pointing crazed fingers at each other and bodies stacking up from the Oss to Pilgrims' Gate, and it didn't have anything to do with *anybody* special, but I couldn't help it. It felt like it was my fault, somehow. If I'd stayed out of the city, if I'd answered Werne's letters, if I'd kept my big mouth *shut* when he'd said, *Do I know you, child* at Bryn Shaer . . .

Outside in the hot morning air, I shook myself out of my stupor. I was heading off to the Keep to visit Durrel again, and the last thing he needed was my good mood infecting the cheery atmosphere of his prison cell. Particularly since I was actually bringing good tidings for once: I had a full purse, thanks to Lord Ragn; I'd talked to a witness; and I had a stack of documents to study. Along with my basket of meat pies and a bottle of local Gerse small beer, it would almost be a party.

. . . Except for the prison bit.

Downriver, visible from the Keep landing, the royal residence of Hanivard Palace gleamed white and stark in the morning light, green banners flying from every window, roofline, and tower until it was hard to see the building itself under all that waving heraldry. Bardolph was ill; a summer fever, the royal physicians claimed noncommittally, and urged the people of Gerse to pray for Celys's most beloved son and our faithful leader. I didn't know what everyone else was praying for, but my entreaties to the gods certainly didn't include a swift return to health for the man who'd butchered thousands of Llyvrins whose only crime was looking to the wrong moon. The same fever was striking neighborhoods in the Sixth and Seventh Circles; who was praying for those people?

When the Keep guards finally cracked the drawbridge and it crashed onto the docks, it was almost a relief to get off that landing and inside the prison. Upstairs, I smiled sweetly at the guard on duty, my grin made brighter by the gold crown I held up to his grizzled face. "I'm going in there," I said sunnily. "I trust you have no objections."

The guard took a slow moment to bite the coin, then spat dangerously near my feet. It was pointless, really. Any counterfeit coin I'd have brought would contain enough gold to pass that silly test — thieves have rules about such things, after all — but I just shrugged and let him have his moment. "Make it a good show," he said, in a slow, Low Gerse drawl. "We don't get much entertainment up here."

When I realized what he meant, I wanted to hit him, but thought better of it. If that's what he wanted to believe of me, all the better. It gave me an excuse to keep coming, to get in and out of Durrel's cell without attracting too much attention. I winked at him, then swished my way down the hall, hitching my skirts a little above my ankles as he followed me.

A sour whistle pierced the cellway's gloom, and I recognized the crude attentions of Durrel's neighbor, watching from the tiny window in his door. "Aw, give Temus a kiss, now, sweet," he purred, smacking his lips. "Can't let that nob have all the fun."

The guard whacked Temus's door with his baton. "Oi!" he cried. "Settle down now, or we'll have you moved to the Rathole where you belong!" The prisoner blew his kiss to the guard instead, and hung in the window, watching us.

"Celyn!" Durrel was waiting at the door, as if he'd known I would come.

The guard unlocked Durrel's cell door. "*Don't* get any ideas, hen," he said before shutting it behind me, his voice low and wet in my ear. "Any mischief, and we might decide to keep you both." The door shut with a clang — but no click. He hadn't locked me in here, and I wasn't sure whether that made me feel safer or not.

"Let me see you," Durrel's voice was raw, like he hadn't spoken since I'd been here a few days ago. "Your cheek looks better." He smudged my face gently with a finger that was cracked and cold, but clean. He wore the torn shirt he'd been arrested in, but it looked cleaner than last time, and now he had a worn but well-made leather jerkin over it. I glanced over the dim cell, and saw that the shirt I'd brought him was hung neatly from the rafters, its arms spread to dry. A rough woolen blanket I didn't remember was folded neatly on the bed. He saw me looking and said, "From my father, who apparently had the same instincts for quality that you did. I gather there was supposed to be more," he added. "Clearly the guards left me the choicest pickings. I hear there were fisticuffs over the horse blanket."

I gave a laugh that turned into a cough. Despite the comforts sent by Lord Ragn, I thought Durrel's cell was actually getting *worse*. The sun had shifted so morning light flooded the room, and the stench of refuse was overpowering.

"This I cannot endure one moment longer," I announced, and walked straight over to the chamber pot. There was nowhere to dump it, so I marched it down the hallway and left it by the guards' station, ignoring their protests.

"Uh — I'm going to need that later," Durrel said mildly when I returned, but he was smiling broadly. "I see you have your basket again. Should I expect more wonders? Soap, perhaps?"

I snapped my fingers. "Damn. And here all I brought were shipping manifests from the Ceid warehouses."

His gaze turned keen. "No. Truly? You *are* quite the conjurer," he said. "Let's have a look, shall we?" He straddled the bench, and I followed him to the table.

"It's freezing in here," I said; dank and chill with an annoying drip echoing through the walls. "Shouldn't you have a fire?"

"Well, you see," Durrel said, looking up at the ceiling, "today the price of a fire is twenty crowns."

"You can't be serious." Twenty crowns was the cost of a horse. He didn't answer, and I thought my first reaction was right. His father's supplies had only punctuated the squalidness of his conditions. "*Don't* get used to this," I said. "Don't let yourself get used to this. You're getting out again."

He gave a shrug. "It starts to hurt less if you forget you were once a human being." He sounded so lost and hopeless I couldn't bear it. "The prisoner in the cell next to me is apparently a spy from Talanca. He spends all night swearing at the guards in Talancan, and all day crying and begging for mercy. He hasn't had any visitors." Durrel shifted one knee to his chest, and still didn't look at me. "He could get out of here, but his government won't pay his ransom. I heard the guards say that his execution has been scheduled for next week."

"Durrel —"

He shook his head. "No, it's all right."

"What about your father? Was there any message?"

"If there was, it went the way of the wine and the gold." He gave a determined smile, his fingers on the edge of his leather jerkin. "The blanket and the jerkin are both his, from Favom. That's message enough."

"What about our friend Temus?" I said, trying to change to lighter subjects. "Next you'll be telling me he's the ambassador to Brionry."

"Our resident entertainer? I'm not sure how he ended up here. They brought him in a few days after me, but even the guards can't agree on what he did — and Temus's story changes hourly. I think he's mad."

I thought of that brown, beady eye tracking me down the hallway, and shivered.

"Hey," Durrel said, turning my face from the cell door. "Don't look like that. It's not so bad. I have clean clothes and company. That's all I need. Show me what you brought."

I pulled the documents I'd nicked from the dockhand from my basket. They hadn't told me much, but I thought they might spark Durrel's memory. "I found Geirt," I said, trying to keep my voice neutral. "She still insists that it was you she saw."

Durrel drew a circle on the table with his finger. "Do you believe her?" he asked quietly.

"Well, she's hiding something," I said. "She got very defiant when I questioned her closely, and Barris didn't want me speaking to her at all. I can have another go." I leaned forward and spoke low. "There's something weird going on at that warehouse. Everyone seemed — I don't know, skittish."

"I think that was just Talth," Durrel said. "Her servants were like that too, always hiding their faces, averting their eyes, as if they were afraid to look at us. Nobody lasted long in her employ either. In the first three months we were married, I lost track of how many different housemaids we had." He looked rueful. "I made the mistake of trying to be friendly with one of the kitchen maids once. Talth sacked her the next day. I still don't know what happened to her."

"Sounds like a lovely woman," I said. No wonder somebody finally put poison in her drink. "I think Geirt liked you, though. I think she'd help if she weren't so scared."

His eyes flicked to mine. "I believe I've had enough of Geirt's help," he said. "What else did she tell you? Did she say Talth and I quarreled?"

I nodded. "But she couldn't say over what." I took a stab. "Was it Koya?"

"Gods, no. Why would you —" He rose and moved away from me, then sank down on the bed, hand against his neck. "That didn't have anything to do with Talth's death. I swear."

"Then what was the argument about?" I pressed.

After a long moment, Durrel looked up at me, his face tilted in the slanted light. "Money. Money I had lost."

"All right," I said. "How, and how much?"

"Five hundred crowns."

Marau's balls. Hardly a princely sum, for the Decath and the Ceid, but more than enough to quarrel over. "Didn't you have your own money?" He was *Decath*, after all; they owned half the countryside.

"Technically, yes," Durrel said. "I had my allowance and the money from the marriage settlement, but Talth insisted on managing it. She considered me an irresponsible child. At the time, it just seemed easier than having another argument."

I was liking Durrel's dead wife less and less. "All right, so what happened to the five hundred crowns?"

"I was an idiot." We'd established that, but I held my tongue. "I — I met this girl. She said she was a Sarist."

I couldn't help a darted glance toward the cell door and the guards outside. "Where was this?" I whispered.

"Some bar on Temple Street. One of Raff's haunts. They don't bother Guards there."

I nodded. I knew the place, or its type. They bothered — or didn't bother — everyone with equality there.

He went on, still rubbing the back of his neck. "I was there with Raffin. He was off duty, and we'd both had . . . rough days, so we had a little more to drink than usual." He winced a little. "We saw this girl in the back, being hassled by a couple of muscles. I was tired, and I just wanted to go home — but Raff was edgy, itching for a fight." I must have made a sound, because Durrel said, "Don't look so surprised. He's stronger than he looks, and he's had Guard training."

"Go on."

"So while Raffin took on the two heavies, I got the girl away from them. She told me they were Ferrymen, and they'd promised to get her and her father to safety, out of the city, out of Llyvraneth, but they'd upped the price and now she couldn't pay."

"And you offered to help." Oh, I could see it all so clearly. Durrel and Raffin, boys still, so eager to rescue the girl in distress. I'd witnessed them play out that very scene myself once. With the king's latest crackdown on dissidents, these "Ferrymen" had crawled up from the muck of Gerse's underbelly — ruthless boatmen or other porters willing to smuggle Sarists out of the city or out of Llyvraneth entirely, for a price, usually an exorbitant one. But it was a desperate gamble for the passengers. Anyone trusting his life to Ferrymen was more likely to end up beaten and robbed — or handed straight over to Greenmen — than across the strait in Corlesanne.

"I had to. You would have too, if you'd seen her." Durrel's voice was urgent, insistent. "She was all bruised, and she had a star tattoo inside her wrist. She was trying to hide it with her sleeves, but —" He trailed off. He obviously knew what it all sounded like, but even now he couldn't help himself. "I tried to get the money from Talth, but she wouldn't pay."

"No soft spot for Sarist refugee girls? Was that the argument?"

"No, the argument came a few days later, when she found out I'd taken the money anyway."

I nodded. "And how did you find out you'd been swindled?"

He looked surprised. "How did you —? Right. Raffin saw the girl two days later, in the same bar — no bruises, no tattoo, drinking and laughing with the same guys who'd been roughing her up. He took her in, but apparently *pretending* to be a Sarist isn't an offense the Inquisition is interested in, and the money had disappeared by then." He looked sick with the memory.

I sighed. "You're like a little girl who finds lost kittens in the street," I said. "Sooner or later one of them is going to bite you."

He lifted a hand up toward the window. "I have a few scarred fingers," he said. He met my eyes and gave me a grin. "But once in a while it works out all right."

I shook my head. "You know I was using you too."

"Then I guess there's no hope for me after all." But the grin lingered, infectiously, and a moment later, I had it too. Still shaking my head, I doled out the remaining contents of my basket, pies, beer, charred ledger page. Durrel stared at the bounty like a starving man confronted by a feast so large he can't fathom where to start eating. He rose from the cot and came back to the table.

"Food first," I said firmly, passing him a pie. "Aunt Grea made these for you particularly, she expects a full report on my return, and trust me, Aunt Grea is not someone you disappoint. So eat up."

"Aye, mistress," Durrel said. He broke into a pie willingly enough, but his fingers and eyes kept straying toward the manifests, until I shoved everything else aside and spread them across the table.

"Does any of this mean anything to you?" I asked.

He gave a mumbled affirmative, leaning over the papers and dropping crumbs everywhere. I showed him the charred scrap from the empty warehouse office.

"Well, this is Talth's handwriting," Durrel said, brushing the burnt paper smooth. "And these look like dates. The other numbers might be, I don't know, ships' registries? Look, here's a repeat. And another." He turned the paper to me, and I saw what he saw, the same number matched up with several different dates.

"See if it's in the manifests," I said, and Durrel laid the papers carefully in order, combing through them swiftly with his broad fingers.

"What else did you see at the docks?" he asked. "Ships, people, cargo, what?"

"I don't know. Barris was there — thrilled to see *me*, by the way — and they were loading royal cargo onto a ship. Food and weapons and cloth for the army." I couldn't quite keep the disgust out of my voice, and Durrel looked up at me, eyes serious.

"Go on," he said. He'd marked one notation on the manifests with the edge of the beer bottle's curved bottom, another with a crumb of piecrust.

"Well, I got into a fight with a dockhand over oranges, and he told me they were waiting for some ship called the . . ." Pox, what was it? "*Belprisa.* Some Talancan vessel."

"Talancan? Are you sure?"

I nodded. "Why?"

Durrel sat back. "We have a commercial treaty with Talanca," he said slowly. "They trade freely with Llyvraneth, even during the war; their ships go through the embargoes, and —"

"And they're not searched," I finished. Durrel was nodding. I felt a little thrill of heat. "It's easy enough to disguise a ship's origin," I said. "False flags, a forged registry . . ."

"How easy?" he asked.

"I could do it."

An altogether strange expression passed over Durrel's face. He laid down the manifests and just *looked* at me, his face a mixture of surprise and — delight?

I fidgeted in my seat. "You do understand I'm not really a jeweler's daughter, right?"

He laughed suddenly, quick and surprised. "Since I met you," he said. But he was grinning. "Forging ships? That's . . . well, I'll just bet you have some stories to tell."

"Milord, you have no idea." And we sat there, watching each other across the dingy, cluttered table, in the sputtering, tallowy candlelight. It softened the too-thin contours of Durrel's face, and made his charcoal-colored eyes look very bright. I grew uncomfortable with the intensity in his gaze and looked away, back to the documents. I heard Durrel sigh once and shift through the papers. After a moment, he gave a low whistle.

"Celyn, look," he said, turning the singed ledger page toward me. "This here, where it's burned away? This could say *Light of Yraine*, which is listed on the manifests. If I'm reading this right, it looks like they were carrying cargo worth nearly forty thousand crowns."

"That's not what they reported to the harbormaster." I showed him the manifests, where the *Light of Yraine*, seagoing carrack, was registered as leaving Gerse on that date with a cargo valued at only ten thousand crowns. We stared at the records together, then flipped through them hastily, searching for other ships' names in the manifests that might match the ledger page. We came across three more — the *Calthor*, the *Ponvi*, and the aforementioned *Belprisa* — all carrying cargo vastly more valuable than what the manifests showed.

"Forged ships' registries? Unreported income? Burned records? What's this all mean?" he said.

I looked up from the records. "There's something on those ships they don't want anybody to know about."

"But what?" Durrel said. "There's no way to tell from these documents, except that the values don't add up."

"Cwalo thought it might be smuggled magical artifacts for the black market," I said. "But these sums we're talking about are much too large."

Durrel's voice was low and grim. "Well, whatever it was, it got Talth killed."

CHAPTER ELEVEN

I lingered in Durrel's cell a while longer, until the pies and the beer were long gone. We swapped wild stories, laughing over his nobbish adventures with Raffin, my near misses on the job in Gerse, as well as a few sweet shared memories of his cousin Meri, managing to keep the conversation well clear of Talth or war or murder. I felt curiously light and silly leaving the Keep, and I could not chase away the image of those deep-set gray eyes or that contagious grin.

We had made good progress with the stolen records. We now knew for certain *something* suspicious was going on with Talth's business, and I was trying to decide what my next step should be, along the path leading to the real murderer. On my way home, I stopped back at Grillig's junk shop, wondering how much I'd have to spend this time for information. If he even had any.

"Glad you made it back here," he said by way of greeting. "Getting worried you weren't going to show again."

I leaned on the counter. "Do you have anything for me?"

"Maybe," Grillig said. "I asked a few quiet questions, and I might have heard about that . . . *merchandise* you were interested in."

"The Tincture of the Moon?"

"Hist!" He waved me frantically to silence, even though we were the only ones in the shop. "I told you, even the *name* of that stuff is outlawed!"

"Then who's been breaking the laws lately, Grillig?"

He scowled, but bent closer to me. "Apothecary up in the Temple District. I hear he's the man to see if you have a rat problem."

"That's it? Where did you hear this?"

"Like I'd tell you that. Nobody'd ever talk to me again."

"You would *love* that," I said. Grillig shrugged, but I couldn't get him to tell me any more. Fair enough; how many potioners' shops could there be in the Temple District?

The day had turned rainy, puddles collecting in the damp streets and making the city seem cooler and gloomy. The Temple District sat in the Second Circle at the heart of the city, where there used to be six churches ringing a round courtyard. Now the ancient chapel to Mend-kaal had become a storehouse for municipal records, and the temple of Sar had been razed entirely. The only ones still standing were the Celyst building, its congregation more thriving than ever, and the temple to Zet, its gilded façade still maintained by generous contributions from the city's noble population. Planted between those two, as grand as its neighbors in its own inebriated way, was Tiboran's house of worship, a massive tavern, theater, and inn known simply as the Temple. I hadn't been down here in months, not since a glance around the area told me nothing had changed here except me.

Since Grillig hadn't given me more specific directions, I spent a fruitless hour poking around the back streets of the district, looking through apothecary shops and accumulating stains on my shoes I didn't want to contemplate. Finally I rounded a corner where Temple Street collided with a nest of tangled alleyways, and saw what I'd been seeking, a shadowed storefront with a begrimed sign hanging outside, showing a mortar and pestle. The red snake twining around the base of the mortar told passersby something important about this potioner's shop: They were authorized to carry poisons.

A bell went off as I opened the door, and the sunlight disappeared behind me when it swung shut. It was dark inside, cramped and tiny — a big man could stand in the aisle and nearly touch each opposite wall, if he didn't crack his head on the low ceiling first. In the dim light, I made out neat rows of shelves holding bottles and boxes and pottery jars, all with dusty, illegible labels. At the sound of the bell, a bespectacled man with a balding head shuffled down the shelves behind the counter and peered at me. His sharp, pinched face and wide, unblinking eyes gave him the look of a mouse. I stepped up to the counter and dipped a hasty sort of half curtsy.

"Yes?" the potioner inquired, staring me up and down. "I've not seen you before."

"No, I, uh — I work at one of the big houses on Castle Street." I pitched my voice shy and low, shook up my syllables to the unrefined accent of a serving girl. "My mistress sent me here for something to kill the rats." I waited — Castle Street was a long way from here; how suspicious would he be?

"You look like a strong girl," the shopman said finally. "I'm sure you have no trouble dealing with rats."

I didn't let him see the sigh, but dug in my dress for one of Lord Ragn's gold coins — how much money would a fine lady give her servant to bribe a shopkeeper? "My mistress says she wants it done clean."

The man regarded the coin for a moment, not touching it. Finally he said in a low voice, "How big a rat are we talking about?"

And here I thought I was going to have to give him a little push. Instead, I looked around furtively, as if anxious, and swallowed.

The potioner regarded me a moment, and then palmed the coin and began rustling under the counter. He brought out a ragged, clothbound book and cleared a space for it. "There are a dozen things that will effectively deal with a rat problem," he said conversationally, heaving open the book. It looked like an herbal, handwritten notes beside drawings of plants and addenda scrawled in the margins. "The question is, how long do you want it to take, and whether you want it, you know, to look natural after. Take monkshood, for instance. Very fast acting, but violent. Distasteful." He gave a little shudder and flipped through the pages. "Or nightshade. A tidier death, but trickier — it's hard to get the dosage just right."

I stared at him. What if I *had* just come in after rat poison? What would he sell me then? I watched the pages turn, but as he pulled his finger down the menu of toxins, the bell on the door rang, and some-body shoved it open.

I jumped a little — fair enough, I was supposed to be a nervous serv-ing girl plotting a murder with her mistress — but the shopkeeper barely looked up. He pushed the herbal my way and turned to deal with the other customers, a pair of older townswomen who regaled him with detailed complaints of their rheumatism and flux. I only half listened, browsing through the book and its pictures of herbs, powders, anatomi-cal diagrams, celestial symbols. . . . I had a passing familiarity with such a volume, having assisted Lady Nemair in her stillroom during my ten-ure at Bryn Shaer.

Even so, I nearly flipped right past it, a color drawing of the shadowy gray full moon of Marau, ringed by a pearly halo. The artist had left out the bright dot of the Nameless One, the tiny moon that follows close behind her father, god of the dead. But that hardly mattered, because he *had* included a title, in bold stroking letters. *Tincture of the Moon of Marau.*

And a recipe: *By the full light of Marau, dissolve in three parts strong red wine, one white pearl and one black. Distill until Marau has turned to new, and strain. Add to this solution three grains of blue monkshood, a drop of quicksilver, and a full measure of ground silver. When Marau is full again, heat over low flame until the liquid glows with moonlight. This decoction may be mixed with any liquid and will retain Marau's power, but it will be especially potent when returned to the liquid of its birth, red wine.*

I read that paragraph over and over, feeling a frown start to form. Silver, pearls, and red wine — stupid and expensive, but not really harm-ful. Quicksilver and monkshood, though, were deadly. This was a nob's poison. I could only imagine what such a dose would cost. Did this guy have any? Did I want to know the answer to that?

I didn't have a chance to decide; the other customers left and the shopkeeper scurried right back to me. I had flipped back a few pages, my thoughts clamped down hard.

"Well?" the shopkeeper inquired. "Have we decided? Maybe a nice preparation of alum?"

I looked around the room and took a deep breath, my finger still lodged in the herbal. "I think my mistress was looking for something a little more exclusive. Exotic. Expensive." With the slightest emphasis on that last word, I turned the book to the page with the recipe that had killed Durrel's wife.

The shopkeeper paused for a moment. "That will take some time to prepare," he said finally. "A month, at least. Can your mistress wait that long?"

A month. Did Durrel have that long? What if the Ceid started pressing for a decision from the king? What if they got tired of waiting? I just bit my lip and nodded. And then I remembered that I didn't actually want any of the stuff myself; I was trying to learn who else might have bought some. How was I going to get this guy to tell me *that*?

"Of course," the potioner continued thoughtfully, "I may have some left from the last batch."

"The what?" I said sharply, forgetting to be the timid servant.

"The last batch." The apothecary turned back to the shelves behind him and wheeled a ladder into place in front of one glassed-in case. Climbing up, he teetered at the top as he fumbled for a ring of keys at his belt. "It's surprising you'd come in and ask for this, you know. It's very uncommon; I don't think I've made up more than one or two batches since I was an apprentice. And I've kept shop here for near thirty years." He reached inside the case and drew out a dark bottle, held it up to the light, shook it a bit. "And then, I get two orders in one summer. Extraordinary."

That was one word for it. I could think of another. "Really?" I said, trying to sound merely conversational. "Who bought the other?"

The potioner seemed to dislike what he saw in the jar, and climbed back down to the counter, shaking his head. "Oh, some fellow. I hadn't seen him around here before. I'm sorry, I'll have to make new." Consulting the herbal, he quoted me a price, asking if my mistress would pay. If the poison wasn't potent enough, the price was.

"How much will that buy?"

The shopkeeper showed me the bottle, a brown vial about the size of my hand.

"And how many, erm, rats will that dispatch?"

"This should fix you up nicely," he said. "It only takes a little" — he held up a smaller vial, no bigger than my thumb — "for your average-sized vermin. It won't work *fast*, mind you, but it gets the job done."

I could feel myself getting breathless even now, and I wasn't really going to buy anything. I'd had it right from the beginning — a nob's poison. Who had spent so much to ensure Talth Ceid such a pricey and rarified death?

"That price is fine," I said faintly. "This other customer, who was he?"

The potioner looked nearsightedly into the distance, frowning. "Nobody I knew. Definitely not one of my regulars. Young fellow, I think. Had a girl with him, tall, pretty. Not like you."

I stared hard at him for a long moment, feeling suddenly cold. "Describe them."

"Well, he was just your average rich lad, noble, at a guess. Quiet. Wore a sword and a big ring, a bowing dog, if I remember aright. She was the looker. Put me in mind of Zet, she did, with all that golden hair and height on her."

"And they bought this poison together." It was hard to get the words out.

"Well, they *ordered* it together, but if you ask me, it was the lady what wanted it. But when it came time to pick it up, he came back alone."

I turned without thanking him, something fluttering loose in my chest, and wandered out onto Temple Street, nearly into the path of an oncoming oxcart. They'd ordered it together — the young nob with the bowing dog on his ring, and the tall blonde who looked like Zet. I felt sick. I knew that bowing dog all too well. It was the seal of the House of Decath.

I was such a fool! The arguments, the evidence, the witness . . . it had all been there, if I'd only *looked* at it.

Koya and Durrel had bought the poison to kill Koya's mother, and then Durrel had gone and fetched it home again.

My friend Durrel Decath was almost as good a liar as I was.

PART II

KEEP YOUR EYES OPEN

CHAPTER TWELVE

After that, I resigned my commission as Lord Durrel's champion — just turned my back on the Keep and kept on walking. It wasn't as if there was so little to occupy my days, after all, that I had to spend them sneaking around warehouses and digging up sordid secrets. There was a war on, and lots of places I could put my talents to better use.

I turned my attentions instead to helping around the bakery. I was objectively one of the worst cooks in Llyvraneth, but I could sift and stir if the need arose, and Aunt Grea didn't protest too strenuously the day I came downstairs, donned an apron, and fell into kneading beside her. Business was thin at the bakery these days, though she didn't like to speak of it; the grain shortages had pushed up the price of bread so high that many Seventh Circle folk couldn't afford it anymore. Grea cut her costly wheat with cheaper grains where she could, but it was hard to ignore the grumbles in the street and the dark looks from her customers.

"It isn't *my* fault," she'd tell them. "Talk to Bardolph." But bakers were an easier target for ordinary folks' wrath; little did they care that Grea struggled too.

"You don't need to do this, you know," she said to me one hot afternoon in the shadow of the blasting ovens. I was up to my elbows in flour that was mostly rye and punching down a ring of dough with enough force to leave dents in the table. "I'm sure you'd rather be doing anything else."

I just shrugged and flung the dough down onto the bread board with a bang that sent flour and cats and bakers flying. The truth was, I was mad as hells with myself, and I couldn't even explain why. It wasn't just that Durrel had lied to me; it was that I had believed him. I'd *wanted* to believe him. I'd looked into his eyes and thought, *He is not a murderer. He can't be.*

What an idiot I was. Didn't I know better than anybody how thin that line was, how easy it was to cross? It would have been the work of a moment for Koya to lure Durrel into helping her; look how easily he'd thrown away five hundred marks on that fake Sarist girl.

Look how easily *I'd* been lured in.

And so I punched and rolled and dragged bags of grain around, hoping the hot, heavy work would sweat all thoughts of Durrel Decath right out of me, until even Aunt Grea finally grew a little alarmed one afternoon and sent me back upstairs "to cool off," she said with a fierce glare that did not brook defiance.

Upstairs, Rat bent over our makeshift table, regarding two bottles of wine with intensity, one blond eyebrow cocked in focus. "Here," he said, handing me a glass. "Taste this."

I wasn't in any kind of mood to refuse a drink, so I downed the shot he gave me. "Tastes like Grisel," I said, recognizing the fine, fizzy Corles wine.

"Ah." Rat lifted a finger, then handed me another, this one in a clay cup.

"Tastes like Grisel," I repeated

Rat gave me a look of disdain. "Heretic." With a flourish he lifted one of the bottles to the light. "*This* is sparkling Grisel, a thirty-four-year-old bottle, in fact, which was entrusted to me by his lordship. And this" — he handed me the other bottle, which looked nearly identical — "is not."

"You're counterfeiting wine? How?" Curious now, I slid into place behind the table.

"Would I ask you how you picked a pocket or got into a nob's bedroom to steal a diamond? I think not. But since you've asked nicely, yes, I am attempting to fill a hole in the lives of our esteemed friends. Thanks to the embargoes against Corlesanne, they are suffering without some of the finer things in life."

I lifted the real bottle from the table and eyed the label. "Interesting." But my voice sounded bored, even to me.

"And you call yourself one of Tiboran's. Can you do the labels?"

I set the bottle down with a clink. "I told Grea I wouldn't bring my work to her house, and I meant it. Besides, I'm helping in the bakery."

Rat leaned against the dry sink, arms crossed over his chest. "This is serious," he said. "I've never seen you like this."

"Like what?" I snapped, glaring at the wine labels instead of him.

"Right," he said, and took a seat beside me at the table. "Look, if you want to help Aunt, then do what you're good at. We don't need a second baker when there's barely flour enough for one. If these grain prices keep going up, she's going to need alternate sources of income." He nudged the Grisel bottle closer to me. "Come on," he said. "You know you want to."

I looked at him. "She could get in a lot of trouble for this," I said, although in truth the risk was minimal. Nobody was going to come hunting a Seventh Circle bakery for smuggled wine, and forged wine? Well, the very idea of it would be so amusing to Tiboran, god of wine *and* forgers, that anyone in the liquor trade who might reasonably complain would no doubt look the other way. Besides, Rat had a point about those Grisel labels — the script had the trickiest little twist to some of the numerals, and it *might* be interesting to try replicating the blue tinge to the edges of the paper, said to be caused by a fungus in Count Grisel's cellars. . . .

I spent a little time on Rat's project over the next few days, selecting inks and paper at a Spiral stationer's, tracking down a glassblower willing to dodge the excise taxes on locally made wine. At night I stayed out past curfew, haunting the shadows near a bar down Bonelicker Way where the pickings were never worth the effort, and did a little halfhearted forgery after getting back home in the mornings. And thus another handful of hot, listless days passed, during which I was pretty damn successful forgetting all about Durrel Decath.

Late in the week, I ran an errand for Rat that took me right past Nob Circle, to a cheesemonger's he liked that *just happened* to be across the street from Charicaux. I halted on the corner, watching the weird guards patrolling the Decath grounds like horseflies. Not my concern; I did not care a whit what those nobs were up to. But before I moved on, the broad arched gateway swung wide, and a handful of riders clattered up the street and into Charicaux. One was Lord Ragn, and the others —

Marau's balls. Lord Ragn's companions were a tapestry of Gerse elite, nobs or gentry all, from the looks of them. I spotted at least one jeweled chain of office around one velvet collar — a member of the Ruling Council. But the one who stole my breath away was tall, rigid-backed, dressed all in green. I didn't recognize anything but her robes. The woman was a Confessor, one of the Inquisition's master torturers.

What was Lord Ragn doing with company like that?

I wasn't stupid enough to hang around trying to find out.

On my way back to Bargewater, I was so preoccupied that I didn't notice the Greenmen trailing alongside me until it was too late to move out of their way. I turned a corner, a nightstick blocked my path, and a slow, entitled voice drawled out, "Papers?"

Pox. My gut curled up inside me. I looked up to see Raffin Taradyce and a thickset partner looming over me. There was no friendly recognition in Raffin's face this time.

"You can't be serious," I said, nicking a little strength from the irritation that had fueled my walk here.

"Is that how you speak to the Goddess's servants?"

I bit back a tart reply; the other guy had a mean look in his eye, like he arrested people just for the fun of it. Still staring at Raffin, trying to figure this out, I dipped my hand into my bodice and withdrew a packet of folded-up papers, which I held past him, toward his partner's waiting hand. Apparently my brother's hands-off order had expired. I tried not to show fear or impatience as Raffin and the nasty-looking thug in green pawed their way through my single most valuable possession. The rattle of market traffic filled the languid air behind us, and the street smelled of horse dung, stale beer, and old cabbage in the low afternoon light.

"Cel-yn Con-tra-*trar* —" the partner read, with painstaking slowness.

Raffin's face betrayed the briefest flash of annoyance, and he plucked the documents from his partner's hands.

"Celyn Contrare," he repeated, eyeing me superciliously over the edge of the papers. "It says here that you are a member of the household of one Eptin Cwalo, Merchant of the Spiral, Third Circle, Gerse. Is that true?" He looked surprised — what had he expected? No house affiliation at all? Maybe forged papers? Mine weren't, but Cwalo would have vouched for me, all the same.

I shrugged. "That's what it says. They're your licenses."

"Should we approach this Cwalo, check your story out?"

"What do you want?" I snapped. On the street around us, people stopped briefly to stare, before ducking their heads and moving on.

"We want what all good citizens of Llyvraneth want," the other guard said, and his voice had gone silky and terrifying. "Peace and order in the streets. Obedience to the Goddess. A return to a state of blessed —"

Raffin cut his partner off. "Suffice it to say, the Goddess cares for *all* her children." There was a weird note in his voice, and I studied his face, trying to figure this out.

"I don't understand."

"Well, peach, why don't you let me explain it to you?" Raffin pocketed my papers, then handed his nightstick to his partner. "Watch this alley," he said, pointing to a dark, twining opening between two squat storefronts. "I'm going to have a private word with the *dutiful* Mistress Contrare here."

And then, as I stood there, confused, Raffin unbuckled his belt and passed it to the other Greenman. I felt all the air just disappear from my lungs.

"Need any support there, brother?" His partner was eyeing me with undisguised lust, and suddenly I wasn't confused anymore.

"Not this time. I'll take care of this." Raffin grabbed me by the arm and half threw me down the alley. I stumbled, cracked my knee on the cobbles, and scrambled to my feet, braced against a rough stone wall. He caught me and cornered me in a doorway, pressing his tall body over mine.

"Stop!" I cried, and to my utter surprise, he eased back a little. The look on his face was fixed and intense — but it wasn't *violent*. It wasn't cruel. "What are you doing?" My voice was shaky. I was shaking.

"I'm going to ask you the same question," he said coldly. "Shouldn't you be in gaol?"

"What?"

"I've been to the Keep docks every morning this week, but Durrel's pretty little spy is nowhere to be seen. What's going on, *Digger*?" There was something nasty in the way he said my name.

"Ask *him*," I said, and my voice was surprisingly steady. "My interest in the matter waned."

Raffin pinched me suddenly, and I cried out. "Sorry," he said under his breath. "Must keep up the pretense."

I glared at him, rubbing my sore arm. "Just *ask* me next time. I can scream as loud as you want. What *do* you want?"

"I want to know where you've been. Why have you stopped investigating Durrel's case?"

"Because *he did it*, Raffin." I sighed. "Or he helped his stepdaughter do it. He's not what we thought."

"You can't believe that."

"His own father believes it." I recalled the odd note in Lord Ragn's voice at the party, the clouded expression I now, belatedly, recognized as *doubt*.

"Never. Decath would move the moons for Durrel."

I shook my head. "No, he told me. There was an incident — something in Tratua a couple of years ago?" I wasn't aware that was a question until I heard the uncertainty in my voice.

Raffin was nodding. "I remember. He didn't do that either." When I just stared at him, he fidgeted a bit and finally said, "You'll have to ask Durrel."

"I'm asking you."

He shrugged. "All right. There was some girl in Tratua."

"*What* girl?"

His eyes darted up the alley toward the street, and he lowered his voice. "Her name was Evalia Mondeci, or that's what she called herself, anyway. She was a courtesan. Pretty, young. Too smart for her own good. Durrel fell hard."

I told myself I *did not care* what Raffin was telling me, but there I was, speaking anyway. "Were you there with him?"

"He wrote me. Long, moony paeans about her crimson lips, her night-dark hair, her — well. The letters stopped a few weeks before he came home. The next thing I heard, she was found dead in an alley near his rooms. Strangled."

I could feel my face contract in a grimace. I tried to relax. This had nothing to do with me.

"The way I heard it, Tratuan authorities were minutes away from arresting him, but Lord Decath paid a fair sum to keep his boy from the gallows."

I pulled away from him. "Thanks for the information." I turned to leave.

His long green arm blocked my path. "Well?"

"Well, what? You realize that story makes him sound *more* guilty, don't you?"

"Don't be an idiot. You know he wouldn't hurt anybody."

"Tell that to Barris. I'm sure he'd find this all fascinating."

"*Barris*? The Ceid know about Evalia? Well, they're obviously using that incident from Durrel's past to frame him."

I shook my head, looking around at the cobbled alleyway, anywhere but Raffin's too-intense gaze. "I'd like to believe that —"

"Then believe it," Raffin said, grabbing my arm again, but with urgency this time, not with malice. "Talk to him. Talk to Koya. Find out what really happened. Because you know as well as I do, Durrel Decath couldn't hurt anyone."

"He lied to me," I said. "*You* talk to Koya. Maybe she'll explain how she and Durrel happened to buy the poison together. Temple Street. I talked to the potioner. You are more than welcome to continue this 'investigation' where I left off." I twisted out of his grasp and straightened my rumpled dress. "Because I am heartily sick of the whole pack of you."

Raffin just looked baffled, wounded. "Look, I'm not saying he's not an *idiot*," he said. His voice sounded desperate. "But he's not a murderer. You have to help him. He needs you."

"He *needs* me?" That drew a laugh. "All the world's power and money and resources at your disposal, and a thief from the back streets of the Seventh Circle is the best you can come up with? You boys really are in trouble." The low sun had shifted, leaving the alley in weary shadows. I was tired and just wanted to go home, and this stupid Greenman was in my way.

Raffin leaned over me again, and his face had gone red. "Look," he said, his voice harsh. "I *told* you, something else is going on here —"

"I've heard that line before. I don't care anymore."

"You would care, if you knew what was really happening."

"And if you have something to tell me, then tell me," I said. "Enough of these games and —" I threw up my hands. "I've had enough, Raffin."

"Please," he said. The word surprised me, but I wouldn't look at him. I was afraid I'd see those sad hound eyes pleading with me. "Can't you at least think about it?"

"Oh, I'm sure I'll *think* about it plenty. Let me go. I'm serious. Your partner will be wondering what's taking you so long, and unless you really do mean to go through with this *pretense*, I'd appreciate it if you'd give me back my papers."

Raffin looked disappointed, but he pulled them from his green doublet. "I shouldn't," he said. "I ought to hang on to these, as a little incentive for you to help Durrel —"

I snatched them back from him. "Help him yourself. You believe him," I said. "Good day, Guardsman Taradyce."

I was tucking my papers back inside my bodice when I passed Raffin's partner, still waiting in the neck of the alleyway. He gave me a leering grin as I stepped out of the shadows. I felt a shudder of disgust; Raffin's ruse had worked in part because it was so common as to be almost beneath notice, but the Greenman apparently read it as something else — and he took the opportunity to slap me, hard, right on my backside. It took everything I had to grip my fingers together and not smack his hand so hard his grandchildren's fingers would sting. I bit my tongue and forced a tight smile.

"The Goddess's blessings on you, Guardsman," I said in a thin voice through my teeth, and edged out onto the street, where I could get away from the whole blasted lot of them.

Nobs. Greenmen. Pox.

CHAPTER THIRTEEN

Despite Raffin's loyalty, I still wasn't convinced Durrel wasn't involved — even a little bit, even perhaps unwittingly. I knew him well enough to guess what his attraction to Koya would have been; even if they were both telling the truth and it never went anywhere beyond sad, longing glances across the Bal Marse court, the fact was, Durrel just couldn't resist a girl in need. And whatever this story about the courtesan in Tratua meant, well, it certainly didn't help my impression of him. Even if I couldn't bring myself to picture Durrel strangling a girl in cold blood, I knew blood didn't always run chill when Marau was nearby. Mine had been *boiling* during that snowstorm in the mountains. Maybe I'd been wrong all along; maybe anyone could kill.

That same evening, as I sat in the stifling top-floor heat of the bakery apartment, soaking wine labels in a mixture of onion skins and rusty water, Aunt Grea huffed her way up the stairs to tell me that "Some tart in a pleasure barge is calling for you."

Frowning, I peered out the window. Sure enough, a familiar boat was moored alongside the Bargewater Street landing, and I could just make out a hem of watery blue skirt over a leg propped casually on a cushioned seat, bejeweled chopine hanging half off a dainty, stockinged foot.

Koya. Just what I needed. With a scowl, I followed Grea downstairs and stepped outside to see what the Ceid wanted now.

"Celyn!" Koya waved lazily from the boat, her slim, graceful body draped like a shawl over the plush seats. The Koyuz boatman, in curious livery that looked green one way and violet another, sat silent and unruffled, his back to his mistress. "You're not wearing *that*, are you?"

I looked down at my linen kirtle, creased and rumpled from bending over the table, working on Rat's Grisel labels. "What's wrong with it?" Even as I said that, I knew it was somehow the wrong question.

Koya just lifted one fair, arched eyebrow at me, and pointed back to the bakery. "Change," she commanded. "That dress you had on at Hobin's will be fine."

"What do you want?"

She jerked upright. "Just to talk. Come with me."

"We can talk here."

That gay, careless laugh. "Oh, Celyn. Don't be like that. It's a beautiful night, the wine is cold, and I have something I want to show you."

I had no interest in following Koya's whims, but it was *hot* in the bakery, and at least out on the water there was a semblance of a breeze. And wherever she was going, dressed like a courtesan, there were probably going to be other rich folk there — meaning jewelry and purses and (usually) good food. "Damn, damn, damn," I muttered as I turned on my heel and went back to change my clothes.

Back at the landing, Koya had shifted aside to make room for me, her silk skirts spread around her. She handed me a molded-paper mask on a long handle, glass beads cascading from its beribboned edges.

"What is that for?" I asked.

"Get in the boat, silly thing, and I'll tell you." She had a bottle of wine open beside her, and I thought the picture would be complete if only the boatman stripped off his doublet and shirt and fanned her with the vast confection of frosty white plumes and gilded ribs that lay in her lap. I lifted my skirts in *nothing* like a ladylike fashion, hopped down into the boat, and grabbed the bottle. I took a long swig before even noticing what it was — some ghastly sweet thing flavored of apples. Shuddering, I handed it back to her.

Koya laughed. "It's from Breijardarl," she said. "Stantin imports it. Apparently it's quite popular in Brionry, though I can't imagine why. Oh, dear Celyn, tell me you didn't have other plans on this *gorgeous* evening." She leaned even farther back in her seat, dropping her head and exposing her thin, pale throat to the air. With a giggle, she straightened. "I am going to introduce you to the best Gerse's nightlife has to offer."

"I can't wait."

"I knew you'd be skeptical. Onward, Henver — to Cartouche!" She announced that last to the boatman like a queen giving a royal order. He soundlessly steered us into open waters, and Koya trailed one hand over the side of the boat. "Barris said you've been to Mother's warehouse," she said. "Have you found any *clues*?"

Had I discovered that she and Durrel had conspired to murder her mother, did she mean? The subject had lost its fascination for me, but I obliged her. "I talked to Geirt," I said.

Barely a flutter of those wispy eyelashes. "Gossipy little thing, but she did know how to dress Mother, which was a feat. What did she tell you?" She sounded eager, hungry — and not because she was desperate to know who killed her mother. More like she wanted to hear the latest scandal, and she didn't even care how it might involve her or her family.

"She insists she saw Durrel leaving your mother's bedroom before the body was found." I heard a dark note creeping into my voice.

"Before the body was found?" Koya sat up in the seat, balancing the wine between her knees. "Didn't anyone tell you who discovered her? It was *Durrel*." There was the faintest tremor in her voice, and for a moment I almost saw a crack in her mask of frivolity. "Can you imagine how horrible that must have been for him? For *him*?"

I wasn't sure what she meant by that, and I really didn't care. "I know what happened in Tratua," I said curtly, and something very much like anger flashed across Koya's face.

"This must be killing him, Celyn. How *anyone* could believe Durrel could murder someone —"

"And I found the potioner's shop."

Her mouth closed, lips pursed together briefly. "And?" she said, her voice a whisper.

"I know you and Durrel bought the Tincture of the Moon."

For a moment there was surprise on her face, and she wasn't quite quick enough to cover it. "Well, it wasn't to *kill* anyone with," she said. "I just —" She gave a wan smile, looking somewhere past me, out into the fading evening. "Don't you ever just get tired, Celyn? Tired of the masks, of the acting? Of nothing being real? Don't you sometimes think, 'I could go to bed tonight, and if nobody wakes me up tomorrow, it won't matter'?"

"What are you saying? That Durrel bought you the poison so you could kill *yourself*?"

"Don't be silly," she said, and her voice was short. "He would never have agreed to anything like that. I didn't tell him what it was for, and that is the truth, Celyn. He just bought it because I told him I needed it. And I *know* you understand that."

Well, she was right on that account. Give Durrel a need to fill, and he would kill himself to fill it. But she still hadn't told me why she'd bought the poison. "All right," I said. "Maybe Durrel didn't do it. Maybe you killed your mother on your own."

She didn't react, just nodded thoughtfully. "But I was at my grandfather's house. And what reason would I have?" She sounded as if this were a plausible theory she was hearing for the first time, and not an accusation of murder. "It wasn't for the money; I didn't inherit anything from Mother, and Stantin keeps me very well. And then what was my plan going to be? Take out Stantin also, but what a shame Durrel was arrested before I could manage it?"

Well, said like *that*, it did sound a little far-fetched.

"I don't know how the poison ended up in my mother's glass," Koya continued. "But I can tell you it wasn't Durrel Decath's doing. Or mine," she added, sounding strangely sad when she said it. "Do I wish Durrel and I had met three years ago, before either of us was married? I won't deny it. Did I conspire with him to kill my mother? Of course not."

She looked out over the water, silent for a long moment. Watching her, I thought she knew more than she was saying. "Maybe it had to do with her business, then?" I suggested, thinking of those falsified manifests we'd uncovered. "Was your mother involved in smuggling anything illicit?"

"Goodness, *I* don't know!" she said, her voice almost merry again.

"You would have to ask Barris. I had exactly one role in this family — to marry well — and once I had done that, Mother hardly thought of me."

"Maybe that was your motive," I said, but Koya only laughed.

"Celyn, my dear, if you had *met* my mother, you would know that having her forget your existence could only be a good thing." She reached for the wine again. "It's good we have that unpleasantness out of the way," she said brightly. "Because we're here!"

The boat had drawn to a stop near a square building, stuccoed pink, with a crowded courtyard outside. Bright banners emblazoned with images of Tiboran and Zet flew above the arched entrance, baldly proclaiming this a pleasure palace for the rich and noble. This must be the infamous Cartouche. People were even now milling about outside, looking alternately bored or curious, as servants in pink livery passed among them with bottles and trays of food.

Koya was obviously well known here; the crowd swelled forward as overdressed young men jostled to be the ones to hand us out of the boat. "Don't forget your mask," she whispered to me, before disappearing into the press of bodies, her hand on the arm of a young man in a bead-encrusted doublet. Wait — she wasn't going to *leave* me here? Shaking off the attentions of a slim gentleman who'd taken my arm, I pushed my way inside, through the tangle of limbs and fine fabrics and the hot smell of wine, smoke, and sweat, and the perfumes heavily applied to mask all of that, but Koya had been effectively swallowed up.

Irritated, I considered going back out to the boat, but that seemed like a waste of a good evening. I was already here; might as well make it worth the trip. I stuck the handle of my mask into my bodice and set off across the club, looking for spoils.

Cartouche seemed to be the domain of Tiboran, run wild. There was a play — I saw performers onstage, looking vaguely put upon — but nobody was paying it any mind. An amorous couple had shifted from their seats to the edge of the stage, where they were in danger of interrupting a dice game between a young nob and an obvious confidence sneak with a deep-bosomed accomplice. I plucked a few gold marks and an uneaten meat pie from a fat man in red, mulling over what Koya had — or hadn't — told me. None of it mattered anymore, but I couldn't shake the image of Durrel and Koya in that potioner's shop together.

As I crossed the crowded common room, a scene in a far corner, away from the bar and near a back exit, caught my eye. A dark-haired beauty leaned over a table, speaking urgently to a pair of young, daft-looking boys in conspicuously expensive clothes. She moved subtly, lifting a hand to shift aside her hair, and I saw deep, smoldering eyes, a smudge of bruise on her cheek, cut by a tear — and a tattoo on the inside of her wrist, half hidden by her sleeve.

Oh, yes. Celys had built this one *precisely* to be impossible for Durrel to resist.

I shoved my way through the cluster of bodies and dropped down into an empty seat beside her. "Well met, Fei," I said cheerfully. She stared daggers at me, and one of the pretty boys at the table said, "Hey!"

I took a swig of his wine. "So I hear you've been pretending to be a Sarist refugee. That's beneath even you, Fei."

The boys looked confused. One of them said, "Do you know this person?" as his companion choked out, *"Pretending?"*

"Go away, Digger, I'm in the middle of something," Fei said, but she knew she was blown, and when the boys packed themselves and their drinks (and their purses) up to leave, she barely looked at them. "Haven't seen you around in a while. How did you find me?"

"Don't flatter yourself," I said. "I was in the neighborhood."

"This doesn't really seem like your sort of place," she said. There was an insult in there, but it could be one of so many that I just ignored it. Fei's accent was real, but nobody was quite sure from *where* — Talancan, Vareni, hells, maybe even Tigas with that coloring. It suited her to give a different birthplace any time she needed one. We'd done a couple of jobs together, back in Tegen's day, and we hadn't liked each other much then either. I wasn't surprised to see her in a place like this, running this kind of scam.

"You took a friend of mine for five hundred crowns," I said. "If the Greenmen hadn't caught you, he'd still be waiting to hear from you and your 'father,' safe in Talanca."

"Oh, him," she said, a languid smile spreading across her face. "I thought he was nice. Very . . . noble."

"He's a big dumb puppy; he'll follow anything that wags its tail at him."

"Well, not just anything," she said. "I see *you're* alone. Did you really come here to tell me to keep my hands off your boy? Again?"

"I think you mean your talons, don't you?"

Her eyes narrowed, and she pushed away from the table, but I put out an arm and blocked her path. "A friendly warning, that's all this is. Find another line of work." I didn't quibble about the money; chances were she really did need it a lot more than Durrel. But still. There were principles.

"Let me go." Her voice was thin and tense, but I didn't budge.

"You're lucky the Greenmen let you off," I said quietly. "I hope you realize that."

Fei tried a different tactic. "Maybe I should speak to them. Maybe they'd be interested to know about a man who paid so much money to help a Sarist. That might be profitable too."

"Maybe, but you're a little late," I said. "Or hadn't you heard he's in jail already?"

When she didn't snap back with a catty reply, I frowned at her. She wouldn't meet my eyes. "Fei? What do you know?"

"Hist! Do you have to be so loud about everything?"

In fact, my voice had been so low it was a wonder *she'd* heard me. But I hid my surprise and dug one of the fat nob's coins from my dress. After five hundred crowns, you wouldn't think a mark would be that tempting, but Fei was a magpie, attracted to anything that shone gold. "You know something about the murder? Tell me now."

She shook her head, and the dark curtain of hair swirled around her face. "Nothing — just. There's a guy, I've seen him around Temple Street sometimes. Big. Scary. One night I was working the Bat, where I met your friend, and I heard him brag about doing some nobleman's wife. At the time everyone thought he meant — well, you know. Not that he'd *killed* her." She gave a shiver. "But afterward, when we heard about Talth Ceid? I don't know. It could have been true."

"What guy? What's his name?" Fei shrugged; she really didn't know any more. With a sigh, I pulled out another coin. "If you see him again, or you hear anything else, let me know, all right? I'm staying at a bakery on Bargewater Street." She looked sullen, and I kept my fingers wrapped around the gold. "Do I have to remind you about that Copper Street job?"

I saw her color deepen, and she gave a single unhappy nod. "Fine."

"Your boys are up at the bar," I told her, rising to leave. "If you hurry, you can probably still catch them. I'm sure you can figure out another way to get them to buy you dinner."

She was still glaring at me as I left her there. I knew there was no reason to believe anything she'd told me; Tiboran's influence was strong here, and that smoke-eyed sneak was clearly a favorite of his. But the look of alarm on Fei's face when I'd brought up Talth's death had seemed genuine. She also had nothing to gain by fingering someone else for the murder, so maybe she was telling the truth after all.

I sat at the Cartouche bar a long time, staring into a drink I didn't want and trying to make sense of things. I'd convinced myself that Durrel and Koya were guilty, but Koya's vague explanations and Fei's story threw everything apart again. What was I supposed to do now? Camp out in the bars of Temple Street, waiting for "some guy" to show up and start bragging about killing noblewomen again?

After a while, a footman in pink Cartouche livery approached me. "Mistress Koya wants you," he said. I followed, not particularly eagerly, until he deposited me at the door of a low room, dimly lit and filled with various types of smoke. I spotted Koya in the shadows, her golden hair practically the only bright thing in the room, her dress of night-dark silk making her look as radiant as the moons.

Or possibly that was the flush of wine on her cheeks.

She waved when she saw me. "Darling Celyn!" she called, and the tide of bodies shifted me over to her. Her eyes were wide, her pupils big and dark as she drew me closer. "Where's your young man?" she asked me, sounding almost comically disappointed.

I just shrugged and said, "Where's yours?"

She gave a merry laugh and fluttered her fingers behind her, where a familiar figure had fallen asleep on the floor beside her cushioned bench. He was missing his doublet and one of his boots. "But wait until you see who I have for *you!*" she said. "Keep your mask on; you're far more intriguing that way."

She clapped her hands, and her retinue parted, and someone gave a gentle nudge forward to a young man — a boy, really — who looked about as happy to be here as I was. He had a shock of dark brown hair that hung over his pale face, and he wore an ill-fitting slashed doublet, too big around but too short in the sleeves. He stumbled forward and took my hand.

"Good evening, mistress," he mumbled. With a surge of sympathy, I tried to draw my hand away, but he held fast to me, as if afraid to let go.

I tugged again. "I won't hurt you," I said, frowning through the cut-out eyes of my mask.

"I know," he said, his eyes darting nervously to Koya, but his hold on me never let up.

Whatever this was, I'd had enough. I marched firmly up to Koya and held out my hand — the one still clutched firmly in the boy's death grip. "I don't think your friend and I will hit it off, after all," I said. "I'm ready to leave."

She was watching me, her expression unreadable. Finally she gave a sigh of utter boredom. "Oh, all right. Vorin, why don't you take our boy back to his room. Sweetling, you can let poor Celyn go now." She shook off the young men surrounding her, and, taking my arm, tottered off toward a bench tucked privately in the corner. I rubbed at my hand, which still tingled from the force of that boy's grip. She settled herself down like a bird adjusting its plumage, and then abruptly said, in a much-too-loud voice, "Is it true you can see magic?"

It took all my control not to start, not to stare, not to blink — not to move a single muscle in my face. "Where did you hear that?"

She gave me a patient smile I recognized — the one that said, *We're the Ceid; we know everything.* But I thought my question actually had a different answer: Durrel. He'd probably thought it safe to tell her, once, assuming she and I would never cross paths. I tried to hand the mask back. "I'm tired, Koya. I've had enough of your . . . entertainment for one evening."

"Show me! Is there any magic in this room?"

"Koya!"

She grabbed me by the skirts and pulled me down beside her. "Is there any magic in this room?" she asked again. Her voice was playful, teasing, and insistent.

With a sigh, I gave the room a cursory glance. "No. I don't see anything."

"Good!" she said gleefully, and I stared at her.

"Why good?" Sweet Tiboran — was I *reasoning* with a drunk?

"Because there's a Greenman here!"

"What?" I was on my feet again and ready to flee, but Koya pushed me back.

"Sit down. He'll see you!" But she didn't sound overly concerned. I turned in the direction she was looking to see Raffin, still in uniform, coming our way. Strange that that sight should be any kind of a relief, but I sent up a hasty prayer of thanks to every god in the heavens.

"Mistresses Koyuz, Celyn, good evening." There was the Raffin I remembered — the smooth, handsome gentleman. He bowed low to both of us and held out his hand to Koya, which she kissed with exaggerated delicacy.

"Have you come to play with us, you pretty boy?" She flung her arms around his neck, dragging him down to the bench almost on top of her.

Raffin gently disentangled himself. He was a little flushed, but still more sober than Koya. "Maybe I ought to take you home," he said, looking closely at her too-wide eyes. "Will you allow me to escort you back to your boat?"

For a moment Koya looked almost belligerent, but Raffin at his smoothest was difficult for even a woman with her head about her to resist. Finally, beaming, she rose and slipped under his arm. Raffin caught her around the waist and steered her toward the stairs. "Celyn, you should probably go too."

Almost dizzy with relief, I stood up and nodded. "Thank the *gods*."

I was so grateful to get out of there that I almost didn't bother nicking the doorman's diamond stickpin on my way out.

CHAPTER FOURTEEN

I slept late and rose later, in a dull and perplexed mood. I tried to shake off (and scrub off) the last residue of my evening at Cartouche, but my thoughts weren't so easy to cleanse. First Raffin with his tale of dead girls in Tratua; then Koya with her poison; and now Fei's story on top of it all. From now on, I'd just have to be smarter and avoid Durrel's friends altogether. A niggling little voice whispered that Lord Durrel was running out of friends by the day, but I ignored it.

It was a hot, heavy day that threatened rain but wouldn't deliver. Grea's customers were increasingly unruly, with their grumbled complaints about the price and quality of her goods. She bore it with a steady patience, but I didn't like the look of some of them, so I lurked about, wiping tables and sweeping, just in case something happened.

And, of course, something happened.

After the noon bells, when the midday crowds started thinning out, I saw a green shadow darken the open Bargewater Street door, and glanced up to see — pox. Raffin.

"Come to strong-arm me into seeing Durrel again?" He didn't answer. His face looked odd, troubled, and abruptly I understood that something was very, very wrong. "Raffin?" I said, alarmed. "Is it Durrel?"

He stepped inside, but wouldn't look at me. "I'm sorry," he said, his voice almost a whisper. I was about to ask what for, but I didn't get the chance. Behind him followed two more green-clad guards, their nightsticks held aloft as if expecting the bakery folk to attack. And behind the Greenmen — I sank against a chair.

It was Werne.

They swept into the bakery, silence falling around them. There were five guards besides Raffin, making His Grace's party number the sacred seven, as always. The Greenmen swiftly cleared the common room, as

Aunt Grea observed silently from the kitchen. There was no question why they'd come, let alone of gainsaying them.

"Wait for me outside," Werne said to his men. One of the Greenmen protested, but Werne flicked his hand toward the doorway, not looking, and they reluctantly filed out. The Lord High Inquisitor stood before me, hands tucked into his heavy green sleeves, studying me. I wouldn't let myself look away.

"Sister, I rejoice in the Goddess's providence that has led me here to you today."

When I didn't answer, he seemed at a loss for what to do next, besides stand there and scrutinize me. He was unchanged from when I'd seen him months ago; still the same slight build, my dark eyes and hair, his brow creased in a look of perpetual disapproval. What was it now, I wondered — the cut on my cheek? The flour on my skirt? Some failing only he could discern?

And then, praise Tiboran, there was Aunt Grea. "Will Your Grace take refreshment?" She held a steaming small loaf of dark bread and a mug of ale — peasant food, no doubt an unforgivable insult to the Goddess's servant. Without waiting for his answer, she set the food down on a table and drew a chair around for him. Werne seemed almost relieved to take it, to thank Grea and give her the customary blessing.

"I'm afraid it's only rye," she said humbly. "Your Grace deserves better, but with the grain shortages . . ."

"It is a worthy offering," he said, but I saw the twist of his lip as he broke the bread to find it coarse and brown. Bowing her head, Grea backed off, but only as far as the kitchen. Annoyance flashed in Werne's eyes, but there was no way that the Inquisitor could quibble with a woman baking bread in his presence. The work itself was Mend-kaal's province, but grain and flour were sacred to Celys.

"Sister." His voice broke into my thoughts, and I snapped my gaze to his sweating face. "Surely you know why I've come."

I said nothing; I had nothing to say to him. Last winter he had quit my presence in disgust, pleading time to pray for guidance on what to do with me. He'd claimed he thought I was dead, and it was possible — but he'd also denied any connection to me when I made my own allegiance, to Prince Wierolf and the Sarists, plain. Raffin had told me the Inquisitor was still debating; had he come to some conclusion about me, then?

"I am here because the Goddess rejoices in your return to her," Werne said. "Thought dead for so long, only to be restored to life by her mercy."

"I think *Celys* knew I was alive all along."

Werne ignored that. "The Goddess has revealed to me her purpose for you, and it is wondrous. She has called you back so that you may resume your work in her holy name."

A chill formed at the base of my spine. I didn't know what he meant, but I was sure I wouldn't like it. Werne leaned closer in his chair, his small hands reaching toward me. They looked like mine, and I curled my fingers into fists beneath my skirts. "You belong by my side at the Celystra. Come and take up your rightful place in your home."

"My rightful place?" I edged to the front of my seat, tense. "They were getting ready to *bleed* me when I ran away. Or don't you remember?"

A shadow passed briefly over Werne's face. "What was once feared an abomination has been revealed to be a gift," he said. "Return to the Goddess's holy bosom, receive her blessing and her sacraments, and consecrate your gift to your Sacred Mother, that she may arm you, as one of her Holy Arrows, to strike down the unrighteous."

The chill turned my backbone to ice as I realized *exactly* what he wanted from me. "Get out." It was barely a whisper, but it carried. Like a Holy Arrow.

Werne the Bloodletter rose and took a step toward me, arms outstretched. "Sister —"

"Don't touch me!" I sounded shrill. "'Unclean,'" I said, moving closer, one hand lifted toward him. At that moment I would have loved to see a flicker of silver from my fingertips. "'An abomination.' Those were their words. Those were *your* words, Werne."

He opened his hands. "Forgive us. The imperfection of men — we misread the Goddess's gift — we did not see the holy and righteous path she had laid before you! We did not know that she had given you vision to see, so that you could seek out and strike down her enemies."

"You told me I would burn." My words made him flinch, just that much.

"Forgive me."

"No." I don't know where the fire came from, but it seared away the chill. "No. I didn't burn. I didn't die. I don't forgive you — not you, not the Confessors, not the entire cursed Celystra." I stood up. "And I will never — understand me: *never* — use my skill to hunt Sarists for you."

"We can compel your return."

"I'm not afraid of you."

Werne smiled, smooth as satin. "Not for yourself, no," he said. "But there are those you care for." His eyes slid past me, to where Grea watched us silently. "I think you will not hold out forever. These are dark days, and people should be among family. You'll make your way home soon enough." He rose in a composed swirl of green robes, and glided out of the bakery. I watched him leave, my fingernails biting into my palms as I squeezed my hands into fists.

I heard Grea enter the common room and I set about rearranging the chairs with a violent passion. "He threatened you," I said, uneasy. "I'll move out. I can go to the Temple."

"You'll do no such thing," she said firmly. "I told you before, lass, we knew who you were when we took you in."

"But —" Grea was unflinching, just fixed me with the gaze that said *don't even* think *about defying me.* I nodded meekly, and grabbed a rag to start wiping down the chairs the Greenmen had touched, but Grea turned me to her and put her great strong arms around me, as if she could close out the whole ugly world.

I helped Aunt Grea scrub every inch of the bakery's common room, but the work didn't soothe me. I kept seeing Werne's smiling, placid face, his conviction that I *would* come back to him, if only he were patient enough. The more I played that scene over in my mind, the more my fear eroded, leaving something darker. My hands shook as I hauled a water bucket across the floor, and I nearly hurled the entire thing into the bakery door, just because. How *dare* he come here, so smug and righteous, and threaten the people I cared about?

When customers started returning, the jostle of tired, anxious people *wanting* things only put me more on edge, so for the good of the bakery, I lit out of there. A quarter of an hour later, I was halfway across town, pacing the bank of the Big Silver river, staring up at the Keep. Somehow my anger at Werne had twisted itself around, tangled itself with the day's other concerns, and found a new target. I wasn't sure what had brought me here; wasn't sure I even *wanted* to be here, but I needed — something. Answers. Information. Something. I didn't know what, but I didn't know where else to get it either.

Up on Queen's Level, I brushed past the guards, dodged the taunts (and aim) of the mad neighboring inmate, and used my lock picks to let myself into Durrel's cell without stopping, without looking at anyone. Durrel immediately sprang from the bed and reached for my hands, but I pulled away before he could touch me. "What's the matter?" he asked. "Did something happen? You were gone so long —"

"Is there anything else you want to tell me?" I said.

He took a step back, frowning. "You're — angry." He sounded confused.

"I spent an interesting evening with Koya last night. And a few days ago, an afternoon crawling around potioners' shops in the Temple District — Oh, yes," I said, as understanding dawned on Durrel's face.

"Look, I can explain —"

"Can you? Because I'd like to hear it."

He stepped away from me, his face unreadable. Finally he said, "I know it's difficult for you to imagine, but Koya hasn't had the happiest life." I let out a strangled laugh, but he went on. "That family, and her marriage . . . I didn't help."

"What does that mean?"

He crossed the little cell and poured himself a cup of stale water, then looked at it with distaste and set it down again, undrunk. "I listened to her. I talked to her. I thought I was being nice. She was my wife's daughter. It's just that —"

"She misunderstood?"

There was a twist to his mouth I couldn't quite interpret. "No," he said. "That was the problem. I liked her. How could I not? She was everything her mother wasn't — young, soft, *friendly*. In her eyes I was a person, a man, not just —" He took an unsteady breath.

"The studhorse?" He flushed, but nodded. "And the poison?"

Durrel's eyes met mine and held steady. "I swear to you, Celyn, I did not have anything to do with Talth's death. Yes, I should have asked why Koya wanted the tincture —"

"Well, what did you *think* it was for?"

He shook his head, shrugged. "I don't know. Maybe some kind of medical use . . ." He sounded unconvinced, and a belated understanding seeped into my thoughts.

"You think she did it."

"No. Not Koya. There's no way."

I nodded, but I saw it now. I might not really know Durrel — but I finally knew him well enough to know when he was lying. If he had proof it was Koya, he'd never tell me. "You have to tell someone you're innocent."

"Tell who? Say what? Admit to buying the poison that killed my wife? Confess to having an inappropriate relationship with my stepdaughter? That's all the Ceid need to send me to the gallows."

And a fairly compelling reason he'd tried to hide it from me, as well. Fair enough. I still wasn't totally convinced, though. "I have more questions," I said.

Durrel nodded heavily. "All right. I'll try to answer whatever you want to know."

"Evalia Mondeci?"

The sudden, heavy silence that fell between us was tangible. Durrel watched me, eyes hard, as if trying to figure out where I'd conjured that name from. He gave a bitter smile. "*Digger*, right. Of course. It doesn't matter. Whatever you've decided to believe, I didn't have anything to do with that."

"What happened?"

"I don't *know* what happened. I —"

"You don't know who killed the woman you loved in Tratua. You don't know who killed your wife in Gerse. Can't you hear how that sounds?"

"You know I didn't hurt those women!"

"How? I don't know you."

"Of course you do!" His voice was low and urgent. "I'm the same man you met last fall. The same man you spoke to on the tower at Favom. You *know* me. As much as I knew you, the moment I met you. You trusted me then, Celyn. Trust me now."

I wanted to close my eyes and turn away. He had lied to me about everything — why did I *still* want to believe him? With a sigh, I said, "All right. Just — explain it to me."

He made me sit beside him on the bed, but it was a long time before he spoke. I watched him, staring down at his own hands, as if studying the grime caked into the cracked skin. He had strong hands — a horseman's hands, a farmer's hands. I stopped myself from thinking my next thought.

"She was like you," he finally began.

"Short? A thief?" *Magical?* "What does that mean?"

"A sort of — spy, I think. Or at least she knew dangerous men, men with a lot of power and secrets, and she learned things that she shouldn't have. She came to me for help —" His jaw tightened. "And I didn't do anything. I didn't know *what* to do. It was already a scandal, we weren't supposed to be seeing each other, and I swear by Marau I did not realize how much danger she was in." Durrel looked out into the cell, his gaze lost somewhere between the shadows and the bricks. "She was strangled with a lace from my sleeve. I'd given it to her to tie her hair back."

And there it was, at last — the haunted look that had been missing when he'd spoken of his wife's death. He may not have strangled the

Tratuan girl, but in his mind he was guilty. She'd died because he hadn't saved her. "Is that —" I swallowed, trying to decide what I wanted to ask. "Is she why you helped me?"

"No." He turned to me, but his look was distant. "Maybe."

I didn't know what to think. Looking at him now, I *wanted* to believe him, but there were too many coincidences. I thought about what Fei had told me — the man she'd heard bragging about possibly killing a noblewoman — but that story seemed to pale compared to the apparent evidence against Durrel. "It looks bad," I said. "But if we have information that could clear your name, we have to tell somebody. You need to tell your father, at least."

"I can't," he said.

"No, listen — I might have a new lead. It's practically worse than nothing right now — just some rumor about a guy boasting in a bar — but if it can help —"

He didn't answer, just stared at his hands.

"I don't understand," I said. "You're acting like you don't want to get out of here."

"Of course I do," he said. "It's complicated."

"Then *explain* it to me."

Durrel sighed. "When Eva died, my father was the *only* person who believed in me. He risked a lot, getting me out of trouble there."

"Then you must welcome the chance to tell him that you're innocent." He was stubbornly silent, and I wanted to shake him. I paced the cell, trying to make sense of this man. "Why won't you do something? Say something? You know you didn't do this. How am I supposed to help you if you won't tell me the truth?"

Durrel's next words were cold. "If you're determined to accuse Koya, then you *can't* help me after all."

"Why are you protecting her?"

"Koya didn't kill Talth!"

"And neither did you!"

"Good," he said curtly. "I'm glad we have that established, because a moment ago, I wasn't sure."

I felt stung. I wasn't even sure what we were fighting about. I rose and moved across the cell, into the shadows at the far end. After a long moment, Durrel spoke again. "I'm sorry, Celyn. I know you're trying to help me."

"At least tell your father. He would help you, I know he would —"

"I can't. Tell him I bought the poison? He'd never understand."

But I did, finally. It had taken me this long, maybe because I didn't have a lot of experience with fathers, but I thought I had it at last. "You would rather risk execution than disappoint him."

He didn't answer, but he didn't have to. I knew his father only a little — and I didn't want to disappoint the man. "You're crazy. You're his son. He loves you."

With his face set, Durrel looked at me. "Exactly." He rubbed his face, looking impossibly weary. "You don't understand, Celyn. He's the Lord of Decath. That means *everything* to him. He would never understand how I could do anything to shame our house. I didn't kill Talth, but I *am* involved. I made a mess of the marriage my father arranged between two honorable houses — the first real responsibility I ever had — and it doesn't matter what the truth is. I've lost his trust, and I've lost his respect."

"I don't believe that," I said, but it didn't matter. Durrel believed it, and nothing else I could say that day would sway him.

Out in the world again, I felt bad for leaving him like that. I was an orphan who'd grown up hating and fearing her only family (witness that afternoon's congenial encounter), but Durrel was a bighearted nob who loved easily and cared deeply for his family's honor, believed in duty and nobility and all those grand ideals that meant little to a gutter rat scraping out a living on the street. He'd looked so lost when I left, like he was losing the people who believed in him, one by one. I should have stayed with him and looked into his eyes and told him I believed him, that I'd find a way to prove his innocence, without implicating Koya or revealing too much to Lord Decath. I should have said everything would work out.

I used to be that good a liar.

I walked all the way back from the Keep, my thoughts wrapped so tightly around each other that I didn't pay attention to where I was putting my feet. At the bakery, Rat had food waiting, thick, steaming rabbit stew (probably *not* rabbit, but I hardly tasted mine anyway). From the look on his face when I sat down, I knew he'd heard all about Werne's visit from Grea.

"You're not here," he remarked after a while, pushing a pitcher of small beer toward me. I shook my head, and he just shrugged and ate in silence. I couldn't put the ugly pieces of the day into sensible order, and I didn't like the direction my thoughts kept pointing. I had every reason not to trust Durrel, and yet —

"I think I've managed to convince myself that Durrel isn't guilty. Again."

Rat eyed me levelly. "Well, that's good, isn't it?"

"I guess so."

"Then what's the problem?" I didn't answer, just played with my food, not eating it. Rat leaned back on one elbow and looked at me appraisingly. "You *like* him."

My head shot up. "Don't be stupid; he's a nob."

"And therefore unlovable on principle?" I made a face and ignored him, but Rat wasn't through. "Admit it, Digger — this isn't just some old debt you're paying back. You *want* to help him."

"Of course I want to help him. But he's been lying to me from the start. About the murder weapon, about Koya —"

"And that bothers a devotee of Tiboran because . . . ?"

"What?"

Rat shrugged. "So he lied to you. Everybody lies. What's the big deal? Unless you feel betrayed for some other reason."

My face *hurt* from scowling so hard. "Not by half."

"You ran straight to him when your brother spooked you," he said. "It's obvious how you feel about him. It's been almost a year," he added, his voice so gentle it hurt. "You can move on."

It felt like he'd kicked me, straight to the gut. "This has nothing to do with Tegen!"

"Right. I forgot, because we can't talk about Tegen. We can't talk about your brother, we can't talk about the prince —"

I shoved my chair back and stood up from the table, but Rat's voice dragged me back down again. "You're not doing yourself any favors with this life you're living. Is this really what Tegen would have wanted for you?"

"He died for me." I pulled away from Rat. "He died for me, and I will not cheapen his memory by flinging myself at the first pretty boy who crosses my path." I slammed the door behind me and stalked out into the deepening twilight.

I knew where I was without even looking; the very *feel* of this place was imprinted on my bones forever. Just a shady street near the palace, where a tidy town house sat circled by a service alley and an arched wooden doorway set back from the cobbles, flanked by potted ferns, long dead. The owner had been arrested, some months back, and the house had the lonely, haunted feel of empty homes all over Gerse. I knelt to the ground and touched my fingers to the road, but nothing happened. There had been no magic here that night, nothing but two unlucky thieves and a company of Greenmen lying in wait.

It had been dark as ink, the moons in shadow, our clothes equally black. We'd come out that door, stepped blithely, carelessly into the night, barely even looking as we slipped outside, Tegen's arm around my waist. He'd laughed and kissed me — and then green-gloved hands had torn him from me. I closed my eyes, and I could *hear* them; my knee throbbed with a remembered blow from a nightstick. And then Tegen's knife — as clearly as if it were happening before me now — plunged into the guard who held me, sealing his fate.

I sank to the cobbles and bent my head to my knees. *Oh, Tegen, why did you do it?* But I knew why. So the Greenmen wouldn't capture the girl with magic. He'd been the only person I trusted with my secret after I left the Celystra, and there was no doubt, no hesitation, not a moment's pause before he drew his knife and shouted my name. And instead of standing and grabbing my own knife and fighting alongside the man I loved, I had turned away into the night, and run.

I closed my eyes, breathing deeply, as if I could catch some part of him that was left behind here, some last wisp of the life I had lost. But the darkness betrayed me, and all I saw were flashes of another man's face. Rat was an idiot — I loved Tegen, would *always* love him, in that deep and soul-searing way that made him still a part of every breath I took. Durrel had been kind to me once, but he was nobody, *nothing* compared to that.

But Rat was right about one thing. I'd been angry and scared, and the first place I'd run to was Durrel Decath's side.

Pox and hells.

CHAPTER FIFTEEN

The weather that week continued sticky and hot, and today's gossip was all about a new company of soldiers being posted in the city. As if Gerse needed more Green Army men at large — we were drowning in them, they were so thick in the streets these days. Barracks were overflowing, and the army had started seizing abandoned properties to house them, or — worse yet — forcing the soldiers on ordinary families, who had to give up a room or a floor or a whole house to billet Astilan's troops. Rat said Hobin refused to talk about it, and he kept his office locked, but it didn't stop everyone else from having an opinion on the matter.

"You've got a visitor," Grea said when I came in that afternoon, pointing a dough-sticky hand toward a corner of the common room. I barely recognized Fei; she'd buttoned her smock up high around her neck and pinned her hair beneath a demure coif. She would have looked respectable, if it weren't for the bite to her eyes or the little twist to her lip. She was seated at a table, picking at a small, round loaf and tapping her foot impatiently. I slid in beside her.

"Well?" I said when she hadn't spoken after a minute. She looked toward the ceiling, past my shoulder, down at her bread — anywhere but at me. "You're drawing attention to yourself," I said quietly. "These are regular marks, and they'll wonder what you're up to. Stop flitting around and tell me what you're doing here."

When she met my eyes at last, I recognized the twitchiness as fear. She pinched a bit of bread between her fingers so tightly I thought she might draw blood. "I saw him again," she said — and we both knew who she meant. The scary fellow who'd bragged about killing Durrel's wife. "Today, at the Bat."

I nodded, my mind a blank. I'd asked for this information; now what was I supposed to do with it?

"He agreed to drink with me. Tomorrow night. At the Temple. You can see him then, see if you know who he is?"

"Uh, yes," I said finally. "Well done."

"Did he really kill that woman?"

"I have no idea." Somehow it didn't seem right to say "I hope so."

"Don't worry," I added, because Fei was biting her lip, dark eyes wide and nervous. "You won't be in any danger."

"What if he saw me with him? With your Decath boy?"

"So what if he did? Fei, I don't think there's a killer out there stalking the streets, preying only on women Durrel Decath shows interest in."

She scowled at me, clearly neither convinced nor amused. "You'll come?" she said finally.

"That's the plan." I was just kind of amazed she'd set it up.

At night, the Temple was all lit up, candles burning in colored glass lamps set into the walls, and massive iron chandeliers hauled up to the beamed ceiling. I almost smiled when I stepped in the great open doorway. (The Temple had doors, but only closed them in *really* inclement weather. Like an avalanche.) It looked like a festival.

I headed upstairs to the upper gallery, at a table just above where Fei was already sitting, her hair now spilling down her shoulders again. She was a little old for such a girlish display, but I had to admit, it worked. If I leaned forward just slightly, I had a wide, clear view of the chair opposite Fei's, while still completely concealed by the balcony floor and railing. Fei had done her job well.

I'd already waved the serving girl away twice by the time Fei's heavy came in, ambling through the common room. He was just as she'd described, big, strong, and scary. He had a curious sort of uneven gait, and as he swung himself into the chair across from Fei, I saw why. The sole of one boot was built up with blocks. Over the noise of the crowd and the unending raucous music, I couldn't hear anything they said, but I saw everything. He looked to be in his sixth or seventh age, a little soft from hard living — but hard enough that I doubted the softness ever affected him much. He had thin, sandy hair, veined cheeks, and an uncertain beard that may have just been from neglecting to shave for a couple days. He planted his meaty fists on the table and ordered a drink.

I was ready to leave as soon as he sat down and I got a clear view of his face, but that didn't seem fair to Fei. I'd roped her into this; I'd stay as long as she would. As I watched her smiling and drinking with him, my impression of her skills only grew. She was a natural actress, and no idiot either. After a few minutes, three more girls "happened" by her table, squealed with delight to recognize Fei, tossed their heads, and grinned a little less than demurely at the heavy, until his grizzled chin was nearly in his ale. If one of them hadn't looked straight up at me, holding eye contact just barely long enough, I'd have thought it was a real coincidence. A minute later, Fei barked out a crass, unappealing laugh, shoved back, and stood up. She excused herself and slipped into the crowd. The other girls slid right into place, and Heavy probably never even noticed the difference.

Impressive. It almost made me miss having a partner.

A minute later, I spotted Fei near the stairs. She gave me one steady, significant look, then took a shadowed table in the back. I fed my way through the crowd and caught up with her.

"Well?" she demanded, her voice low and rough. "Did you see him?"

"I saw him," I said evenly.

"His name is Alech Karst, and he works —"

"I know where he works," I interrupted her. She looked surprised — but not quite shocked enough. "He works for Ragn Decath. He's a guard at Charicaux."

Fei's expression was so wary and guarded that as soon as the words were out of my mouth, I realized she'd been going to say something else entirely. "Fei?"

"I don't know about Decath. You might be right."

"But that's not where you saw him."

More fidgeting. A decision, a deep breath. "He's a Ferryman."

I let out all my breath in one rush. She was serious. "Did you know that when he bragged about killing Talth Ceid?"

"I don't know. Maybe. They come into the Bat sometimes, because it's near the water. I hear them talking, usually about the money or the runs they do, out to Wolt or sometimes Tratua. Once I heard him say something about leaving a cargo locked in the hold of an impounded ship. They never went back for it."

She said "it," but I knew, from the haunted look in her eyes, that she really meant "*them*." Sarists, or other unfortunates desperate enough to trust their fates to Ferrymen, trapped in a cargo hold, for days or maybe weeks. If they were lucky, Marau had gotten to them before the Greenmen did. For a moment, I couldn't decide who I hated more — the Inquisition's thugs who forced people to such desperate actions, or the Ferrymen who took advantage of them.

"Do the Ceid have dealings with Ferrymen?"

She drew a circle on the table with a nervous finger. "I never heard that," she said. "But some of them — they're local crews, but run by a bigger operation."

A powerful family like the Ceid would be just the outside support a crew of Ferrymen could use. "What *have* you heard about the Ceid?"

Fei shrugged. "I don't know about Karst, about Ferrymen, but once I heard someone bragging about how he'd ripped off a shipping family on the Silver. Said he and a couple of skells took them for some cargo that was supposed to go to the army. Medicines, I think. They sold them right out of the crates on Temple Street. Temus never said the name of the family, but it wasn't hard to figure out."

"Wait — did you say *Temus*?"

She glanced past me, as if waiting for a threat to melt out of the shadows. "He's just a Temple Street lowlife, nobody special. I haven't seen *him* in a few weeks, though, so don't even bother asking."

"No," I said slowly. The hum of the crowd seemed to dissipate, until all I could hear was a shrill, nasal voice crowing, *Give Temus a taste, sweetling!* "I can track him down. Did Karst tell you anything useful just now? Anything else about killing Talth Ceid?"

She shook her head. "I asked him, but all he would say is that the job wasn't finished yet. He also said Lord Durrel would never go to trial, but I couldn't get him to tell me what he meant."

I didn't like the sound of that one bit. I palmed a gold crown from my sleeve and slipped it into her hand. "You can go. I don't think you'll have to worry about Karst. He won't bother you."

"I made sure he won't," Fei said, her voice fiery. "And this finishes the debt between us. Don't come looking for me again."

I nodded, watching her slip back into the bar. As she crossed the gallery, her skirts slipped, the hem falling lower, and she twisted her dark, loose hair around the back of her head and tightened up the laces of her bodice. With that closed, prim posture she could walk right past Karst's table, and he'd never even see her. I wondered what she'd do now; she might not be able to go back to the Bat for a while. But I didn't worry. Fei had a way of working things out for herself.

What did it all mean? Why were *Ferrymen* patrolling the Charicaux grounds? There was no way I could believe Lord Ragn was involved with those people. But Talth? That was a much more credible leap. Though what did Durrel's neighbor at the gaol have to do with any of it, and what had Karst meant when he said Durrel's case would never make it to trial?

The next day I was back at the Keep as soon as they lowered the drawbridge. Something was wrong here; very odd, and I should have seen it days ago. The top floor of the gaol was for prisoners like Durrel, nobs and courtiers, gentlemen, ambassadors. Not a seldom-bathed gutter boil like Temus. Some local trash ripping off the Ceid, and getting a prince's accommodations at the Keep in return for it? No wonder he'd seemed so cheerful as a prisoner. Maybe he'd hit on a way to cancel his debt against the Ceid — by spying on the man accused of killing one of the family. At any rate, Temus was involved, and I was going to find out how.

I paid off the guard and rushed down the cell ring, almost eager for Temus's entertaining abuse today. Not that I thought I had a rat's chance in a Gerse kitchen that he'd answer my questions, but —

Things were too quiet. I could still hear the Talancan spy, weeping piteously down the row, and that annoying drip of the rooftop gargoyles, but no rotten vegetables flung into my path, no rude whistle, no screeching cackle as I approached. I stopped to peer inside Temus's window, bracing myself for the slam of his filthy, wiry body against the door, but there was nothing. Raising myself up on tiptoe to look into the cell, I saw that it was empty.

Something was *very* wrong.

Slowly I turned to Durrel's cell and tapped gently on the door. After a pause, I heard the sound of Durrel peeling himself off the bed, then leaning heavily against the door. His breath was ragged as he coughed out my name.

"Where's your neighbor?" I demanded, not bothering with greetings. "What's happened to Temus?"

I heard the quirk of amusement in his voice, even now. "He said you'd miss him."

"You're not funny. What *happened* to him?"

"He got out. What in Marau's name's the matter?"

I yanked myself up to the window. "He got out? When? How?"

Durrel was staring at me as if I were the deranged one. "Yesterday. Said it was time for his hearing, and a guard I'd never seen before led him away."

"What kind of guard?"

"Celyn, what is this —"

"What kind of guard?"

Durrel looked at me, a furrow beneath the fall of hair. "Big fellow, ruddy, losing his hair."

"Karst," I breathed. "Pox, pox, *pox.*" *The job's not finished yet.* I spun back to the hall, looking down toward the guards' station. It took so little — a gold crown, a couple of silvers — for me to bribe my way into Durrel's cell whenever I wanted. What was the price of a guard's uniform and a blind eye? "That wasn't a guard," I said. "He's a Ferryman. And he's been claiming to have killed Talth."

He was silent for a moment, just looking at me through the bars, digesting this. "Then what does he want with Temus?" was what he finally said.

"That's what I want to know." Were Karst and Temus. working together? "I have to go."

"Celyn, wait —"

I turned back.

His face was set as he gripped the iron grille, but all he said was, "Wherever you're going, be careful."

I didn't linger long enough to respond. Back at the guards' station, no amount of coinage could persuade the guard to tell me who Karst really was or where he'd taken Temus, but from the chilled expression on his normally greedy face, I was pretty sure they *weren't* headed to any magistrate's hearing. The hearing that never, ever happened.

I tore down the long spiral staircase, but halted abruptly halfway down. There was a sound trailing me on the stairs — footsteps behind me, trying not to be heard. I ducked back into the shadows, tense and ready. When a pair of filthy boots came into my sight, followed by scrawny legs and a stained red uniform, I made a grab for him.

"Mmph!" I had my arm around the neck of a small guard — no older or bigger than me — who was struggling in protest. I let him go, and, coughing, he sagged against the closed stairwell wall.

"I'm sorry!" he gasped out. "I didn't mean to startle you!"

"What do you want?" I didn't recognize him, but he had an indecisive and furtive air. "You look like you have something to say."

The little guard nodded, rubbing his throat. "I work the dock level, round back," he said. "Usually. My name's Stotht. I've seen you visiting more than once."

"And?"

"I heard you asking about that prisoner who was transferred yesterday."

"Do you know something?"

Stotht glanced past me down the stairs, back up where he'd come from, then leaned in closer. "I saw them together, heading down through the cellars. A while later, the guard came back alone and told me he'd give me a gold crown if I could deliver a message."

"What kind of message?" I asked, my blood cold. "What did it say?" Belatedly I realized Stotht probably couldn't read.

"No, it weren't a letter," he said. "He give me a little pouch, said to take it to this big house on the river, and be sure to wear my uniform."

"Do you know which one?"

"Not who lives there. Just some big house in Nob Circle with a red roof and guards outside."

"Charicaux." Stotht looked surprised. "What was in the pouch?"

"I didn't look," he said. "But it weren't coins; I could tell by the weight. Something soft, wrapped in cloth, maybe."

I could feel myself frowning. What did it mean? "Thank you," I said. "That's very helpful." I made to move on, but Stotht's little body was in the way.

"I've seen you in and out of here," he said again, conversationally. "Who're you visiting? Your brother?"

"My — what?" I had to get rid of this kid. I dipped into my bodice for the last of my meager supply of bribery money, not quite liking the way Stotht's eyes followed my hand, and pulled out a couple of copper marks.

"I don't want any money," he said earnestly. "But . . ." he paused. "Can I call on you at your home?"

I blinked, incredulous. Well, why not? "Fine," I said. "I'm in the Temple District. My name's Fei."

He was still thanking me as I headed back down the stairs.

A message to Charicaux? To Lord Ragn. This was getting more and more tangled. My thoughts turning in on one another, I followed the stairs down to the cellars, where Stotht had seen Karst take Temus, drawn on by a sickening thought. What if Karst hadn't grabbed Temus to free an accomplice — but to silence one?

The stairs continued downward, into service passages, unused kitchens, and the charnel. Moving deliberately so I didn't call more attention to myself, I followed the steps down into the dank, dripping darkness.

Unlike the prisoners' floors, the cellars were unguarded, full of hidden, empty rooms, with stores of weapons nearby — knives in the kitchen, bone saws in the charnel. Karst could have taken Temus anywhere down here, but there was said to be only one exit from the cellar levels: Marau's Door in the charnel, where executed prisoners were sailed back to the city. The charnel was a low-ceilinged room with niches carved out of the brick walls and the doorway on the river. I grabbed a lantern from the hallway and pulled my smock up to cover my face. Inside, there were two bodies waiting to be hauled away on the coroner's barge, wrapped neatly in linen shrouds. I hesitated, considering one dark possibility after another. One corpse was far too large to have been Temus, but the second . . . Steeling myself not to gag, I peeled back the cloth from the face of the narrower body.

And saw nobody, just some poor, famished soul who'd no doubt died of starvation or disease in the Rathole. A dark, bearded face, too old to be Temus. Weak with relief, I pushed myself out the service door, onto the little outside landing. I gasped in great lungfuls of fresh, fishy-smelling air and leaned my head back against the curving brick wall of the Keep. I could tell by the angle of the view that I was on the same side of the tower as Durrel's cell, and if I looked up —

I didn't look up. A little rowboat was moored nearby, bobbing merrily on the sunlit river. Beneath the surface of the water, I thought I saw a shimmer of white. Coming closer, I gave the boat a little kick with my foot and sent it out into the river a few feet. The white shape bobbed higher through the murk, getting larger as the light struck it, until it turned over in the water, and I had to bite back a yelp of shock.

Temus's wide, dead eyes — already partially nibbled by fish — stared back at me, his white, bloated body bumping the edge of the landing. I gave a squeak and stumbled back against the building. The waterlogged hair floated away from the ghastly face, and I saw an injury that was not attributable to Big Silver fish.

Karst had cut off Temus's ear.

My heart lodged in my throat, I scrambled back inside the Keep, ran through the charnel — making the sign for Marau — and sprinted back up the staircase to Queen's Level. I hit Durrel's door at a run, and I heard him jump from the bed.

"I found him," I gasped out. "Temus. He's dead."

Inside, Durrel paled. "Are you sure?"

I recalled the ragged gash across his neck, the blank stare. "Someone slit his throat and dumped him in the river."

"Who? Why?"

The first question we already knew the answer to; the second was the more worrisome. "I don't know, but we have to get you out of here." I tumbled the lock on the cell door and slipped inside, closing it quietly behind me. I told him what Fei had related to me, that Karst had boasted of killing Talth, that Temus had boasted of ripping off the Ceid; and what Stotht had just told me about his delivery to Charicaux.

"Why would Karst need to send a warning to your father?"

Durrel pulled away. "I don't know," he said. "I — he wouldn't."

And yet he clearly *had*, in language plainer than a letter: *We can get to anyone, even inside the Keep. We can get to your son.* I thought furiously, frantically. Right now the priority was getting Durrel safe. I backed off a pace, hiked my skirts to my knees, unbuckled my knife, and passed it to Durrel, sheath and all. "Keep this on you. If anything happens, if anyone comes —"

"Celyn, slow down." But he took the blade and slipped it into his own scuffed boot. "Maybe we're overreacting. This might not have anything to do with me."

"The Ferryman who murdered your wife just killed a man and sent his severed ear to your father. I don't know exactly what's going on here, but I don't mean to keep counting the bodies. You *need* to get out of this place and somewhere safe."

Durrel still hesitated. "I don't know," he said. "Won't I be more secure in here than loose on the streets?"

The way he said that made me pause, the logic of the argument sounded familiar somehow, and infuriating. "No, that —" I shook my head, frustrated. "No. They know exactly where you are right now, and that's bad."

"All right," he finally said. "If you're serious about this, then let's think it through. What are our options? You can buy me out —"

"We don't have the money." I was pacing, sure I could hear Karst's heavy footsteps banging down the cellway, even now.

Durrel nodded. "Or *break* me out."

I shook my head. "Not enough resources."

"Then it looks like you'll have to sneak me out. Fortunately I just happen to know the city's foremost authority on sneaking." There was a glint to his dark eyes, as if he found some part of this madness remotely amusing.

"What do you want me to do, hide you in my skirts?" But even as I said it, the thought spiraled out, twisting itself into an idea.

"There have to be plenty of ways. What about forging a pardon, or a transfer order?" I could tell he'd given this some thought, and no wonder. "You've been able to get inside my cell," he added. "And this Karst fellow pretended to be a guard to get Temus out —"

"That's it," I said. "That's *exactly* it. We need a guard."

Durrel leaned against the cell door, arms crossed over his chest, and cocked his head at me. "It would appear that an overabundance of guards is actually part of our current dilemma."

"Oh, but I know one who owes me a favor. It's almost perfect." I knew I should leave quickly now, get our plan underway before — I wasn't going to think about what came after *before*. And yet I didn't move. "I don't like leaving you," I said. "Promise me you'll be safe."

Durrel put a hand against my chest, as if to feel the flutter of my pulse at the base of my throat. "With you to protect me? How could it be otherwise?"

My heart gave a little squeeze, but I shook him off. "This is serious. Once I leave here, you'll be all alone, and I'm afraid that little knife won't be much help against somebody like Karst. If he's the man we think he is —"

"Don't *worry*." Durrel brushed a strand of hair from my face. "Contrary to appearances, I have not spent my entire life locked in towers. I *can* wield a weapon to defend myself. Granted, I'd prefer a sword or a pistol, but you and I have had good luck exchanging knives before."

"Don't remind me." I didn't consider any part of what had happened with Lord Daul to be lucky, but I had to admit, without Durrel's dagger, that skirmish on the cliff would have had a different ending. "Anyway, you're in close quarters. A knife is more useful than a sword."

"You see?" he said softly. "I feel safer already."

I finally pulled away from him and let myself back into the hallway, making sure I set the locks, just in case. Durrel had followed me to the door; I could barely see him through the high window. "Just —

sit tight and wait for me. I will figure something out by tomorrow. I promise."

His fingers curled around mine on the bars. "I'll be waiting," he said, and though he tried to disguise it, I finally heard the fear in his voice.

CHAPTER SIXTEEN

After leaving the Keep, I turned toward the city center and made myself walk straight to the Celystra as fast as I could. I had sworn I would never come back here, and this week I'd reaffirmed that vow — but today it had something I needed, something I didn't want to waste time hunting down elsewhere. Something I was just mad enough today to go fetch from my enemy's doorstep.

It took two hours, but he finally showed up, ambling up the long High Street toward the temple complex, his green uniform almost aglow in the low, angled light. His partner walked beside him, looking hulking and gruff and mean, and the look he gave me had all kinds of ugliness in it, and promised all kinds of ugliness if he got his hands on me. I steeled myself to meet his eyes.

"What's this, then?" he said, a sneer twisting his thick lip.

"Go on inside; I'll take care of it," Raffin said. His partner shrugged and swung open the tall side gate, iron ivy twined through stalks of corn, that led into the Greenmen's headquarters. I suppressed a shiver as my eyes followed him inside.

"All right, peach, you've got my attention. Should I change my uniform?" Raffin fell into step beside me. "Put on something a little more casual?"

I made a face. "No, we're going to need it."

"Sounds amusing. What do you have in mind?"

I glanced around. The great temple building loomed over us, its green tile roof seeming to devour the entire sky. I felt breathless and a little sick here in its presence. "We can't talk here."

"All right." Raffin steered me across the street toward a bustling, polished tavern with big glass windows and tables outside. The place was crawling with green uniforms. I halted in the middle of the road.

"You can't be serious. A Greenmen's bar? I'm not going in there."

"Suit yourself," Raffin said, turning away from me. "But you'll never know what I might have said."

It took a great deal of restraint to behave myself. "Oh, trust me. You're going to agree. You *owe* me, Raffin Taradyce. First for that night of hilarity at the prison, and second for bringing the Inquisitor *to my home*." I was surprised by the venom in my voice, but Raffin sobered.

"About that," he said. "I —"

"If you're so eager to make amends, then help me."

"All right," he said. "What seems to be the problem?"

I was already exhausted from this conversation. "I need help rolling Durrel."

Raffin gave a snort. "Not from what I hear, pet."

That was it. I smacked him, right in the jaw, right there in the middle of High Street, with a dozen Greenmen looking on, not even caring it was a hanging offense. "From *prison*, you idiot!"

Raffin took the blow with equanimity, rolling backward on his heels and laughing, but he grabbed me by the back of my bodice and dragged me into the tavern as several men in green turned toward us, rising up from their benches.

"Just a little dispute with my lady, boys," he said. "Nothing to get your dander up."

I kept my head turned toward Raffin's broad green shoulder, and for his part, he pulled me securely into a table far in the back near the noisy kitchen and the fires. Nobody else was stupid enough to sit near the ovens on a hot evening like this, so we had a fair amount of privacy. I took the seat that had my back to the Greenmen, but regretted it immediately. The presence of all those dogs of Celys, where I couldn't keep an eye on them, made the skin on the back of my neck crawl.

"Easy there. These men aren't the type to notice it's a lady slapping their friend around. Try to stay calm if you don't want to make enemies here." He was right, and I knew better. I took a deep breath and nodded.

Raffin ordered a pitcher of beer and a plate of stew, but I shook him off when he asked what I wanted, waiting impatiently for the server to leave us alone. Finally he leaned over his food and said, "All right, let's hear it. You've got some plan to spring our boy to freedom?"

"I don't know about freedom," I said. "I still can't prove he didn't kill Talth." But I explained about the Ferrymen, and Karst, and the murder of Temus inside the Keep.

"Marau's balls." He poured himself a little more beer, his knuckles white on the pitcher's handle. "So what's this plan that requires my uniform?"

I almost didn't have to explain it. Before I got half a sentence out, he was sharp enough to catch on. Nodding easily, he said, "I'm in. Just say when."

I tapped my lip with the stub of my finger; he watched with distaste but made no comment. "I was thinking tomorrow. The guards would normally interrogate a prisoner during the day, right?"

"Yes," Raffin said slowly, stirring the broth of his stew with his knife. "But we're less likely to be questioned about it at night. Better do it tonight. How many guards on duty every shift?"

"Four during the day, I think just two in the evening, and they don't pay very close attention up there."

"Are they armed?"

"We're not going to fight our way out!"

He looked at me, eyes hard and narrow, and for a moment I saw the Greenman *inside* the uniform. I didn't like it. "Are they *armed*?" he repeated coldly.

"Not officially. A couple of them carry blackjacks — big, nasty things with a shaft of iron in them. Mostly they subdue the prisoners just by intimidation."

"Well, that's fine," said Raffin, a grin breaking through his cool Guardsman's mask. "Intimidation's my favorite weapon." He actually sounded pleased by the thought of ordinary prison guards trying to outstrip the Acolyte Guard in a contest of arrogance. "Now, who exactly will *you* be in this little masquerade?"

"I can't really be anyone else," I said, although Tiboran knew a disguise wouldn't go amiss. "They know me."

"We can work with that," he said. "Now, when do you want to leave?"

"Already?" For a moment I felt panicky. There wasn't any time to waste, and the longer we delayed, the more danger Durrel was in — but what was I going to do with him *after* we got him out of the Keep? I couldn't bring him home, and it wasn't like he could very well go back to Charicaux or Bal Marse.

Raffin was drawing patterns in the stew left on his plate. He leaned back casually, his long limbs thrown out like he owned the table, the bar, and the whole damn city. The Taradyce always had that air of entitlement, of *ownership*, and life in service to Celys certainly hadn't tempered Raffin's attitude any.

"You could get in a lot of trouble for this," I said. "This could finish you with the Guard."

He shrugged. "I doubt it. You and our boy do your jobs right, and nobody will raise a peep. Besides, what's the worst they can do?"

"Send you home to your father without refunding your commission? Have you arrested for treason? Torture —"

"All right, enough! I said I was in; you don't need to sweeten the pot for me, peach." He took a swig of his beer. "I say we wait until Zet rises. That's a couple of hours before midnight, at the beginning of the night shift. It's also the time when we're the least likely to be missed or noticed doing anything . . . untoward." He gave me a critical look, then nodded. "I'll meet you at Market Bridge at her moonrise and we'll go from there."

I agreed, and after that there was no reason for us to linger there together, but neither of us moved.

"How is he?" Raffin finally said, and I shook my head.

"Still alive. I hope." I watched him watching the strong drink in his cup, and I thought about the first time I'd seen him at the Keep docks, a few weeks ago. "You told me there were questions about Talth's murder. Do you have anything to add to that story?"

He hunched lower in the seat, his long arms spread behind him. "What have you learned?"

It was madness to talk about these things here, in a nest of Greenmen, but what choice did I have? "Magic, at Bal Marse. Secret shipments in and out of the Ceid warehouse, on a disguised ship. Lord Ragn threatened by a Ferryman. Just a lot of pieces that don't match up. What can you tell me?"

Raffin had looked up sharply. "Lord Ragn? You can't think he's involved in this. I don't like that idea one bit."

"I don't either. Now you tell me what you know."

His head shook. "Nothing," he said firmly. "But I'd say at least one of those things you've mentioned definitely bears closer attention. Ah, peach. I should go. Things to do before our little fete tonight." Raffin rose to leave, throwing a couple of coins down on the table, but he hesitated. "You know, you should really be careful," he said, and for the thinnest moment, he actually sounded serious.

"What do you mean?"

He watched me, his face impassive, before finally saying, "Girls who share Lord Durrel's bed have an ugly habit of winding up dead."

My mouth dropped open and I stared at him. When I could speak again, I said, "Not that it's *remotely* your concern, Guardsman Taradyce, but for the record: I'm not sharing his bed."

"Oh, you will be," he said, sounding resigned. "You're exactly his type."

"Really?" I said. "And how's that?"

He took a deep sigh and met my eyes. "Cosmically unmarriageable."

The hours until Zet's rising were intolerable, and I thought *I* would kill someone if I had to wait much longer. I couldn't help wondering what Durrel was doing right this minute, and then right the following minute. Was Karst coming back? Could Durrel hold his own in a fight? Karst was big and heavy, and Durrel was thin and weak from hunger and inactivity. Would my scheme with Raffin work, or was I making a bargain with a devil in a green uniform? It was an insane risk, but I lingered outside the Greenmen's bar for some time, plucking coins from guards as they filed in and out. But eventually my hand started shaking, and I gave it up.

I wanted to run straight back to the Keep and wait there, but realistically I knew it wasn't any use. I couldn't surveil an entire prison by myself; if Karst wanted in, he'd have to get there the same way as everyone else, by way of drawbridge or boat. I did make a stop back at Grillig's rag shop, giving up another ten silver marks for a decent secondhand knife more suited to Durrel's size than my little blade. After taking it to be sharpened, I found myself across town at Charicaux, and just stood in the shadows as the sun set and the moons rose, watching the hired guards patrol the property. I recognized some of them from my last visit, but tonight, Karst was not among their company. What was going on here? What was the connection between Karst and Lord Ragn? I'd thought that Karst worked for Ragn, but I was beginning to doubt that. It wouldn't make much sense for Karst to threaten his own master. There had to be more between them. The incident with Temus suggested that Karst was a Ceid henchman instead, and I remembered Koya saying that the family wouldn't wait for the king's justice. Had they sent someone to get their own kind of justice for Talth? But why Karst, who claimed he'd killed Talth himself? And why Temus, if they were actually after Durrel?

The hot, heavy sky grew thick with moisture. Scudding gray clouds settled in, obscuring stars and moons alike, and a wet, stormy fog scented the air. Hells — was Celys going to pick *tonight* for it to finally rain? Jobs were always harder (not to mention less enjoyable) in bad weather, and smart thieves usually packed it in when it looked like rain. The first fat drops fell as I trotted toward the Big Silver and the Keep, and it was pouring by the time I tucked myself against the arch at the base of Market Bridge. Somewhere in that clouded sky, the bright disk of Zet was waking up, but I couldn't see her. Eventually I heard whistling, and Raffin appeared in the shadows, still wearing his Greenman's uniform —

this time with a wide, green hood and mantle pulled up to protect him from the rain.

"Lucky weather," he said as a crack of thunder shattered the sky. "Shall we get on with it?"

"After you," I said, and Raffin surprised me by grabbing my arm and dragging me out onto the landing toward the guards' station. I stumbled along with him, wondering whether I should be worried. It was *Raffin*, but I was still trusting Durrel's safety and future to a Greenman — and one who now had me in a grip so tight I couldn't pull away.

"You're hurting me," I gasped, but he ignored me, just whipped out his nightstick and banged the tip of it against the station door.

"Open up in the name of the Goddess!" he bellowed.

I heard a creak, and a cross, squinting face appeared through the bars. "What's this, then?" It was the same ugly guard who'd been on duty the night of my arrest. I ducked my head, grateful for the brim of my hat for more than rain protection.

"The Court of Blessed Inquiry has dealings with a prisoner in your custody. In Celys's name, I demand to be let through."

The guard hesitated. "What about her?"

Raffin pulled himself up to the limit of his very imposing height, leaning over the guard inside. "None of your concern," he said. The guard finally ushered us through and cranked down the drawbridge (Greenmen had their own boats, but thankfully the Keep man didn't ask why we hadn't just *sailed* here). When he offered us an escort across the bridge, Raffin waved him away with a sweep of the nightstick.

"Don't bother," he said. "I think I can find my way across."

He practically flung me before him onto the bridge, and I scurried ahead, trying to twist out of his grip. "What are you *doing*?" I said. The bridge was slick in the rain, and I half hoped Raffin would pitch into the river.

He pulled close to my ear. "You're Tiboran's girl, so *act* like it. You're a witness I'm bringing on my investigation."

"Do you treat all your 'witnesses' like this?" But I already knew the answer to that. His grip slackened a bit, at least, and finally we reached the island. Inside the Keep, the performance was much the same, Raffin imperiously demanding to be let through, and the steel in his voice and the green on his back granting us safe passage all the way up to Queen's Level. I started to worry again. Would *Durrel* be able to pull off that air of dangerous entitlement on our return trip? At last we arrived at his cell door, and the guard on duty just stood there with us, staring pointedly at me. I glared back — until I realized he was expecting me to let myself in as I'd done often enough.

"Well?" Raffin said, breaking the tense silence. "Open the door and begone." And he swept a dismissive hand in the guard's direction, as if brushing away a fly. Once we were inside the cell, I shut the door behind me by sagging against it with relief. It was dark inside, and the whole tower seemed to shake with every clap of thunder. Lightning flashed, and I saw Durrel, braced against the wall near the window, knife in hand, ready to lunge for Raffin.

"Somebody call for a Greenman?" Raffin said cheerfully, and Durrel's lunge turned into a clumsy embrace.

"Boyo!" he cried. "By Marau, how did you — never mind. I think I'm having more fun imagining how you two got together than whatever it is you might actually tell me." He reached a hand down, found mine, and pulled me to standing. "All right, you two miscreants, what's your brilliant plan for getting me out of here?"

Raffin had unearthed a candle and tinder, and was now surveying the cell with dismay. "It's not seeming quite so brilliant at the moment," he said. "By the gods, man, how did you end up in here?"

Durrel met his friend's eyes, and I saw there all the long years of their acquaintance, their *knowledge* of each other. "I did not do this thing," Durrel said, almost formally, and Raffin nodded once.

"That's good enough for me. Peach, care to explain to our boy what your plan is? Or shall I do it, while you help me undress?"

For a moment Durrel looked perplexed, and then it was as if another flash of lightning lit up the cell. "Oh. *Oh.* Are you sure you want to do this?"

"Absolutely, old boy. All for a good cause, and all that." But I could tell he was having second thoughts. We were counting on his rank and name to get him out of here tomorrow, but there was really no guarantee that the rest of this plan would work. Raffin was taking a huge risk, and we all knew it.

"So the idea is that Celyn and I overpowered you and stole your uniform, is that it?"

"She's half mad, but she's so adorable, I couldn't resist."

I shoved his hands away before he could tousle my hair again. "You're supposed to be *interrogating* him."

"I mean, is that *it*?" Durrel said again. "You expect me to just — walk right out the front gates? Without being noticed? Shouldn't I — I don't know — hide in a wine barrel or get smuggled out in a food cart?"

"The best plans are the simplest ones," I said. "The fewer moving parts, the less potential there is for breaking down."

"She's right," Raffin said. "Better get on with it." He shrugged out of his green tunic and passed it off to me. "Wouldn't want to get blood on the Goddess's sanctified raiment." Cracking his knuckles, he said, "Make it look good, brother."

"Oh, can I do it?" I said. "Please let me hit him at least once."

Raffin made a face at me. "I liked you better as a runaway nun."

"Play nicely, children," Durrel said mildly, and we both shut up. He hastily climbed out of his own clothes as Raffin stripped off the green breeches and boots. I got to hold the nightstick, and it was so tempting to hit a Greenman with his own weapon that I almost scared myself. I had to lay it beside his uniform on the bed and step back a pace.

I checked out the cell-door window, just to make sure none of the Keep guards had gotten suddenly curious about the Acolyte Guard's interest in Durrel, and when I was sure we were clear, I said, "Now would be a good time."

Durrel took a deep breath, and before I was quite ready, slammed Raffin in the gut with his closed fist. Raffin gasped and doubled over, his eyes bulging. He stumbled backward toward the bed, but Durrel pulled him upright and hit him again, a round, solid blow to the cheekbone. Something cracked in Raffin's face, and I flinched. Blood sprang from his nose, and Durrel wiped his knuckles on his bare leg. "Sorry, brother," he said, surveying the damage. Raffin was crouched on one knee, breathing heavily, but he took Durrel's offered hand and pulled him into an embrace. His words were slurred, his voice muffled, but I thought I heard, "You get to the bottom of this, understand?"

When Durrel finally broke away, I passed him the pieces of Raffin's uniform, breeches, tunic, cowl, boots, the knife I'd bought. He wasn't as tall as Raffin, and while he once might have been broader, he'd shrunk while in prison, and the uniform was ill-fitting. He'd never pass muster with other Greenmen, who paid a pretty coin to have their uniforms tailored precisely to fit — but on a stormy night in the Keep, it was all we had. He tugged the hood low over his face, but Raffin, holding his bloody nose, shook his head and winced.

"Leave the hood down," he instructed. "You don't want people to think you're hiding."

"But I am hiding," Durrel said. "Won't they recognize me?"

"No," Raffin said. "No one ever sees the man inside the uniform."

". . . But stand up straight," he and I said at the same time.

"Yes, milords," Durrel said, giving the two of us a half-amused look. "Good now?"

I straightened the cowl, brushed a little straw off the green tunic's shoulders. Raffin gave a dismissive wave of his hand and stretched out on the too-short bed, one arm bent lazily beneath his head, the other holding the balled-up remains of Durrel's spare shirt to his nose.

"You two lovebirds clear on out," he mumbled. "I'll just have a little rest here, enjoy His Majesty's finest accommodations."

Durrel, now the picture of a very sloppy Greenman, lingered at the cell door. "Raffin —"

"Go!" It was almost a roar, muffled through the shirt and the possibly broken teeth. Durrel grabbed my hand and we got out of that cell together.

CHAPTER SEVENTEEN

Outside the cell, rain drummed thinly on the Keep's lead roof, sounding like hollow pistol-fire. Durrel followed me down the passage, but I stopped him. "Don't *slink*," I said in a low voice. "You're a nob and a Greenman. You own the world, remember?"

Immediately Durrel stood taller, and the hand he rested on my shoulder was just heavy enough to signal his control without resorting to driving me forward at the point of his nightstick. We passed the guards' station unmolested, and I led him down the stairs from Queen's Level, feeling the tension in his arm. When we finally stepped out into the world, Durrel stopped in the arched doorway and sucked in a mouthful of wet air. Breathing out again, he had the ghost of a smile on his face.

"We did it."

"Not yet we haven't," I said. "Try not to fall off the drawbridge."

Across the river, we still had to pass through the bankside gatehouse. They never bothered me there, and I steered Durrel through as invisibly as I could, but the gatekeeper was in a chatty mood tonight.

"Did you get what you needed?"

For a split second, Durrel looked blank, and stood frozen, staring at the guard.

Fortunately the man took it as typical Greenman arrogance. "From your prisoner," he said, his voice an obsequious squeak. "Did he confess?"

I opened my mouth to speak — which would have been pointless and stupid, since I was supposed to be an anonymous, worthless witness — when Durrel glared at the guard. "No," he said in a curt voice. "Typical lying Sarist trash. We'll need to persuade him more strongly. I'll send a contingent here tomorrow to effect the transfer to one of the Goddess's Inquiry Chambers."

I couldn't help flinching. Inquiry Chambers — he meant dungeons, the secret underground cells where the Inquisition tortured their prisoners in Celys's name. But the guard nodded eagerly. "We'll make sure the prisoner is . . . prepared, Your Grace."

I *felt* Durrel's sudden alarm, but he kept calm. "We'll expect to see him in pristine condition," he said firmly. "Anything less would be a grave offense to the Goddess. We would hate to present one of her children before her in anything other than the perfection with which she made him." Never mind that Durrel himself had already beaten Raffin bloody. He lifted a hand, as if in blessing. "And I'm simply a humble guard, like you. The Court of Holy Inquiry thanks you for your devotion and duty."

The gatekeeper hauled up the portcullis to let us back out onto the street, where we stumbled out almost on top of each other in our haste to leave the Keep behind us.

"Don't run," I murmured. "Just a nice, easy, brisk pace. We don't want to call attention to ourselves."

"All right."

"But you can let go of me now," I said gently. Durrel's grip slackened and I rubbed at my shoulder.

"Now what?" he asked.

"Now we get you safe." I pointed toward a narrow side street, where the only light was the reflection of the moons in the puddles. The rain had slowed and the sky was clearing, and we trotted down alleys and back streets, places nobody had any business being after midnight on a wet summer evening. When I finally judged us far enough away from the Keep, halfway to Markettown on the way to the Temple District, we paused to rest a moment.

Durrel sagged back against a wall. I'd forgotten he'd had inadequate food and no exercise to speak of for the last few weeks and probably wasn't up to hiking the span of Gerse. But he surprised me. Standing up straighter, he caught me bodily and pulled me to him — so suddenly I wasn't immediately clear what he was doing. My face was against his scruffy neck, and I felt his chin rest gently atop my head.

"Thank you," he breathed into my hair. "Celyn, thank you."

And maybe because I was anxious or weary or spent from the day's heaped-up crises, I didn't move away immediately, just closed my eyes against the soft, damp wool of his tunic, listening to him whisper my name into the night.

Finally one of us came to our senses and broke away. Durrel lifted his face to the stars and scrubbed at his beard with his hands, as if washing his face in fresh air. "Gods!" he cried, and I wasn't sure of everything that was in that low, rough utterance, but I could guess at some of it. "Do you do this sort of thing often?" he asked, his eyes bright but sober.

I swallowed my laugh. "You handled the guard back there nicely."

"I didn't want it to seem strange when Raffin's cohorts show up tomorrow to get him out of there."

If they show up. I said, "I'm sure he'll be grateful. But for future reference, it's the Court of *Blessed* Inquiry."

"Ah," he said solemnly. "I'll have to remember that."

"You do that."

"Should we keep moving?" Durrel finally said, and I nodded, but we just stood there together, dripping wet in the moonslight, staring at each other. I meant to go, but I couldn't seem to make my feet obey me.

And then I heard sounds — footsteps, voices — heading our way. "Hist!" I pushed Durrel deeper into the shadows, up against the building.

"What is it?" He barely mouthed the words.

"Soldiers, I think." We were out past curfew, and though Greenmen had the run of the city at all hours, there was no sense tempting chance. "Damn it, I should have gone another way. Markettown is too heavily patrolled at night." I tugged on Durrel's sleeve and pointed toward the mouth of the street. He nodded silently, and together we stepped out onto the common road, turning the corner.

Straight into the Night Watch, heading toward us up the long stretch of roadway.

I skidded to a stop in the wet cobbles, and felt Durrel freeze behind me. Three of them, local heavies in their own dark doublets and red sashes. One sword, one cudgel, one pistol. I saw the look of stilted panic on Durrel's face, and thought fast. Slipping my arm around his waist, I looked up at him sweetly.

"The Goddess's blessings on you, good gentles," one of the Watchmen called out. "What's a servant of Celys doing abroad on such a foul-weathered evening?" I snuggled closer to Durrel, trying to make our purpose abundantly obvious.

But Durrel didn't follow me. "Just — taking a walk," he said stiffly.

"In the rain? After curfew?" The second guard put a hand to the hilt of his sword.

"Pox, they want to throw their weight around," I said, my voice low. That was all we needed. "Don't let them provoke you."

I felt Durrel's hand reaching for his knife. His breath came faster as the Watchmen drew closer. "I *know* that guard," he whispered, his eyes fixed on the men. "He was there when they arrested me."

"Are you *sure*? He won't recognize you," I said, praying I was right. "Just let them go by." I held fast to him as the men caught up to us.

"Good evening," Durrel said — like a cordial nob greeting his social inferiors, not like a Greenman.

"You're a little far from your neighborhood tonight, Guardsman," the Watchman with the pistol said. His words were friendly, but there was a challenge in his voice.

"I don't have to explain myself to you," Durrel said.

"Of course, of course," the one in the middle said smoothly. "It's just unusual seeing one of your ilk down here at this hour."

The third one, leering and fat, leaned closer to me. "Need any help with your prisoner, then? We'd be happy to take her off your hands." And where he put his own hands next made it perfectly clear exactly *what* they'd be happy to do to me. I twisted away, willing Durrel to stay calm.

"Don't touch her." Durrel's voice was cold as iron.

"Easy, brother, I meant no disrespect," the Watchman said, his voice oily. "Just thought you'd be willing to share, that's all, in the name of friendly coop —"

He didn't get to finish. Durrel's fist stopped his mouth and sent him reeling backward into his partners.

For a horrible moment, nothing happened — the five of us stood immobile, staring at one another. I think my jaw had dropped open in surprise. I felt it snap closed just as Durrel's guard righted himself. I caught Durrel by the belt before he could strike again, and spun him the other direction. "*Now* you should run," I said, shoving him down the street and taking off after him.

"Stop! Hold in the king's name!" Behind us, the Watchmen swore and gave chase.

Pox, pox, *pox*! We flew down the street and around the first corner, dodging a parked wagon and landing squarely in a puddle that soaked us to the knees. I pointed toward the black hollow of an alley just ahead. Durrel skirted inside; I followed, nudging him onward. "Keep going, keep going, keep going!" Footsteps thundered up the street behind us, close on our heels.

I was sure our footfalls could be heard through the entire city, that the Watchmen would call for reinforcements from their Watch and the Guard and the Green Army, if any soldiers were convenient. We had to get off these open streets. There was a low wall at the end of the alley; I swung atop it and helped Durrel pull himself over, just as two of the Watch rounded the corner behind us. The wall might stop them; it depended on how motivated they were. Not much, on a night like this. I hoped.

An explosion cracked through the wet night air, and a chunk of brick came flying off the building above Durrel's head. "Are they *shooting* at us?" he cried, but I yanked him onward when he tried to look back. We ran doggedly on, twining through streets and turning wild, random corners, until even I wasn't sure where we were anymore. I saw the glint of water up ahead — one of the rivers. By Marau, if he'd led us *back* to the Keep —

It was the Oss, spread before us like a sweet, blue banner. "Which way?" Durrel said, looking up and down the long, empty riverside street.

"There!" I said, pointing to the footings of a wide stone bridge, just as Durrel said, "Here!" and headed toward an empty skiff roped to the pier.

"No," I said, low and harsh. There was a hollow under the bridge that led along the river; the Watch would never look for us there.

"The boat is faster."

"You've just broken out of prison, assaulted and robbed a duly sworn servant of the Goddess, struck a member of the Night Watch, and ignored a command to halt in the king's name." I took a breath. "Do you really want to add hijacking a boat to the night's offenses?" I'd do my penance to Tiboran for that blasphemy later.

"But —" He looked desperately toward the water, his labored breathing turning into a cough. He held a hand to his side, bent almost double.

Gently I touched his back. "Trust me," I pleaded. "Under the bridge with you, milord."

He gave me a sharp look, but nodded reluctantly and followed me to the hidden landing beneath the bridge. It was almost dry, tucked under the span of stone, though the river lapped close to our feet. We squeezed together against the arched footings, catching our breath. Durrel couldn't stop coughing, and hugged his knees to his chest, burying the sound in Raffin's green breeches.

"What the hells was that?" I said. "You almost started a street war between the Night Watch and the Greenmen! If he'd *shot* you —"

"I'm sorry," Durrel said. "But he had no right to touch you."

I fell silent. I felt oddly warmed by that. It had been a long time since any man cared about my virtue. "Well, thank you," I mumbled. "I'm sure he got the message. But in the future, try to keep track of who's saving who."

He watched me silently a long moment before nodding. "Agreed."

I peered out past the edge of the bridge, but the docks and the street were empty. "I think we lost them," I said. "Still, we should stay covered for a while. They won't find us here."

"No, we should keep moving," Durrel said. He started to stand, but another spasm of coughing pulled him back down again. "Damn."

"Sit *down*," I said. "You're no use to anyone in this state."

"I know. It's just — all I've been doing for the better part of a month is sitting." He rubbed at the back of his neck. "That guard — I'll never forget his face. And the thought of going back there —"

"I know." There were three Greenmen I still saw clearly in my nightmares. "Well," I said cheerfully, "look on the bright side. If he didn't recognize you before, he will now."

That teased half a grin out of Durrel. "That's something," he said.

CHAPTER EIGHTEEN

We sat under the bridge as Tiboran shifted from phase to phase. I'd figured out more or less where we were, and I plotted out a new route — quicker and more direct — to our destination. Eventually judging it safe to move on, we hastened into the night again.

"We need to get you out of that uniform," I said. "They'll have spread the word to look for a Greenman with a girl."

Almost uncannily, Durrel's panicked path had pulled us in the right direction, and we hit the Temple District within minutes of leaving the shelter of the bridge. I felt safer as soon as we stepped into the glow of the big tavern, but Durrel looked perplexed.

"Where are you taking me again?" he asked.

"The Temple," I said.

"Temple? Which temple? I don't need a church, Celyn —"

"Not *a* temple," I said, sweeping my arm toward the massive, round public house with a flourish. "*The* Temple. The House of Tiboran. They're bound by sacred oath not to ask questions, and guards are forbidden from coming in here to look for anyone." Unfortunately that protection didn't extend to Ceid henchmen sniffing around, but I didn't say that out loud.

Inside, I waved down a woman at the bar, a dark-skinned beauty in a raven black wig that cascaded curls, winking with jewels, to her waist. She gave a dazzling smile behind her mask when she saw me, but her eyes narrowed briefly when she took in Durrel's green uniform.

"Now, Digger," she said in her lilting voice, "you know we can't have Greenmen coming in here. It upsets the Masked One."

"Oh, I'm not really —" Durrel began, lowering the green hood.

The woman's grin widened. "But he loves a man in disguise," she said. "I am Eske, High Priestess of Tiboran. Be you welcome to this place, stranger." The note of amusement in her voice said she knew exactly who this man in green was, and, in keeping with the long-honored tradition of the Lying God's hospitality, found it highly diverting and didn't plan to do a thing about it.

"He needs a room," I said over the din. *A place to hide*, I didn't need to add.

Eske took Durrel by the arm. "It is our duty and our honor to provide one," she said, her rich voice warm and genuine. Like all high priestesses of Tiboran who had served at the Temple, she was named for the mythical original Eske who had held the role, back in the Nameless One's day. Our present priestess was a tall woman whose beauty owed more to artifice than nature, and her ecclesiastical costume made her look even more striking, from the gown's open neckline showing off her night-dark skin, to the vast mask that covered almost her entire face — tonight's version made of feathers, the peacock plumes that were Tiboran's favorite, but also sporting a few spiky violet shafts I didn't recognize.

Since this Eske had taken the mantle of high priestess, the followers of Tiboran had sported Sar's colors more and more openly. Long-standing truce, and hefty bribes billed as taxes, kept the Inquisition from interfering with Temple business. Tiboran's devotees controlled Llyvraneth's wine and spirits trade, which even Celys's people relied on for their rituals and their everyday lives. Vintners outside the city, not to mention coopers, glassblowers, and all the other people who made a portion of their living from Tiboran's bounty, wouldn't stand for interference in their trade either. The Celystra left the Temple and its denizens alone, for the most part. And so Temple folk could sometimes get away with things other people didn't dare do, like show open defiance toward Bardolph and Werne.

Eske led us up through the second-floor gallery where I'd watched Karst with Fei, to a curving corridor of guest rooms, her beaded skirts brushing the dark floorboards. Some of the doors had colorful silk masks hanging from the knobs. I saw Durrel give them a look, and then cast a questioning glance my way, but I pretended not to notice.

The priestess stopped before a room at the back of the Temple. "It's not quiet, but it's private," she said. "No one will disturb you here." She produced a key out of thin air, a slim length of ornamental iron fashioned into the shape of a mask, and handed it to Durrel. A moment later the door swung open into a fair-sized room. "But understand, Tiboran's sanctuary only applies *inside* our doors. We can't protect you if you go outside."

"But —" Durrel objected.

"He's not going outside," I said hastily. "I'll make sure of it."

"I'll leave you now," Eske said, bowing to Durrel. "I'll have my staff send up some food, and my dear boy, you're going to need new clothes."

"*Normal* clothes," I stressed. "Nothing — outlandish. He's supposed to be in hiding."

Eske gave me a wink. "Digger, darling, *nothing* is going to make that boy look like anything other than the pretty nob he is. Even the Masked One has his limits." In the candlelight, under the grime from the gaol, I thought I saw a flush of pink color Durrel's face.

Almost before we were inside the room, a procession of masked serving girls carried down the hall, linens and platters and clothes in their arms. One of them lit the lamps, casting the room in a merry glow. It was well-appointed but not lavish, with a feather bed and a couple of cross-frame chairs, a large window overlooking the river (with a wide sill below it, convenient for Tiboran's servants to come and go as necessary), and a bottle of wine on the prayer stand. Durrel grinned at that.

"There's no hot water till tomorrow, milord," one of the masked acolytes said apologetically. "But Her Grace has ordered you a bath come morning."

"*Morning* means almost noon," I murmured to him.

The acolyte continued. "There's rosewater with mint in the washbasin, and fresh clothes for you. Would you like us to dispose of the uniform?"

"Ah, no. I think the owner's going to need this back," Durrel said.

"Very good, milord. We'll just have it cleaned, then." The girl stood back expectantly, but when Durrel made no move to strip in front of her, she nodded. "We'll pick it up in the morning. Good night, milord." And she and her fellows slipped out in one masked stream.

Once they were gone, Durrel stood in the middle of the room, looking faintly lost. I sat on the bed. "A wash?" I suggested gently. His weeks in the Keep had him smelling like something that wouldn't pass inspection at the Favom Court stables. Absently Durrel shrugged off the green tunic, and his shirt with it. A smudge of blue still showed up on his back, where someone must have kicked him. When he was arrested, probably. I looked away; men had a disturbing propensity to take their shirts off in my presence. Eske had been right about the noise; the sounds of tavern life down below us rattled through the floorboards, a merry clamor and din in the distance. I tried to ignore the sound of Durrel splashing in the background. Once cleanish, he put on an embroidered shirt the serving girls had left, with vaguely rude designs at the cuffs and collar, then sank down to the floor, his legs folded neatly under him. With a lavish sigh, he tipped his head back against the bed, eyes closed, and sat like that for a long moment, not speaking. I watched him, his throat tilted to the ceiling, the bronze of his beard glinting in the lamplight, until I was sure he'd fallen asleep.

But a moment later he sat up, grinning, and lifted down one of the trays of food. "I think we should share a celebratory feast," he said, uncorking a bottle of wine. He hooked two glasses from the tray, then pulled the clay cover from a dish. Inside was a steaming platter of stew, thick with meat and onion. Durrel looked like he could drown in the *smell* of it. He speared a chunk of meat with his knife and popped it into his mouth. "Oh, gods," he said, sagging a little. When he recovered, he poured me a glass of wine, then toasted me with the bottle.

"To Raffin Taradyce," he said.

"Raffin," I echoed, lifting my goblet.

"Is this Grisel? I thought it had been banned."

"That depends on what you mean by 'Grisel,'" I said noncommittally as Durrel polished off his glass and poured another.

"I think I like this god of yours."

I took the wine from him and refilled my own glass. "Most people do. Maybe you should have some food with that."

"You too. Eat. I feel like a glutton with you just watching me."

"I had a decent meal this week. I live at a bakery," I reminded him. "It's going to take more than that entire pot of stew to get you back to not looking like a half-starved hound."

"That bad?" He winced. "I guess it's been a while since I've seen a mirror." He set down the plate and rubbed at his chin.

"Not so bad," I said softly.

He gave a choking laugh. "Try to say that with a little more enthusiasm! I know I'm not at my peak at the moment, but I'll be back to racing form in no time, thanks to my favorite servant of Tiboran."

"Eske?"

"*Not* Eske," he said, so solemnly that a moment later we were both grinning. We finished the meal and the wine, merrily managing to ignore the crisis that had drawn us here as the candles burned lower and the room felt warmer. Finally though, Durrel grew serious again. He set down his empty glass and stretched his lean body past me, reaching for the pile of Raffin's clothes. He retrieved a roll of papers from them and spread the pages on the floor.

"You saved the manifests?" I said. "Well done."

"I've been studying them. I wish we could have recovered more of Talth's papers. The Ceid keep records of everything — docking fees, licensing, records of payments made or received. Whatever they were doing, they weren't *invisible*. There's proof somewhere."

I was thoughtful, looking at the documents, now covered in notes and scribbles. He'd made lists of the ships and their cargoes, their routes and arrivals and all the money that went with them. "You told me about Talth," I said, "how she kept you out of her business. But you're *good* at all this; it's obvious you know what you're doing. Why would she ignore an asset like that, right in her own house?"

Durrel eased back, watching me curiously. "What are you saying?"

"I'm not sure," I said. "Months ago, she was eager to marry the heir to Decath, but after the wedding she shut you out of everything? I don't think it's because she thought you were ignorant or immature. She didn't *want* you nosing about in her business. I think she was doing something she didn't want you to see, and she knew you'd do exactly this. You'd figure it out."

Durrel's face was impassive. Finally he sighed and shuffled the papers back into a neat stack. "I wish she would have trusted me," he said. "Because whatever she was hiding, it got her killed."

"We'll work it out," I said with more confidence than I felt. "We just need to know how Karst fits into all of this." There hadn't been time yet to explain everything I'd learned from Fei, but I filled in the details now. Durrel seized on the idea.

"We have to find him, then. If he's involved — if he killed her —"

"I don't think it's that simple," I said. "It sounded like he might be connected to the Ceid somehow. Would they just take your word for it that he was guilty, instead of you?"

He looked stubborn, and for the briefest moment I could tell what he was thinking. The word of a nobleman weighed against a street heavy and Ferryman? But he finally shook his head. "We'll need evidence." He glanced back through the documents. "Were you able to learn any more about the magic that you saw at Bal Marse?"

"No," I said, "and it's even more confusing now. I haven't seen him up close, but Karst doesn't seem the magical type to me. Maybe I was wrong. Maybe the traces I saw didn't have anything to do with the murder."

Durrel just gave me a *look* at that. I suppressed a yawn, and the look grew concerned. "You need some rest," he said. "You've been running around town all day."

"You too," I said, dragging myself upright. "But you're right. It's a long walk back to the bakery."

"You're not leaving?" Durrel stood and reached for me, his hand falling before making contact. "Don't go." I thought I heard a thread of something else beneath the lightness. "I'm going to need help fending off those servants of Tiboran in the morning."

"So you'll want me here for backup, then?"

His arm was on the door above my head now, and he was leaning over me, grinning slightly. "It couldn't hurt," he said, but that easy charm faltered just a little.

"I can't." I sighed. "Grea and Rat will worry, and I still have to let the Greenmen know about Raffin. He can probably manage to get out of there on his own, but we shouldn't risk it. I'll be back in the morning."

"The morning?" he said, a little quirk to his lip.

"The *real* morning," I promised. My hand on the doorknob, I grew sober. "Listen, Eske was right. You can't leave the Temple, and it's probably a good idea if you don't leave the room. At least for a while."

He nodded finally. "Good night, then," he said.

At the last minute, I almost didn't leave him. The lamplight behind him flickered against his shoulder and sparked through his beard, and his gray eyes were in shadow as he watched me. But he was safe as he could be for the night, and he had a friend out there taking an awful risk for him. My job wasn't finished yet tonight. As the door clicked shut, I caught a glimpse of Durrel sinking back to the floor among the remains of our feast, his empty glass in one hand.

CHAPTER NINETEEN

On my way home, I tipped off the Greenmen at Raffin's station, using the anonymous speaking-box outside the wall, which was meant for citizens to accuse their neighbors of heresy without being identified. Although they'd been told one of their own was in the Keep, it might be a day or more before they actually *believed* it. Raffin would have to miss at least one shift before anyone would register his absence, and who knows how many more before they did anything about it.

The next morning, I descended the bakery stairs feeling oddly unsettled. I had slept poorly, worried about Durrel. He'd traded one cell for another, and though we'd dodged the immediate threat from Karst for now, we still weren't any closer to clearing his name. Downstairs, Rat was in the common room, making his way methodically through Grea's leftovers. "Letter for you," he said through a mouthful of bread. "It came by courier. You owe me two marks for the tip."

Now what? There was no seal and no signature; whoever had sent it wasn't concerned about the message being intercepted. But I immediately recognized the small, neat hand as Cwalo's, and his message was typically cryptic.

Shipment of Talancan oranges arriving tonight. Come to the docks to inspect cargo.

"You're smiling," Rat said. "Love letter?"

"Better." I memorized the address Cwalo had included, then handed the note back to Rat. "Burn that when you're finished," I said, breezing out the door.

I heard Rat's voice behind me. "Secret riverside rendezvous? Clearly I've underestimated you."

As I crossed the city, I grew almost cheerful. Last night's rain had left the air light and fresh, and everything looked brighter. Durrel was free, Raffin would be fine, and now Cwalo had come through with a lead on those secret shipments he'd told me about. Maybe I'd be able to connect them with Talth's burned records and the discrepancies in the Ceid manifests, and see what they had to do with the magical stains on the Bal Marse floor.

This news buzzing in my thoughts, I hurried back to the Temple District. Was it my imagination, or were there more guards on the streets today? Up in Markettown, I saw red-sashed Day Watchmen mustered by a public fountain, distributing broadsides. I drew back into a shadowed alley and turned to take another route. It was a safe wager those papers had Durrel's portrait on them. And possibly mine, as well. Pox. I took to the river paths, which were always crowded in the morning, and kept my head down as I hurried along the water.

Upstairs at the Temple, Durrel swung open the door, half dressed in steel gray breeches and a blue jerkin that made him look like a yeoman farmer. Eske's girls had chosen well; the clothes fit his smaller frame better than anything I'd seen him in yet. "Good morning," he said cheerily. "Sunshine, new quarters, new clothes. I am a new man."

I looked up at him, and he was right. He did look like a new man. The light scattered across his damp hair and clean cheeks and — "Oh, you shaved," I said.

He gave a little frown. "You sound disappointed."

"Of course not." That was ludicrous. Why should I care whether Durrel had a beard or not? "But it makes your cover a little trickier. You're harder to recognize with a beard."

"Oh," he said, fingering his chin. "I hadn't thought of that. I just wanted it gone — it made my whole body feel grimy."

I came inside the room. He'd been busy since I'd left; in addition to the bath, the shave, and the new clothes, he'd apparently wheedled a box of tacks from Eske's girls and pinned the shipping manifests all across one wall of the room. They'd sent up breakfast too, simple fare, a jug of mead and a loaf of hot, brown bread. The bread was untouched, but he'd started on the mead. I tore off a hunk of bread and helped myself.

"I'm going to thank you again," Durrel said, sitting beside me on the bed. "I'd almost forgotten what it felt like to be a free man."

"You're *not* a free man," I reminded him. I strode to the window and pulled the shutter closed. "You've got to start thinking like a fugitive. Don't let people see you, don't call attention to yourself. You need to learn how to be invisible. Karst and the Ceid are still out there."

"Of course," he said quietly, staring into the distance. "Anything else?"

Pox. When I'd gotten here, Durrel had looked the best he'd seemed for weeks, and now I'd deflated him. "Ignore me," I said. "I'm used to living like this. You're not. I can't expect you to master all the secrets to fugitive behavior overnight."

Durrel looked grave. "You live like this all the time? Don't you ever feel safe?"

I didn't know how to say what I was thinking, but it came out anyway. "Not *unsafe*, exactly. Just cautious. Like a mouse." My mouth had a little trouble with the last word. It was an old nickname, and those memories were painful ones.

"That's an awful way to go through every day." He reached for my hand. I meant to pull it away, but it had its own ideas.

"It's not so bad," I said, but my words sounded a little hollow. I couldn't help looking at him, at the way he sat, holding my hand like it was fragile and precious, like the scars were beautiful. Eske was right. Even in the drab and well-worn workman's clothes her servants had procured, there was still something unmistakably noble about Durrel. He made the title seem like it meant something.

"I'm sorry about last night," he said. I looked at him quizzically, so he added, "I didn't mean to insult your virtue by asking you to stay."

Oh. Surprise hit me like a blow, and for a second I wanted to laugh. "It was nothing." I paused a moment, deciding, then added, "I don't have anything to insult."

His freshly washed boyish face turned pink. "I'm sorry," he said again. "I had no right to assume —"

Seventh Circle boys never embarrassed that easily. It was oddly endearing. "Where I grew up, down below the Big Silver, life can be short. There's not always time to wait." There hadn't been, for me and Tegen. I bit my lip and shoved that memory aside. "And sometimes you don't get to choose. There's always some Greenman patrolling your neighborhood, and plenty of fathers scared enough to give up their daughters in return for spotty protection from the Guard. Not to mention all the girls ready to give up their lives and bodies for the Goddess." My own mother had been one of those.

He was watching me calmly, too much going on behind those dark eyes for me to make out. "You lost someone." It wasn't a question, but it was a long time before I could answer.

"Tegen," I finally said, hating the way I had to whisper it.

"Meri told me something of it," he said. "I'm sorry."

I didn't want to talk about Tegen. Not here in Tiboran's temple, not to this kind-eyed nob I'd just plucked from prison with the help of a Greenman. It seemed wrong, somehow, given how he'd died. But Durrel *knew*, he understood; I could see it in his eyes, in the long shadow there that belonged to a dark-haired Tratuan girl, and somehow I found myself telling my fugitive nob about the man I had loved and lost, and how.

"This can't be easy for you, then — with Raffin, I mean." I saw his eyes go past me to the folded-up Greenman's uniform on the bench near the door.

I just shrugged. "Everybody has a story like that."

Outside, we could hear the soldiers marching through the circle. They were becoming more and more a part of the music of the city. Why were we talking about this when there were Ferrymen and murderers on the loose? I shifted to another side of the room and took one of the chairs. Durrel lifted his mead cup, but, seeing my eyes follow his hand there, set it down again and took some of the bread instead.

"All right," he said. "What comes next?"

"We keep you away from Karst," I said. "And I will be going back to the docks tonight." I explained about Cwalo's note.

"Well, I'm coming too," he said.

"Like hells! Every guard in the city is looking for you. It's too dangerous."

"Damn it, Celyn!" He rose and paced the room. "You can't expect me to just *wait*, while you're out there taking all the risks." I opened my mouth to object, but he went on. "Look, I have to do something. If this Karst really is out there, and he really did kill Talth, I have to know. Not just to clear my own name, but —" Durrel trailed off, but his eyes were fierce. "She was my wife; she was my responsibility."

I fidgeted, but I knew he was right. If our positions were reversed, there was no way I could simply sit still and wait for answers. I understood that, at least. "All right," I said. "Just as long as you don't plan on starting any more fights on my behalf. I can take care of myself, milord."

Satisfied, he nodded. "Well," he said, "I'm not making any promises."

I supposed that was the best I could hope for. Nobs.

Durrel went to the documents pinned to the wall. "We have a few hours until then. Let's review what we know. First, the magic you found at Bal Marse." He pointed to a mark on one sheet of paper. "Second, Talth and the Ceid were running clandestine shipments in or out of the city on falsified vessels. Third, a man called Karst claims to have killed her. Fourth, Karst is a Ferryman." Durrel turned a sober face to me. "I think the implication is clear," he said. "The magic, the shipments . . ."

A dark feeling stole up my spine and made my skin prickle. "The Ceid are involved with Ferrymen."

Durrel studied his lists, his jaw set. "I'd like to believe there isn't any truth to it, but — I lived with Talth. I saw what she was capable of." His brows drew together grimly, as if he was remembering too much. "Maybe your Cwalo's information can shed some light on things."

"It's just a rumor about some undeclared shipment," I warned. "It's a lot more likely to be a load of Vareni marchpane or cloves for the spice trade, and it might not even have anything to do with the Ceid." I got up from my chair to look over Durrel's lists. He'd been thorough, marking the connections between everyone so far, from Karst and Talth to Barris and Koya, and even himself. Still, something was missing. I hesitated a moment, then said, "What about your father?"

"What about him?" Durrel's voice was sharp. "He doesn't have anything to do with this."

"Durrel, Karst sent him an *ear*. That's not a gift you give a stranger."

"You said yourself — that was just a warning, to stay out of their business."

Maybe. "Look," I said. "I don't know what it means, but I've seen Karst before, and it wasn't with Ferrymen or the Ceid. He was there when I went to Charicaux."

Durrel looked like I'd struck him, an expression of surprise and confusion on his face. "I need to see him."

"Who? Karst?"

"My father."

"You can't," I said, although I did think, rather belatedly, that someone ought to let Lord Ragn know his son was well, and *not* the owner of the ear delivered to Charicaux two days ago. "It's too dangerous."

"No." Durrel looked stubborn. "I must speak with him." He turned and rummaged through the clothing Eske's girls had brought, but absently, as if he couldn't find what he needed. "And if you don't take me, you know I'll simply walk out that door the second you leave here."

I believed him. I nodded. "I'll try and arrange it."

He still looked set and worried. "Good," he said. "Thank you. You're taking as much risk as anyone, and I want you to know how much I appreciate it." That *noble* tone was back in his voice, all solemn and weighty.

"It's nothing."

"No," he said. "It's *everything*."

A few hours later, I presented myself at the Charicaux gates. Last time the guard — or *Karst*, rather — had summarily dismissed me, but now a stone-faced retainer ushered me through as soon as I gave my name. He led me into the house like an errant child tardily returned from some high adventure, finally depositing me in an interior courtyard with a curt warning that I was to wait there until Lord Ragn became available. He gave no indication of when that would be, however, and after a few minutes of pacing between a fountain and an iron bench, I grew restless. Since this was probably my only opportunity to get a glimpse at what those guards were keeping so well protected, I decided to make the most of it.

I could hear voices from the second story above me, and saw a series of closed doors in the courtyard level below. Swiftly I passed from door to door, testing them. I ignored the unlocked ones — kitchens, work-rooms, a covered walkway to the stables — and set my attention (and my lock picks) to the ones that wouldn't open to a visitor's casual curiosity. The first two were useless, a music room and a cluttered storeroom that held spare furniture and bolts of cloth. The third, however, granted me access to a broad chamber of bookcases, desk, and a chest of many tiny drawers and doors. An office. Perfect. I slipped inside, leaving the door open a sliver so I could hear my guard return with Lord Ragn.

It was dark and hot in the office, the tall windows closed behind heavy damask drapes, like the room was hunkered down and hiding from something. I went straight for the desk; a closed ledger sat atop a blotter, with a neat row of pens and inkwells. Very tidy. Very Decath. The desk drawer held a stack of correspondence and an accounts book from a banking house. The book was smallish, and though it would have fit very nicely in the bodice of my kirtle, I resisted. Lord Ragn would miss it straightaway, and Durrel would hardly welcome it. Nobs and their honor.

Instead I contented myself with leafing through the entries, and I was surprised to see the withdrawals outnumbered the deposits. By a lot. The records went back a little more than a year, and the sums in Lord Ragn's accounts seemed to be dwindling rapidly. There was one large influx of cash at the end of the winter, around the time of Durrel's marriage to Talth, but after that, the decline continued. I wondered if Durrel knew his father was losing money. But how? Bad investments? Gambling? Women? None of the usual reasons for nobs to go broke seemed to fit what I knew of Lord Ragn. I tucked the account book back into place and combed through the letters, my fingers stalling when they came to a fold of green parchment in the drawer. Loath to pick it up, I flipped it onto the desk with a letter knife, and spread it open.

It was a note from the Matriarch at the Celystra, thanking Lord Ragn for his recent gift of a set of gold candlesticks for the convent's chapel, and a donation of ten thousand crowns. I frowned, feeling dull and sick in the stuffy heat. Could famously *neutral* Lord Ragn, the man who had raised Meri, be secretly a Celyst? It would explain the company he'd been keeping, at least, the Councilor and the Confessor I'd seen riding with him into this very house.

I heard the thump of footsteps coming down a flight of stairs outside, so I ducked back out to the courtyard, not even bothering to replace the letter. I did pull the office door shut behind me. Lord Ragn appeared at the base of the stairs, looking uncharacteristically rumpled, his face flushed. He stalked over to me. "Where is my son?" he said, his voice harsh.

"Safe. For now." My heart was pounding; between his cold greeting and the letter from the Celystra, I didn't know what to think about Lord Ragn's loyalties.

"This isn't a game," he said. "You have no idea how much danger he's in. Lord Raffin was taken to the Celystra infirmary with broken ribs! He's facing discommendation for this little stunt."

My breath caught. "Is he —"

"What were you two thinking?"

"Karst was going to kill him!"

Ragn fell back like I'd struck him. "Karst? I don't know what you're talking about," he said stiffly.

"What does he have on you?"

He took a moment, pacing across the tiled floor, past the fountain and a bench with a blue velvet cloak puddled in the seat. He tugged and smoothed his doublet, rubbed the back of his neck. "These are not matters I have any intention of discussing with you," he finally said. "You must tell me where Lord Durrel is."

I could be stubborn too. "No."

"Damn it, girl, if they find him —"

"They won't," I said firmly. "I told you, he's safe for now. But he'd be a whole lot safer if I understood what was going on."

"It's no concern of yours," Lord Ragn said in a tight voice. "The situation is under control."

"He wants to see you."

Lord Ragn's eyes closed briefly, and he nodded. "I — I would appreciate that very much. You haven't brought him here, surely?"

"No, milord." I outlined my plan, which had grown legs on my walk over here. "This afternoon, can you book passage on a ship to Tratua?" Nobs could still travel freely in Llyvraneth, so far as I knew. "Withdraw a reasonable sum, say, five hundred crowns, from your banking house. Send one of your men to a tailor's — your normal one — and buy a suit of clothes and a traveling cloak."

"Shall I buy a horse, as well?" There was almost a trace of amusement in Lord Ragn's voice.

"No," I said. "That would look suspicious, since the Decath already *own* the best horses in Gelnir. But a good sword and a pair of boots, and perhaps a falcon."

"You want him to run."

"I want it to *look* like he's run. Can you do that?"

Lord Ragn looked into the distance. Lines creased his forehead and feathered the skin at his eyes. "And he'll still be here in the city? Do you think that's wise?"

"If I could have convinced him to leave, don't you think I'd have done it already? He's determined to clear his name."

"But this is madness," Ragn said. "To break out of prison, to —" His voice broke and he fought for composure. "You're *certain* he's safe?"

I felt a surge of pity. "As safe as I can make him, your lordship. But, please, if you know anything about what's happening to him —"

"I asked you before to stay out of this," Lord Ragn said, but he sounded tired now, not angry.

"What does Karst want from you?" There was no question in my mind that I'd seen Karst *here*, at Charicaux, and that Lord Ragn *must* know him. So what was he hiding?

Lord Ragn sighed, shadows crossing his face. "It has nothing whatever to do with the death of Lord Durrel's wife, but since I don't expect you'll accept that for an answer, I'll try to explain. Sit down." He pointed me to the iron bench, and I shifted aside the velvet wrap. "You know that I fostered my niece Merista for five years."

"Of course."

Ragn continued. "You have no idea how costly that was for us — for the Decath. Keeping her safe, keeping her secret. The bribes alone nearly bankrupted the estate. And then when she came out as not only magical, but a party to Wierolf's rebellion . . ." He touched his fingers to the bridge of his nose, wincing slightly. "If she had been my blood relation, and not just my late wife's niece, we would have lost everything. There were inquiries. The king was not pleased. We convinced him we knew nothing of Lady Merista's magical nature, but it was a near thing. We're lucky we still have our title, let alone managed to hold on to Favom Court *and* Charicaux. Only my wife Amalle's connections, and a very great fine paid directly to the king's coffers, as well as sworn oaths of loyalty to His Majesty, saved us at all."

I suspected Lord Ragn was sparing some of the details. Hang the estate and the title — he was lucky he still had his *head*. Meri's parents had been in exile for much of her childhood for their role in a previous rebellion. "And Karst?"

"I'm getting to that. As you can imagine, the Decath estate has fallen into debt since all this began. I couldn't approach a bank for obvious reasons, so I turned to old, old family friends."

"The Ceid?"

"The very same. Mistress Talth's first husband and I had worked closely together for many years. His heirs were more than willing to negotiate a settlement with the Decath, but their fee was steep."

"Talth wanted to marry Durrel."

He nodded. "It was an excellent match, and Lord Durrel seemed amenable as well, so we struck the bargain." Lord Ragn shifted position, his face grim. "Unfortunately it was not the happy marriage we had all anticipated, and with the untimely passing of Mistress Talth, there has been some . . . dispute regarding the settlement. The family Ceid has demanded I return the money from Talth's dowry, and their requests are developing a certain uncharacteristic urgency. This Karst you've mentioned is employed by the family."

"They sent him to recover the money from the marriage settlement?"

"He's a bit thuggish and uncouth, and he's been flexing his muscles a little more than I'd like," Ragn said, "but it's been — relatively — civil. They've filed a claim with the magistrates, and we're simply waiting on the court's judgment. Some of us more patiently than others."

So Karst wasn't a Charicaux guard after all, just a Ceid heavy who'd been hanging around the Decath house, leaning on Durrel's father. But he was also a Ferryman, which reminded me that something was still off here. There was more that Lord Ragn wasn't telling me. "What about the ear?"

"I beg your pardon?"

"The *ear*. The severed ear that Karst had sent here the day before yesterday."

Lord Ragn looked genuinely perplexed. "I can't imagine what you're referring to. Now, if I've answered your questions to your satisfaction, when can I see my son?"

I knew *that* noble tone well enough; there was no use trying to get more information out of him today. "I can arrange something for this evening," I said. Before my errand to the docks.

"Not tonight," he said. "I have another engagement, and it can't be missed." What could possibly be more important than seeing his son? Lord Ragn must have read the look on my face quite clearly, because he said, "Dinner, with the minister of the exchequer and the master of the king's horse. And there is no possible way I can get out of that without arousing extreme suspicion. It will have to be another night. Tomorrow."

Grudgingly I admitted he was right. That would also give me more time to make sure the details were in place. "I'll send word when everything is arranged. Give my regards to Lady Amalle," I added, rising to leave.

"Amalle?" Lord Ragn looked surprised. "Certainly, but it will be a while; she's at Favom Court for the summer."

I smoothed the blue velvet wrap across the arm of the bench. "Oh, I thought — never mind. It wasn't important." As I turned to go, Lord Ragn caught my hands.

"Celyn, wait. Tell Durrel —" He faltered. He looked weary and spent and ground down by concerns I could only begin to imagine.

"Tell him yourself," I said gently, squeezing his arm. "Tomorrow night."

CHAPTER TWENTY

I made my way back across the city, my thoughts a tangle. Did Durrel know about his father's debts? And Raffin — had Durrel really hit him hard enough to crack bone, or had Karst turned up to "finish the job"? Lord Ragn had said Raffin would receive an official reprimand, but broken ribs and a dressing-down were hardly the worst of it. Unbidden, my list of consequences for his participation in our scheme sprang to my mind again: the loss of his commission, arrest for treason for the escape of one of the king's prisoners, and worse. I wasn't convinced even Raffin was a match for the wrath of the Acolyte Guard.

Back at the Temple, the place was as crowded as ever, and I saw a handful of masked barmen and servers hauling up a huge gold-and-orange banner to one of the balconies. I stopped to watch them, and one of the figures hanging over the balcony rail, a coil of rope over one shoulder, paused to give me a broad wave. Evidently Eske had put Durrel to work. With the mask, he'd be as anonymous as the rest of the Temple staff, and I wondered if she'd have him serving drinks next.

As the snapping silk unfurled, it revealed itself to be a device of a golden lion, silhouetted against the rising sun. Prince Wierolf's banner.

Eske was at my shoulder. "What do you think?" Today she was wearing orange to match, a shrieking concoction of flame and citrus, with a mask of spangled gold fur, and golden feathers tumbling through her wig.

"Of the banner or your new assistant?"

A wink. "Oh, he was too pretty to keep locked up in that room all day. Do you know he looked at my accounts and discovered a way to adjust our wine orders so we save six hundred marks a week? You keep that boy around, Digger."

"Um, I will," I mumbled. "Where did the banner come from?"

"Another friend of yours, in fact." She gestured toward a figure seated across the circular bar, his back to us. "You're filling up my common room with all sorts of tasty new company today, my girl. The Masked One is very pleased indeed."

I frowned, perplexed. I could count my Gerse friends on one hand, and half of them were already here in the Temple common room. Eske walked me around the bar and the stranger turned toward us — a tall, young man with dark eyes and hair, one arm in a sling.

"Berdal!"

At the sound of my voice, the Nemair's groom and guardsman, now one of Prince Wierolf's soldiers, rose from his seat and bent low to scoop me into an awkward, one-armed embrace. "Celyn! By the gods, you're looking well."

"And you!" I said. "What happened? What are you doing here?" I gestured curiously to his injured arm.

He gave a grimace. "Shot. At Cardoc Field a few weeks ago. It's nothing, but I can't ride and shoot with just one arm, so I've been furloughed."

I was brimming with questions to the point I didn't know what to ask first. "How — what?"

Berdal grinned. "Let's sit." He looked roadworn and weary, but intact and as robust as I remembered him, considering his injury. Better fed than many Gersins, certainly. Maybe some of the grain that didn't reach the city had found its way to the prince's army. "You told me if I ever came to the city, I could look for you here."

"I did?" I settled in across the table from him.

"Aye, but you didn't warn me of the size of the place — or the weather! By Marau, how does anyone live in this heat?" He plucked at the collar of his doublet.

"Welcome to the south," I said. I couldn't help grinning. Berdal hailed from the Carskadon Mountains, and had kept up an infuriating jollity last winter when we were all snowbound and chilblained. "How is everyone?"

"Very well," Berdal said, but didn't get to finish, for at that moment a cheer went up from the crowd. We looked up to see Wierolf's banner fixed in place proudly at the gallery rail.

"Well?" Eske had returned, and set a bottle of wine between us on the table.

"What will you do if someone sees that?" I said.

"But of course people will see it! Long live Prince Wierolf!" And she cried that last so loudly, in her echoing stage voice, that I flinched — but an answering roar rose up from the Temple's patrons and Berdal's booming voice.

"Long live the prince!"

"It looks good," Eske said to Berdal. "I think we might just leave it up there permanently." She was awfully nervy, I thought, to flaunt the prince's colors so brazenly, and yet seeing my god's temple displaying the enemy standard made me fiercely proud. Tomorrow it might have the Greenmen breaking fifty years of truce between Bardolph's and Tiboran's people, but for now, the Temple had just declared its allegiance.

Durrel came down then and joined us, doffing his mask and looking curiously at my companion. I introduced them, and Berdal gave Durrel a brief bow. "I've heard many fine things of your family, sir," he said. "It has been an honor to serve in the guard of your cousin, the Lady Merista."

"I'm glad to hear it," Durrel said. He pulled over a chair, turned it wrong-way around, and straddled it casually. "Is my cousin well?"

"Very well, milord," Berdal said. "Indeed, better than well. She is a wonder."

Durrel gave a broad smile at that. "What brings you to Gerse?"

Berdal's own levity faded. He glanced around, carefully poured himself a drink. "Can we speak freely here?" he said pointedly to me.

"Lord Durrel is a friend, and the Temple is as safe as any place in Gerse," I said, and as if to punctuate that, the musicians in the gallery struck up a lively tune hailing Bonny Prince Wierolf. I heard the men laugh. "Or we'll all burn together, I guess."

Berdal's voice was low. "You know the front draws nearer to the capital. We have the support of Tratua, and we are gaining ground in the plains of Gelnir. The prince has sent me to seek out his friends in Gerse, to determine how quickly he may take the city."

I felt a chill wash over me.

"So soon?" Durrel said. "It's been less than a year."

"I think the king has underestimated how tired his subjects are of the present rule," Berdal said, looking toward the banner he'd brought us. "We hoped to get word long before this, and His Highness was concerned when no one heard from you, Celyn."

There was no reproach in his voice, but I heard it anyway. I'd never promised to keep playing spy once I returned home, but I supposed that wouldn't stop Wierolf and the others from hoping. "There's little rebel activity in the city," I said. "Just rumors, really." I told them about the dead Greenman we'd discussed at Hobin's dinner party, the purple handprint beside the body.

Durrel nodded grimly. "There've been other stories like that," he said, and I stared at him. "Attacks on the Guard, those purple marks left behind. Stuff that Raffin's told me. They don't publicize it outside the Guard."

"And what of your own people, milord?" asked Berdal.

"Most of the gentry still openly support Bardolph — they can't afford to do otherwise — and the Council has declared its fealty to the king. Those nobles suspected of nursing Sarist sympathies have been cast out of the city." Or so heavily fined and intimidated they didn't dare make a wrong move, if Lord Ragn's tale this afternoon was any indication.

"Everyone is too scared," I said. "Bardolph is squeezing the city until it suffocates, and the people are too afraid to speak up. We might not have any organized resistance left, but I can't see many ordinary Gersins lining up to oppose Wierolf." I thought of the Greenmen and the soldiers patrolling every corner, the food shortages, the arrests and public executions and seizures of property. Even people who might be afraid of magic and Sarists on principle would probably welcome a change from Bardolph's starving police state.

Berdal took this in. "Who can speak for the city on this matter?"

I glanced at Durrel, but he frowned. We were the wrong people to ask. "Maybe Eptin Cwalo?" I suggested. "He might know."

At the mention of Cwalo's name, Berdal looked pleased. "Excellent. I remember Master Cwalo well. My lady trusted him completely." He shifted his long body in his seat, looking eager to get moving. "I'll be staying here while I'm in town. Celyn, do you think you could arrange a meeting with Master Cwalo and whatever friends he deems suitable?"

"Of course," I said. "Tell us more about the war."

Durrel and Berdal and I sat together for the next few hours, in the golden shadow of Prince Wierolf's banner, as Berdal shared tales of our friends at the front. Through the Temple's broad, open doors, I watched the day vanish and the night rise, until it was nearing time for our appointment at the docks.

Finally we took our leave, promising to bring word when I'd heard from Cwalo. Durrel and I returned to his room and changed into dark clothing, more loans from Eske. I dressed in breeches and boots, my hair tucked into a man's cap. A man and a woman walking together at night would be much more conspicuous than two young men, and Durrel was known to have left the Keep in the company of a woman, so this was an increased measure of protection for him. It was also just a little easier to go climbing about on docks if I didn't have to worry about trailing my skirt hems in the brine.

Durrel eyed me strangely when he saw me. "You look —"

"Like your little brother?"

He grinned down at me, his hair in his eyes. "Not by half."

"Well, *you* look like you've never dressed yourself before. Do I need to have Eske provide a manservant?" I shifted the laces on his jerkin so it hung properly. "You should have a sword."

"I believe I mentioned that," he said. "Do you think Eske could track one down?"

"No, I was thinking a real one. If we run into trouble, how are you at hand fighting?"

"You have already extracted my promise to behave myself."

That would have to do. I'd just have to keep Durrel away from anyone who might take his sudden appearance on the Gerse streets as the opportunity to kill him.

The rain that had blown through earlier had cooled the air, and the early moonslight tinted the deepening sky with rare summertime colors. Durrel loped easily along beside me, and I almost had to scurry to keep pace.

"Do you wish you were out there?" he asked as we walked. "Fighting, I mean? In the war?"

The question stung unexpectedly. "What about you?"

"A Decath in the army? Perish the thought." But he hunched into his black doublet, and I couldn't see his face. "Gersin youths of my class never join the military," he said. "Certainly not first-born ones. It is considered beneath our station to scuff about in the dust with the rabble and get our hands dirty. And where would my father have sent me? Which side do the Decath support? Impossible."

I wondered. Those peculiar payments to the Celystra, the visits from Confessors and Council members. . . . Which side did Lord Ragn take? "But what if you'd wanted to?"

"I told you before, remember?" he said. "I'm not allowed to have thoughts of my own."

"What if you hadn't wanted to marry Talth?"

Another shrug. "He would have chosen someone else. But I could never have actually refused to go through with the match. Father had acted in the best interests of the family; what was I going to do? Throw that back in his face and disgrace the House?" He shook his head.

"So that awful woman would become Lady Decath? Your father can't have thought that was best for anybody."

Durrel made a sound that was half sigh, half bitter laugh. "We didn't know her as well as we thought. I think we're here."

We had reached the address Cwalo had sent, a quiet dock on the Big Silver, a few blocks away from the busier ports where I'd seen Geirt and Barris. The pier was empty and the property seemed abandoned, but a harbormaster's station stood a few dozen yards down the shore, with a man on duty. We could see a light burning in the little hut.

"This is a Ceid property," Durrel said, looking it over.

"How can you be sure?"

"I recognize the address," he said. "And there's this." He strode to the edge of the pier, where a sigil had been burned into the boardwalk, the stylized initial of the House of Ceid. Gentry weren't permitted heraldic emblems like the nobility, so Gerse's wealthiest merchant families had turned their monograms into house symbols. I remembered the sign from Bal Marse, where it was tiled into the Round Court floor.

"We should check the place out," I suggested. There was a boat shed, but no warehouse; whatever cargo moved through this pier moved quickly.

Durrel gave the boat shed door handle a jiggle. "Locked, of course."

Really, people just can't seem to remember how *handy* I can be. I had the lock tumbled and the door opened before Durrel even registered what I was doing. I pushed past him into the shed while he stared at the lock. "I've seen you do that half a dozen times now," he said, "and it still catches me by surprise."

It looked like an ordinary storage shed inside, just a single room cluttered with ropes and nets and broken oars. "There's a chest here," Durrel said, picking through the mess toward a heavy trunk on the floor near the back, buried under an assortment of sailcloth and pitch jars. "It's locked too."

This was a strange place to hide anything, but Durrel's box was completely out of character. With its shiny brass fittings and embossed leather top, it was too nice, too new, and too clean to belong here. Durrel hauled it up onto a bench, and a corner caught on something, a length of cloth that spiraled out behind the case as he dragged it across the shed.

"What's this?" I said, catching hold of one end. It was a string of flags, the small, colored pennants required by Gerse harbormasters to identify a vessel's home port. "Brionry," I said, fingering the triangle of blue-and-white silk. "Talanca," a yellow-and-red-striped square. "Varenzia," a white ground with a black lily.

"Just like we thought," Durrel said. "False flags to disguise domestic ships." Scowling, he set the casket on the bench, and I popped the padlock holding it shut. "What is all this?" He sifted through a stack of papers inside. But I recognized them immediately.

"Passports," I said. "That one is from Brionry." I pulled it out of the mix and carried it to the doorway, where some of the moonslight made it just possible to make out details. "I'm pretty sure it's forged. The royal seal doesn't look quite right."

"There's more in here," Durrel said. "And — sweet Tiboran . . ." He trailed off, but hoisted the other discovery high for me to see, a heavy leather purse, bulging with coins. He shook a couple into his hand. "Wait, these are all —"

"Foreign?" I guessed, holding out my hand. A silver Brion coin, a couple of gold ones from Talanca, even Vareni money. "This must all be for the Ferrymen's — uh, customers. New identification to get out of the country, and money to bribe the officials at their destinations." So the Ceid's mysterious secret cargo wasn't magical artifacts after all — it was magical *people*.

Durrel was silent, looking at it all. "Five hundred crowns," he said softly. "That's what she said. It cost five hundred crowns to ransom her father from the Ferrymen."

I didn't remind him that Fei had invented that sum — and the father. I knew what he was thinking. A fee that large would be a lifetime's savings for most Llyvrins, a price only the truly desperate would pay.

"And that was just for the passage," he said. "Another, what, five hundred for the passports?"

"Maybe," I said. Good forgeries were costly. "Assuming they don't raise the fees on arrival, to cover delays for bad weather, or because they decided you ate more than you paid for."

"And if you can't pay?" he said, coins raining through his fingers.

"I don't know," I said, but I did. Fei hadn't made up the story of cargo the Ferrymen had abandoned before delivery, all those people left to die or be captured by Greenmen. The dark look on Durrel's face told me he knew as well.

"I was married to —" He shook his head. "I almost wish I *had* killed her." He flipped through the documents, pulling one from the stack. "We should take some of these with us for evidence." He faltered. "What's wrong?"

I was frowning at the stack in his hand. "Documents like that are expensive," I said. "If they discover that some are missing —"

He drew in his breath as he realized what I meant. "They'll take it from their clients. Damn, you're right." He hesitated, and I knew how reluctant he was to let go of any scrap that might prove his innocence. I came to his side and fanned through the papers.

"Here," I said, plucking free a badly worn paper in flawed Talancan. It was more obviously a forgery than the others, and since it was just an identification letter, not a passport, it wasn't as valuable either. Durrel rolled it swiftly and tucked it inside his doublet.

"Anything else?"

I stared at the pouch of coins in his hand, sorely tempted by the glitter of that gold Vareni *scuto*, but I shook my head. We packed up the chest and returned it to its square of dust on the floor.

"What now?" he asked, brushing off his hands.

I looked around, but it seemed we'd exhausted the storage shed's clandestine contents. "Now we wait," I said.

"We need somewhere to watch from," Durrel said. "Can't see much from in here." Outside, traffic on the river was starting to slow, and I wondered how long the harbormaster would stay in his little hut. All night, if it was also his home. Crouching low, we crept onto the docks, squeezing tight to the deep shadows along the sides of the outbuildings. Durrel pointed to a rowboat moored to the dock, partially covered in canvas. It had a deep enough hull to conceal us, and it was close enough to the water to give us a plain view of anything that happened. I gave a nod and dashed across the open dock toward the craft. Durrel hastened after.

We stripped back the canvas and Durrel climbed down softly, barely making the boat bobble in the water. Once he was settled, I had second thoughts. That was a *small* boat, and I was a small person — but it was still going to be awfully cramped in there.

"Something you're waiting for?" Durrel's voice was low, and I took one last hopeful look around the docks, but it was the rowboat or nothing. I eased down beside him, hotly aware of the thin sliver of space between us. If the boat rocked even a little, I'd be jostled into his lap. I clutched the rail, my forearm like a brace of iron.

"Hey, relax," Durrel said. "There's plenty of room."

There wasn't, but I couldn't hold this posture all night, so I let out a small sigh and untwined my legs a little, until they were just barely nudging into Durrel's knees. "Let's hope they weren't planning on using this boat to unload their cargo," I said.

Through the crack between canvas and boat, we watched a sliver of sky, the moons rising in the distance. Marau was nearly full, a fat blob of gray that seemed to swallow light instead of give it off, casting a long, low shadow against the river.

"I can't believe I was in there almost a month," Durrel said. "Marau was full that night too — the night Talth died. I noticed it when they took me away, and I remember thinking how odd it was, to die on the night of Marau's full moon. Like a bad omen."

I pictured him dragged off by clumsy guards who didn't care that he was a nob, who hadn't even let him finish dressing. "Didn't you say anything? Didn't you struggle, try to get away?"

He was silent a long moment, staring into the stars. "I didn't really believe it at first," he said. "I couldn't make myself believe that she was dead. And once I was in the cell, I thought *surely* they knew they'd made a mistake, and it would all be straightened out by morning."

His voice, his eyes, his whole being were far away, but his body was lean and warm against mine, his breath moist and warm against my cheek. With a shiver of alarm, I realized that wasn't as annoying as it should have been. I pulled myself in tighter. I was close enough to count his sandy eyelashes, trace the curve of his jaw and the long, cool line of his neck. He turned his face toward me, lifting his fingers to smooth aside a strand of hair that had come loose from my cap. The water brushing the hull sounded impossibly loud in the silence between us, like the whole world was holding its breath. His hand fell away from my cheek.

"I'm sorry," he said, and turned that boyish face away from mine again. "I didn't mean —"

"It's all right," I said, but my voice cracked and nothing actually came out. I pulled my knees up to my chest as a kind of heat washed over me. Oh, gods. Rat was right. I was out of my depths, and sinking fast.

Durrel twisted his fingers together in his lap, and I think we were both relieved when a moment later, we heard a sound and I slid upward against the boat rail. "What was that?"

"What?" he whispered, but by then it was clear — hoofbeats, and the accompanying rattle of a wagon. We lifted the canvas a little more and peered out. The harbormaster had heard too; he'd stepped out of his little hut and stood waiting outside, as if expecting them. "Is it Karst?"

The horses arrived, one man riding, another driving a wagon draped with black cloth. I moved closer to the gap and tried to get a better look at the wagon, but it appeared to be empty. The rider dismounted and crossed the pier in long, determined strides to meet with the harbormaster. He wore a nondescript dark doublet and trunk hose; anyone who saw him in a well-lit tavern would think nothing of the clothes. Out here on a moonslit night, he blended right into the shadows.

But not well enough. As the rider stood and spoke to the harbormaster in tones too low to make out, I thought he looked familiar, and I felt Durrel stiffen beside me. I held his arm hard with my fingernails, lest he propel himself out of the boat, but he just stared grimly ahead, his jaw set.

Cwalo had told me about suspicious Ceid shipments, and we were on a Ceid dock — so what in Marau's name was *Lord Ragn* doing here?

CHAPTER TWENTY-ONE

I whispered Durrel's name, but he ignored me, just sat still and stony in the boat, watching his father with an expression I couldn't begin to make out.

His lordship was still speaking to the harbormaster, both men gesturing at the water. Ragn dipped a hand inside his doublet and passed a packet to the official, who took a moment to verify the contents before tucking it inside his own clothing. From the size and shape of the object, I had a good idea what it was — banknotes, tucked inside a courier's pouch. *The bribes alone nearly bankrupted the estate.* What was he up to?

Durrel's frown intensified, and I thought he'd forgotten I was there. Back near the street, the hooded wagoner absently stroked the cart horse's sturdy neck. A workhorse, but very fine; I could see the gloss on its hooves from here. From the Charicaux stables, no doubt. The wagoner, then — a Decath servant? He was dressed like his master, in colorless dark livery and hat. It wasn't Karst, that much was clear. This man was slimmer, slighter, moving with an easy grace around the horse.

What were we waiting for? A boat, obviously, but which one? I strained my gaze through the darkness, trying to make out a likely craft from among the traffic. Near the opposite shore, a wealthy family's canopied barge dragged easily through the water, its lanterns bobbing like tiny moons as music and conversation drifted across the river. Docked at a neighboring pier, a tall-masted merchant ship sat silent and hulking, the only movement on its decks the irregular passing of the sailor who'd drawn the night watch. Occasionally one of the small, swift hired boats so common in Gerse cut through the glittering current but did not stop. Finally a shadow shifted on the water, almost unseen, and I turned my head to watch a low, blocky craft staining the reflected moonslight. I sat up straighter in the rowboat.

"There," I whispered, pointing. The vessel was dark, its cargo a formless mass on deck I couldn't make out clearly, but I felt a twinge of certainty as it came within sight.

"Which one?" Durrel peered in the direction I indicated. "Where? I don't see it."

"That little barge," I said, "with the striped hull —" But Durrel shook his head, though he was looking right where I was pointing. A few minutes later, the boat pulled up to the Ceid pier, and Lord Ragn strode forward to grab the lead ropes and help the boatman steer into the dock. Someone moved on board; I leaned in closer, caught a murmur of greeting, a stifled cough, perhaps a yawn. The servant with the wagon turned just slightly into the scattered moonslight, and I saw him raise an arm to stretch or readjust, a pistol held easily in that hand.

The mooring ropes secured, the boatman climbed ashore, and his voice broke through the night. "Easy there. We've made it. You can get out now." Wordlessly the shapeless lump in the boat shook off the dark blankets concealing it, and revealed itself to be three human passengers, a man, a much younger woman, and a small child. With their faces cast up to the moons, I could see worry and relief in their expressions.

"Come." Lord Ragn motioned to the passengers, who climbed awkwardly onto the dock. The young woman reached behind her to scoop up the child, and the moonslight caught something on her wrist, her neck, and flashed it back to us. Long silver chains, heavy silver bangles — the sort worn to dampen magic.

"There you go. You're almost there. You'll be safe soon." Lord Ragn steadied the woman as her footsteps wavered, gave the man's shoulder a friendly squeeze, tousled the child's hair, and finally stooped to retrieve a bundle of belongings passed up by the boatman. His lordship led the family to the wagon, where the stable hand helped them aboard.

I was confused, and judging from the tension rising off my

companion in the boat, he was just as nonplussed. *Lord Ragn* was the Ferryman? How was that possible? But the evidence seemed clear. The documents at the ready, the bribe for the harbormaster, this late-night landing where no one could see. . . .

He couldn't be stashing refugees at Charicaux, though. These imported oranges would have to be moved along in the market fairly quickly for this operation to remain undetected. Decath would need allies, associates — someone to produce those documents we'd found, shuttle the refugees through the city, ferry them off to foreign lands before the Acolyte Guard picked up their scent, and encourage their silence and cooperation along the way. Allies like Karst and Talth Ceid. Lord Ragn had the connections, the Ceid had the money and the ships, and Karst had the muscle. And judging from the money we'd seen in the boat shed, it turned a tidy profit for everyone. I felt sick. I didn't want it to be true.

"We should follow them," I said, moving to climb out of the boat, but Durrel's hand held me back. He was silent, watching his father and the servant ride off into the night. The expression on his face scared me — a mixture of disbelief and something far past anger. Betrayal. I nudged him gently, but Durrel didn't move, just kept staring into the darkness with enough force to bring down the moons.

"Durrel!" He finally snapped back and saw me. "That *can't* be what it looked like," I said desperately. "There must be some —"

"It all looked pretty clear to me," he said, and there was a faint tremor in his voice, like a bowstring after a shot. "My father is a Ferryman."

"I don't believe it."

"Then you're an idiot," he said, and I flinched back, stung. "I'm sorry, Celyn. I didn't mean that. I'm just —" He gave up.

"Let's go talk to him," I said. "I'm sure he'll explain it to you. He'd have to, with the evidence right in front of us."

"We don't know where they've gone," he said heavily, and I bit back my reply that if we'd *followed* them like I suggested, we might have that figured out. "And we can't risk it, anyway. What if the Guard or the Ceid are watching my father, waiting for me to show up? I'd bring the authorities right down on top of those Sarists."

I sat back, horrified. Of course he was right. Even if Lord Ragn *was* a Ferryman, that young family had trusted him to get them to safety. Our interference now would only jeopardize them. What could we do?

"What about Bal Marse?" I said abruptly, pieces finally clicking together. The movement of Sarist refugees could explain the magic I'd seen there. "Maybe they've been using it as a kind of way station."

"You said it was empty, though. They can't be using it still." We stared at each other, neither of us speculating about who, precisely, "they" might be. Finally Durrel shoved aside the canvas covering to the rowboat and stood up. "Let's go, then."

I felt a twinge of guilt. I'd never mentioned tailing Lord Ragn to the Bal Marse warehouse — there hadn't been time, and then it hadn't seemed relevant, and now *certainly* wasn't the right moment for it. I scrambled up after Durrel, who had stalked off across the docks, not even pausing to help me out of the boat (not that I needed it, but still. He was a nob, and usually nothing could make him forget that). He was silent and cold all the way across the city, moving at a pace practically fast enough to catch Lord Ragn's party. I would not have been entirely surprised to see those horses tethered outside Bal Marse, still sweating.

But we didn't. From the outside, the residence and its warehouse were as desolate as they'd been on my last visit. The grounds were streaked with mud from last night's rain, and there was no sign of wheel tracks or hoofprints. Lord Ragn had taken his Sarists somewhere else.

While my back was turned, Durrel had scaled the stone wall surrounding Bal Marse and was straddling the decorative ironwork at the top. Pox. I hurried to catch him, but he was over and down and halfway across the barren courtyard by the time I closed the distance between us.

"What are you doing?" I called softly, and was ignored. Durrel skirted the house and came to a stop at last below a window overlooking a jut of stone. Before I could reach him, he had lifted his foot and was kicking violently at the stonework with the sturdy heel of his boot. "Durrel!"

Nothing. As he lifted his heel to strike again, I grabbed him by the elbow. "Stop!"

He shook me off, and the stone tumbled free from the wall. He hefted it with one hand, and I had a sickening, belated understanding of what he was planning. *"Stop!"* I caught him by the sleeve again and held fast, and he finally seemed to see me. "You're scaring me."

"The window," he said simply. I tried to pry the stone from his fingers, but his grip was unbelievable; it was a wonder that rock wasn't *dented* from it.

"The door is *open*," I said, pointing behind us, to the unlocked kitchen door I'd used before. He looked at me for a moment, uncomprehending, then pitched the rock underhand across the courtyard, as if disappointed he hadn't gotten to fire it through a window after all.

"Fine," he said, shrugging away from me.

I let him go and followed him into the house. Once inside, though, he was subdued. The place was as silent and empty as it had been several days ago, but tonight the full moon of Marau shone through the windows, bathing the empty rooms in faint grayish light. He stopped inside the barren kitchens, tracing his fingers along a cupboard, a wall, a dry sink. It was strange to watch — almost like me searching for traces of magic. But I think he was looking for something familiar, some sign that the months he'd spent living here, married to the owner, had really happened.

I followed mutely as he walked dully through the rooms like a sleepwalker. Something pinched in my chest, watching Durrel pause in doorways, or at the foot of the stairs, and stare into the vast, unfurnished rooms.

"I don't understand," he finally said outside the abandoned Round Court. I could still make out the traces of magic on the floor, the spilled-looking stain, the brushstroked skirt-sweep, and I pointed them out, though I knew he couldn't see anything. "Why gut the place?"

"He sold it," I said abruptly. "The furniture, the tapestries, the candle-sticks, the silverware. To make money —"

"For the refugees," he finished, his voice taking on new life. A frown narrowed his forehead. "Wait. *Who* sold it?"

My frown matched his. "I don't know." I'd been thinking Lord Ragn, who could have had access to the building once Durrel inherited it, but it could just as easily have been Barris Ceid or Karst.

Durrel said, "Let's keep looking."

He led me through the back stair to the floor with the series of darker-on-darker rooms that I'd decided were Talth's suite, and paused in the landing, looking around. Moonslight flooded the corridor from tall arched windows at both ends.

"My rooms were over that way." Durrel pointed. "And Talth's were there —" He took a step down the corridor. "That's a lot of moonslight," he said, and I instantly knew what he was thinking.

"It's after midnight, close enough to the time Talth's maid claims she saw you." With enough light out here to plainly make out the set expression of his face.

"Stay there," he said, and moved down the hall, closer to Talth's door. As he stood in the light from the windows, I could see him clearly. "No, I can easily identify you," he said. "It's a little hard to imagine how she might have been *mistaken*."

"So she must be lying. Maybe it was really Karst she saw, and she doesn't want to say. He is a lot scarier than you," I added.

The corner of his mouth twitched. "Glad to hear it," he said. "Let's check Talth's rooms."

I was oddly reluctant to follow him inside. Even in the impenetrable darkness, even with no furniture to speak of, I couldn't help the ridiculous and inappropriate thought that this was *his wife's* bedroom — the bed-room he had, on occasion, as required, shared *with* her. That had nothing at all to do with me, but I balked in the doorway as Durrel disappeared into the tangle of chambers. I didn't join him until I heard a muffled thump and an oath, and found Durrel inside, sucking on his knuckles.

"Slammed my hand in a drawer or something," he said. Very little light filtered into these rooms, so it was a matter of distinguishing one black lump from another, and it was easy to see how someone could trip over or bang into something. The fixture that had given Durrel trouble turned out to be a panel near the stone fireplace in the biggest chamber. I traced my fingers around the door, feeling out the shape of the opening. It was big enough to step into, and it cast pale light into the rooms, striping the floor with shadows.

"How did you find that?" I asked.

Durrel gave his hand a shake, wiped his knuckles against his breeches. "It found me. I tripped into it and it just popped open."

I stuck my head inside. There was no ceiling, just a small square of sky very far up there. "A skylight," I said. "And stairs. This must go out to the yard down below."

Durrel peered in over me. "But why?"

"Wait." I pushed my way inside. There was a platform just big enough to stand on beside the opening for the stairs. "Now swing the door shut," I said.

"Definitely not! What if you get stuck in there?"

I made a grumble of impatience. "Presumably you'll let me out again." But I didn't wait for him, reaching around the edge of the door to tug it closed. It gave a disconcerting click, but I was still bathed in moonslight, so it wasn't immediately alarming. My fingers searched the panel, and there, a little above my head, I found it — a tiny hole in the wood, not quite big enough for my little finger. A squint. "I should have had you come in here," I said. "I can't see through it."

"See through — Celyn, what?"

I found the catch for the door and tapped it open again. "It's a watch-hole," I explained, pointing to the squint. "For spying on this room. It probably used to be a garderobe, but they walled it in when they built these rooms. Bryn Shaer was *riddled* with them."

Durrel was moving the door back and forth, peering through the squint at various angles, as if trying to guess what view of these rooms anyone hiding in that space might have had. "This is all fairly disturbing," he said, and I didn't press him to elaborate.

"But it's not very useful, is it?" he added — but I didn't answer, because I was kneeling in the little watch-hole, my fingers brushing the thin floorboards. "Celyn, what is it?"

"I don't know, but I think there's something here." I bent closer to the floor, peering down the narrow stairs. There was an odd shadowy glint, almost invisible in the moonlight — but my searching fingers coaxed it into the light, teasing out pairs of shapes, poorly matched, scattering just the smallest trace of magic. "I think it's footprints," I said finally. They were all muddled together, as if the owner had shuffled his feet while standing in the cupboard. "They go down the stairs here." I couldn't see the whole set, not without touching them, but I descended a few steps, trying to make things out more clearly.

"Somebody magical was hiding in there?" Durrel asked, poking his head around the watch-hole door.

"I don't think so. It's — like a residue. Like wet boots from walking through a puddle." I came onto a landing, where the footprints straightened themselves out, and I could see their shape plainly, though they got dimmer with each step. "This is odd. The left print is easy to make out, but the right one — it's all scuffed."

"Maybe he had a limp," Durrel suggested.

"What did you say?" I skittered back up the steps. "A limp? Like from somebody wearing blocks in his shoe?"

"I guess. Why?"

I almost felt like smiling. "Karst has boots like that," I said. "He was here."

A slow grin brightened Durrel's shadowed face. "Oh, you are good. We got him."

I shook my head. "It doesn't help us much, since I'm the only one who can see them. We'll need evidence that's not invisible. . . ." I trailed off, because the wash of moonlight had finally showed up something helpful — a tiny glimmer of natural light in the corner of the watch-hole, in the shape of a curve of glass. I reached for it, and my fingers closed around a little vial, stopperless, that had somehow rolled into the depths of the cupboard. I straightened, then held my hand in the light, slowly uncurling my grip, and knowing with a cold, dead certainty what I would find.

A tiny brown bottle, bearing a potioner's seal of twining red snakes and a neatly inked label: TINCTURE OF THE MOON OF MARAU.

"But —" Durrel said, "they said they found the bottle that had poisoned her."

"They found the bottle you bought for Koya," I said slowly. "So what is this one?" I held the vial up, looking at the moonslight shining through it. It reflected off a single droplet still clinging to the curved glass bottom.

We were both silent a long time, looking at my find, before Durrel spoke up again, his voice soft and measured. "How do we prove that was Karst's?"

"I don't know." But at least it was something — something real. I tucked the bottle inside my doublet and we made our way back downstairs, lingering in the bright Round Court. I tried to picture the room with all its furnishings back intact, but no matter how many tapestries I hung on those curved stone walls, no matter how many candles I set burning, this room, this house was still cold, dark, and forbidding.

"Tell me again what you see here," Durrel said, crossing the cold marble to stoop a few feet from where I'd pointed out the magical residue. I touched the floor, describing the scattered lines, the swish of somebody's hem, the spreading stain.

"What kind of stain, I wonder," Durrel said, studying the spot almost as if he could see for himself. "Like —" He turned to me. "Could it be a bloodstain?"

I froze, my fingers bare inches from the floor. I was kneeling right in it, the wavering glow like an eldritch pond at my feet. I scrabbled backward, falling over my boots and landing hard on the floor. By the gods, Durrel was right. That was exactly what it looked like, as though someone had felled a magic user right here, spilling his blood — his magical blood — on the Bal Marse floors. What else could make a stain so bright and large?

"Hey, you've gone white. It was just a thought. It could be anything. Somebody dropped an inkwell or something."

I swallowed the bitter taste in my mouth, but something still thumped uneasily inside me, a rhythmic throbbing that did not quite keep time with my heartbeat. "Right," I said gratefully. "Of course you're right." But neither of us believed that. I thought hard. "What did Talth keep in the warehouse across the alley?"

Durrel shook his head. "Was it hers? I never saw her use it."

"What about anyone else? Barris? Karst?"

"The only time I ever saw Karst was at the Keep, when he was disguised as a guard."

"Maybe we should check it out anyway," I suggested. I wasn't hopeful, but I wanted to get out of here, out of the invisibly bloodstained Round Court, out of Bal Marse altogether with its secrets and memories and its empty vials of poison; and the idea of seeing what lay behind the warehouse doors suddenly seemed urgent.

"Good," Durrel said. "Let's have a look."

We left through the kitchen door and had to pass along the dead gardens and through the back gate, crossing the little cobblestone alley behind Bal Marse before we got to the warehouse, and I felt more anxious with every step. There was a murky, swampy smell down here after the rain, like the river was too close, and I heard the rustle of a rat or a cat in the rubbish at the end of the street. Without even waiting for Durrel to catch up, I stopped at the same door Lord Ragn had used and picked the lock.

"A light would be nice," Durrel said, coming up behind me. "You're not hiding some candles and a tinderbox in those clothes, are you?"

But I didn't need the light. I knew what I would find inside; it tugged at me like an impatient child until I gave it my attention. I swung the door wide, and the room flashed bright like a lightning strike. I flinched back.

"What is it?"

"Magic." I pushed my way into the warehouse, and I had only to touch my finger to the wall beside the door, and a glow like moonslight spread throughout the space, dotting the floors and windowsills and door frames with the flickering residue. It all lit up at once, and it was like a lute being tuned — the weird thrum inside my chest fell into rhythm with my breath and pulse and disappeared. I took a deep breath and turned through the space.

It was as empty as Bal Marse, a spacious room with no crates, no furniture, just the cold streak of magic left behind. Inside, a lantern hung on a bracket near the main doors, the tinderbox stashed behind it. Once lit, it gave a depressing sallow light to the space and dulled the brightness from the magic in a way that was an odd relief.

Durrel followed me in, surveying the room with a look of doubt. "Well," he said. "I expected a little more, frankly."

"Wait," I said, and handed him the lamp. "Could you — turn that way?" I pointed back toward the door. "And cover up the light? Yes, that's better."

"What are you doing?"

I rubbed at my chest. The funny little tremor in my breastbone was back, faint and annoying. It turned me toward the back of the empty storeroom, and I saw a trail of blots that might have been footprints leading to a door. I followed them, and heard Durrel keeping pace behind me. The door led to stairs, and the stairs led to a cellar, a cavernous room with stone buttresses in the arched ceiling and a drain in the brick floor.

"We're above the sewers," I said. Last night's rain hadn't fully dried away, and there were puddles on the floor that shined the ceiling back at me as Durrel moved the lantern. The strange insistent tug subsided.

"Celyn, look." Durrel had crossed the room. He crouched in a corner, a thick chain in one hand, an open shackle in the other. "They're silver."

Alarmed, I glanced into the other corners, and saw matching sets of chains and manacles, all silver. There was a crude, stained mat like a pallet and a couple of threadbare blankets, and in the flickering light from the lamp and the magic, I made out the quick disappearing shadow of a roach, the vile black specks of rodent droppings. I realized I wasn't breathing.

"They were holding magic users here," Durrel said, his voice thick with horror.

"It's worse than that," I said, barely whispering. "Your father was here."

CHAPTER TWENTY-TWO

The silence in the wake of my words was so cold the very air seemed to stiffen.

"What did you say?"

I was committed now. "That first night I spoke to him — he left the party early, so I followed him. He came here." I made myself look at Durrel, and his expression was so closed it frightened me.

"I see. My wife, my father. It all makes sense."

"No, it *doesn't*." I caught at his arm. "We don't know what he was doing here —"

He wheeled on me. "Really? The chains don't make it clear for you? If you have some other explanation, I'm dying to hear it."

"Karst —"

He gave a brutal laugh. "Of course, the mysterious Karst with the limp. Your answer for everything."

"That's not fair," I said. "We *know* Karst is a murderer, and we know he's a Ferryman. And we also know that your father did not bring those Sarists here tonight."

Durrel took a shaky breath and nodded grudgingly. "You're right. Hells, let's get out of this place."

We got out, and fast. But I couldn't get that picture out of my head — those silver chains, the filth and squalor — all the long walk home. There had been three sets of chains in that dank basement; if they weren't for the family of Sarists we'd seen Lord Ragn take away earlier, then what?

As we crossed back to the Temple District, we turned the night's other discoveries inside out and upside down, until they were all tangled into one great, incomprehensible knot. Some things were confusing, like Lord Ragn's connection to Ferrymen, and the stains at Bal Marse. And some had meanings all too clear — the chains, the poison bottle, Karst's foot-prints leaving Talth's bedroom. Though we were tantalizingly close to answers, they were more disturbing than I'd imagined, and we still had no way to prove Durrel's innocence.

"We have to find something that connects Karst to the murder," I said. "Something we can show people, I mean. Besides this little bottle, which could have gotten there any number of ways."

"We can't exactly bring the Day Watch to Bal Marse and point out Karst's invisible, magical footprints," Durrel agreed, visibly trying to shake off the mood from the cellar. "How did you do all that, anyway? At the warehouse — you looked just like a bloodhound on a scent trail. *And* you knew which boat they were on, long before you could have picked it out of the traffic on the water. Before I could even *see* it."

"I don't know." I looked off into the starlit distance. Durrel was right; somehow I had followed the nagging tug of the magic from the warehouse like a tether reeling me home. I could still feel the sensa-tion, an echo in my breastbone, and I didn't like it. I rubbed at my chest again.

"Hey," Durrel said. "You're shivering. What's wrong?"

I shook my head, but found myself wanting to tell him. "Werne came to see me a few days ago." The words sounded strained and unreal.

"Your brother? The Inquisitor." I had never spoken to Durrel of my connection to the Bloodletter, but everybody knew. Everybody knew that now. "Celyn, what happened?"

"He —" I rubbed my fingers against my clothes, but they still glinted with magical light. "He wants me to come back to the Celystra and hunt magic users for the Inquisition."

"Black Marau," Durrel swore. "Oh, Celyn. Digger. I'm sorry."

I shrugged, but Durrel's hand fell gently on my shoulder, and his dark eyes were all sympathy. "They had people in *chains*," I said. "That's what he forces them to. To trust their fates to Ferrymen —" I faltered, because

I couldn't go further without touching on Durrel's father again. What a pair we made. I hunched out of Durrel's grasp and kept walking, and it was a moment before I heard his footfalls beside mine again. Frowning, I recalled another incident. I had shrugged it off at the time, but now I wondered about it anew. "That evening with Koya — she wanted to know if I could really see magic."

That brought Durrel up short. "Why in the hells would she ask you that?" he said.

I looked into the moonslit sky, and three heavy orbs looked back at me. "I have absolutely no idea."

Durrel was sober but calm as I left him that night. "You'll see your father tomorrow," I said, lingering in the open threshold of the Temple. Lamplight poured into the street where we stood. "I'm sure he'll be able to explain everything."

"I hope so," he said with a little shrug, and then disappeared into the masked crowd inside. I stood there in the pooling light for a long moment, but he never turned back.

That night I was still uneasy, and as I undressed for bed, I tried to work out what was bothering me, beyond the disturbing revelations at the river and Bal Marse. I'd set the little bottle near the window, where it glowed amber in the moonlight. I looked at it, my thoughts turning back to Lord Ragn's servant from the docks, and the way the slim man had moved and stood. He felt — familiar, somehow, but I couldn't place him. Frowning, I unlaced my oversized doublet, and my hands slowly froze on the ties. That was it. Lord Ragn's accomplice had seemed familiar not because I knew the *man* — but because I knew the stance, that posture, that slight difference in bearing under the clothes. I laid the doublet aside, feeling more and more certain. The figure with the pistol had been a woman, dressed in men's clothes, just like me.

Exhaustion from the week's late-night running around kept me in bed late the next morning. When I finally pulled myself together to appear downstairs at the bakery, the hot yeasty scent of bread baking engulfed the whole building — and, apparently, much of the street outside. The common room was as crowded as I'd ever seen it, certainly busier than it had been the last several weeks. Grea was up to her elbows in customers, and even Rat bustled about the kitchen, handing out loaves.

"What's going on?" I asked, squeezing between clamoring bodies to get behind the counter. I reached for a stray bun that had rolled into the flames and gotten singed on one side.

"They heard we had flour," Grea said.

"You have flour? How? This I want to see for myself." Grea nodded toward the back room, the pantry where she kept her supplies. Rat must finally have managed to track down a couple of stray bags that could be diverted from their intended destination. I wondered how much *that* had cost. Inside the pantry, beside Grea's sad supply of cheaper barley and millet, sat two huge sacks of white flour tagged with her name and the Bargewater Street address. When I saw them, my appetite shriveled up to nothing, and I set my singed bun down, untasted, on a shelf. The bags were stamped with a symbol of a stalk of wheat against a green circle. Grea might not recognize the emblem, but I knew it immediately. This flour came straight from the Celystra.

I banged back out into the kitchen and flagged Grea down. "Who brought this to you?" I had to half shout above the noise of the customers and the roar of the ovens.

"Two workmen just delivered them yesterday," she said. "Said they were told to bring it direct to me. I have no idea who sent it or why, but I'm not complaining!"

"What kind of workmen?"

Grea looked at me quizzically. "Workmen. What's this about, Digger?"

I waved her back to work, scowling. There was only one way that Celystra grain would find its way to a tiny bakery in the Seventh Circle, and it left me feeling confused and defeated. Werne was too shrewd. He hadn't bothered to include a message for me; he hadn't needed to. I couldn't even be *angry* about this. Who was I to begrudge Grea and the hungry people of Seventh their bread?

That evening, when the moons were low and the traffic on the river was dying down, I fetched Durrel for the meeting with Lord Ragn. Eske had clad him in a fine doublet of gray velvet, much like the one he'd worn habitually before his arrest; and freshly shaved and dressed in black damask trunk hose and soft leather shoes, he looked every inch the nob again. Though I was in my copper satin gown to match, I felt awkward, and hesitated before crossing the Temple common room to meet him, pausing first to leave a message for Berdal at the bar that Cwalo had agreed to arrange a time in the coming days to meet with influential Gersins who might be sympathetic to Prince Wierolf's cause.

"We'll need to be careful tonight," I said as Durrel made his way toward me. "You look — like yourself."

His face was unreadable as he lifted fingers to the brim of his hat. "I don't feel like myself," he said softly. "Where are we going, dressed like this?"

I had enlisted Rat's aid in arranging this rendezvous, as I had more confidence in his ability to select a venue suited to Lord Ragn's station. Although that station was becoming less and less clear by the hour. "A theater in the Second Circle," I said. "There's an opera." When Rat had given me the tickets, he hadn't said as much, but I gathered they were meant to have been his and Hobin's. I owed him one. At least.

"Master Breem's?" Durrel asked, and I nodded. "I know it."

The theater was a long way from the Temple District, but we took it on foot; it was easier to duck into an alley to avoid a patrol of guards than it was to secure a hiding place from a boat. A pall fell over the walk as we passed through a public circle where one of the gates had been barred off. A uniformed guard of the Watch was tying strips of yellow cloth to the bars, and we slipped deeper into the shadows.

"Plague flags," Durrel said when the guard finally passed us by. Fever must have struck that quarter, a crowded, working-class neighborhood, from the looks of it, and the Ruling Council had quarantined them. No one could cross the boundary of the yellow plague flags — in or out — for at least the next four weeks, or until the court physicians declared the risk over. I doubted the court physicians had ever set foot down here, nor the Celystra healers turned their prayers to the unfortunates locked behind those gates. The penalty for trespass was death, either from the fever itself or from the Watch, if you were caught.

"Talth rented out houses in that neighborhood," Durrel said grimly as we set off again. "I never saw them, but I can guess what they must be like."

I thought of what he'd said the other day during our conversation with Berdal. "What you mentioned before, about Greenmen being killed by Sarists — is that true?"

He lifted his hands. "Who knows? It could just be rumor — which is plenty of reason they wouldn't want it spread around. But Raff told me they were cracking down on anyone who might have been involved, either in a real crime or rumormongering."

Talk of Greenmen made me uneasy. That afternoon I had asked Rat to look into what had become of Raffin. I was increasingly alarmed by the silence on that front, and I hoped Rat's connections would have better luck turning up some information.

We were mostly silent the rest of the way, relying on Durrel's familiarity with the district to lead us to our destination. I kept my eye out for Watchmen, but as we approached the theater, the streets filled up with other well-dressed young couples and clusters of nobs and gentry out enjoying the evening. Anyone looking closely would notice immediately that Durrel and I stood out. We were the only ones not making merry.

We followed the queue into the theater, beneath garlands of grape-vine draping the arched entry and past a respectable-looking footman who exchanged theatergoers' tickets for silk masks. It was precisely the sort of event a man like Ragn Decath would be expected to attend. Rat's tickets had secured us a box overlooking the stage, as well as a pair of more elaborate, sculpted-paper masks, and there we waited for Durrel's father.

"Leave that on," I said as Durrel fidgeted with his mask. "If somebody sees you —"

"Stop reminding me," he said, but he sounded tired, not angry. His sandy velvet mask had a bulldog's face whose mournful expression so matched Durrel's own that I couldn't help smiling. He lifted its velvet edge and peered out at me. "A bulldog? Really?"

"Rat picked them out," I said.

"Yours is beautiful."

"It's Zet," I said. "It's ridiculous" — an absurd concoction of white silk and gilded scrollwork that would *never* make me look like a goddess. "I'm just grateful it isn't a mouse."

Durrel leaned back against the box rail and regarded me through his bulldog's eyes. "A mouse? Certainly not. But a cat, perhaps . . ." He brushed a hand toward my face, where a strand of hair had come loose from its arrangement. "You have a whisker out of place."

We didn't get a chance to say more, for at that moment, the box door creaked open. "Durrel? Celyn?" Lord Ragn stepped inside. He wore a strip of blue silk across his eyes, which were lined with concern.

Durrel started to lift the edge of his mask, but my hand on his elbow stopped him from removing it. "It's us," I said, and Lord Ragn's shoulders slumped with relief.

"Thank the gods," he said, reaching for his own mask. It was almost comical, how swiftly Durrel and I moved together to forestall him.

"Keep them *on*," I said. "That's one of the reasons we're here, after all." And not meeting in some public circle with our faces exposed to everyone.

Lord Ragn nodded, stepping forward to embrace Durrel, who stood stiffly beside me. I gave him a nudge, but he held fast to the balustrade

221

and did not move. "Go to him," I whispered, my mouth concealed behind Zet's painted one. Reluctantly he stepped into his father's arms, though their hug was awkward and swiftly broke apart again.

Ragn stood silently, his mouth turned down, looking at a loss for what to do. Durrel had paced away again, staring out into the audience. "Lord Durrel," Lord Ragn said, too formally. "I — Thank the gods you're well."

The pain in his voice was palpable, and Durrel softened. "I didn't kill her," he said, and for a moment he was the lost and desperate young man I'd found in the Keep a few weeks before.

"I know," Lord Ragn said. "Of course you didn't. I know." He pulled his son to him again, and this time, Durrel did not resist.

It was a private moment, and I felt clumsily out of place in the middle of it. I wanted to hear Lord Ragn's explanation for what we'd seen last night as badly as Durrel did, but I settled quietly in the back of the box. The space was designed for discretion; they could speak normally, and the curved walls and velvet would soak up the sound till it was no more than a whisper.

Watching them together, both of them masked, I had a sudden sense of disorientation. Durrel was the bulldog, Lord Ragn the blue silk, but if I hadn't known that, I would have been hard pressed to tell father from son, younger man from older. They were the same size, the same compact shape, with the same gentle curve to the bottom of the jaw. They even had the same gestures, the way they put a hand against the back of their necks when they were vexed, or slumped forward with relief or weariness.

At first I was touched by the similarity, but as I watched them, I felt a sick, dreadful heat wash through me. I was sitting no more than half a dozen paces away, and I could barely tell them apart. In the moonslight, from a distance, down a shadowy corridor — could someone who did not know them distinguish one man from the other?

Talth's maid Geirt had seen someone matching Durrel's description leave Talth's bedroom in the middle of the night. She had sworn to the hour and the identification, but who wouldn't? Durrel had every reason to be in his wife's bedroom. And yet he swore he was not.

Maybe Geirt wasn't lying. Maybe she *had* seen a Decath nobleman in her lady's chamber.

Just not the one she thought.

Oh, *pox.*

PART III

KEEP YOUR
MOUTH SHUT

CHAPTER TWENTY-THREE

I sat in that box for the rest of the show, as small and still and invisible as I could make myself, wishing every minute I could sink into the cushioned seat and disappear. Father and son were reunited, nobody was in gaol; my work was done and I could leave them to flee to Talanca together, if they were smart.

My skin felt too tight, the air too thick to breathe. It didn't matter what Geirt had seen or said she'd seen. Karst had *admitted* to killing Talth, and we'd found his footsteps and the murder weapon. Even if Lord Ragn had been in Talth's rooms that night, for *whatever* reason, Karst was still the most logical suspect. He was the known Ferryman and Ceid employee with the history of violence and murder, after all. Lord Ragn was — Lord Ragn. That's what I told myself, but the memory of what we'd seen on the docks and the warehouse reared up and shook my certainty apart.

"You're awfully quiet tonight," Durrel said to me as we made our way back across town. We had a little money on us, thanks to Lord Ragn, and we were both tired, so Durrel hailed a coach from among those waiting at the theater. It was actually a smart move; probably the last thing any contingent of guards would expect was two fugitives dressed up like nobs and riding in an open carriage through nob streets in the moonslight. Lord Ragn took his leave reluctantly; he was leaving the city for a few days on Decath business, and I could tell he longed to take Durrel with him and never look back.

"What did he tell you?" I asked, biting back all the questions inside that one.

Durrel scowled into the night. "Nothing," he said. "Mostly it was a lecture on how reckless I'm being."

"He cares about you." When Durrel didn't say anything, I persisted. "Did you ask him about — what we saw, last night?"

"Oh, yes. And he was not well pleased to hear we'd been spying on him, in case you wondered." That seemed supremely unfair to me; it wasn't as if we'd gone to those docks *looking* to discover Durrel's father involved in some odd business. "I asked him who those people were, in the boat, and he told me they were friends of the family who needed a little help getting safely out of the city. Servants of one of Amalle's aunts, so he says."

"You don't believe him."

"I don't know *what* to believe. When I told him we'd found evidence that suggested Talth was working with Ferrymen, he was outraged. Called the Ferrymen common street scum and a low-city spook story, and asked how I could possibly imagine that anyone as dignified as the Ceid family could have any association with such people." He held a hand to his neck and scowled out at the wide, curving street passing below us.

"He could be telling the truth," I said. "Maybe this *was* just what he said, and he was helping Lady Amalle's friends get to safety. It does seem like what he would do." A lot more than keeping magic users chained in the basement of a warehouse, anyway.

"I'm not sure of anything anymore, Celyn," he said heavily. "All I wanted was to clear my name, but the deeper we dig, the more confusing it all becomes. I'm not sure I even *want* to know anymore. Maybe I should have the coachman take us to the nearest Watch station and turn myself in."

"Don't say that!" I said. "Don't give up. Not now. We just need that one piece of evidence that proves Karst and Talth were working together —"

"As Ferrymen? Do you really think the city magistrates will care that they extorted and maybe held captive fugitive Sarists?" His voice was bitter.

"No," I said honestly. "But Talth *was* the victim of murder. And the Ceid will certainly care if one of their employees killed her. When we can tell them who really did it, you'll be free."

He was silent as the coach bounced along, his hand braced against the rail. "Look," I said, "I'm going to have another peek at the Ceid docks tomorrow, see what I can find out about Karst. I doubt he'll recognize me, so I should be reasonably safe."

Durrel just gazed sullenly at the back of the coachman's head, lost in his own dark thoughts. He didn't speak again until the coach dropped me off on Bargewater Street — and that was a long, long ride indeed. I hadn't voiced my real reason for tomorrow's mission. I had to find Geirt again, ask her again what she'd really seen — *who* she'd seen. Would she have recognized Durrel's father? There's not much cause for a visiting gentleman to meet a lady's chambermaid, so it certainly seemed plausible that she might have mistaken father for son. But had she done so deliberately? A curious possibility wormed its way through the questions. Could Geirt be the woman working with Lord Ragn?

The next morning, almost itchy from all the doubts and confusion, I went down to the dockside warehouse where I'd met her before. Today the place was hopping, three ships at anchor at the pier, a bevy of deckhands and roustabouts carrying cargo from shore to ship — and a brace of Day Watch guards strolling along the waterfront, looking like stocky, armed seagulls in their gray uniforms. I pulled back behind a shed, hoping they'd pass, but they delayed, stopping to chat with a man on board one of the ships. If I kept my head down like a good little thief, they'd have no reason to notice me.

From my hiding place, I looked over the moored ships. One sported a yellow-and-red flag hanging limply in the still air from her bowsprit; a Talancan ship, or one pretending to be, her name scribed in red about the prow: *Belprisa*. I slipped along the river's edge, drawn toward the *Belprisa*'s graceful, sweeping hull. The Watchmen still chatted with the deckhand, and I rubbed at my collarbone as I gazed up at the looming ship. There was a shout from the deck of the nearer craft, and I jumped, realizing I'd wandered out onto the open dock, in view of anybody. I swore and tucked myself back behind my shed until the Watchmen finally moved on.

Geirt, having come from her soft position as a lady's maid in a fine home, was probably inside the warehouse building, taking inventory or working on the books. But I found the little office locked and empty, and the warehouse itself was staffed only by men, that I could see — including Barris Ceid. I spotted the friendly Tratuan dockhand who had been here before, making notes on a crate improbably labeled ORANGES.

"I see you have my oranges," I said brightly. "My mistress will be *so* pleased."

Confusion gradually gave way to recognition — and then alarm. "You again! Master Barris gave us strict instructions not to speak to you."

My eyes flicked to the office. "Did he say why?"

The dockhand looked me over briefly, as if trying to guess. "No," he finally said, and the tone of his voice told me Master Barris did not infrequently give orders without explaining himself, and that Dockhand made his own decisions.

"Where's the girl who helped me before?" I asked. "Maybe your Geirt will be able to get my oranges delivered properly."

"Doubtful," Dockhand said. "She doesn't work here anymore."

The heat pressed in on me from all directions. "Where did she go?" I asked slowly.

He shrugged. "Your guess. Just up and disappeared one day a week or so back. Left after her regular shift one evening, then didn't come in the next morning. Master Barris was fit to be tied too. Said she has a new post in Yeris Volbann or some such place, but he didn't seem too happy about it. If you ask me," he added, "it's good riddance to that girl. There was something weird about her. Uncanny."

I almost shivered, even in the breathless heat. First Temus, and now Geirt. My witnesses were disappearing one by one. I was almost afraid to ask my next question. "Did you ever see her talking to someone called Karst — a big fellow with a thin beard?"

"Karst? Of course. He's our superintendent here. In fact, I think I saw him with Master Barris earlier. Let me get him." And before I had a chance to decline that very generous offer, Helpful Dockhand had waved over a thickset, stoop-shouldered heavy in a shapeless dun brown jerkin, his thick boots clomping the boardwalk with every uneven step.

"Master Karst, this — lady's been looking for Geirt. Something about oranges."

Pox and bloody hells. Now what? Karst turned, and I stood there stupidly, staring up into the cruel, gray eyes of the man who had killed Temus and probably Talth Ceid.

"Yeah?" Karst growled. "What's this about oranges?"

"I —" I squeaked, and then I had a positively *terrible* idea. "That is, I need to move some cargo, um, *quietly*?" Karst's eyes narrowed as he scowled at me, clearly trying to make out just what variety of imbecile I was. I sent a quick prayer of forgiveness to any god listening, and said, "Fei sent me? She said you knew how to get people out of the city. For a price."

Karst regarded me implacably, arms folded over his chest. I held still as he stared me down, probably judging me a respectable, if naïve, serving girl who *might* be able to gain access to enough coin to make this conversation worth his while. There was a cold appraisal in that gaze, and it was hard to stand there and look right back at him.

Finally he grunted and gestured vaguely toward a corner of the docks well away from the ships and crowds. He set off across the boardwalk and I scurried after, telling myself to be calm. Karst was just an ordinary city thug, no different than guys I'd known all my life, and I wouldn't get another opportunity like this one, so I'd better learn as much as I could.

"What's this, now?" Karst's voice was thick and gravelly, tinged with an out-city accent that might have been Yerin. "You're asking about passage past the gates?"

"Aye," I said, remembering my own lost accent. "I heard you could do for that."

"You heard," he echoed, his eyes sliding down my kirtle. "Where would you hear anything like that, now, a little girl like you?"

I gave a shrug and turned away. "If you can't do it, that's fine. Sorry to waste your time."

One long, beastly arm curled around, not quite touching me. "Hey, now, I never said that. I *may* be able to arrange something, for a fee."

"And it's quiet?" I said. "I don't want attention from the Watch." I said that deliberately, to see his reaction, but he was a solid lump of stone. "How much is it?"

"Depends. Where you going?"

"I never said it was for me," I said. I edged closer to the building; I wanted that wall behind me. "But let's say Tratua." Tratua was the closest port city on the sea; the "Talancan" vessels almost certainly sailed that way when leaving Gerse.

He shook his head. "Tratua's bad. Too many checkpoints. You don't want a river crossing. We go up to Yeris. Easier to get the licenses, make it look like grain or livestock."

And a longer trip, and probably a higher fee. But it didn't track with what we thought we knew of his operations with Talth. "But that's an overland route," I said without thinking. "Isn't that more dangerous?"

Karst grinned and flexed his big hands. "We got plenty of protection," he said. "Now, about the fee. It's seven hundred crowns up front, another seven on delivery. You bring your own food, and luggage is extra. If you can't pay . . ." he trailed off, still grinning, and drew his index finger straight across his throat.

"Do — do you have a lot who don't pay?"

"Not anymore."

I believed him. "I guess I can manage that," I said. "I heard other crews were charging a lot more —"

"*Ain't* any other crews but mine!" The words just — *exploded* out of him, and I flinched back against the shed. "Not that matter. Not anymore."

What did that mean? "But don't you have competition for this kind of work? It seems, uh, very profitable," judging by the exorbitant sums from Talth's burned records.

He shrugged, and I half expected the man to whip out a knife and start cleaning his fingernails. "I did. But that's all been taken care of. I'm my own man now. Got my own ship, my own men, my own route."

I looked into his face, and let all my breath out at once. *That's* why he did it. Get rid of Talth and out from under the thumb of the Ceid, strike out on his own, keep the profits for himself. Oh, sweet Marau. Kill one rival, threaten another's son . . . Did it also explain why Lord Ragn might have paid a late-night call to Talth? If he had tried to warn her about Karst, but too late? And now Karst was threatening Lord Ragn — but Lord Ragn apparently had ignored the message, and was continuing to move people through the city. It gave me a chill like a fever in the steamy morning, and I had the sudden firm conviction that I should probably be on my way.

I pretended to dither. "Fourteen hundred crowns is a lot of money."

Karst leaned over me. "Less than your bail if you're arrested by Greenmen."

Well, that was a sales pitch. I nodded faintly. "Let me think on it?" I said.

"Think *quietly*, little girl," he said, and accent or no, there was no mistaking the menace in his voice. I tried to slip away from him, but that thick arm came up and blocked my path. I didn't like the way he was looking at me — as if there were more to be gained here than my fourteen hundred crowns. "All kinds of dangers in the city these days. You wouldn't want to fall in with the wrong folk, now, would you?"

Well, no, I certainly didn't want that. I shook my head vigorously, and he finally let me go. I hastily headed for the nearest street leading away from the river, as Karst turned back toward the docks. But then I heard a very unwelcome voice from the warehouse behind me.

"What's *she* doing here?"

Pox — Barris. I flashed a look over my shoulder, and saw that Karst had halted at Barris's voice as well. "Don't you know who that is? Stop her — don't let her leave!"

Ah, hells. I hiked up my skirts and skittered off down the street, but

Karst, for all his size and gimpy leg, was surprisingly fast. Fighting for breath in the muggy air, I turned deeper into the city, away from the water, where the buildings were thicker. Damn — he was right behind me. I swung around a tight corner, caught the edge of a stone corbel on the first handy building with an overhanging roof, and hauled myself up to the tiles. I pulled myself flat, heart banging painfully against the slates, as Karst pounded into view. He stared around the intersection, hands curling as if he'd already caught me.

Not even breathing, I eased toward the peak of the roof so I could slide down soundlessly to the other side. A broken tile snagged my skirt and tore my hem, but I swallowed my curses as Barris caught up with Karst. He pointed around the corner, and they charged down the street below me.

"Marau's balls, she's gone." Karst's voice was gruff and breathless.

"Damn it." I saw Barris sheath a dagger — expensive, by the look of it, and I hoped he wasn't as practiced with it as he appeared just then.

"Who was she?" Karst said, looking down another street.

"That girl I told you about." Barris swore again.

"You mean the one —" Karst's expression shifted. "Oh, *aye*. Wouldn't mind getting my hands on her, then. I bet she'd be worth a pretty coin to our friends." I stiffened, fingers cramping from their grip on the narrow slates. What did he mean by that?

"Don't get ambitious," Barris said, turning back the way he'd come.

I didn't breathe again until Karst's scuffing footsteps disappeared after him.

CHAPTER TWENTY-FOUR

When I got back to the bakery, after taking a ridiculously circuitous route to shake off any possible tails, I had another note from Cwalo, this time arranging our meeting with Berdal and certain "friends" who would be amenable to just such a conversation, set for the following afternoon.

I couldn't help puzzling over what had happened on the docks. It was possible Geirt simply had gotten a better post in a different city, but I doubted it. Still, why would anyone want to get rid of her? She was the best witness against Durrel. Had those sharp green eyes seen more than the silhouette of a Decath leaving Talth's rooms after midnight? And Karst's statements about ridding himself of rivals to his Ferrying operation seemed awfully ominous as well. I had one dead merchant, one dead prisoner, and now a missing chambermaid. Bodies were piling up (or at least disappearing on me), and the connections among them still weren't making themselves plain. I was looking forward to the meeting at Cwalo's — I could do with a distraction now, and the war seemed just the thing.

The pretty house in the Spiral was in an uproar when Berdal, Durrel, and I arrived late the following afternoon.

"Impossible!" Mistress Mirelle was bellowing, although Master Cwalo sat well within earshot. Mirelle was a tall, striking woman with black hair and at least six inches on her husband. I had liked her instantly when I'd first met her in the spring.

"What's impossible?" I asked, poking my head into the snug drawing room.

Mirelle just flung her hands skyward and stalked out. Cwalo grinned his odd, sinister smile and greeted Durrel and Berdal. "Well met, milord, Captain." He turned to me. "Garod has announced his intentions to marry, if you believe it."

"I *don't* believe it," I said. Garod was Cwalo son number two, the one his parents most despaired of settling down. "Who's the bride?"

"A chorus girl from the Well!" Mirelle cried from whatever room she'd disappeared into. I wasn't sure what "the well" meant, but from her inflection, I gathered it must be some kind of less-than-reputable establishment in Yeris Volbann.

"He, uh, sounds a lucky fellow," Durrel suggested tentatively. He'd been sullen and brooding on the way over here, but the lively chaos of the Cwalo home was enough to shake anyone out of misery.

"He's a libertine!" Mirelle said, but stepped back into the parlor to have a look at my companions, pinning the boys into a corner for examination. I felt a sudden empathy of terror for her sons, enduring that intense scrutiny for a lifetime. "You're too thin," she told Durrel. "Go into the kitchens and tell Runa to give you a pie."

"But you're just about to serve —" Seeing Mirelle's expression, Durrel gave it up and slinked away in the direction Mistress Cwalo was pointing.

"And *you*," she said severely to Berdal, examining his wounded arm. "Blackberry and dock tisane," she pronounced with disapproval, as if the sling had done her a personal injury. "We have some in the kitchen."

Berdal was nodding, smiling his broad smile. "Aye, we use that in the mountains, mistress." He followed her out of the parlor, leaving me with Cwalo.

"I have a treasure for you, lass," he said, producing a folded paper from an inlaid chest. It was a letter, clearly much traveled, judging from the wear around the corners. "Though it took its own time making its way to us."

The letter in question was from Meri, a single, folded sheet, its seal long broken; it had obviously begun its journey well before Berdal had left her side. For a moment I felt a twinge of anxiety, picturing the many hands this letter must have traded, and all the eyes that had taken in its contents. But Meri was too smart to write anything incriminating, and the note was breezy and newsy, with very little substance to be alarmed over.

> *Lady Merista Nemair of Bryn Shaer sends these tidings to her sister-by-heart in Gerse, Celyn Contrare:*
>
> *We have spent a very busy summer here, with much time upon the horses and with traveling here and there. We see friends everywhere we go and count ourselves lucky to meet so many kindred souls along our path. I am sure back at home you are busy as well, with festivals and with moving, as they tell me you have done now several times, but I would have you please put pen to page once in an age, as you have friends here who wonder after you.*

It was all very typically Meri, frothy and upbeat and full of happy nothings. But there was more to the note that was *also* unmistakably Meri — its secret content. Somehow she had covered every inch of the back of the page with tiny, invisible writing that sparked to life when I touched it, a letter not only in invisible ink (smart little Meri!), but in *magic*. She had taken a chance that only I would be able to read it, and the fact that the letter had made it to me confirmed her faith in herself and whatever network she'd entrusted it to. It was risky and brilliant, and enough evidence to condemn this entire household to the Inquisition.

I looked over the edge of the page to see Cwalo watching me solemnly, so I came and sat beside him, and read out Meri's *real* letter:

> *Celyn, there hasn't been much time to write with all the fighting going on. It is all happening much faster than anyone suspected, and they are saying we shall be near you by the end of the season. They have put me to work as we expected, and I am honored to do my part, but it is much harder than I had thought and I often wish there was someone else here to relieve me. We have had one or two new recruits in our little battalion since summer*

came, and they are welcome, though none yet who can share my task. But they do take good care of me! You should see the food they've been shoveling into me; I am the only one in His Highness's army who has grown fat this summer! The prince says I must remind you to eat, because he thinks you will not; but I heard that you were living near a bakery, and I told him you would not starve if there was bread nearby.

Hereupon Cwalo interrupted the account with a snort.

Mother has organized the surgery, of course, and complains constantly that her aides do not have half your skill at a sickbed. But I think she is just weary and afraid like the rest of us, for she and Kespa save more than they do not. They have sworn me to secrecy because you will only worry, but I think you should know that the prince has been injured, though not seriously and he is on the mend — or he would be, if Mother could get him to lie quietly for more than a half hour at a time.

I must go now; I am running out of paper and I do not dare send a second page. But I would bid you to stay away from this strife if you may, and that if you are not too busy, perhaps you would look forth and see if you might not find another like me and send him our way, because we could sorely use him now.

The prince says to "watch your flank." Do you know what that means?

— M

"The best of tidings," Cwalo said, and I nodded absently, tracing my fingers across the bright letters. "Not all warriors are on the battlefield, my girl. You are where you are meant to be." He gave my knee a squeeze, then rose from his seat. "I'd best go check on the squab; Mirelle has been immolating them of late."

I watched him leave, then saw Durrel standing in the doorway, listening. I waved him over, and he held out his hand for the letter. I let him take it, with the feeling his thoughts were too near my own.

"He raised her, you know," he said after a long moment, stroking the blank-to-him back side of the page. "My father. For five years he kept Meri safe, kept her secret. How could he be involved in —" He gave up, lost in Meri's letter, as if the invisible swirls of power on the paper were hiding all the answers.

Mirelle called us to eat a few minutes later, and we fell to a happy enough meal of roasted pigeons and a delicate seafood stew. Even at Mirelle's table the food shortages were evident; there was no bread, the squab were city-caught, Cwalo's spices couldn't disguise that the broth was mostly water, and Mirelle's expression of distaste as she served out every portion said the rest. Still, it was a jolly meal, with Berdal and Cwalo trading unbelievable stories of their travels, and Durrel even joining in with the odd tale of hilarity at Favom Court.

About halfway through dinner, we were cut off by a knock at the door. I looked up, uneasy.

"Don't fret, girl. It's just another guest," Cwalo said, rising to meet the new visitor, who was just then being ushered into the crowded dining room by the serving lad. I blinked and dropped my spoon. It was Lord Hobin — Rat's Hobin — now greeting everyone with low bows, and dressed improbably in a poorly matched leather doublet and linen trews that were apparently meant to make him look common. And on his heels, giving me a broad wink, was Rat.

"I see we've interrupted your meal," Lord Hobin said, stooping through the arched doorway. "Have we come at the wrong time?"

"Not at all," Mirelle said warmly. "Come and have a plate."

I was too dumbfounded to say anything, but Durrel had no such qualms. "What interest does a member of the Ministry of War have in this company?"

Berdal looked perplexed and alarmed, but Cwalo just moved his chair aside to make room for Hobin. "One might ask the same of a Decath," Hobin said smoothly as he sat. "But for my part, I am ever partial to a perfectly cooked squab. A rare delicacy indeed, Mistress Cwalo. Digger, my darling girl, you're looking much healed from when I saw you last."

My fingers flew to the cut on my cheek, and I nodded dumbly. "Well, I'm offended," Rat said cheerily, squeezing beside me on the bench. "We invited Digger to dinner, but she did not return the favor, and we had to crash. *Tsk, tsk.*"

I glared at him, but Cwalo broke in. "I asked Lord Hobin to join us because these matters we discuss affect his interests and his work, and I felt it critical to have someone here to tell us how things stand with the king."

Mirelle gave her husband a quelling look that plainly said, *No politics at the dinner table.* But Hobin spoke up. "My loyalties are to Llyvraneth and the city of Gerse," he said. "*Not* the king. If I am in a position to help my country and my city, I will do so."

Everyone was looking at me expectantly. "I —" I frowned. "Rat trusts him," I finally said. He had never given any hint that Lord Hobin was anything other than the most steady of officials, without a streak of zeal for any particular cause or faction. And I trusted Rat with my life. Even if he was currently picking food off my plate.

"Very well," Mirelle said as if that settled the matter. "Your lordship, do try the citron marmalade. Cwalo brings it from Talanca. Halcot, how are your parents?"

After that, the rest of the meal passed smoothly, conversation touching on only the lightest topics. Hobin roared with laughter at the account of Garod Cwalo's betrothal and Cwalo's efforts to pair up the others. "Merciful Goddess," he said. "You make me thankful my own son is well settled, and that I had only the one!"

"You have a son?" I said, surprise making it sound a little rude.

"Dear girl, of course! I'd hardly be allowed to go on with Halcot if there wasn't already another Lord Hobin to come after me."

"He's not in the war, I hope," said Mirelle, whose two middle boys, Andor and Viorst, fought with Wierolf.

Hobin shook his head. "No, thank the gods. He's well out of it, reading law in Talanca. I'd like to bring him home to a country at peace with itself and its neighbors."

The meal had rounded out, and apparently Mirelle judged this an appropriate time for the discussion to turn serious. The remains of dinner were cleared away, and she decamped for the kitchens, sliding the dining room doors closed behind her.

"Well, now, we all know why we're here," Cwalo said. "Captain Berdal, if you'll begin?"

Berdal gave a cough and shifted forward in his seat. "I'm not at liberty to reveal anything about the prince's position or strategy." I wondered if that caution would have applied without Lord Hobin's presence.

"Of course," Lord Hobin replied. "You've come only to discover how things stand in the city, and I'm sure you've seen much for yourself."

Berdal nodded grimly. "The food shortage is worse than reported. Celyn has said that the people are restless, and many would not resist an invasion, but Lord Durrel says the city's noble population and gentry rulers are still loyal to the king."

Hobin looked thoughtful. "We are *required* to be loyal," he said. "It isn't exactly the same thing. And we pay dearly for the privilege."

I held up a hand, thoughts clicking. "Lord Decath told me he paid heavy fines for keeping Meri all those years. But every other noble who ever showed any signs of Sarist sympathies was exiled, or worse."

Durrel sat up straighter at this. "Bardolph needs *money* more than he needs another enemy." He scrambled for a piece of paper, supplied by Cwalo from the chest in the other room, and began jotting notes. "The whole war effort's got to be fantastically expensive." Hobin and Cwalo leaned over the paper with him, and they fell into calculations together for several tense, quiet minutes as the rest of us looked on in bemusement. Rat refilled our glasses. Finally Durrel stuck his head up again. "That's why he's been diverting grain and meat from the city markets. Not so he can feed his troops with it, but —"

"So he can sell it on the black market," Rat finished. "Not a bad business, really."

Cwalo looked up sharply, dark eyes alight. "Damn, lad, I think you're right. And from what I've heard, Bardolph's also been charging the city billeting fees for housing soldiers here, while at the same time taking it out of the troops' pay and calling it a lodging tax."

Hobin watched us stonily. Finally he said, "That would be a violation of the terms by which the army has been mustered. They're to be lodged in common homes only when barrack space is unavailable, and they — and the household — are to be paid allowances by the army. If this is correct, the troops are owed quite a bit of back wages."

"But there are unused barracks all over the city," I put in. "They've been building them for years. Don't the soldiers care?"

Berdal gave a shrug. "Most common troops — especially Green Army — wouldn't even know their contracts weren't being honored. And besides, the king does what the king wants."

"And if they learned about this?" Rat asked quietly, looking at Hobin. A long moment passed, and it was Berdal who answered.

"An army has to have faith in its commanders, and a breach of trust like that wouldn't go over well."

"If even a portion of the Green Army fell to discord," Hobin said slowly, "Astilan's attention would have to be diverted to deal with the uprising."

There was silence in the wake of this suggestion, a chasm too immense to be filled with words. Finally Cwalo spoke up. "And that might be enough to give Wierolf the final advantage he needs. March on the city and take Hanivard Palace."

"The soldiers in the city aren't happy either," Berdal said. "I had a few drinks with some local Green Army boys, and they're mad as hells about back pay, no food, and having to bunk with civilians."

"How in the world did you manage that?" I asked.

Berdal grinned. "They come into that public house where I'm staying. They see the arm, and nobody even thinks to ask which side I fought on. I was at all the right battles, after all. Anyway, they complain about everything. Even saw one of them toast that great banner. Course, I also saw one lad drop his pants to it."

"How tasteful," Lord Hobin said. "I'm glad to see our beloved city is defended by only the finer sorts of people."

"The question is," Cwalo was saying, rubbing his bald head thoughtfully, "how to use this intelligence to our benefit. If we could stir up this discontent among a few key-placed battalions . . ."

"Start with the troops inside the city," Hobin said. "They seem to be the most unhappy. And then maybe . . ." He turned one of Durrel's sheets of paper around and started sketching a quick, crude map that swiftly became Gerse's western wall and the lands around it. "Maybe the Third Artillery, here."

Durrel leaned forward to study Hobin's map. "If those troops were to mutiny, that would leave the Green Gate undefended, right?" He pointed to a gap in the city wall, and the wide road leading to the heart of town. "Prince Wierolf could practically march straight down High Street and knock on the king's door before anyone could stop him."

We all fell silent, staring at one another. "Would it work?" My voice was a whisper.

"My dear, I think we are obligated to try," said Cwalo.

Lord Hobin looked grim, but he finally nodded. "If it brings the war to a swifter close, it will mean less bloodshed in the end. I would prefer either your prince and his friends turn around and go home, or that Gerse throw open her gates and welcome them with open arms, but since neither prospect seems likely to be forthcoming, I must lend my support to any action promising to end the conflict sooner."

Berdal was scowling a little, obviously uneasy at the idea of *deliberately* brewing disquiet among fellow soldiers, even if they were the enemy. "How do we do it, then?" he said. "Convince the other side to mutiny? Right now there are just grumbles, complaints. I'm not sure even this bit about barracks pay is enough to spark a real flame."

"Well, then, lie to them," I said. "Tell them something they'd get *really* mad about."

While we pondered the possibilities, Cwalo called for another bottle of wine, passing it around the table. It stopped at Rat, who turned the near-empty bottle over in his hands, picking at the edges of the label. "Shoddy workmanship," he said mournfully. "Even the labels are going downhill these days."

That sparked an idea. I plucked the bottle from Rat's hands. "Let's take away their wine," I suggested.

Hobin looked momentarily horrified, but Durrel and Cwalo leaned forward, appreciative smiles turning up the corners of their mouths. Berdal's grin widened. "Tell the lads their ration's been cut off because of money shortfalls? It'll be the end of them."

"It's going to take more than a rumor to make them rebel," said Rat.

Cwalo's lip quirked. "I think among the six of us, we can probably manage to exert some influence over the movement of wine in this city."

"Plant the rumor, forge a letter or two to the wrong people, and then delay a key shipment by a few days. Rat? What do you think?" I said.

"I think it's despicable," he said. "But the vintners in the Third Circle have the army contracts. I'm sure they could be persuaded to let a few of their barrels go to a higher bidder, but they'd want some protection."

"I'm not entirely sure that can be arranged," Hobin said. "This is still a war we're playing with, my boy."

A shiver went up the back of my dress at the scope of what we were proposing, but the conversation continued, long into the evening, as we fine-tuned the plans. The prince would have to approve the scheme, and establish a time frame for setting it in action, coordinating his troops' movements with the rumor we were intending to plant among the Green Army garrisoned in the city. But we had the means to set it all in motion from inside Gerse's walls.

When we finally said our good-byes that night, Cwalo gave me a quick, firm hug. "Lass, you have a gift, you do, though Mirelle will swear I've corrupted you."

"Thank you for bringing me," Durrel said to me as we walked out into the night. "Even though I know you only did it to keep me out of trouble."

"And to meet the Cwalo. They're almost like family. What would your father think of you dining with rebels and plotting a mutiny?" I added softly, and Durrel's expression went closed and hard once more.

"My father the Ferryman? Ask me if I give a damn."

I looked into the night sky. Tiboran had gone into hiding, but Zet was rising, fierce and bright, and I wondered how the goddess of war would like her brother the trickster interfering in her domain. And would Wierolf want to end the war by trickery? Suddenly I felt bone weary of death and deceit, but it seemed every step I took these days carried me deeper in.

CHAPTER TWENTY-FIVE

We met again the next day, Berdal, Rat, Durrel, and I, in a back room at the Temple, to work through our parts of the plan. One of the critical components of the scheme was producing an accurate enough map of Gerse and her defenses to send to the prince. Wierolf had been exiled from Gerse as a child, and current intelligence would be vital to any engagement in town. But when the war had started, Astilan's troops had stormed bookshops and printers and private collections across the city, seizing every map they could find and burning them all in a great public bonfire in Market Circle, lest any make their way past the sealed gates to the enemy. Durrel had a quick and accurate hand, and a good memory, and between us — with occasional input from Eske — we put together a sketch of the town walls and her main streets and gates, as well as the locations of the Green Army troops stationed throughout (thoughtfully provided, for the public service, by Lord Hobin).

"You'll want to hold that carefully," Eske remarked to Berdal. "That'll not be an easy thing to take out of the city, and woe if they catch you with it."

"Oh, they won't," Rat put in. "Digger has a plan."

I explained how Cwalo had contributed a case of local Gelnir wine, which *could* pass unmolested through the city gates and roadside checkpoints, and how, with the application of a little egg white and lemon juice, the backsides of the innocent-looking wine labels would become a secret patchwork map that the prince could reconstruct back at his camp, "when he holds the labels up to a flame." I used the table's candle to demonstrate how the fire warmed the hidden ink and made it visible.

Eske's wide smile signaled her approval of this scheme, which involved the three things Tiboran loved best: wine, secrets, and deception.

Durrel was focused and intent, and I was relieved he'd found some distraction from the mystery of his father's involvement in smuggling Sarists. I would have liked Cwalo's opinion on the matter, but Durrel had made me promise not to mention it until we knew more for certain. In the meantime, I was getting even more concerned about Raffin's lingering absence. Rat had turned up nothing, and even Lord Hobin had made a few discreet inquiries after a fellow lord's son, to no avail. Rat tried to sound casual when he broke this news, but I felt a current of concern beneath the words, and it made the skin on my neck tighten uncomfortably. What had happened to him? I couldn't believe how much I longed to see a Greenman step casually out of the shadows and pin me into a conversation, and I was starting to be worried that I might actually have to *do* something about it.

As for our plot to foment rebellion among the king's troops, Berdal had taken the first steps already, drunkenly announcing to his new soldier friends that the next thing they knew, old Bardolph would be cutting off their wine supply. It had produced the expected cries of outrage. I'd caught Eske's look of momentary alarm at that, but eventually she'd grinned wickedly behind her mask of night-dark satin spangled with silver stars. I'd been prepared to forge a quartermaster's report declaring the new ration, but it turned out to be unnecessary; Lord Hobin, after all, was a minister of war and had legitimate access to any documents we'd need, and he assured us that a "clerical error" like a misdirected wine shipment would bring very little risk to him. Berdal was still officially furloughed from the prince's army, but Lord Hobin had smoothed his passage licenses through the proper channels so he could depart the city freely, and he'd be leaving us again in the morning.

I said my good-byes to him that night, wishing him health and good speed. He'd offered to carry a letter to Meri, but what news would I send? *Durrel has been accused of murder? He and I are fugitives for breaking him out of prison, and Raffin Taradyce has been swallowed by the Inquisition.*

And as for your Uncle Ragn — I just shook my head and said, "She knows what I wish for her."

Durrel was left alone at the table, still scribbling doggedly on a stack of papers, and I peered over his work as I slid in across from him. He was making a list of figures. Two hundred thousand crowns, one entry said; the price of his marriage settlement to Talth Ceid. Sixteen hundred sovereigns — a vast figure whose value I wasn't even certain of — for the farm at Favom Court. Another eighty sovereigns for Bal Marse.

"What are you doing?"

"I don't know," he sighed. "Nothing. It's pointless. It doesn't matter." Durrel set down the pen and rubbed a hand over his bleary face. "If he needed the money — Why didn't he just *tell* me?"

"He didn't want you to worry. He probably knew you'd do something like this."

"He didn't trust me." There was a weight and conviction to those words, like a stone rolled into place that wouldn't budge again.

"No," I said, but Durrel pushed the papers aside and bent his head wearily to the tabletop. "I talked to Karst," I said tentatively.

He gave a bitter laugh. "Did he explain their operation to you, then? How they chain women and babies in the cellar of the home I shared with my wife?" I heard a dark slur to his voice that wasn't all drink.

"Your father is not a Ferryman!" I said with a fierceness that startled me — maybe because I was afraid I was lying. "We're not done here, you know. We still have to find proof that Karst killed —"

"Why?" He interrupted me. "We're not learning anything good."

"Because this isn't right," I said. "None of it. Your father is a good man, and you don't belong here. What's your plan? To camp out in the Temple the rest of your life? You're not Tiboran's — you're not built for all this lying and sneaking around."

"You're right," he said, standing up abruptly. "But apparently you are, so go ahead, Celyn, go off and dig up more dirt from my life." And he pushed aside a chair and stalked away toward the stairs, leaving me standing alone in the little back room.

When I got back to Bargewater Street that evening, almost the last person in the world I wanted to see was waiting for me. Koya's boatman, moored at the landing in the *Davinna Koyuz,* turned his gaunt, sepulchral face to me and solemnly intoned, "My mistress requests your company at Cartouche this evening."

I still hadn't recovered from Koya's last salon, and I hardly relished the prospect of another night in that smoky fleshpot. But I was still fuming from that stupid, *pointless* argument with Durrel, and I didn't feel like going straight back to home and bed at the bakery, where Werne's grain sat patiently in the pantry, its very presence a silent rebuke. So I climbed willingly into the skiff and let the gloomy boatman carry me across the city.

Tonight the party was all upstairs, as I was told in a languid hand gesture by a lazy footman, and I let myself up into the inn section, drawn along by the seductive music and the rising heat gathered in the upper floors. At the end of the hallway, one of the private rooms had its doors thrown open to the corridor, spilling smoky shadows into the passage. A single lamp teased the chamber with hazy light, and a lute player crooned out a sophisticated melody that concealed ribald lyrics. Koya was at the center of a cluster of lively, laughing attention, draped elaborately across a padded bench, eating some sort of confection from the fingers of a slight, well-dressed boy kneeling beside her.

"Celyn!" she called out gaily as I crossed the threshold into the room. "Andros, give my friend a taste." Her eyes were hooded and indolent, and she looked plump and well-stewed and ridiculously pleased with herself.

The slim, young man rose and held out one of the sweets he'd been offering to Koya. "No, really — that's all right," I said, ducking away from him.

"Oh, you're so *boring,*" Koya said. She rolled up from the bench and took me by the shoulders. "You need to learn how to relax, Celyn. Loosen up a little —"

Apparently she meant that literally, because she actually gave the laces of my bodice a tug and began pulling my kirtle open. Glaring at her, I swatted her hands away and hastily yanked them closed again. "Koya!"

She ignored me utterly. "Oh!" she said suddenly to everyone gathered around her. "I know what *you* would like — come with me!" With a swoop of arm she gathered her blue velvet cloak to her and dragged me off before I could argue, before anyone from her cluster of admirers could follow. Babbling a stream of one-sided conversation I barely followed, she led me from the crowded room and up a narrow flight of back steps.

"Koya, where —" I began, but gave it up and just stumbled after her.

". . . Durrel the most boring person I knew, but you may be even worse!" Still dragging me by my dress and chattering loudly, Koya stepped off the stairs into an empty hallway of low light and plush, patterned carpets, checking up and down the passage. "There," she said, closing the stairwell door behind her. "Now we can talk privately." Her voice was low and serious — and sober.

"What is this, Koya? What's going on?"

"That's what I was hoping you'd tell me." All traces of the overly buoyant Koya had slipped away, like she'd stepped out of a too-warm cloak.

"You're not drunk," I said stupidly.

She gave me that indulgent, patient *Ceid* smile. "I've found a mask useful, at times. Not always, but on occasion it serves its purpose."

"Which is what, exactly?"

She ignored that. "Did you think the Ceid just wouldn't *notice* that Durrel disappeared from prison? Celyn, don't underestimate the family. If they find him, they will kill him."

"Then they won't find him. And you can tell *the family* that we know who killed your mother. It's a man called Karst, and —"

"Karst?" She sounded uncertain. "Do you have proof?"

"Not yet." I couldn't very well tell Koya about the footprints in Talth's bedroom. But if she knew anything . . . "Did you know your mother was involved with Ferrymen?"

"Yes," she said after a long moment. "Not at first, of course, but — yes. And you think that's what got her killed?"

"You had to have suspected something."

She hesitated, lifting one graceful arm to adjust her wrap. "I can't talk about this."

"Damn it, Koya —" I broke off. She stood there before me, tall as a young man, that blue velvet draped over her shoulder — and I had it at last. "You're working with Lord Ragn," I said. It was *Koya* I'd seen on the docks that night, dressed as a stable hand and carrying a pistol, her velvet wrap discarded on the bench at Charicaux.

"Clever girl," she said, a faint smile flickering to life again. "I told him you'd figure it out. But it isn't what you think. We're not *Ferrymen*. We're just in a position to help people, sometimes."

"*Desperate* people. Sarists. Magic users."

She was nodding urgently. "People like you. Like Lady Merista. And Geirt."

"Geirt?" At once I remembered that afternoon at the warehouse, the strange, strong urge I'd had to touch Geirt's arm, and the surprise I'd felt when nothing happened. "Geirt's missing."

"No she's not." That Ceid smile again.

"I see." I wasn't sure whether to be relieved or concerned by this revelation, that Lord Ragn had spirited away the witness who might identify him as the man in Talth Ceid's bedchamber. "How did you get involved? I'm guessing Talth didn't raise you to rescue refugees." I didn't entirely believe her yet, but I wanted to keep her talking.

She gave one sharp laugh. "Hardly. *Her* only interest in a Sarist would have been how she could make a profit from him." She shifted her wrap and continued, "About a year ago, one of Mother's housemaids became pregnant. I found her crying in the Bal Marse kitchen one day, and she told me she was afraid of what would happen to her and the baby."

"Sent to the Celystra." It was the usual fate for ill-gotten babes and their mothers; just how Werne and I had ended up there, in fact. I shoved that thought from my mind. "Did you know she was magical?"

"No, that was just brilliant dumb luck. I found her a post in another house, but it wasn't far enough. She needed to get out of Gerse. And I knew that the Decath had a property outside the city, and so one day I simply asked Lord Ragn if he could help her. He'd always been kind to me, the few times I'd met him with Father.

"So he sent the girl to Favom Court." Koya paused, remembering. "I couldn't stop thinking about her, how brave she was. And how I had, for the first time in my life, defied my mother. And for such a noble cause! It was intoxicating. After that, it was almost easy. A neighbor's footman asked about the girl I'd sent to Favom; his cousins were being watched by Greenmen. Ragn found them jobs in Brionry. And it's been like that ever since. People just find us, and we help them move on. And more than that! Some of the people we've saved have gone on to join Prince Wierolf's army."

"All right, so you're running your own operation," I said, still a little skeptical. "In defiance of the Ferrymen."

"Yes! And don't you see how important that is! Those people who fall into the Ferrymen's clutches, Celyn, there's no hope for them. They keep them like prisoners until they work off their debts. And when they can't work them anymore . . ." She swiftly drew a slashing fingernail across each wrist, pantomiming severed hands, the punishment for accused Sarists, under the cruel method of execution used inside the Celystra. Their hands were cut off and burned, their eyes put out, their skin flayed, their bodies finally hung upside down in a public circle to bleed to death as Goddess-fearing Gersins watched in smug, satisfied horror.

Koya swept up her skirts gracefully and paced the narrow passage-way. "Everything was going smoothly until my mother died. I think something's gone wrong, but Ragn won't tell me."

"What kind of something? Gone wrong how?"

"I don't know. He's — nervous, like I've never seen him. Secretive. I want to say it's because he's worried for Durrel, but that's not it."

"What do you think happened? What changed?"

252

"A month or so ago Ragn had dinner with someone from the Celystra — he has to do that, to maintain appearances — and something spooked him. Since then he's been increasingly evasive. When I ask questions, he won't answer me. He makes arrangements without telling me, and changes details at the last minute. I'm worried for him. I'm afraid it might have to do with — everything else."

From the way she said that, I understood well enough what "everything else" meant. "I *know* you know more than you're saying about your mother's death."

Koya shook her head. "Only that it wasn't Durrel or me who killed her. Beyond that — nothing, I'm afraid. I'm telling you the truth."

"Then at least help me find something that implicates Karst. Records, letters — you could get access to your mother's business papers."

"It's not that easy," she said. "Barris does all of that now, and it would look awfully suspicious for frivolous, *ridiculous* Koya to suddenly start snooping around in Mother's affairs." She took a breath. "But I'll try."

I looked at her, all gown and shoes and careless, reckless beauty. "Why do you do — all of this?" I waved a vague hand at her dress and hair.

She gave a weary sigh. "It's impossible to keep a secret in Gerse society," she said. "Gossip is the currency that keeps this town running, after all. And silly, drunken, dissolute Koya who's in love with her stepfather? Better they think that than learn the truth."

"That she's smuggling Sarist refugees to safety at great risk to herself?"

"Why, that's just incredible!" she cried in a gay voice, loud enough to be overheard. "What a delicious imagination you have, Celyn! What other scandalous adventures have I been up to?"

"I think Tiboran must have laughed at your birth," I said.

Her smile dipped a bit. "Well, I do seem to have a natural capacity for playing the brainless coquette," she said.

"Not brainless," I said. "Never brainless. Lonely, maybe. But you're plainly no fool."

She regarded me through shadowed eyes, and I couldn't tell what she was thinking. "Thank you," she finally said, and for the first time that night I thought I saw a crack in her mask. "I will see what I can turn up, if you promise to be careful. I must go now, but will you tell Durrel I'm sorry?"

"For what?"

"He knows."

That night it was too hot and muggy to sleep. People all over Gerse were dragging pallets onto rooftops, balconies, and airy sleeping galleries. Rat was at Hobin's, where there was actually a chance to catch some breeze from the river. I lay awake beneath the open window, thinking about Koya's revelation. It was incredible to me that someone like her — who had every advantage possible in our fair city — would even bother to help a few poor Sarists to safety. *People like you*, she'd said. What would I do with a rescue like that, swept out of Llyvraneth, somewhere Werne couldn't track me down? Somewhere his grasping, magic-hunting fingers couldn't reach? But I'd tried that before, running away with the Nemair, and I'd just ended up right back in Gerse, wasting my days while *Koya* risked everything to save people like me.

The tiny vial of Tincture of the Moon still sat on my windowsill, drinking in moonlight and spilling it back like an amber prism. I studied the little bottle. There was scarcely a drop left swirling inside the dark glass. It had a milky, metallic gloss to it, like quicksilver. I remembered the ingredients from the herbal in the apothecary's shop — the pearl, the wine, the *tsairn*, or silver. The silver. From my apprenticeship with Lady Nemair, I had a passing knowledge of some medicine, and the healing (or otherwise) properties of various preparations and their ingredients.

But clearly I was an idiot, because here it was staring me in the face. The *silver*.

I sat up and grabbed the vial. I knew what Koya had wanted this tincture for. And it wasn't poison. Not exactly.

Feeling hot and cold all over, I held the little bottle up to the light. Silver dampened magic, which was why Lord Ragn's refugee had worn heaps of it — heavy chains and belts and bracelets wound about her limbs. And why the Bal Marse dungeon and Inquisitors' torture chambers all over town had been outfitted with silver shackles. But it only worked so long as you had the silver in contact with your skin. Take off the necklace, the rings, and you'd light up like a candle flame, for anyone with the power — or the tools — to see.

Was it possible? Could this work? If so, Koya was half brilliant, and I needed to know. There was one way to test it. Ignoring the fact that the only person I knew of to actually ingest any Tincture of the Moon was now *dead* from it (but she'd had most of a whole vial, I told myself), I swiftly upended the bottle, letting the single silvery drop swirl down to the lip of the glass, and into my mouth.

CHAPTER TWENTY-SIX

As soon as I did it, I knew it was a mistake. Only a drop of the stuff, barely enough to survive on my tongue, but the burn from the silver knocked me to my hands and knees, gasping from the searing pain that shrieked through my throat and mouth. *Water.* Suddenly, desperately, thirsty, I tried to crawl toward the kitchen, but my legs wouldn't hold me, and I spilled to the floor, unable to move. *Hours of silent agony* — why did that sound familiar? A cramp seized my limbs, and I tried to cry out, but couldn't open my mouth to scream.

I lay there, immobile but writhing inside, the floor shifting in weird, smoky patterns under my cheek. As the cold took my feet and hands, my shins and wrists and forearms, the room seemed to change size around me, and I reached out for the water pitcher — now close at hand, now half a league away. My fingers curled and uncurled uncontrollably against the wooden floor, trying to grasp the handle. Somewhere, one of the moons, maybe, a god banged on the earth, making the whole building shake.

So this was what it felt like to die. I was just getting used to the idea, my lungs boiling in my icy chest, when thunder split the sky, and horses crashed into me — and then somebody was peeling away all my skin. And I'm sure I screamed.

Everything hurt. And then nothing hurt, but everything was too *loud.* And then I was horribly, horribly sick, and someone was holding a damp cloth to my face, and someone else was yelling.

"Are you out of your *mind*? What in hells were you thinking, Celyn?" That voice, unmistakably, was Durrel. I tried to move, to look around, but strong arms held me down. I blinked, almost the only thing I had strength for, and through the haze of my vision, I thought I recognized . . .

golden hair, blue sleeves. *Koya?* I struggled to sit up, but Koya was surprisingly strong, and she held me down with considerable force.

"You won't be able to move much for a few hours," she said softly, and her voice next to my ear was like being sanded to death by wool wadding. "It's always like that after. But yes, what *were* you thinking?"

I stared at her, at the red face of Durrel swimming in and out of my vision, and I couldn't remember. "I —" My voice was a choke, a rattle, no sound at all.

"You could have *killed* yourself!"

"Enough. Stop. She needs to rest." Koya rose from the edge of the bed and I watched a blur of blue put something that might have been an arm around something that might have been a person, and move out of my field of vision.

I couldn't sleep after that, just lay in a fog of alternating clarity and confusion, feeling cold through to my very bones, and trying not to panic. I clearly remembered *what* I'd done — I'd swallowed the last of the Tincture of the Moon from the bottle we'd found behind Talth's fireplace — but what escaped me now was *why*. Something important, something to do with Koya . . . but that didn't seem right. And now I'd almost killed myself and couldn't even remember the reason. I stared up at the unfamiliar ceiling, which advanced and receded as I watched it, wondering where I was. Koya's house, perhaps.

Finally, when I imagined feeling returning to my hands and feet, Durrel came back. Alone this time. And quieter. He knelt beside the bed, and his face was lined with concern. With effort, I fixed him clearly in my gaze, and he gave what was obviously trying to be a smile, and failing miserably.

"I'm sorry." I don't know which one of us said it, but his fingers came up to brush a damp strand of hair from my forehead, and it was everything I could do not to shriek from the pain of his touch on my skin.

"How —" *How did you find me?* I wanted to say, but lacked the energy. He understood anyway.

"I had to see you. I — after you left the Temple, I was angry and so *sick* of being cooped up in there, so I went for a walk. And somehow I found myself down in Seventh, outside your building. I know, I shouldn't have gone out — but damn the gods, I'm glad I did!" He took a moment, let the fury subside. He tried a smile instead. "I realize you were upset, but suicide? Over me? Celyn, I'm touched."

I coughed out a painful laugh, and Durrel sobered again.

"Koya says you'll be fine. Eventually. I don't understand. What were you doing?"

I tried to shake my head. "I — I can't *remember*," I said, and my voice sounded strained and whiny. "Why —?" It was too much effort to put into words. Why would Koya be so knowledgeable about the effects of the poison? The answer was somewhere; I'd had it a moment ago, before I'd gone and nearly killed myself trying to prove . . . *what*?

Durrel took my hand and held it to his face. His breath was hot and gentle on my cold fingers, and I closed my eyes with a sigh. "I'm sorry. It was stupid."

"Don't do anything like that again," he said. "I couldn't stand it, when I found you, lying there on the floor, the vial still in your hand. . . ." His voice shook, and I opened my eyes, to see him staring at me, an odd brightness in his charcoal-colored eyes.

"It wasn't a fatal dose," I said.

"You didn't *know* that."

I shook my head. "No, I —" But it was gone again. "I know what it was for. I mean, I *knew* what it was for. Why she wanted it —"

"Hist. It doesn't matter."

Of course it mattered! The only reason for my colossal idiocy, and now I'd lost it. Helplessly, furiously, I felt hot tears spring up and blot my cheeks. I turned away from Durrel.

At that moment, Koya returned, carrying a basin of water, with a length of linen draped over one arm. "Lord Durrel," she said rather formally, "if you'll excuse us, I have a patient to tend, and feminine modesty to defend. Out."

Obviously reluctant, Durrel rose from my side and edged toward the door, staring back at us, at me, until finally the door whispered shut behind him.

"Do you have to do that?" I asked, nodding toward the basin.

"No," she said. "I just wanted him out so we could talk." She settled beside me. "Normally we give it with a preparation of poppy, to ease the effects of the poison. It is still a poison," she said. "And you're luckier than you know."

"What is it for?" I asked. I had known, earlier.

Koya gave me a sad smile. "You'll figure it out."

They made me stay at Koya's for two more days, during which the numbing effects of the tincture held me fast to the bed. Durrel hovered nearby, alternately attentive and restless, until his own edginess nearly drove me crazy. Koya and I finally made him promise to return to the Temple and keep out of sight and off the street.

"She can't hide you here," I insisted. "What if Barris shows up?"

"I know," he said. "It's just — I don't know what to *do* with myself, all day, with you —" He stopped that sentence still unfinished, but I knew what he wanted to say. We'd been on the verge of proving Karst's guilt and Talth's connection to the Ferrymen, and I'd gone and blown everything by my own stupidity, and until I was well enough — or at least remembered what the hells I'd been trying to prove — our investigation was at a standstill. "I need my protector," he said softly.

From across the room, Koya made a face, but eventually he gave in, with Koya promising that her own boat would deliver Durrel safely back to the inn, where Eske would no doubt keep an eye on him. "You two are worse than the guards at the Keep," he said, and Koya and I exchanged looks of satisfaction.

Sometime on the third day, I woke to find myself blessedly alone, at last. I was hot and weary and *starving*, but mostly I felt restless, tired of being tied down to a sickbed and anxious to get back and figure out whatever it was I'd been trying to do. Gingerly I peeled myself off the mattress and, bracing myself for the vertigo, carefully stood.

I was naked. Of course I was. I turned my head slowly, looking over the room for my clothes. It had been night when I'd drunk the poison; I'd had on just my smock, which was probably ruined. Well, Koya appreciated outrageous behavior. I tugged the damp sheet from the mattress and wrapped it around myself, then shuffled out into the corridor. Amateurs. They hadn't even bothered to *try* locking the door. Although I did have to step carefully over one of the huge, shaggy sighthounds, which had stretched itself across the threshold and refused to budge when I opened the door.

The maid, Vrena, was just outside. Perfect. I couldn't remember why I'd tried to kill myself, but the name of Koya's servant was *right there*. She let out a little screech when she saw me, and tried to usher me back inside my room. I was small and sick, but I resisted. "Fetch Mistress Koya," I suggested.

"She's not home," Vrena said. "Oh, lady, she'll kill me if she finds you gone" — this, as I tried to push past her into the corridor.

She wouldn't if she found Vrena knocked unconscious and tied to one of the atrium pillars, but I didn't have the energy to suggest it. "Just . . . get me some clothes?"

She nodded her agreement and hurried off down the hallway. I went the other direction, seized by an idea. I was half mad (and more than half naked), but this was the best opportunity I was likely to have to search Koya's house. Maybe she hadn't killed her mother — but she knew more than she'd admitted about Talth's death, she was neck-deep in her own involvement with smuggling Sarist refugees, and she was *definitely* withholding key information about the Tincture of the Moon. If she wouldn't tell me, then I'd have to figure it out myself.

I found her bedroom easily, the most ridiculously opulent suite in the house, every inch of it gilded or colored in blue silk. She had left that door unlocked as well. I went in, my sheet trailing behind me like a train. Koya appeared to share her mother's penchant for darkness; the room's large windows were hung with heavy drapes, and I realized that these were the rooms of someone who often worked nights and needed to sleep during the day. I shoved one set aside, bathing the chambers with hot afternoon sun and stirring up a cloud of spicy-scented dust. Though there were three vast silken pillows on the floor, the damask counterpane on Koya's bed was covered with gray hairs from the dogs. Near the window was a spindly desk with outsized carvings dripping gilt, and I had only to turn halfway to reach the matching dressing table with its bounty of conveniently placed hairpins. My hands only shook a little as I popped the fragile gilded lock. I steadied myself against the edge of the desk, breathing hard.

The desk was mostly empty, but I pushed aside the quills and various invitations to society events to locate the spring that released the hidden panel inside the drawer, where the real secrets lay. It would have been nice to discover a memorandum detailing the uses of Tincture of the Moon, but I was none so lucky. Only a letter or two from contacts in Brionry or Wolt, offering positions as clerks or nursemaids for reliable workers. Under the letters was a ledger book, with monetary notations — some of them astronomical — carefully detailed, but without a single identifying word. Certainly nothing that said, "Cost of forged Brion passport, twenty crowns." I rubbed at my chest, where my heart still banged unevenly, relieved at least that Lord Ragn and Koya's plans for their smuggled Sarists didn't stop at the Gerse dockyards.

Tucked inside the ledger, its crease weak from wear, was a letter to Koya from her mother, a spewing, vitriolic rant accusing Koya of every conceivable offense, from ingratitude over her marriage to Stantin Koyuz, to trying to bilk Talth of her fortune, to "base designs" with Durrel. I tossed it back inside the hollow of the desk like it had burned me. Why would anybody keep such a nasty thing?

There was nothing in the room, however, that explained my stunt with the poison. I leaned heavily against the bedpost, feeling a little dizzy. What now?

There was something else missing, as well, I realized, staring hard at the blue and gold furnishings. In all this vast room, with Koya's bed and Koya's clothes and Koya's books, there was no trace of magic — nothing at all from the Sarists she must have had contact with. I turned about the room, frowning. I should find at least a faint spark here and there. Footprints. Fingerprints. *Something.*

I wanted a closer look, but at that point Vrena reappeared. With a firm shake of her head, she pointed me out of Koya's chambers, closing the door with a sharp click behind me. The clothes she brought me appeared to be her own castoffs, a threadbare smock about my size, and a plain brown kirtle with a stained skirt. I decided not to push my favor with Tiboran (or Vrena) and didn't ask for shoes.

The maid followed me anxiously to the riverside doors. "Tell your mistress I had business to attend to," I said. The urge to get out of Koya's house was overwhelming, like insects crawling along my insides. I just hadn't decided where I wanted to be instead.

"She won't like that at all."

At that moment I wasn't sure I cared what Mistress Koya liked or not.

I'd told Koya's boatman to take me back to the bakery, but as we skirted through the murky water toward the center of town, the feeling of dread and panic I'd felt since taking the poison only intensified. I couldn't help tallying up the crises in my mind as we traveled. How to prove that Karst killed Talth? What had Koya meant when she said something had spooked Lord Ragn? Would Berdal make it safely through to the front with his secret maps of Gerse? Would Durrel stay put at the Temple until we figured out our next move? And what had become of Raffin? Troubles twisted in on one another until I felt seasick from them. I looked up into the sky, where the green dome of the Celystra loomed over the city. Koya had said Ragn's puzzling behavior had started after he'd dined with somebody from the Celystra. And back when this had all started, Raffin had made that curious remark about not asking questions of other Greenmen.

It seemed that everything, as always, came back to the Inquisition.

I chewed on this for a bit and then gave Koya's boatman a new direction. He frowned, dubious, but took me there at my insistence, and a few minutes later we pulled up alongside the Celystra's beautifully maintained riverside promenade.

I dragged myself up onshore, dizzy from the effort and the heat. The boatman offered to accompany me and then promised to wait as I shook him off, stepping tenderly over the sunbaked cobbles in my bare feet.

Across High Street, the bar where Raffin had taken me was a little emptier this time of day. Standing there, surrounded on all sides by green, I almost changed my mind. *Don't be an idiot*, I told myself. Greenmen or no, a tavern was still Tiboran's domain, and I had nothing to fear.

Or at least I'd see if there was any truth to Raffin's claim about Werne's order to leave me alone. It was the height of idiocy to present myself, neatly gift-wrapped, to a room full of guards, but it still wasn't the dumbest thing I'd done this week. Half a dozen pairs of eyes swung my way as I pushed open the tavern doors, and for a moment I felt like I was still wearing nothing but Koya's sheet. I took a shaky breath and came inside.

"I'm looking for a friend," I said, trying to pitch my voice calm and level.

"I'd like to be your friend," said a gangly young guard in the back, rising from his seat, but his tablemate pulled him back down again and whispered fiercely in his ear. By the way the first guard's face turned scarlet, I had an ugly suspicion what was said. I forced myself to take a few more steps inside.

"I'm trying to locate Raffin Taradyce," I said. "Some of you may have seen me here with him before. Does anyone know where he is?"

That was met with a stony, chilling silence, and for a sickening moment I was all too afraid what had happened. But finally an older guard, neat as a nob in his uniform, turned from his fellows and met my eyes.

"I know him," he said. "Partners with Brum, right?"

I didn't know Raffin's partner's name, but I gestured with my hand to indicate the burly size of the guard I'd seen patrolling with him.

"I haven't seen Taradyce in a few days," the guard said. "But we can ask around. Were you trying to get a message to him?"

"Just looking," I said with as much dignity as I could muster. "He knows how to reach me. If you see him, can you let him know I need to speak to him?"

Expressionless faces pulled together across tables, things were whispered, a few hands went for nightsticks, but eventually the Inquisitor's order must have prevailed. The spokesman turned to me again.

"We have your message. You may wish to leave now."

And with that, I could not have agreed more. I fled back to the street and into the boat as fast as I could, stubbing a toe on a cobble and tearing my toenail. The whole litany of recent abuses threatened to overwhelm me, and I sat the rest of the ride home a small, sniffling bundle of misery.

CHAPTER TWENTY-SEVEN

When I stepped back inside the bakery that afternoon, it was to absolute dead silence, shocked faces turning my way, and at least one customer getting up and leaving. In fairness, I was barefoot and wearing somebody else's clothes and my hair hadn't been combed in *days*; I probably did look like the Allegory of Wantonness from a cautionary play. But it was Grea in the kitchen, slowly setting down her knife, whose expression stopped me cold. Rat hurried over to me, his own face drawn with concern.

And before I knew it, he had flung his arms around me and was absolutely crushing me. "You had us scared to death," he said. "Aunt had no idea where Lord Durrel carried you off to."

Minutes later, having finally released me and shuttled me to privacy at a table in the kitchen, Rat and Grea shoveled loaf upon bowl of hot, hearty food into me. I had to give them a detailed accounting of my last two and a half days before they would really believe I was actually back home and safe. "But what happened?" Rat demanded. "Aunt said you were sick."

I shook him off, not yet ready to explain to *everyone* that I'd been testing Talth Ceid's murder weapon on myself. When I was sufficiently fed, in their opinion, Rat turned a pointed gaze to Grea. "We should tell her. You know she'll find out." At her nod, he continued. "The Watch was here. The day before yesterday."

"With Barris Ceid," Grea's voice was thick with disgust. "Acting like they owned the place. Pawing their way through the rooms and helping themselves to a whole night's product."

"Through the rooms?" I asked. "Our rooms? Did they find anything?"

"What's to find?" said Grea. "They were looking for you and Lord Durrel, who we were obviously not concealing. Told them your clothes were mine, left from when I was a slim young girl," she added with a wink. Grea had a good eight inches on me, but apparently it had convinced the guards.

I scowled at this news. "What if they come back?"

"They probably will," Rat said. "Our explanations were hardly satisfactory, and I doubt they'll lose their motivation to track down the missing Decath any time soon."

The day was getting better and better. I pulled myself up to go — somewhere else, but the look Grea fixed me with was severe. "Upstairs with you. To bed. And if anybody shows up asking after you, you're my niece."

"I've been sleeping the last two days," I objected as Rat half pulled me up the stairs. I stopped him in the snug landing. "My clothes weren't the only thing in that room," I said quietly. I had never taken Reynart's magic primer back to its hiding place in the roof.

"I know. Don't worry; it's safe."

"Where?"

"I took it to Hobin's."

"Hobin's!"

"Marau's balls, I'm only kidding," he said, trotting up the rest of the stairs. "I sold it to Grillig."

I stared at him a moment, that cheeky, unconcerned grin, then dissolved into helpless laughter.

The rest of that day and the next dragged out hot and intolerable. Grea fussed, Rat kept his ear to the ground, and Durrel came by to visit, bringing word that Koya was still concerned, and would I consider coming back to stay with her? I declined, reminding Durrel that *he* was supposed to stay put at the Temple. He merely shrugged, and I let myself ignore the signs that he was behaving recklessly.

But as for reminders for myself? They didn't come. Though I searched every inch of Rat's well-swept floor, I couldn't find the tincture bottle again, and I was no closer to remembering what I'd thought I'd discovered about Koya's poison. Was it that Koya had killed Talth? That awful letter I'd seen would certainly give anyone motive for matricide — but somehow that wasn't right. It didn't click any tumblers in my brain, which was as dull and sluggish as if still fogged with poison.

Around dusk on the following evening, when the dinnertime crowd was thinning out, Rat scurried up to the apartment to fetch me. "You'd better get down there," he said. "Your brother's back."

I just stared at him stupidly, momentarily unable to fit this latest development into the week's catalogue of torments. But finally I hauled myself to my feet and followed dumbly after, down the stairs, and into the common room, where the remaining customers were tripping over themselves to depart. I didn't see Werne at first, so I pushed through to the doors, and caught a glimpse of a low, green boat moored outside, where two big Greenmen were lifting something — somebody — to shore. Tall and bent with exhaustion, their charge wore nothing but a rough, gray tunic belted to his knees. As he tried to straighten, I caught a flash of sunlight on bright hair.

"Raffin!" I cried.

He looked ragged and weak — with a spectacular bruise all across one cheek from where Durrel had punched him — but he found a sleepy grin for me. A third Greenman held the bakery door open for Raffin's guards to drag him inside. Grea was right there, slipping one of her great strong arms around him. He winced and sucked in his breath as she eased him down into a chair.

"What is this?" I said loudly, because everyone was ignoring me. The Greenmen parted, and Werne finally came forward. He gave me a little bow, and I backed up a couple of paces, bumping into the bread counter.

"Well met, sister," he said. "Mistress Grea, it gives me great pleasure to see what fine use you have made of the Goddess's bounty. May you continue to enjoy her blessing."

Grea looked up from Raffin and nodded uncertainly. "What's going on here?" I asked, a cold edge to my voice.

Werne gave a little cough. "It, ah, came to my attention that you had made certain inquiries into the location and condition of one of the Holy Mother's servants. I feared you would not heed a message from me, so . . ." He trailed off oddly, his hands lifted halfway between me and Raffin, as if he weren't sure exactly what to do with them.

"What did you do to him?" I demanded. "I was told his *ribs* were cracked. But he looks like —" Something sharp hit me in the foot, and Rat was at my side, his face expressionless.

Werne's lips thinned, and there was a deep line between his thick brows. "Unfortunately there was some miscommunication regarding his — treatment while in our care at the hospital ward." The note in his voice, the expression on his face, didn't track. If I didn't know better, I'd almost say he was uncomfortable. Apologetic, even.

I knew better. Raffin was hunched forward slightly, breathing shallowly, which seemed right for cracked ribs, but I didn't like the too-loose way his limbs fit together, as if he were afraid to move his arms. I was afraid I understood why. "Did you torture him?"

"Of course not!" Werne said hastily. "But discipline was called for. He abused the authority of his uniform —"

"The authority of his uniform? Do you know what those thugs of yours *do*, in back alleys, because everyone is afraid of the uniform? Why don't you discipline some of *them*!"

"Silence!" One of the Greenmen barked at me. "Do not raise your voice to His Grace!"

"Guardsman!" Werne held the palms of his hands to his forehead, breathing evenly. "Captain, I think the mistress of this place has our, ah, patient well in hand. Take your men and wait for me outside."

"You can go with them," I said, kneeling beside Raffin. I couldn't read the expression on his face, beyond the grimace of pain with every breath. "We'll take him from here."

"Sister, please — Mistress Grea, perhaps you ought to get this young man to bed. I believe his wounds are paining him."

I burst to my feet, outraged, but Raffin managed, "It's all right, peach," and a weak nod. Everyone filed out of the common room at once — Grea and Rat with Raffin between them, the Greenmen ushering the remaining customers outside — leaving me alone with the Inquisitor. I was pressed up against the bakery counter as Werne advanced on me. I tried to pull back —

And he eased off, a frown creasing his forehead. "Will — will you sit?" he said, indicating a chair. I shook my head.

"What do you *want*?" I said. "You can't think that returning Raffin will buy my cooperation."

"No. I —" He paused, frowning deeper. "I handled our last encounter poorly. I should have realized you would not understand the situation as I did."

"I understood you perfectly."

"I only wish to speak to you," he said, sliding into a chair. "Can you not manage that much civility for a few moments' time?"

I scowled, my chest tight. He was right; I was not particularly good at staying calm and civil in his presence. It gave everything he'd always said of me a little truth — that I was wild, uncontrollable, *a corrupt thing unworthy of the gods* — and I didn't want that. So I scrunched into the seat opposite him, feeling damnably like his misbehaving little sister. He reached his hands across the table, but I kept mine folded tight in my lap.

Now that I was seated calmly, Werne didn't seem to know what to say to me. For a long moment he just *looked* at me, staring intently, searching my face for — I don't know what. I made myself stop biting my lip.

When he finally spoke, it was nothing I'd expected. "You look like our mother," he said.

One hand flew to my face, my fingers brushing over chin, lips, scarred cheek. "You never told me her name," I said, then wished the words back. Treacherous tongue; this was nothing to me. I was technically Werne's half sister, born in the Celystra to his mother by some unknown sire. Having achieved the ultimate glory for the Goddess, she had then died in grace, to be remembered, sanctified, an anonymous saint. And I'd stopped caring about any of this years ago.

"You always hated me for that," he said. There was a question in there, buried deep. I kept my mouth shut this time; he wasn't going to get anything more from me. "Very well," he said softly. "It was Fenna."

I sat still, impassive — but inside I was turning the word over, looking for openings, seeing if it held any secrets for me. It was nothing, just two soft syllables that slipped in and out of the world.

"I know you bear rancor for me," Werne said. "You think I should have protected you better at the Celystra, and you may be right. I —" He took a deep breath and leaned toward me. "I am sorry for whatever passed between us, and I want to mend it."

I pulled back as if he'd struck me. "You don't even understand what you've done," I said. "Not to me, but to *everyone*. Did you see the burned house down the lane? That was your handiwork. And now you bring Raffin in here half dead from beatings that your men gave him, and you can't even see the trouble with that! There's no mending what's wrong here."

"Sister — Celyn." Werne paused briefly, and in that moment I had never hated that cursed alias more. "The things I did, have done — I wished only to protect you. It's hard for you to see that, I understand."

I was silent, looking everywhere but at Werne. I didn't want to have this conversation, with him trying to play the penitent one, all the while looking at me and only seeing the corrupt thing who'd lost his Goddess's favor six years ago. I knew what he wanted from me; my mother's name was just another bribe, like the flour and the release of Raffin.

A moment later, there were footsteps on the stairs, and Grea descended into the common room. Werne rose. "I know you've never understood the price the Goddess has asked," he said. "This work she has called me to, but believe me when I say I am only her tool, the instrument of her work."

"Her Holy Arrow." But he'd never hear the irony in my voice.

"*Exactly.* And it is larger than me, or you, or any one of us — but you are my blood kin, and Celys cherishes family above all else."

I pulled away from the table. "I don't have a family," I said, my voice as calm and *civil* as his.

There was something in his face that hurt to look at, but I did it. "Celyn, please." He took a step forward, his voice almost plaintive. "I'm not the monster you imagine me to be."

"No," I agreed. "You're worse." And without waiting for whatever poison would come out of his mouth next, I turned and went straight back upstairs.

Up in the apartment, the one inadequate bed had been given over to Raffin. He lay facedown, breathing shallowly, his back a mass of bandages, stained and stiff with blood and ointment. I hung back in the doorway until Rat pulled me inside.

"'S'all right, peach. It's not as bad as it looks." Raffin's voice was muffled, a little slurred.

"Not anymore, anyway," Rat said. "Thanks to a little poppy. The wounds look to be a few days old."

"What did they do?" I made myself ask, made myself come forward to see how badly Raffin was hurt. I was painfully aware of my share of the blame for his injuries, and I would not flinch at the sight of them.

"Cane," he said. "Fourteen lashes. Fourteen! And I bore them like a man, Father."

"How much poppy did you give him?" I asked Rat, mostly to blot out the image of Raffin strapped to the Hanging Ash in the Celystra courtyard, flogged with a switch from the sacred tree. I had seen it before, and hoped never to witness it again.

"There may have been some wine too."

"Aw, don't fret so," Raffin said more clearly this time. "They don't like to be too rough on their own. I will be" — he winced — "fresh as milk in a few more days, and then the ladies will have fourteen impressive scars to admire. And I have a shiny new Writ of Discommendation to match them."

I felt sick. Beaten and drummed out of the Guard for what we'd done! Regardless of how I felt about the Greenmen, this wasn't good news.

Raffin's father would probably disown him. "You sound almost proud of yourself."

He managed the start of a grin, though I could tell it hurt his face. "Come closer, peach. I have to tell you something." I knelt beside the bed. Raffin's eyes were too bright, his face glossy with perspiration. "Your man came to see me at the Keep," he said, voice low.

"Karst? Did *he* hurt you?"

"No, that's the thing." Raffin turned his face to me. "We recognized each other."

"I don't understand."

"That's what I've been trying to tell you," he said. "I'd seen him before, making deliveries at the Celystra."

CHAPTER TWENTY-EIGHT

"Deliveries?" Durrel frowned, looking down at Raffin. It was hours later, night; Raffin had recovered enough to sit up in bed and recount his tale as if it had been a heroic adventure. Rat had fetched Durrel back to the bakery, and his relief at seeing Raffin almost equaled his performance at my sickbed earlier in the week. After a brief reunion and a simple meal, I had Raffin repeat what he'd told me.

"He means *people*," I said, my voice harsh. "Karst is selling out his Sarist clients to the Inquisition!"

"How many of these 'deliveries' did you witness?" Durrel asked.

"Only the one. I was on duty at that gate just once, but the things I've heard — there were probably others." Raffin's face was expressionless, and I felt my guilt at him losing his post slipping away.

"But it doesn't make any sense," I said. "The Inquisition doesn't pay bounties on heretics. They consider informing on your neighbor to be a devout Celyst's moral duty."

"I told you," Raffin said, "something rotten is going on up there. If you're getting closer to figuring out whatever it is, be careful. Or, well." He gestured weakly at his own injured body.

"He's right," I said to Durrel. "We've been much too visible lately. We need to get you back to the Temple. The bakery isn't safe." Not with Barris and the Watch lurking about, and the Lord High Inquisitor popping in for a friendly fraternal chat anytime he felt like it. *I* wanted to leave, with a Greenman in my bed and the taint of the Inquisition downstairs.

Durrel didn't budge. He was still watching Raffin, the same cold expression on his face, jaw set. "Was my wife involved in this?" The words were thin, forced through his lips with effort.

"Brother, don't do this to yourself."

"*Was my wife involved in this!*" Durrel's hands had curled into fists, and he was scaring me a little.

Raffin met his friend's gaze evenly. "I heard her name —"

Durrel made a cry of rage and rammed his fist into the wall, hard enough to shed plaster. He turned on his heel, grabbed a bottle of wine from the makeshift kitchen, and stalked toward the stairs.

I ran after him. "Where are you going?"

He wheeled on me. "Don't worry, Celyn. I'm not going to do anything *stupid*," he said savagely, and slammed the apartment door in my face. I grabbed the handle and yanked it open again.

"Peach." I turned back. Raffin was watching the door, looking pale and weary. "Let him go," he said.

"But —"

"Sometimes a man has to be on his own," he said. "He won't welcome you, not in that mood."

Everything in me screamed at me to go with Durrel, but Raffin's voice, so tired and reasonable, held me back. Scowling deeply, I shut the door, planted myself back on the floor beside his bed, and said, "Tell me *exactly* what you know."

It wasn't much, in the end. Just what he'd told us already, that he'd seen Karst turn over two people, both women, to guards at the Celystra, in exchange for payment in banknotes. The women were chained in silver, and they'd been taken to a plain cell on the main level, before being fetched away again by Confessors the next day, to *disappear* into the clutches of the Inquisition like so many others.

"We were ordered not to touch them, not to let any harm come to them," Raffin said.

"Strange orders for Greenmen. And you don't know what became of them? You never saw another exchange like that again?"

He shook his head. "It was only my first week there, before they assigned my street patrol. But I heard about other cases like it. Not many, just once or twice more while I was there."

I nodded, thinking this through. "And what did you hear of Talth Ceid?"

Raffin's bruised face twisted. "Nothing specific. I think they mostly dealt with your Karst, or men like him. But I saw her name once in a record book; you know how they love their records at the Celystra. And when I tried to ask about her — just casual curiosity about my friend's wife, mind you — they dropped the discussion like a hot pot and reassigned me to another post."

It was something, at least. Finally, a tangible link between Talth, her killer, and "rotten" doings at the Celystra.

"One more thing, peach. I don't know if it's important, but —"

"What is it?" I was trying to figure out how to get my hands on those Celystra records — or a matching set of Karst's, perhaps.

"That hands-off order they gave for those girls he sold us? It reminded me of the one they set for you."

A chill washed through me. My last conversation with Werne echoed in my brain, when he'd said the Celystra had work for me. I didn't like the sound of whatever arrangement Raffin had seen, and it made me even more suspicious of my brother's motives. He might claim his only desire was to renew our family ties, but I'd known him long before he was the Inquisitor, and he knew how to get what he wanted, by any means necessary, not always by force. It had been the same when I was a child at the Celystra, and it hadn't changed in all this time. Werne wanted me to hunt magic, to use my skills to supplement the methods of his Confessors. Only once had I made the mistake of pointing out a magic user to my brother, and I would never be able to make up for that.

When Raffin was finally asleep, I tracked Rat down in the bakery. He was closing a low storeroom door partially concealed behind the pantry shelves.

"Did they get anything?" I asked. Though we never spoke of it, I knew Rat kept some of his merchandise down there, in the bakery's unused beer cellar. The last I'd seen of our counterfeit Grisel had been Rat toting a crate down through that little door.

"Nothing important," he said, and passed a small, cloth-wrapped bundle into my hands. "Kept safe, as promised."

I unwrapped the object, knowing from its slight weight in my hands exactly what it was: a tiny velvet-bound book, its dark plush cover worn away almost to nothing from centuries of hands touching the edges. Reynart's chronicle on magic. I closed my eyes, my fingers curling around the little volume, feeling a ridiculous urge to kiss the thing.

"Rat, they could have —" I didn't finish the thought. Something was wrong. I stroked the binding, ran my finger around the uneven pages.

"Digger? What is it?"

The book cradled in one hand, I fanned it open, touching page after page; flicked my fingernail beneath the endpapers; lifted it to my face and blew into the spine. And nothing happened.

There wasn't really all that much magic of its own right in the book — it was mostly *about* magic, not actually magical — but usually enough power sparked to life from all the magical hands that had handled it through the years to make it a challenge for me to read. But now — I squeezed the book tight, but no spark of glitter, no swirl of shimmering dust motes, no invisible light to brighten the pages awoke to my touch. I took a sharp breath. Maybe the magical residue had finally run out or worn off.

But I knew better. It wasn't the book that had changed.

It was me.

And all in that one moment, I finally remembered what I'd figured out about the Tincture of the Moon. That it dampened magic — from the *inside*.

"Digger?"

I slammed the little book shut and tucked it inside my bodice. "Thank you," I said. "I have to go."

Turning to leave, I felt Rat's hand brush my shoulder. He was looking at the roll of clothes I'd stuffed under my arm. "You're not coming back, are you?"

"Time to move on," I said, then softened. "At least until this thing with Durrel is settled."

There was a quirk to his lip at that. "You'll have to find somebody else to bail you out of gaol," he said.

I gave his shoulder a companionable punch. "So will you."

I had to see Koya. I hopped a boat for Cartouche; if she wasn't there, at least I could lose myself for a while in the crowds, and not have to think about what I'd done to myself.

During the sail, my thoughts flitted wildly. I finally understood about the poison, and what Koya was using it for. Essentially I'd drunk a silver cocktail; what had I *thought* it was going to do to me? I gave a flick of my fingers, watching sparks not fly, and felt curiously bereft. I'd spent most of my life hiding my magic, not even recognizing it for what it was, an extraordinary power, unique to me. A year ago I might have been glad to be rid of it — but now? I was just learning about it, about myself, what it might be. What *I* might be. I wasn't ready to give it up, but it seemed I might have thrown it away.

I found Koya in her usual spot, surrounded by her retinue. Her long hair was looped and braided elaborately, and she wore the blue gown she'd had on when I'd first met her. A long-handled mask rested gently in the crook of one arm. I recognized the costume now. She took one look at me, barreling through the crowd, and waved her friends away with a sleepy hand.

"Why, Celyn, what a surprise!" she said just a little too loudly. I wasn't fooled anymore, and I just squeezed in next to her.

"You might have just *told* me."

Koya glanced past me briefly, then led me away from the bar to a more private space back near the stage. "It isn't permanent," she said gently. "I should have warned you, but I never expected you to do anything so . . . insane." She had an expression on her face that might almost have been admiration. "Durrel thinks you're marvelous, by the way. He'd never admit it, but he's completely smitten with the way you charge straight into things."

"He ought to get to know *you*, then."

Koya gave a short, sharp laugh, but sobered quickly. "I couldn't tell him," she said, but wouldn't elaborate.

"The potion — it was for you, then?"

"Gods, no. *I* don't have magic."

I looked hard at her, searching, but — "I can't tell now. How can I be certain?"

"Well, for one thing, you can be *certain* my mother would have found a way to make a profit from it," she said bitterly.

She was probably right about that. "How long?" I said. *How long do the effects of the tincture last? I meant. How long until I get my magic back?*

She watched me carefully. "It depends. Not long; a couple of weeks, usually. Long enough to get safely out of the country."

Everything was starting to line up: Koya, Lord Ragn, the poison, and their mysterious midnight shipments at the docks. "Explain."

Koya spoke quietly. "We discovered it a few months ago. A passenger brought it; he'd been using it on his daughter. I saw instantly how valuable it could be to our work, but Ragn was skeptical. He didn't want to risk it. You saw how dangerous it is, how tricky to get the dosage just right." She looked uneasy. "But I went ahead."

"And had Durrel get it for you."

"Yes, after the original batch our passenger brought with him was gone. As you saw, it doesn't take much at all to work effectively. I hardly thought someone would use it to murder my mother!" she said. "That was just a horrible coincidence."

But I wondered. Talth being murdered with the very same elixir that Ragn and Koya were using to strip their refugees of their incriminating magic ... that was too much coincidence for even one of Tiboran's devotees to swallow. I pulled up a seat next to Koya's. "Walk me through your — operation. How does it work, what you and Lord Ragn do?"

She gave a wan smile. "Thinking of taking a trip?" When I didn't dignify that with an answer, she went on. "How it *did* work was just like I told you — people would come to us, quietly, and Lord Ragn would just as quietly send them on their way again. But it's expensive — all the little details that have to be taken care of, the new passports and lodgings and transportation, not to mention the bribes for officials to look the other way. Demand for our services went up when the war started and the Celystra started cracking down even harder on suspected Sarists. Ragn needed money."

"Your mother's?"

She nodded. "At first it seemed like a perfect plan. The Ceid are discreet, after all, and they can afford a little risk. I think Mother even liked the adventure, although her main interest was obviously financial, not humanitarian." She took a sip of her drink, loops of gold hair swaying gently around her face. "Things were going well. And then Durrel entered the picture, and after that, everything got *very* complicated."

"How does Karst fit in?"

"I don't know," she said. "He was just one of Mother's employees. Sometimes he went along to guard the shipments. But you think he killed her?"

"When did you learn they were involved with Ferrymen?"

"Not until after she died!" Koya looked so distressed there that I believed her. "We heard that Karst had been hassling some of the passengers, leaning on them for extra money, but Ragn told me Mother promised to take care of it. Maybe she didn't get a chance," she said. "They quarreled, and Karst killed her."

"It's more than that," I said, and explained what Raffin had told me, about Karst selling some of his Sarists to the Celystra. Karst clearly had ambitions of his own, and maybe Talth had wanted a piece of that little side business with the Inquisition. Or maybe she'd merely been in Karst's way. From everything I'd been told, killing Talth did seem the only way to budge her.

"What are you thinking?" Koya asked, her voice tentative.

I frowned at my lightless fingertips. "That this almost makes sense. And *almost* means something is wrong."

I probably should have stayed at Cartouche, and Koya suggested it, but I wasn't ready to sit still yet. There were too many jumbled thoughts buzzing around in my head, and I needed time and movement to sort through them. I was dodging curfew, but tonight it didn't seem to matter. As I crossed through Markettown, there were people abroad like I hadn't seen in months. A cluster of townsfolk with jugs and laundry baskets gathered by a neighborhood fountain, chatting into the night; people argued outside a closed stall in Market Circle . . . It was all so bustling and odd I wanted to stop and ask someone what was going on, but I spotted a patrol of the Night Watch in the crowd, and ducked into the shadows.

In the Temple District, it was just as lively. Before I was in sight of the tavern or the churches, I heard shouts and banging, the whinny of an alarmed horse.

A gunshot.

Somebody smart would have taken off in the other direction, but I ran *into* the circle, where a knot of men in military uniforms hassled a wagoner. His cart was overturned, and in the light from the Temple's open doors, I made out its cargo of casks of wine or ale, no doubt destined for Eske's customers. Two of the soldiers had the wagoner by his collar, while the others raided the barrels, hoisting them aloft or tapping them in the street. One knelt on the ground, lapping up spilled wine like a stray dog.

Another gunshot broke the night, followed by a sharp, clear shout in a voice I recognized, and this time the soldiers heeded it. Eske stood in the Temple threshold with a musket, her dark mask and wild hair making her look more like the Nameless One, delivering the swift, fiery justice of the gods, than our ever-jovial high priestess.

"Halt!" she cried, and her voice alone was enough to stop the soldiers short. "That man is a servant of the gods on sacred business of Tiboran, and you will unhand him now or suffer the Masked God's wrath." She lowered the barrel of the musket straight at the soldier holding the wagoner. He dropped the man's collar so quickly the wagoner stumbled.

But these were king's men, trained soldiers in the Green Army, and it was a hot summer night in Gerse, and they were angry. I heard the whisk of a sword drawing, saw an arm flick in Eske's direction —

"You don't want to do that, friend," said a low, even voice, and another masked Temple worker melted out of the shadows, a long, steel blade leveled at the armed soldier's head. "Come back into the Temple and let this man get about his work."

"But that's *our* wine," somebody groused.

"And you're welcome to it," Eske said smoothly. "But it leaves the Temple in your bellies, not on your backs. I have no say in the new rations, but the taps at the Temple are always ready, and we've never turned away a man yet."

Amid this, the wagoner had slinked away, and Eske's man had easily circled around the back of the crowd. Finally the armed soldier lowered his own weapon, and the group broke up, still grumbling. Most of them crawled back into the Temple, but a handful left across the circle, while at least one paused to help right the wagon and rescue the stock. Eske stood in the doorway, shaking her head.

Her frown intensified when she saw me. "I understand this plan of yours," she said. "But all I can say is, it had better work fast. You've put us right in the middle of the fight, and I'm not sure that's where we want to be. And *you*, young lord," Eske said severely, then beamed. The masked barman with the sword had stepped up to us and was sheathing his blade. "I should kiss you, but I doubt our girl here would approve."

I spun around. Durrel — of *course* that level voice and blade had been Durrel's. He gave me a crooked half smile. "I'd better make sure they're not in there causing trouble," he said, and jogged easily up the short stairs.

Eske smiled, but there was a shadow across her face as we watched Durrel move through the bar. "I like him," she said. "And we're happy to keep him here as long as necessary, but that boy is not meant to be one of Tiboran's. He belongs to Zet, and the sooner you get him back in his rightful place, the better."

I understood what she was saying; Zet was the patron of nobility, and as much as Tiboran liked things topsy-turvy, the world had its proper order, and it was dangerous to defy that order for too long. "I'm working on it." I sighed, and followed her inside.

Durrel had found a table upstairs and doffed his mask. He looked hot and disheveled, his eyes rimmed in red, and I remembered that the last time I'd seen him he'd been heading off to get drunk. He linked his fingers together on the table, the knuckles of his left hand raw and bloody.

Neither of us spoke for a long time, but Durrel finally broke the silence. "How's Raffin?"

"He'll be fine." I didn't know what to say next. There was so much going on, and I wanted to talk to somebody — to Durrel — but I couldn't decide where to start. "Where did you go?"

He shrugged. "Just — here. Along the water. I went past my house, but . . ." he trailed off. "I knew she didn't like me," he said, and it was obvious he meant Talth. "And I accepted that. I knew she was cold, and hard, and never let a drop of warmth or affection go to waste. I even knew she was a terrible mother. But to find out that she was involved not just in extorting and exploiting vulnerable people, but — this *thing* that Raffin told us . . . How could *anyone* do that?"

"I don't know."

He turned those dark, anguished eyes to me. "And my father?"

"*No*," I said, my voice rough with relief. "He wasn't involved. Koya explained it to me."

He looked perplexed. "Koya?"

I had forgotten Durrel didn't know that Koya and Ragn were working together — because I'd only just figured that bit out before poisoning myself. I recounted what Koya had told me tonight, finishing with, "It was only Karst and Talth who were involved with the Inquisition." Koya had just said Karst, but she hadn't had the benefit of Raffin's intelligence regarding her mother's involvement. "Your father didn't do anything wrong."

He nodded slowly, still looking troubled. Eske appeared at that moment, bearing a ewer of mead. "Busy night?" she asked, and I choked on my drink.

"You have no idea," I said before she slipped away again. It had started with a visit from my brother and ended with the discovery that I'd killed my own magic, and it seemed unbelievable that everything that had happened between could fit into the same evening.

"Hey, what's wrong?" Durrel reached for my hand and I pulled it back. "Did something else happen?"

I shook my head. I didn't really want to talk about it, but I told him anyway. "I figured out what the poison was for. It — quells magic."

"Quells?" Durrel looked hard at me for a moment as this sank in. "Damn, Celyn. Are you all right?"

"Koya said it's temporary," I said — but she couldn't know for sure. Koya had never dealt with a magic like mine. There was no telling what the Tincture of the Moon might have done to my singular power.

"I'm sorry," he said. He looked helpless, and there was concern threaded all through his voice. He did take my hand then, refusing to release it when I tried to tug away.

"I'm sure I'll be fine," I lied. "Is there any more mead?"

CHAPTER TWENTY·NINE

The rest of that night involved a great deal of the Temple's best offerings and a concerted effort to blot out our mounting mysteries for a few hours. I woke late and muzzy-headed and just a little surprised to find myself alone in what seemed to be my own room at the tavern. I got myself more or less put together, in time to see a note slip through the crack beneath the door. We'd had a message from Koya, calling Durrel and me to a meeting at an address I didn't recognize. I was suspicious, but Durrel confirmed the hand and knew the house, so we set off that hot, drowsy afternoon, squinting against a damnably bright sun.

"What's this about?" I asked, as if Durrel knew any more than I did.

"I don't know," Durrel said, "but I'm glad to finally be doing something besides sitting around the Temple waiting for something to happen."

"I'm sure it's very onerous," I said crossly. "Being anonymous among all those masked women."

"I'm only interested in one masked woman," he said, and was rewarded with my most withering scowl.

The address Koya provided was in a middle-class district, on a street with a view down the Oss to the city wall. I felt a stab of concern as I saw that black iron bars were lowered over the river.

"They've closed the gates?" Durrel's disbelief mirrored my own. But the queue of vessels backed up thickly in the water, and the frustrated buzz of conversation all along the riverside, was plain enough. To protect the city from invasion by Prince Wierolf's troops, Bardolph had ordered all the gates sealed, cutting off transit in and out of Gerse, closing docks, and shutting down shipping. It had been hard enough for ordinary people to enter or leave town for months, but at least we knew food and goods and information still passed through the gates. Now I felt my chest constrict a little, as if Bardolph's grip was literally closing around me, and not the city.

Durrel stopped to question a merchant standing outside his shop and shaking his head at the sight. "Been some kind of incident," the fellow explained. "A fire at a house down Sixth Circle way — burned half a dozen soldiers in their beds, *and* the family they were staying with." At this last, he spit on the ground.

A woman drawing her washing in from a cramped courtyard told us more. "They say it were deliberate," she said. Somehow the home's doors and shutters had been fixed shut, ensuring that there would be no survivors. "And a purple handprint, right there on the front door."

Durrel and I exchanged alarmed glances. "That purple handprint again," he said in a low voice as we moved on. "Just like those dead Greenmen."

"Well, whoever they are, they've progressed to killing civilians," I said grimly.

Eventually we turned down along the river and stopped at a modest town house painted sky blue, its narrow balcony overlooking the water. "We're here," Durrel said.

"Where?" I looked the place over; I saw no wall, no guards, just a well-tended patch of garden and a sleepy, white cat draped sinuously across the doorstep. What was Koya up to now?

"Ah — this is Stantin's house," Durrel said, his voice a little tight. "Koya's husband."

I drew back in surprise, but the door swung open, and a tall man with white hair stepped over the cat and bowed briefly to Durrel. "Your lordship," he said in a smooth voice like warm wine. "And Mistress Celyn. The others are here. Come."

"Others?" But Koya's husband just ushered us inside, making polite inquiry about the weather, as if we were ordinary visitors. He led us upstairs to a cozy sitting room overlooking the river. The balcony doors were thrown wide, lightweight curtains lifting in the air. Koya and one of her sighthounds had taken over a delicate, turned-wood bench, and she was deep in conversation with Lord Ragn and another man about Stantin's age (Claas, Durrel quietly informed me). In her beaded velvet she looked utterly out of place here, but turned a relaxed face to us when we entered.

I felt Durrel tense up beside me when he saw his father, but Lord Ragn rose and embraced him firmly. "Is he being careful?" Lord Ragn demanded of me. He looked windblown and weary, as if he'd ridden hard to get here. "This will be over soon," he added — and I wanted to ask what he meant, but was forestalled by Stantin bearing a dish of fruit and a pitcher of wine.

"How did you get strawberries?" I asked instead.

"I've been at Favom," Lord Ragn said. "They're falling off the vine, they're so ripe, and the fields are black with crows feasting on them. I'm afraid they'll rot, since there's no way to get them from the farm anymore."

"Lucky you made it back before they sealed the gates," Durrel observed.

"Only just," his father agreed.

"How are Lady Amalle's friends?" I heard the edge in Durrel's voice.

Lord Ragn stiffened. "Safe," he said curtly. "If you'll excuse me, I need to speak with our hosts."

He turned away, but his path was blocked by Koya. "Ragn," she said softly, "let them help." Leaving him no room to object, she steered us all toward the sitting area. "Tell him what you've told me," she said to me, and Durrel and I explained what Raffin had said about Karst and the Sarists he'd sold to the Celystra.

Disturbingly Lord Ragn's face betrayed no surprise or alarm at this information. "We'd feared something like this might be going on."

"Something like *what*?" I said.

Instead of answering me directly, Ragn shifted in his seat. "Your ability to sense magic seems to be unique in the world, Celyn," he said.

286

"But there's always been the question of how the Inquisition seeks out and identifies magic."

"Beyond random accusations, you mean?" Durrel said.

"Right. But we know from firsthand accounts that their techniques do occasionally turn up an authentic magic user or artifact."

"The lodestones, the treated silver," I said. The Confessors had tools to detect the presence of magic, but they were only a noninvasive first step. The other *techniques* came later and weren't so kind.

"Exactly," said Lord Ragn. "But *I* wouldn't be able to work the lodestones; Lord Durrel wouldn't know how to tell the difference between altered silver and ordinary."

"And altered how?" Durrel put in, obviously tracking his father's line of thought. "You'd need —"

"Someone like me." Listening to the Decath's analysis, I felt cold all over. They were right. How would ordinary people craft a lodestone to respond to magic in a room? The stones themselves weren't inherently magical, so how did they work? "Somebody inside the Inquisition must have magic."

Lord Ragn's face was set, and I realized he must have come to this conclusion ages ago. Why had I never thought about it?

"Well, I can hardly imagine Werne putting very many wizards on his payroll," said Durrel.

But I could. What had he wanted *me* to do, after all? I looked between father and son, willing it not to be true. "Karst's prisoners."

Lord Ragn nodded grimly. "It would appear that at least some of the Ferrymen's clients who come short of their ransom aren't killed outright by the Inquisitor's men."

"Wait," Durrel said. "You think Talth and Karst turned people over to the Greenmen, who subsequently put them to work charming chains and rocks so the Confessors could track down their fellow Sarists even more efficiently?"

It was a horrible thought, and one that had too much of the ring of truth about it. "We know Werne's tried to recruit me," I said. "And it explains what Raffin saw."

Lord Ragn gave me a barely perceptible nod, but Durrel looked alarmed. "And this is why Karst killed Talth? Some dispute over this — arrangement with the Celystra?"

"We've been trying to find evidence," I added. "But all we have right now is the word of a disgraced Greenman."

Koya's cool voice broke into the conversation. "We actually called you here for a more urgent matter." She rose from her seat and drew closer to us, giving Lord Ragn a pointed look. "*Tell* them."

He looked stubborn, but finally acquiesced. "There's been a delay in the arrival of one of our shipments," he said.

It took me a moment to understand what he meant, and then I wished I didn't. "You have missing Sarists?"

"The last clients we contracted to move through Mother's firm," said Koya. "There was an arrival the day she died, but there were — people absent. Passengers we know had arranged for the journey somehow did not reach Gerse with the others, and we fear there may also be others we were unaware of, people she added on her own."

Something heavy settled on my chest as I took this in. "They'd already turned them over to the Celystra?"

"Fortunately I don't think so," Lord Ragn said. "It was Talth's habit to put them to work in her own enterprises while bleeding them of their money. Only when they were worked half to death or the gold had run dry did she turn to the Inquisition." There was a bitter edge to his words, and I couldn't blame him. "No, as far as we can tell, they just never arrived."

"So they're still out there?" Durrel sounded horrified. "It's been *weeks*! They could have suffocated in some cargo hold, or —"

"Let's not jump to conclusions," Lord Ragn put in gently. "But that is one reason Koya and I have been so concerned."

"We have to find them," Durrel said, an accusatory note to his voice.

Koya reached for him. "That's what your father's been trying to do," she said. "He's been traveling, making inquiries —"

"But unfortunately the one person who definitely knew what happened to them is dead, and her colleagues have not been forthcoming either." Ragn stood and paced behind the bench. "I've tried to suss out information from sources inside the Celystra or the Council —"

"And I've asked what I could of the Ceid," Koya added.

"But it's delicate work, inquiring after Sarists, and I've found no sign of them. I'm afraid only Talth's close associates know where they are."

"How many?" I asked, my voice very small.

Ragn took a breath before answering, looking over my head to the river outside. "At least six."

"Hells," Durrel said. "What can we do?"

Here Koya looked at me. "That's one of the reasons I reached out to you, Celyn. I thought you might —" She broke off, shaking her head.

In a sudden, awful rush I understood what she meant. "I can't," I said.

"We wouldn't ask you to expose yourself," Ragn said. "But if there were some way you could turn your gift to this matter, you would be doing a very great service for the cause of good."

I stared at him. Why hadn't Koya mentioned this? "No, I mean I really *can't*," I said. "I took the tincture."

From the look of dismay on Lord Ragn's face, I knew he understood precisely what I meant. "And you're sure — you sense absolutely nothing?"

"Father, please. If you knew what she'd been through, you wouldn't ask her. There's got to be another way." Durrel leaned forward in his seat. "Are you sure the refugees made it to the city?"

Ragn lifted his hands in defeat, but said, "To the best I could figure out. I've been able to trace them as far as a checkpoint outside Tratua, but after that the trail runs cold. But Talth preferred to keep her assets close; she didn't like to leave things unaccounted for."

"The city it is, then," Durrel said. He shoved aside a pile of books on a little table and started to trace a figure on the table's surface — a wide circle representing Gerse. "You've already checked the docks, I hope," he said.

"Of course," his father said, sounding cross. "All Talth's shipments have been accounted for. And the warehouse near Bal Marse, where we know she'd held people before." He marked a spot on the table with the stem of a strawberry.

"Here," said a low voice, and there was Claas, spreading a rolled-up parchment across the little table. "It's a bit dated," he added apologetically, as the image of Gerse opened before us. "Which is why we were allowed to keep it." He was being generous. The fragile document lacked at least two major bridges crossing the Oss and the Big Silver, and Markettown appeared to be a pasture. Still, it was good enough for our purposes.

"Didn't you tell me Talth owned houses in Markettown?" I asked Durrel, pointing to the general area on the map. "Where we saw the plague flags?"

Koya slipped in closer. "Barris told me he sold those properties. Ragn?"

Durrel's father frowned at the map. "It's something," he said, not sounding particularly hopeful.

"Let's go look." Durrel stood up, but his father shook his head.

"We can't simply rush straight into a quarantine," Ragn said. "We need to consider our next move carefully."

"How much time do you think they have?" I asked. "If Karst realizes we know what he's doing, he'll get rid of them. I'm with Durrel on this."

"Karst *won't* realize, because I have gone out of my way to keep from arousing his suspicions," Ragn said.

"But we haven't," Durrel said heavily. "He's seen Celyn, and I'm obviously not where the Ceid put me for safekeeping. We need to find those refugees."

Their argument continued, Durrel wanting to leave *now*, and his father urging caution. I was starting to feel a little sick, from the heat, and last night, and the whole awful weight of what this meant finally settling on me. The idea that I could somehow use my skill to track magic users had always repulsed me, but now that I absolutely *couldn't* do it, when it might have been used to save people instead of condemn them — I squeezed my eyes shut and bent my head to my knees, wishing all of this would just go away.

A few moments later, I felt a gentle arm around me. I looked up, expecting Durrel or Koya, but it was Claas sitting beside me, offering me a drink. He was watching me, a strange, sad kindness in his warm eyes, and there was something here that I almost, *almost* understood. I swallowed hard, rubbing at my chest.

"They're gathering for dinner," he said. Lord Ragn and Durrel had disappeared to the dining room next door. "Why don't you step outside for some air? There's actually a breeze this evening."

It was so bland and simple it was comforting. "Thank you."

Outside on the balcony, Koya and her dog gazed out over the glassy water, and I went to join them. She turned and leaned against the balustrade, her gaze tracking back inside the house, where Durrel still spoke with the other men.

"Stantin and Claas seem . . . hospitable," I said tentatively, to break the awkward silence.

A weak smile flickered across her face and was gone again, fast as a darting bat in the dusk. "They are all good things," she said, and there was a trace of the old, arch Koya in her voice. "They didn't even flinch when I asked if I could bring you here, just threw open their doors and steamed some oysters." She cast her head back, as if to soak up the night. "Koyuz is like an overindulgent uncle, happy to give me anything I ask for."

"Except a divorce," I said baldly, and her laughter clapped through the night, too harsh.

"No," she said. "Not that."

The moons hung heavy in the thick sky, over a chorus of crickets and frogs. After the longest moment, Koya spoke again, her eyes on the sky above us. "I want a child," she said. "If I have one, Stantin will say it is his. But as you may imagine, it's not been easy finding potential . . . candidates. I thought Durrel, but —" She shook her head. "He wouldn't. Mother overheard us that night. I was crying. Durrel was Durrel. Gallant, defending me. Mother banished me from Bal Marse. *That's* what their quarrel was over."

"Oh," I said, not sure how to respond to this revelation. The moment had curled tight around us, and neither of us realized we weren't alone until the dog's scrabbling toenails and whisking tail worked into a frenzy of greeting. We looked up sharply as Durrel let himself through the gauzy curtains onto the balcony with us.

I thought I saw Koya color slightly; she turned back to the view of the water. For all the talk of what stood between Koya and Durrel, I had seen them together only rarely, and their awkwardness was palpable. Durrel moved to stand beside me, and his hand gently brushed my shoulder. It was an affectionate gesture — a possessive one, and Koya saw it instantly.

Her bright smile signaled the return of the careless Koya persona once more, and it was almost painful how seamless the transition was. "I must thank Stantin for hosting us," she said merrily, and swept back into the house.

"I don't really understand her," I said, although, strangely enough, I thought I did.

Durrel's hand dropped, but he didn't move away from me. "She's . . . complicated," was all he said, and there was a world of meaning in that one word. At least I understood now why Durrel had lied about that last argument with Talth. He was the sort to hold a girl's secrets close.

Darkness had fallen, silhouetting him against the night. In the dark water behind him, I saw the lights of a boat, coming nearer. I took two steps backward, toward the house.

"Durrel," I said carefully. "Move away from the edge."

He shifted aside immediately. "What is it?"

"I don't know." I wasn't certain — just an odd feeling about that boat. I peered over the balustrade, but the vessel had drawn beneath the balcony. When it didn't reappear, I felt a prick of unease. "Something's wrong."

Clinging to the shadows, I leaned farther over the railing. The boat had pulled to a stop outside Stantin's house. A handful of men were disembarking stealthily onto the bank, and in the light of the boat's lantern, I could just make out their mismatched gray doublets, crossed with red sashes.

I yanked myself back inside, and waved to Koya and the others across the room. Claas saw me first, nudging Stantin to attention. "We have a problem." I pointed to the river outside. "Guards."

"What?" Alarm colored Koya's voice, and she hurried the other direction, toward the front of the house. A second later she reappeared. "Damn it," she said. "It's Barris. He's brought the Watch."

Durrel looked from Lord Ragn to me. "What do we do?"

"How many are there?" I asked Koya. "I saw about six out back."

A bang and a shout from downstairs interrupted whatever anyone might have said next. "Open up in the name of the king!"

"Pox. We'll have to hide." I appealed to Stantin. "Do you have a cellar or something?"

He was shaking his head. "That's the first place they'll look."

Koya touched his arm. "I'm so sorry," she said. "I brought them here."

"And I'll send them away again," he said. "Have no fear. In the meantime . . ." he said nothing more, but gave a significant look to Claas, then headed down the cramped stairway.

"I'm coming with you." Lord Ragn was quick on Stantin's heels.

When they'd gone, Claas herded Durrel and me gently into a corner near the balcony. "You can climb?" he asked us. Surprised, I nodded. "Good," he said. "Wait for my cue."

"What?" Durrel said, but fell silent as footsteps pounded up the stairs. Koya grabbed her barking dog by its collar, and for a moment she looked just like the goddess Zet, warrior and mighty huntress.

"You can't go up there," Stantin was saying, with altogether too much calm, as Koya joined him by yelling, "Barris! What the hells do you think you're doing?"

"Hist," Claas said in a voice so low it was little more than a whisper beneath the breeze.

Gray-clad Watchmen poured into the tiny sitting room, tripping over books and knocking aside furniture. Koya gave a convincing scream, and the dog lunged forward in her grip. I had the feeling she wasn't trying terribly hard to restrain it.

"We are here on official city business," one of the Watchmen announced. "Stand aside and let us conduct a search of these premises."

"What could you possibly expect to find here?" Stantin asked, but the guard elbowed past him.

"Don't play stupid. We're looking for *his* son."

I tensed, but Lord Ragn said with great dignity, "My son is in Tratua."

I stared at them. His son was in the *corner*, in plain view of everyone. Maybe they didn't recognize him — but that was stupid; Barris knew Durrel. I felt Durrel stiffen to one side of me, and Claas's hand squeezed mine. I looked past them, into the room, where the guards' eyes crawled across every inch of the space, coming to stop everywhere but *here*, the corner where Claas stood with Durrel and me. It was as if they couldn't help but look past us. I tugged on Claas's hand, and he turned his solemn, deep-set eyes to me.

"It's you," I said, barely more than a movement of my lips. "You're doing this."

Claas said nothing, but a corner of his mouth lifted in the beginning of a smile. He pulled us back slightly as the Watchmen stormed through, some of them inches from us, but no one seeing, no one hearing the race of my heart or the too-swift measure of Durrel's breath. I strained my vision, searching around Claas for a hint of shimmer or a glow or a fog I couldn't see — but there was nothing. I was as blind to the magic as anyone else here tonight.

"Now see here," the Watch captain was saying, "we've come to search for two fugitives from the king's justice, and we'll tear every stone from these walls if we have to."

"You're welcome to search," Stantin said genially. "But you'll see for yourself that we're not harboring anyone."

Apparently that was Claas's cue, because he squeezed my hand hard and pointed toward the balcony. We shifted as a unit, tight together, until we stood at the railing.

"The climb is not bad," Claas said. "I've done it before." Durrel regarded him with utter disbelief, and he gave a faint laugh. "The cat got stuck on the roof. Now down you go. There's a path to the water. Stantin and his lordship will keep them occupied. And I will keep you obscured as long as I can."

I didn't know what to say. Too much was happening all at once. But Claas squeezed my hand one final time, and it said everything we needed to. I nodded and pulled away gently as Durrel swung one leg over the balcony.

CHAPTER THIRTY

We could still hear the Watch yelling and stomping through the house, even as we lowered ourselves from the balcony. There was a window one floor down, with a wide ledge above it, and from there it was an easy drop to ground level. I hit the mossy earth a moment after Durrel, and he pushed me back against the house, one finger to his lips, the other hand pointing toward the water.

A lone Watchman had remained with the boat and stood guard at the river. I looked quickly up and down the banks, but it didn't seem as if any of Stantin and Claas's neighbors were the sailing types.

"We have to take out that guard," I said in a low voice. "Can you manage?" I could do it, but Durrel was bigger than me, and could probably accomplish it with a little less fuss and noise.

"Gladly," he said, stepping out of the shadows and drawing his knife. He slipped up behind the guard and had his knife arm around his throat, the other hand over his mouth and nose, before the poor fellow could react. I counted the painful heartbeats, watched the frightened concentration on Durrel's face as the pinned guard struggled futilely in his grip, until he finally slumped in Durrel's arms, unconscious.

We dragged the man well away from the water, and left him hidden behind a bush. I ran down to the river and grabbed the lead ropes of the Watch boat. "Help me," I said, pulling the prow around to the water. "We'll take this."

Durrel took the other end, but hesitated. "Why are we stealing their boat?"

"Because we don't have time to scuttle it!" As the body of the vessel hit the water, I climbed inside, and Durrel hopped in neatly after me. I was too short to row effectively, but Durrel was an experienced boatman, and had us in the Oss's swift evening current in moments. I dropped the boat's lantern overboard, its light swallowed up by the swirling water. Claas still stood watch on the balcony; how long would the cloak of darkness and silence he'd produced protect us? Or had it faded as soon as he'd released my hand? Nobody came running around the side of the house, shouting about stolen boats, so I guessed the spell lasted long enough. I raised my lightless hand in farewell, but I didn't know if Claas could even see us anymore.

Durrel was frowning as he looked back at the Koyuz house. "I've never done anything like that before." He sounded troubled. "Choking that guard, I mean."

"You didn't look like a novice."

"It's a wrestling hold," he said. "But you usually let go after the other man begs for mercy."

"You showed him better mercy than they would have shown us," I said, but Durrel rowed silently, his gaze far away. A moment later he scowled again.

"Damn. I thought, standing behind Claas . . . I was sure they had us. What *was* that? Was it magic?"

"I'm not sure. I thought it took two people for a spell like that, but maybe it was just a small magic." It explained Koya's odd attachment to her marriage, at least; the heroic rescuer of magic users was hardly likely to expose Claas and Stantin's secret by petitioning for divorce. I studied the shoreline and water for any out-of-place movement, straining backward to hear the shouts of the Watchmen as they discovered their boat was missing. "We have to get rid of the boat. That Watch insigne on the prow might as well be a giant sign that says *Boat Thieves*."

"Where exactly are we going?" Durrel's shoulders strained with every pull of the oars, but we skimmed along the water swift as a dragonfly. All the more reason to get to shore, before *more* of these swift little boats came after us.

"Away from the gates," I said, thinking of the tangle of vessels clogging the route beneath the great bridge. "No, turn around. Go *toward* the gates. It'll take them days to find this boat in that mess."

He nodded, steering easily in the direction I'd indicated. "And then what?"

"I'm thinking," I said irritably. "If they tracked you to Stantin Koyuz's house, of all places, they've surely already searched everywhere we'd frequent. So that means both the Temple and the bakery are out."

"I thought they couldn't search the Temple."

"No, but they can stand outside it."

"All right, what about Cartouche?"

I pondered this, but dismissed it. "They'll tie that to Koya. It needs to be somewhere they'd never suspect you of going."

"Your friend's house," he said, but for a second I wasn't sure who he meant. "Where you took me a few days ago. Not his house; we don't want to lead the Watch there, but —"

"His warehouse," I finished. "Cwalo. That's brilliant. It's on the Big Silver, though. We'll have to head downriver, where the rivers join."

"Quicker to walk from Oss Bridge," Durrel said. "And the more space between us and this boat, the better. Let's go."

We ditched the boat in the river, in the queue for the locks; the Oss was so thick with vessels, many abandoned, that we could leave the boat midstream and climb almost to shore across them. We dropped into the shallows at the bank and waded ashore, the water dragging at my skirts. Heads bowed, we trotted away from the river, dodging pools of light and taking as many back alleys as we could. Once I spied a brace of Greenmen strolling toward us, and shoved Durrel behind me, under a shadowed archway.

Finally we crossed to the Big Silver side of town. No doubt its gates were sealed as well, those tall ships trapped at harbor. Cwalo's warehouse was deserted, not even a sleepy dog guarding the property; apparently the owner's reputation for swift revenge was enough to protect it. I popped the lock on the main door in a hurry, a little careless with the tumblers, and I think one snapped. Pox. I'd have to pay Cwalo back for that later. Inside, the warehouse was crowded with crates and casks and bales of cloth, very little moonslight streaming through the small, high windows. There was a flaw in our plan; our hiding place gave us excellent cover but no effective way to see out. If we wanted to know what was going on in the world, we'd have to poke our heads back through the door again.

I paced, making a canal of Cwalo's floor with my soaked skirts, until Durrel stopped me. "Take your dress off."

"What?"

"You're shivering. You'll catch cold in those wet clothes. But it's an oven in here; they'll be dry in no time."

I saw the logic in this, but I hesitated. "You too, milord," I said finally, and Durrel shrugged off his doublet and kicked his boots into a pile in the corner. Then we stood there, trying not to look at each other in our wet smocks, and I was painfully aware how little mine concealed, even in the dark.

"We, uh, might as well get some rest," I said. "We should be safe here until morning."

"Good idea." Durrel glanced around and pointed to a bundle of cloth by the wall. He dropped beside it and pulled his knees to his chest, resting his cheek against them. I followed suit, a few feet away.

But sleep was elusive. It wasn't that late, first of all, and despite the warm evening, the warehouse was dank, and a chill seeped through me from the stone floor. "How can I be *cold*?" I said.

"Shock. Come over here." Durrel lifted his arm and beckoned me to him. I hung back, but my *teeth* were chattering, so I finally scooted over and let him put an arm around me. He smelled strongly of river wet, and a hot, salty scent I remembered from his days in the Keep. It wasn't a bad smell, tonight. I told myself I should edge away again before I did something stupid, but I was very weary and disinclined to move. Light fingers stroked my hair, and I didn't push them away.

"I'm sorry about your magic," he said, and that was so much the strangest and the *least* of the troubles facing us just now, that I didn't know what to say. "I can't imagine what it must be like. We always knew Meri had it, of course, but most of the time it didn't mean anything. But for you . . ." he trailed off, but I didn't have anything to fill up the gap, and besides, I liked the sound of his voice, low and soft in the big hollow space of the warehouse. "I broke my arm when I was a boy. For one entire summer I couldn't ride or hunt or even write. I *hated* it, but this — it must be like losing a limb."

I flexed my left hand, where I had lost the tips of two fingers fighting Daul last winter. Was it the same? When I'd hurt my hand, had I felt this desperate panic, like there was a *rend* in my soul? "I never wanted magic," I said, my voice halting. "All I knew was that it hurt people — having it, using it. And for the longest time I had to pretend I didn't have it. But now, with the war —" and a dozen other things I couldn't say aloud, meeting the Nemair, and knowing Meri, and coming back to the city alone, and then being courted by the Inquisition . . . I bent my head back and pushed those thoughts out of reach. "It's a poxedly inconvenient time for it to go missing."

Durrel laughed, warm and sweet in the darkness, and his fingers curled around my small, damaged, unmagical hand.

We were still sitting that way, hours later, as a pale, watery light filtered through the high windows. I blinked awake, disoriented for a moment. I thought we were back in gaol, and I jumped a little, but a gentle hand on my arm held me down.

"Our clothes are dry," Durrel said quietly. His face was very close to mine.

"Is it morning?" I whispered.

"Almost."

"We should get dressed, then."

"We should."

But nobody moved.

"I was thinking of the day we met," he said, his voice low and breathy. "When you fell asleep in the boat with us? I think that's when I first wanted to."

"Wanted to what?"

"Kiss you," he said, and tilted my face to his, to do just that.

His lips were warm, and I felt a rush of heat from my hips to my belly. I twined my fingers in his, in his damp hair, and was shifting to my knees — when a noise from outside snapped us apart again. Breathless, Durrel held up a hand, and I edged silently aside, my heart banging as I eased to my feet and fumbled in the half dark for my dress.

The noise turned itself into footsteps, and then a hand jiggling the warehouse door. Cwalo? Or the Watch? Durrel's hand found mine and together we slipped through the maze of boxes and barrels, toward what we both apparently hoped was a rear exit. The warehouse door cracked open, and a saber of light cut through the darkness. Durrel and I flattened ourselves against the wall, as if we could make ourselves invisible again just by willing it. I looked around, frantic, but the door was swinging wide, and there wasn't another way out that I could see. I held fast to Durrel's hand, until my fingers tingled from the force of my grip.

I glanced down, and nearly dropped his hand in surprise. He felt the movement and turned quizzical eyes to mine. "You're *glowing*," I whispered, and he looked down at himself, but could see nothing out of the ordinary, of course. I held my own hand up, and saw the faintest vibration in the darkness — some residue from Claas's spell, or whatever that had been. We'd been cloaked in magic, and now, for some reason, I could see it again.

"It's back, isn't it?" he said, and I felt myself grinning foolishly. "You should kiss me again. Who knows what might happen?"

But what *did* happen, just then, was the door snapped shut, and a thin voice drifted through the storeroom. "Digger?"

I stiffened and peered over the barrel we were hiding behind. "It's Cwalo. What do we do?"

"I don't think it matters much at this point," Durrel said, and he stepped out of the barrels, his balled-up clothes in one hand. "Good morning, sir."

It's *really* hard to surprise Master Cwalo, but the look on his face that morning was worth sovereigns, as he beheld Durrel and me, in nothing but our small clothes, lurking in the back of his warehouse.

"I take it your courtship with Piral is off," he finally said.

"We got wet," I said indignantly, pulling away from Durrel.

"Evidently."

"Escaping the Watch," Durrel said.

"Stop helping."

Cwalo said, "Why don't you two get dressed, and then step into my office so we can have a chat." There was the very slightest emphasis on *dressed*, and I had the distinct feeling he was trying hard to conceal a laugh.

We followed him to the smaller room, and I realized how stiff and hungry I was. "I'm sorry about your door," I said.

"I recognized your handiwork, but usually you're a little neater." Cwalo sat at the desk, and Durrel and I took the chairs. For a moment we three just looked at one another, all at a loss for words. But it wasn't long before Durrel and I were pouring out our story — not just of our wild flight from the Night Watch at Stantin's, but everything. Talth, Karst, Ferrymen selling refugees to the Celystra, all of it. I even included Werne's visits to the bakery.

"Lost magic users? Here in Gerse?" Cwalo frowned as he poured out a measure of a hot, spicy drink for each of us. The drink was thick and sweet and fortifying, and I held fast to the warm cup.

"We need to find them before Karst does something with them," Durrel said. He didn't need to specify what *something* meant.

Cwalo was tapping his fingers together. "If they're not inside the city wall by now, they won't be, not with the gates closed. Have you followed this Karst's movements, to see if he'll lead you to them?"

"We're too conspicuous," Durrel said. "He's already suspicious, and the Ceid have men watching my father."

"This might be a matter I can help you with," said Cwalo. "I have a man I trust. But it could take a few days before our efforts turn anything up."

"They might not *have* a few days," Durrel said. "There has to be something we can do right now."

I shared Durrel's restlessness, and pushed away from the desk. "First we need to get word to the others," I said. "We have to make sure they made it out of Stantin's safely, and let them know we're putting a tail on Karst. I'll also see if Koya knows anything else about where the Ceid might hide their prisoners. You stay here and help Cwalo."

"You can't go out there alone," Durrel said. "And what am I supposed to do — spend the next few days just hiding in Master Cwalo's warehouse?"

"You'll be fine," I said. "He keeps a room here."

"That's not the point."

"I've been dodging guards since I was eleven years old," I said, though a growing part of me really wanted Durrel by my side. "I know what I'm doing. I can't have you hanging about, throttling everyone we run into."

"Listen to the lady, your lordship," Cwalo broke in. "Besides, I'll need you to tell me all you can about your late wife's operation. Maybe we can uncover a lead you two have missed. You'll not be idle."

"You're still a murder suspect and a fugitive," I added gently.

"Damn it, stop reminding me!"

"When you start acting like one!"

"All right, easy there, both of you." Cwalo stepped between us. "Milord, I hate to admit it, but our girl's right. She's the best person to send word to your friends, and you have a very important job to do here."

"What's that?" Durrel asked sullenly.

"Don't get caught," I said.

"All right," he finally said, and followed me to the doorway. But I didn't leave, just stood there, staring up at his fathomless dark gray eyes, the hair that wouldn't quite stay in place, the smooth contour of his jaw. I wanted very badly to kiss him again, but Cwalo was looking over us like a brooding chaperon. Instead I put a hand against Durrel's chest. He touched his fingers to my wrist.

"Go," he whispered. "And come back soon."

I went. Out into the bright, hot morning, the kiss of his fingertips still lingering on my hand, but a knot of worry pushing itself to the front of my thoughts. My chest felt curiously tight as I hurried along the docks, and I couldn't shake the feeling that I was missing something, somehow. We had a plan, and now with five of us searching, a better chance of finding Lord Ragn's lost refugees. So what was wrong? I squeezed my hands into fists as if I could coax my magic sense back even more quickly. But that odd anxiety only intensified when I left the river behind.

All the same difficulties I'd enumerated to Durrel last night were still in place, but I hazarded a visit to Cartouche, thinking it was probably the place least likely to attract Barris and his thugs, and where I could most easily get a message to Koya. It was a long trek, made longer by my twisting route as well as the unusual crowds abroad. It was as if the whole city had just opened out onto the streets for a festival — but the mood was anything but celebratory. I saw soldiers clotting the entries to public circles, and angry citizens arguing with them, and city guards hanging back, doing nothing to intervene.

Cartouche was quiet during the day, the public rooms all but empty, and the indolent company I did see had more on their minds than calling down the Watch on me. I found no sign of Koya, but a pink-clad footman went to look for her. While I waited, I stole up to the bar to buy the first real meal I'd had in two days. When the barman turned to take my order, I almost didn't recognize him. He had filled out a little, and lost that panicky look he'd had the last time I'd seen him, but he was unmistakably the lanky youth Koya had tried to foist upon me my first night here. The wariness in his eyes said he recognized me, as well.

"Mistress Koya's out today," he said. His eyes darted across the room, and I saw he wasn't quite as nonchalant as that pink uniform made him seem. Before he could engineer an escape, I leaned forward.

"If I put my hand on your arm," I said quietly, "what would happen?" Even before taking the tincture, I hadn't detected his magic, and I still couldn't tell anything, yet I knew, with solid certainty, that I was right.

"Are you trying to get me in trouble? No one here knows, all right? I'm just working here until my family gets to town."

"They're still with Ferrymen?" My voice was as low as possible, but the boy still flinched at the word. "With Karst?"

He scrubbed at the bar determinedly with his rag. "I can't say any more."

"Do you know where they're being held?"

He looked up sharply, and the fear was back in his gaze. "They're late, aren't they? Koya said not to worry —" He shook his head. "But I'm *sure* they're coming. We paid our fares."

"How did you get separated?"

"I came ahead," he said. "In the first group, with my uncle. My mother and my sister were supposed to follow after. My sister was sick when I left, and they couldn't travel with her. But I know they set off," he added with conviction, "because I got a letter from them saying Meis was better, and they were coming in the next transport."

"And you haven't heard from them since."

"It's been over a *month*," he said. "And every day Mistress Koya promises that they'll arrive soon. Something's happened to them, hasn't it?"

"No," I said. "I'm sure they're safe." What was I going to say?

"Marau's moon was full when we arrived in Gerse, and I remember our guard making morbid jokes about us, because of it." He gave a shudder, remembering. "Karst was the worst. He'd torment the women, touch them, pull their hair and — and worse things."

"You won't have to worry about him much longer," I said. "We're sure he killed his boss among the Ceid, and he'll hang for it. Lord Ragn is doing all he can." But the promise was hollow, because none of us had the faintest idea where this boy's family was, and chances were good that Karst wouldn't be anywhere near as patient as Talth had been.

I started to leave, but something tugged at me as I slid from the bar stool. "Wait —" I turned back, and the boy looked up, still wary. "When did you say you arrived?"

"About a month ago," he said, gesturing toward the shuttered window. "When Marau was full."

The full moon of Marau, which fell at the same time as the new moon of Celys, and upon which Durrel had commented, when we were hidden together in the rowboat. *I remember thinking how odd it was, to die on the night of Marau's full moon. Like a bad omen.* The night of Talth's murder.

"Are you sure? You saw the full moon?"

He nodded. "They moved us from the ship to a — some kind of cellar that night. It was the first time I'd seen the sky in weeks."

"And Karst was with you the whole time? Did he ever leave? Get relieved by another guard? Leave you alone for a couple hours, maybe chained up?"

"That one *never* left. Not even to use the privy," he added with such obvious distaste it didn't take much to figure out what he meant. "Kept us all at gunpoint until dawn. I think he was waiting for somebody. . . ."

I didn't hear the rest of what he said. If Karst was with a shipment of refugees all night, then he couldn't have been at Bal Marse, slipping poison into a drink.

He couldn't have killed Talth.

CHAPTER THIRTY-ONE

I left Cartouche feeling hollow. I had *wanted* Karst to be the murderer; he was cruel and ruthless and guilty of so much else that it only seemed fitting that he had killed Talth. Yet somehow I had ignored the signs that he was blameless in that particular crime — that *someone else* was responsible.

There was no conceivable reason for Koya's pink bartender to give Karst an alibi. He could have been mistaken, no matter how confident he felt about the date. That's what I tried to tell myself, anyway. With Talth dead, Karst could move in and seize control of the Ferryman trade, and how better to make a name for himself than by killing his ruthless boss to get her out of the way? But as I walked into the slanting sunlight, I knew I didn't believe it. Karst's boasts to Fei and his cronies had been nothing but bravado, lies told to impress his men, to establish his own reputation as a cold-blooded Ferryman — and a more entertaining story than the official version of murder by unhappy husband. It was possible, I supposed, that *another* Ferryman had killed Talth, but I doubted it. No self-respecting Gerse criminal lets another man take credit for his work, and if someone else in Talth's crew, or some rival organization, had done it, he'd have spoken up fast when Karst started bragging. That left me with one suspect, and a sick core of dread when I thought about it.

I walked aimlessly through the city. My feet led; my head was some-where else. The mood of people in the streets had grown thin and tense, as if everyone was waiting for something. All around me were soldiers, the king's Green Army, ambling through the dusky evening, but they were scattered, disjointed, not the lean, organized regiment mustered to bring order to Gerse. I heard a shout, two, a dozen, and when I finally made out the words, I was too weary and distracted to notice them at first.

"Take a torch to the cursed place, that's what somebody *ought* to do."

"Burn old Werne to ashes. It's his damn fault we're at war in the first place."

"Too much control over Bardolph, and his green dogs grow fat and lazy while we're doing all the work and starving in the streets!"

I halted at a corner. Had I heard them right? The king's army was planning an assault on the *Celystra*? What did that mean? I found a high place, a shop rooftop where I could see across the city, to the green tiles of the temple's massive dome. For a moment, I thought it was aflame, but that was only the reflection of the setting sun off the glass. But the streets everywhere were full of soldiers — and for once they weren't harassing ordinary Gersins. These were fighting men on a mission, and it could not be one that boded well for the city.

I sat on that roof for what seemed like hours, the sun slipping lower behind the city, trying to make up my mind. I should do something. That was a nagging certainty, but what? Walk back to the warehouse and tell Durrel what I'd learned? Definitely not that.

I got to Koya's house when I ran out of places to go. It was a guess, but it felt like the right one tonight. She answered her own door, the dogs peering curiously from behind her. She was dressed informally in a loose, dark robe, her hair in a long plait down her back, and relief washed over her face when she saw me.

"Celyn! We were so worried! I'll never forgive that bastard Barris."

"I need to speak to Lord Ragn," I said.

For a moment she hesitated, obviously trying to decide whether to dissemble, ask why I would think to find Lord Decath at her house, but finally she stepped aside and said, "Outside."

Lord Ragn was on the terrace landing, seated at a stone table and flipping through maps he couldn't possibly read in the dusk. I slipped out silently and stood beneath the limp white mourning banners, watching him. How could I have missed it? I hadn't. I knew the truth, *had* known it for nearly two weeks now. Since the night of the opera when I'd looked at Durrel and Lord Ragn and not been able to tell them apart. I should turn back. Why couldn't I just ignore the Cartouche boy's story? He'd been traumatized; surely it was possible that he was mistaken about the date?

But he wasn't. I knew he wasn't, and I watched Lord Ragn now, studying the river as if scanning the water for some vessel's distant approach. *Stop*, I told myself. *Don't go, don't speak, don't ask the question.* Because I already knew what the answer was — and I also knew, somehow, that he would tell me. If I didn't say anything, didn't force him to respond, we could all go home and keep telling ourselves that Talth had been killed by some Ferryman thug she'd ripped off.

And not by her innocent husband's father.

I stepped down into the moonlight, and Lord Ragn rose and caught me by the shoulders, crushing me in a hug. "Celyn, thank the gods!" he cried. "The Watch didn't find you? Where's Durrel?"

"Safe," I said, but that was all. I gestured toward his maps. "Any more leads on the missing Sarists?"

"None," Lord Ragn said, but he was still looking at me with that devastating concern. I had to move away from that compassion before I forgot why I'd come. Ragn frowned. "It's almost enough to tempt me to call in the Night Watch myself, have them raid the Ceid's warehouses."

"Don't do that," I said, alarmed. "If they found the Sarists —"

"Of course not," he said. "But it would put a stop to this endless waiting, at least."

"And prove Karst's guilt?"

He looked at me sharply. My next question was a knife, and I aimed it precisely. "Where were you when Talth was killed?"

Lord Ragn breathed out slowly, as if he'd been waiting all month to hear those words, and he was almost relieved someone had finally asked him. The Celystra bells tolled through the muggy night, and the nearby water seemed to make the hot air even thicker. The moons shimmered through the damp, and no breeze teased off the water to pretend that anything besides more heat was coming downstream.

"You don't understand." His face looked cool in the moonlight, but I could still see the darkness of his eyes, and the shadows, deeper still, that lingered there. "I owed her money, you see," he said. "The smuggling operations were getting more expensive. Bribes went up as security tightened with the war. I'd had some dealings with Grensl Ceid, Talth's first husband, and knew him to be a good man who'd left a fortune to his wife. I had no notion of the kind of woman Talth was."

"She hid herself well," I said.

"Too well." But Lord Ragn continued, "When I decided to expand my operation, I needed more cash. I was cautious at first, didn't tell her what the money was for, and she was only too happy to grant me a loan. Plus interest, of course." He paused, his lips tightening. "Eventually she wouldn't lend me any more until I told her what it was being used for. She'd invested a lot in our operations, so I brought her into my confidence."

"Did you kill her?"

"I had to do something! You know what she was, what she was doing to those innocent people who trusted her. I had married my son to a *monster*. It was my responsibility. I had to take care of it."

"And leaving Durrel the blame? That was how you took responsibility?"

"Of course not! I've always intended to turn myself in, but before I could do anything, we learned of the missing passengers. With people delayed, possibly trapped, I had to do what I could to save them, first. It never occurred to me that —" He broke off.

"That Geirt would see you, and mistake you for your son?"

He closed his open hand, a brief fist of frustration. "When Durrel was arrested —" He faltered, a shadow crossing his face. "I swear by Marau, at the time it seemed like the safest place for him. Talth's thugs wouldn't care if she'd been murdered by a disgruntled husband — they weren't going to come after him."

But they did. They nearly did, and we'd only just saved Durrel in time. "You have to speak up," I said. "Barris's men are still after Durrel, and the Ceid are calling for his blood."

"I never meant for anything like this to happen," he said. "You know that." He sighed and shook his head. "I keep wondering how it all could have gone so wrong. Amalle was not in favor of the match. She felt Talth was too old, that Durrel was too young to be married, particularly after what had happened to him in Tratua. But I thought I knew better, that marriage to a woman like Talth would give the boy some stability in his life. I should have listened to her." He sounded weary, resigned. "But at first, things seemed to go well. I had no idea how unhappy my son was."

"Didn't you check on him? Go to him, see how the marriage was working out?"

"I thought to leave him alone, to adjust to married life on his own, that it would be better for him to be independent. I thought the problems they were having were normal for noble marriages. No one of Durrel's rank marries purely for love, and seldom do we have much say in who our partner is. What happened to him is no different than what countless other young noblemen, and women, have gone through."

"Except he was your *son*."

"He was my son," Ragn agreed, and we both heard what neither said. *I should have done more. I should have protected him better.*

"When did you realize what Talth was up to?"

"It was slow," he said. "After we confided in her, Talth insisted we use her ships, her warehouses for the shipments. Initially it seemed a blessing from the gods. Resources we'd had to scramble for before, now at our least bidding. But then I heard — from dockmasters or border guards we were on good terms with — that she was starting to change the terms of deals, withholding bribe money, charging the passengers. . . . I tried to break off my dealings with her, and that was when she threatened to expose us. She had me trapped. She had Durrel trapped." He examined the rim of his tankard carefully, before looking skyward once more. "And then we learned that Talth had been taking on passengers of her own, making them work as slaves in her house and businesses."

"And that she was turning over those who could not pay to the Inquisition."

He nodded grimly. "I went to Bal Marse to reason with her." He paused to take a breath, but I was breathless, motionless. "It was late, and none of the servants was about; I remember thinking she must have sold them off already, and I was blind with rage by the time I found her. When I confronted her about the Inquisition, she laughed. I offered to buy her out of her share of the operation, but she told me she'd found more lucrative partners." Lord Ragn's mouth was set, his face hard. "She'd gotten all she ever wanted from me, after all. She had my son." He gripped the edge of the table tightly. "And then she looked at me and said she hoped the son would turn out as profitable as his father.

"I — I'm not sure what happened next. She turned away from me, and her glass was sitting right there, and I had the Tincture of the Moon — Koya had insisted I carry some, earlier in the week, for the passengers we had coming in. I had never removed it from my purse, and it seemed so simple suddenly, so obvious what I had to do." His face twisted painfully, but he went on. "I stayed long enough to watch her drink it, then I left. I must have thrown the bottle in the river. I didn't have it with me when I got back to Charicaux."

"You dropped it in her room," I said. Where it rolled into the watch-hole. "It was almost empty." *Just a single drop left.*

"But why did Durrel have any?" he asked. "I still don't understand that."

"He bought some tincture for Koya," I explained. "When you resisted the idea of using it, she approached Durrel. She knew he'd do anything for her."

"I didn't realize," Lord Ragn said. "And of course when they found the bottle in his rooms, and with the rumors that their marriage was troubled —"

"And Geirt seeing you leave Talth's chamber and mistaking you for Durrel —"

Lord Ragn pressed his eyes closed briefly. "It was all a terrible mess, and I just needed time to fix everything."

There's never time to fix everything, I thought, but held my tongue. Lord Ragn was silent too, for a long moment. Behind me, I sensed one of Koya's hounds snuffling at the terrace doors, pressing its nose to the glass and wondering why its visitors had secluded themselves outside.

"How does Karst fit in?" I asked.

"He was one of Talth's enforcers. She'd send him to make sure her clients paid up when promised. We've been trying to negotiate with the Ceid, get Barris to let us take the shipment off their hands, but Karst has been suspicious. He's been sniffing around lately, threatening us."

I pulled back against the low stone wall and looked up into the sky. Pinkish clouds swallowed the moons, leaving us in shadow.

"What will you do?" Lord Ragn asked.

"Do? What do you mean?"

"Will you tell my son?"

"I have to," I said. "I don't want to turn you in, but Durrel's life is at stake. I can't let him die for a murder that he didn't commit. And neither can you." A cold, dark thought stopped me. "Koya doesn't know."

"She knows," he said sadly. "She just won't admit it to herself."

"You've told her?"

"No, but she knew I was there to see her mother, and she'd given me the poison."

He was right; Koya *had* to know, had to have known all along, and she'd hidden the truth from all of us, all this time. Maybe even from herself. But what about Durrel? How would he take the news that his father was a murderer?

"Grant me one favor, Celyn."

I wasn't in any position to be generous, but I heard him out.

"Give me time to find Talth's last passengers. We may still be able to rescue them. But if I'm arrested . . ." He turned his anguished eyes to me.

They were all Lord Ragn's responsibility, all children he'd delivered into the clutches of a monster, and he had to save them.

"All right," I said. "But only if you agree to something in return." When he nodded, I said, "*You* tell Durrel the truth. He deserves that much."

There was a long silence, a thick haze hanging over the river, and bull-frogs singing their low, brooding song to the moons. Lord Ragn traced an endless circle with one finger on the papers before him. "Durrel is my only child, you know. After he was born, his mother was very weak, and we knew there would be no more. When he was just a boy — eight years, maybe nine — he fell ill while I was away on business for the Crown. He and his mother were at Favom Court, and he'd broken into the stables early one morning and taken one of the horses to ride. But he fell, trying to jump the paddock wall, and he injured his chest. A fever set in, and for a week, they tell me, our physicians thought we'd lose him. I had forbidden him to ride that horse; it was the last thing I'd said before leaving for the city. He wasn't defiant, but there was something — somehow I knew, the way he'd been eyeing it the past weeks, like he was ready for a challenge. But I was sure I knew better, and it never occurred to me that he would disobey me."

Of course it hadn't. *I'm not allowed to have thoughts of my own.* Lord Ragn shook his head, remembering. "I was tied up at court and couldn't return, though my wife told me he called for me endlessly, in the delirium of fever. When I was finally dismissed, the spectre of Marau had departed, and he was well on the mend, with nothing but a broken collarbone to show how near to death he'd come. I sold that horse when I got back, and I promised myself I would never put my son in harm's way again. And until Talth Ceid, I kept my word."

I waited, watching Ragn stare blankly at his maps.

"It is harder than you can imagine to do good in this world," he said, so quietly I wasn't sure he was speaking to me. "To know what *the right thing* is, all the time. To choose the better of two bad paths, always wondering if you have chosen wrong." He sighed and met my eyes. "Do not judge too harshly actions taken out of love."

I didn't understand, and there wasn't a chance for him to explain, for at that moment Koya's dogs pushed through the terrace doors, followed by Koya herself. "I'm sorry to disturb you both," she said, and there was a chord of tension in her voice that suggested she knew or had guessed the content of our conversation. "But there's been a messenger, and he's brought a note."

"No bother," Lord Ragn said, reaching for the paper she carried.

Koya shook her head. "It's for Celyn."

"For me?" I took it, unfolded it in the moonslight and read it swiftly. "I have to go," I said. "It's from Cwalo."

"Cwalo — who?" Lord Ragn asked, but I was banging up the steps. "Where are you going?"

Reluctantly I turned back. "He says Durrel knows where the refugees are."

"But that's wonderful," Ragn said, rising, but I forestalled him.

"And he's disappeared."

CHAPTER THIRTY-TWO

"What? Where would he have gone?" Lord Ragn's voice was harsh. "You must have some idea."

"No, I —" I faltered, uncertain. "I'm not sure. What did he say to you at Stantin's? I know he was curious about Talth's properties in Markettown —"

"Damn." Lord Ragn was pacing now. "I told him it was madness to go down there."

"It's possible he went somewhere else," I said. "Master Cwalo might know more."

He nodded, his face drawn. "Good. You go there, and I'll check Markettown. It'll take all night, the way traffic is. If I don't find anything, I'll meet you back at —?"

"The docks." I gave him Cwalo's address, and he nodded, looking distracted. I felt like I should say more, but I didn't know what, not after everything he'd told me tonight. Instead I just turned away and darted back up the stairs.

"Celyn —"

I didn't look back.

I took the quickest route I knew across the city, with the rivers jammed and the streets clogged with angry soldiers: over the roofs. Full dark had fallen, the sky awash with moonslight and tinged with the scent of gunpowder. It gave me a chill and hastened my climb across the slates and tiles and occasional thatch of the city's rooftops. I was out of practice and badly dressed for such a mission, but at least the weather was dry and the roofs weren't slippery.

Terribly.

I picked myself up from the dusty cobbles, my hands scraped painfully, and shook the limp out, racing the last of the way to Cwalo's property.

All sorts of dire scenarios proposed themselves, but they all distilled to one simple explanation. Durrel, tired of waiting and chafing at being confined yet again, had broken free and gone looking for the missing Sarists. Alone. With the Watch after him, and Karst still out there.

I was breathless and sweating, my palms stinging with blood, by the time I skirted the last corner and barreled out onto the Big Silver boardwalks. I felt a little dizzy, probably from not eating for two days, and bent against a flamboy to catch my breath, rubbing my chest to ease my heartbeat. But the sensation didn't subside, and I only felt more anxious as I hastened along the docks to Cwalo's. I couldn't shake off the sense I was heading in the wrong direction.

The warehouse was in chaos. Green soldiers swarmed the dockyard, toting guns — theirs or Cwalo's, it was hard to tell — and casks of beer. Crates had been torn open, their contents scattered on the boardwalk, tossed aside into the water. I reeled back. What had happened here? Where was Cwalo? Where was Durrel?

I made my way inside the warehouse, and found Cwalo in his office. "We planted the seeds, my girl," he said, glaring at the soldiers even now sacking the storeroom. "We must bear up through the harvest. But that's not why you've come." He gestured me closer, and I shut the door behind me. "I'm afraid our boy slipped away when the soldiers arrived. We'd been going over some records when we were distracted by the marching outside. I gave him a pistol, for his own protection, but he disappeared the minute my back was turned."

"You've *armed* him? I have to find him."

"Not out there, lass! Half the Green Army's coming down on this town. They are mad with drink and armed to the teeth, and they are not under anybody's control."

"Durrel is out there." My voice was calm, but inside I was pleading with him to understand.

And he was Cwalo. Of course he understood. Wordlessly he took a case from his desk drawer, flipped open the lid, and began assembling an inlaid pistol, gathering shot and powder. "I presume you still remember how to use this," he said. I nodded, but I was looking at the books splayed open on his desk.

"Are these the records you were going over?" I asked.

"Aye," he said, peering sternly at the pistol's working parts. "Troop musters from Hobin, in and out of the city."

I shifted papers aside. "That may have been what *you* were reading," I said. "But Durrel was looking at these." Tucked inside a stack of royal army recruitment rolls, corners bent to hide its different size, was another document, now a little rumpled and edge-worn from being dragged to and fro across the city, stuffed in sleeves and doublets. I turned the Ceid harbor shipping manifests around, looking them over for . . . what? Whatever Durrel had seen, whatever had sent him out into the night with a gun.

"Lass, what is it?"

"I don't know," I said slowly, drawing my finger down the rolls. What — *there*. Familiar names, scrawled in the margins: *Belprisa, Ponvi, Light of Yraine*. I pushed a hand against the neckline of my bodice, wishing that my pulse would settle. Was this what Durrel thought he'd figured out? The Ceid shipyards, where tall ships were trapped at harbor because the city was sealed off from invasion. How many vessels were docked there tonight? Did he think he was going to search them all himself?

"They're on a ship," I said with urgent certainty. "I have to go."

"I hope you know what you're doing," Cwalo said gravely, handing me the pistol. I didn't bother reminding him how very seldom that was the case. I just strapped the pistol snugly to the sheath on my leg and dropped my skirts over it. Cwalo would have been welcome company tonight, but I could hardly ask him to leave his warehouse while it was being looted by the king's army. I gave him a quick, firm hug and took off into the night.

It didn't take me long to reach the Ceid dockyards, even dodging soldiers making disturbingly merry with the contents of the river's warehouses. Soon I was back at the familiar port, gazing up at the tangle of vessels packed together at the harbor. They seemed curiously unguarded; the warehouse itself was standing open to the night and the elements, and it looked like someone had been interrupted in the process of unloading cargo. But where was everyone?

Where was Durrel?

I recognized the *Belprisa*, still anchored beside a low-slung caravel with no flags, and a big, new merchant galleon, which was liable to get stuck in the summer muds if it had to linger in the Big Silver much longer. The *Ponvi*. Was the *Light of Yraine* among that crowd of vessels, and how was I ever going to figure out which ship Durrel had identified?

I paced the abandoned dock, distracted by the annoying quiver in my pulse, thinking hard. What had he seen? I tried to picture him here, finding the right ship — but another thought came to mind instead, from that night we'd watched Lord Ragn receive his refugees. Durrel saying to me, *You knew which boat they were on before I could even see it*; asking how I'd tracked the magic from Bal Marse to the warehouse. . . . I turned slowly, looking over the ships, blocking out the buzz of mob traffic in the distance and the urgency of my throbbing pulse. Straining through the darkness for some sign, some faint shimmer on a curving hull or furled sail, I settled my attention at last on one small brown craft, swirling Talancan script spelling out a name on the prow. All the wild turmoil inside me settled abruptly, like iron filings snapped to a magnet, orienting in the same singular direction — my strange magical compass calibrating itself.

Belprisa.

There was no logic to it, but I knew. However Durrel had discovered this, he had done it without the benefit of magical aid, but I no longer had any doubt, not with the arrow in my blood pointing unequivocally at the ship. Lord Ragn's missing Sarists must be aboard the *Belprisa*. How long had they been there? I thought back over the last fortnight or so, all the times I'd stood right here. When had I seen the *Belprisa* before? Had I felt anything odd? Had I missed them, trapped so close, and merely walked right by?

Not this time. I crept toward the water, behind crates stacked up on the shore, ready for someone to come and carry them off. A movement on board the *Belprisa* caught my eye and I glanced upward. A lantern swung from the mast, and the sails were pulled high and tight. Through the still night, over the lapping water and the murmur of sleepy gulls, I thought I heard voices, floating down through the darkness.

I hesitated, but the snatch of sound was gone as quickly as it had come. I edged closer. The gangway was still in place, and in the wide-open silence, I simply walked on board.

Crouching low, I moved as fast as I could along the deck rail, trying to follow the murmur in my chest, but it was now curiously silent. Either it was satisfied that I knew where I was going, or it was overwhelmed by the proximity of magic, or —

Or the prisoners were gone. And their magic with them, hauled away to the Celystra to be enslaved.

I swallowed that thought, refusing to believe it. And what, by all the gods and hells, had become of Durrel? I reached a hand toward my leg, only slightly reassured by the heavy presence of Cwalo's pistol. Low voices carried on a sudden breeze, and this time I finally saw somebody: a lone sailor on the upper deck, the skipper by his dress, engaged in conversation with someone I couldn't make out. The skipper was a big man with a brace of pistols and a short sword at his belt, and I had the firm conviction I should steer well clear of him.

Cautiously I ducked down behind a row of barrels lashed together and found a stair leading down into the cargo hold — and here, at last, proof that the niggle in my blood was more than imagination. There was enough magic strewn around — handprints on the railing, long streaks like somebody's skirt brushing against a wall — that it was bright enough to navigate the depths of the vessel. I felt all that power rushing back to me, stronger than anything I'd experienced since I had taken the Tincture of the Moon — or before. I had only to brush my fingertips against the smooth, wooden planking of the ship's hull, or catch hold of a rope handrail, and a glittering path woke up before me, lighting the way for me alone.

Now. Where were the *people* who had left these tracks? I paused at the base of the steps, looking into the sparkling gloom, but seeing only barrels and coils of rope and two sad hammocks strung limply in the stern. Above me, footsteps on the deck made the ship creak as we bobbed gently in the current.

I swiped my hand against a glittering wall to pick up some of the magic left behind, and shined it before me like a light as I had once seen Meri do. I was half amazed that such a thing was even possible. I went deeper into the hold, now hearing the muffled voices above me as I moved astern through the ship. The holds were small and dirty, but I could tell the vessel had once been well appointed; Talth's ships would no doubt have been newer, nicer, faster, and better than what ordinary Ferrymen had had access to before her. My foot scuffed over something on the floorboards, and I looked down. As I cast my hand in a slow arc at my feet, I saw long, straight lines of magic join into a neat square — illuminating the edges of a door set into the floor.

I knelt down, picked the lock, and flipped the hatch open, and the invisible light from the depths below nearly knocked me backward with its brightness. Blinking it away, I squinted through the glow to the hold beneath — and found at least a dozen wide, frightened eyes staring back at me.

"It's all right. I'm here to help you. I'm —" What should I say to them? I took a reckless stab in the dark. "I'm called Digger. I'm not with the Ferrymen."

There was no glimmer of understanding, of recognition. They just *stared*, as if wondering what I might do to them next. "I think they're gone," I said. "If you come with me now, we can get out of here."

Nothing. Pox and hells. Someone in the group was incredibly powerful, and it was hard to see naturally with that distracting glow around them all. I was going to have to touch them, douse their light a little. I gave a little flick of my hands, scooting them all backward, and then dropped myself down into the hold with them.

I heard a sob, a whimper, a sharp intake of breath. *"I won't hurt you,"* I said. "I just — you're too bright. How many are you?"

The knot of people finally sorted themselves out and a woman about Lord Ragn's age stepped forward. She should have been pretty, with black hair and pale green eyes that filled her narrow face, but she looked haggard and worn. "Nine. I'm Irin, and this is Meis," she added, indicating the child at her side. I recognized her now, the lean features, the long, thin wrists, the guarded hazel eyes. She must be the mother of the boy at Cartouche.

"I've seen your son," I told her. "He's safe here in the city. I can help you — all of you. But we need to get off the ship before the Ferrymen come back."

"They said they were off to fetch their buyers," Irin said. "What does that mean?"

Nothing good, I thought with alarm. But I just shrugged. They all shifted uncertainly in the small space, and as they parted, I saw a boy a little younger than me tucked in the back, alone and wary. He was the source of all that power, bursting up through the cracks in the wood, blinding me. His magic had a strange, slightly off-kilter tinge to it — yet it was familiar, and as I reached for him, my fingers barely brushing his arm, I understood why. *"Reijk-sarta,"* I said, surprise coloring my voice. "You're a Channeler."

He looked back at me blankly, as if he couldn't understand Llyvrin. I wasn't sure he'd be capable of understanding *anything* after being crammed into the tiny hold of a ship for weeks, and who knows what horrors and abuses before that. I knelt beside him in the smoky darkness. "Your magic is different." My voice was as gentle as I could make it, but he cringed away from me. "No," I said, and tried to smile. "It's a good thing. Really. Look." I lifted my hand to his, and when he touched me, *I* flared brighter. Sometimes they couldn't see their own magic without my touch. The *Reijk-sarta* were incredibly rare, even among magic users. Master Reynart had only known of one: Meri. The discovery of a second Channeler would revolutionize magic in Llyvraneth, could turn the tide of the war decisively in Wierolf's favor. *Look forth and see if you might not find another like me for we could sorely use him now.*

Or this boy would go peacefully into the countryside, or the seacoast, or the city — or to Corlesanne or Talanca or Brionry, and live out his own life in quiet anonymity, unmolested by Ferrymen, Inquisitors, or wild thief girls who popped in from nowhere, spouting all kinds of nonsense about magic. I bit my lip and drew my hand away. Before he could make that choice, I had to get them all out of here.

"All right, let's go. I didn't see a ladder or a rope handy, but I can pull you up after me, with your help." I squeezed back through the jumble of bodies. A thick, musky scent filled the cramped hold, fear, as palpable as a fog, seeping from their pores as surely as their magic did. I was just about to jump for the edges of the opening and haul myself back out onto the cargo deck when I heard footsteps rattling down the narrow stair. I dropped back, motioning the refugees into the shadows.

"Don't get your breeches in a knot, I'm going," said a disturbingly familiar voice. *Pox.* Smooth black boots stepped toward the opening, bringing a bobbing circle of light with them. Durrel stumbled into view, knocked off balance by a sudden shifting of the rolling ship and the butt of a musket rammed into his back. The armed Ferryman moved into the light, and every single one of us pulled back deeper into the darkness. It was instinctive. *Karst.* He bent his leering face low to the crammed hold and grinned at us.

"Looks like there's room for some company down there," he said, and shoved Durrel hard over the edge of the hatch.

I caught him — barely. It was more like he landed on me, flattening me into Irin and the others, and we tumbled back against the wall together.

"Sorry," he mumbled, trying to stand, and I realized his hands were bound behind him. "I usually fall with *far* more grace."

"Enjoy your new quarters," Karst called down. "You won't be in there long." He kicked shut the hatch door above us, sealing out all the real light. I heard Durrel take a hiss of breath, the shuffle of bodies shifting fearfully into position.

I heard the snap of a padlock on the trapdoor hasp.

"Oh, bloody *pox*."

"Celyn?" Durrel hauled himself to his feet, with the help of a tall, older man whose eyes were dark with haunted shadows. Durrel bore an expression of utter disbelief — and something else that faded too fast for me to see. "I'm glad you're here. I think. Can't you pick any lock?" he added.

"I can," I said. "But I have to be able to *reach* it first. And that one is on the other side of a locked door."

CHAPTER THIRTY-THREE

There was a dead, crushing silence following my words, as the reality of our situation sank in. Well, for Durrel and me, at least; the others had lived for days, weeks without hope. Having us locked in here too didn't change anything for them.

"Well, this is inconvenient," Durrel said, looking around the hold. "Now what do we do?" He made a halfhearted jump for the hatch. "Celyn, do you still have your knife? They took my weapons."

"And a pistol." I fumbled it from my leg, found the shot and powder at my belt.

"Better yet. Are you a good shot?"

"Not by half. Why?"

Durrel edged backward, pushing us deeper into the hold. "Maybe we can shoot our way through."

A murmur of hope whispered through the group, but the tall man spoke up from the back. "Are you mad? That hatch is two inches thick. You'll never shoot through it."

"It's worth a try, though," argued Irin.

"Right," Durrel said. "Celyn?"

"You'd better do it," I said, passing him the gun. "I'm liable to miss and take somebody's head off."

"Who *are* you?" the older Sarist demanded.

"Vorges!" Irin said, as Durrel looked at them in surprise.

"Sorry. Of course. I'm Durrel Decath, and this is — a friend, Celyn Contrare."

"Decath?" Another man, who hadn't spoken yet, pushed through the crowd. "Lord Decath was supposed to meet us." There was a darkness in his voice, and I was suddenly alarmed for us.

"You've been deceived," I said firmly. "Unscrupulous people used that name to convince you to trust them. The real Decath has been searching for you. He's on his way now. This is his son. We've come to help you."

I spoke clearly, slowly, trying to make them — *all* of them — believe me, but a dissatisfied grumble rose up from the others, while Durrel's knuckles whitened around the pistol grip.

"Some help," Vorges said. "You've gotten yourselves trapped as well."

"It's all part of my clever plan." I sighed. "How do we get out of here?"

Durrel was studying the trapdoor. "Maybe we could dig away at the hinges, see if we can't pry the pins out? Celyn, your knife?"

"That's a good idea," Vorges said reluctantly. He stepped forward. "I'm tall; I can help."

It was a good idea, except that the hinges were with the lock on the other side of the hatch. "Wait," I said, having the worst idea ever, and everyone stopped and looked at me. "Which one of you is the best trained?"

There was a blank silence. "In *magic*. Nobody? None of you even played around with it a little bit? Hells." Not that I could really blame them; why should I expect any more from these people than from the girl who'd fled the Celystra six years ago? There *was* no safe place to practice magic.

"I know a little," a tiny voice finally piped up, and a girl just as small to match wriggled forward out of the group.

"Good. What can you do?"

She gave a shrug. "Um, I can make a light —" which she demonstrated, and Durrel smiled at her in appreciation. "And swirls —" Pretty, but impractical. "And sometimes I can make a room smell like lilies."

I reined in my impatience. "Anything else?" I said encouragingly. "Fire? Wind?"

"I can light a candle —"

"Perfect! What's your name?"

She smiled shyly at me. "Teina."

"You, in the back —" I held my hand toward the Channeler. "What are you called?"

"Jos," he said, edging forward suspiciously. "What are you going to do?"

The proper question, I thought, was what *he* was going to do. "I'm going to show you how to use your magic." Or I was going to kill everyone. Even chances. But Teina and Jos watched me eagerly, and even Durrel gave an encouraging nod.

I moved Teina closer to Jos as the others shuffled aside. "Jos, you have a special kind of power, and it can magnify Teina's." I couldn't believe I was standing here, locked in a ship's cargo hold with a band of refugees, giving a primer on magic. But as I watched the group, curious faces drawn into the circle of Jos's light, I realized these people were as desperate for knowledge as they were for freedom. I was no Master Reynart, but I'd do what I could.

"All right," I said. "This is how magic works." And I briefly sketched out the fail-safe system Reynart had once explained to me, how magic was the power of the gods, lent to mortals; how Sar had split her gift, so that no one mage could wield more than a lone mortal could handle, into Channelers and Casters; how the magic was buried deep within the earth, and it took someone with Jos's gift to pull the power up from the land, and someone with Teina's gift to shape that power into a weapon.

"Or a tool," I amended, considering what I was about to attempt. I took a breath. "So, Teina, if you touch Jos, you should be able to make a brighter light, *bigger* swirls —" *Larger fires.* "Let's practice first on swirls."

Beaming, Teina slipped her hand inside Jos's, who flinched slightly, but then grabbed her almost fiercely. "Easy there," I said. "Now give it a try."

Teina drew her hand through the air, and a glittering pattern of vines and curlicues followed, but nothing much greater than she'd done on her own. I felt my eyebrows pull together. What was I missing here? Jos, frustrated, yanked his hand away. Ah! That was it. All of Reynart's students had worn tattoos, as if the ink conducted the magic more efficiently.

"Teina, I don't suppose you have a tattoo, do you?" She giggled and shook her head. Nobody was carrying pen and ink either. I stared up at the ceiling for a moment. Teina certainly wasn't powerful enough on her own to budge that door. We *needed* Jos for this plan to work.

"Durrel, can I have my knife back?" I asked, and felt it slip into my hand as naturally as if it belonged there. I rolled up my smock sleeve and touched the tip of the blade to the crook of my elbow, near the long scar that already snaked down my forearm, but Durrel caught me by the wrist.

"Wait," he said. "Let me." And he shucked out of his doublet and shoved his sleeve halfway up his arm. It seemed a shame to mark that smooth, beautiful skin, but I did it. I nicked as tiny a cut as I could manage, right where the blood welled up at the surface of his skin, as good as charmed violet ink. I dipped my fingernail into the blood and turned to Jos. The boy seemed to realize what I was doing, and he swiftly rolled up his own tattered and filthy sleeve, revealing a painfully thin, bruised arm beneath.

"You're not going to *cut* him," a woman's voice objected.

"No." As carefully as I could, with my glittering finger, I traced a crude seven-pointed star with Durrel's blood on Jos's arm. I hoped we didn't actually need *magical* blood; blood freely given in sacrifice seemed sensible as well. When the Mark of Sar was on Jos, with Durrel breathing on it to dry the blood, I traced the same symbol on Teina's palm.

"Now try," I urged, and Teina carefully put her hand on Jos's arm, matching star to star. She pulled back like she'd been shocked, and giggled. Jos turned stunned eyes to her.

"Do that again," he said, almost the longest sentence he'd yet spoken.

Suppressing a grin, Teina grabbed Jos's arm, harder this time, and before I could say anything, she swept her hand in a glittering arc through the dark air, and a brilliant tracery of light and smoke flared into the space like fireworks. Gasps and murmurs greeted this display, and I could feel the longing, hungry people in the hold pressing closer, wishing for their turn with Jos.

"That will do," I said, gently separating them. "Now, let's see if we can't get out of here. Teina, I want you to try and break down that hatch."

"How?" Jos spoke up.

"With fire," Teina said with solemn understanding. "We can shove the fire through the door, and it will come off."

Jos stared at her, at me. "Will it work?"

"You don't need to ask me," I said. "Feel it for yourselves." But I was worried. I had no doubt those two could blow the door right off its hinges — the key was not blasting the hatch straight through the hull of the ship.

"Careful," Durrel said, apparently having the same thought. "Everyone, get back. Cover your heads."

"I have no idea what's going to happen next," I warned. But I hoped at least some of them could swim. "Teina, can you picture the lock, clasped on the other side of that door?"

I held my hands up to show her the lock's size, and imagined sending a strand of my own magic floating through the crack around the door to find the target. Teina had her head cocked thoughtfully to one side, her gaunt face screwed up tight in concentration. Jos looked patient, ready. At last Teina nodded and clutched Jos's arm once again. The blood was smeared and flaked now, but that didn't seem to affect either of them. Teina lifted her free hand and pointed one slim finger toward the trap-door in the ceiling.

I held my breath, and didn't even realize Durrel was squeezing me as tightly as Teina gripped Jos, until he bent my head against his shoulder, turning his face into my hair. I held him hard, bracing my body against his, hearing the anxious breathing of the refugees, the lapping of the waves against the hull, the creak and shift of the wet boards — and, suddenly, a tiny explosive *crack* of shattered metal. Sparks flew everywhere — visible, invisible, and Teina stood frozen in the middle of the hold, hands clamped over her mouth, dark eyes huge and surprised in her little face. Beside her, Jos frowned up at the ceiling.

"Did it work?" somebody asked, and Durrel peeled away from me, to give the trap a gentle shove. It came loose, crashing down into the hold, nearly on top of Teina and Jos — but Durrel swept the girl up in his arms and away from the falling wood. She gave a shriek of laughter, and the other refugees broke into spontaneous applause. Jos stared at the opening, at me, in wonderment. I grinned back.

"That was impressive," Durrel said. "And — loud."

"Is anyone coming?" I edged forward to peer up through the darkened hatch. We could probably shoot the first Ferryman who came to investigate, but we'd lose the advantage after that. "How many men are up there?"

"I only saw Karst and the captain," Durrel said. "But I heard another voice as well."

"Karst usually has three men with him," Vorges said. "I've seen at least five different faces, though."

I glanced at Durrel, whose brows were knitted together in a mirror of my own concern. Our sad little band of refugees, against possibly six armed Ferrymen? "So we're outnumbered," I said — practically, if not technically. "And almost certainly outgunned. The captain is armed with handguns and a sword, at least. We've got one knife and one pistol."

"And us." Irin's voice was firm.

I admired her bravery, but what were we going to do? Fend Karst's men off with *swirls*?

"What are we waiting for?" Vorges demanded. "The longer we wait here, the better the chances of them coming back."

"Right," Durrel said. "Up we go, then." He made a stirrup of his hands for my foot, boosting me up and out of the hold. I landed lightly, crouched low beside the broken hatch, my fingers tracing the darkness for signs of Karst and his men. They must have judged the lock sufficient, for there was no one in sight on the cargo deck. From the decks above came a clatter of footsteps and agitated voices.

"Hist," I said. "It's clear. On this deck, at least." I reached down into the hold, and my hands met Irin's; she was balanced awkwardly on Durrel's linked fingers, and I pulled her out beside me. One by one, all nine were handed up, Durrel waiting until the very last of the refugees was out of that cramped hold before climbing out himself.

"Now what?" I asked him, once we were all assembled, a little glowing knot of bodies huddled in the shadows. "This is your plan, milord."

"All right," Durrel said. "Let's get these people to safety. Upstairs, everyone."

"We'll have to cross to the opposite side to get to the gangway," I said. "Lord Durrel will cover us. Big ones protect the little ones."

Durrel nodded, his face solemn, and we got answering nods from the refugees. My heart was banging in my throat, and my hand was so slick with sweat I was afraid I would drop my knife, but their faces were aglow with hope. I prayed to any gods listening we wouldn't let them down.

"Ready?" Durrel asked, and launched himself up onto the deck, pistol at the ready.

I climbed after him as fast as I could, the others behind me. We emerged in a fog of smoke and haze, which even so seemed impossibly bright after the darkness of the ship's hold. As I stepped onto the open deck, someone rose up out of the smoke ahead of me, but reeled backward, arms raised, at the sight of Durrel's gun.

He gave a shout, and with that we lost our stealth. "Get back!" I cried to the refugees, but there was nowhere for them to go. The deck was swarming with men, deckhands, even a couple of Greenmen with their nightsticks drawn, and — sweet Tiboran — Lord Ragn, armed with a short sword and clambering over the side of the ship like he belonged there. He grabbed the nearest deckhand by his clothes and yanked him overboard into the roiling water below.

"Stop them! They're getting away!" Karst's bellow came from the upper deck, and a moment later the man himself appeared, sliding down the steps to the deck and shoving his own men aside to get to us.

"Quick!" I cried. I could see the gangway, and a twining path that crossed the deck and dodged the masts, but we'd have to skirt the worst of the fighting. I dashed toward the curving deck rail, Irin and her daughter on my heels. Lord Ragn had seen us, and was making his way in our direction, fending off a sailor armed with a rod of iron and waving a pistol wildly.

I was almost to the gangway when I heard the first shot. "Go, go, go!" I said, shoving my Sarists before me. "Make for that little boat!" Down below the ship, hidden in the shadow of the *Belprisa's* curving hull, I'd caught a glimpse of an elegant, painted skiff, moonslight frosting its cushioned seats. The *Davinna Koyuz*. Koya herself was crouched by the *Belprisa's* gangway, her own pistol drawn, looking preternaturally calm. She scarcely nodded as the Sarists scrambled past her down the ramp.

A green shape suddenly loomed up before me, and I barely had time to register the length of wood crashing toward my head when I heard a shriek of rage. A beam of moonslight shattered the air by my ear, hitting the Greenman squarely in the chest and hurling him backward against the mast. I whirled around and saw Vorges beside me, a look of fury on his face. One arm was raised — and the other clutched Jos hard up against his body. I stared, mouth half open, until the man loosed his hold on Jos and showed me his hand.

"I have a tattoo," he said simply. Not much of one, just a circle of faded ink on his palm. I think I nodded, dazed, as he guided Jos more gently down the gangway guarded by Koya. The other Greenman fell to the deck beside his injured partner and flung his nightstick down in surrender.

Durrel had joined his father on the deck, calmly loading and firing the pistol, as Lord Ragn fended off Ferrymen with his sword. Durrel wounded at least one of them, and Lord Ragn had succeeded in disarming the guy with the pipe — but there was Karst, thundering toward them, a knife the length of my forearm clutched in one meaty hand.

"Celyn, *go!*" Durrel shouted. In the moment that Durrel looked away, Karst lurched forward, slipping awkwardly on the wet deck, his great arm reaching to seize Lord Ragn from behind, that huge knife sharp against his lordship's bearded neck. Ragn's sword fell, landing with a ring at his feet.

"Durrel —" Ragn's voice was calm, assured, but his face had gone a little pale.

"All right," Karst said, edging backward with Lord Ragn. "Everyone just be easy. Drop your weapons, and I'll consider not killing this nob."

I heard something clatter to the deck. Durrel had dropped my pistol, and at the anguished look he gave me, I knelt and laid my knife beside it.

"Good," Karst said. "Now, if you'll excuse me, we'll be taking that boat there."

"Karst, it's too late!" Ragn said. "There's nowhere to go. Just put the knife down and surrender."

Karst gave a coarse laugh. "It's time you learned you're not in charge here." He dragged Lord Ragn toward the gangway, toward the waiting boat full of Sarists. The second Greenman hauled himself to his feet again and retrieved his club. I heard a whimper from the boat below, and saw Koya, hands up in surrender, step aside.

"We can't let him take them!" I cried, but I was out of ideas. After all we'd done, we'd only managed to neatly package the hostages into a nice, easily deliverable bundle, with the Greenmen right here to carry them off to the Celystra.

Koya backed away from the ramp, and Karst moved to disembark. When he reached the gangway, he shoved Lord Ragn away from him, and Durrel's father stumbled slightly, trying to regain his footing.

Or did he? In the swirling mist, I caught a flash of silver, and somehow, Lord Ragn had a blade in his hand again. But Karst was turning —

"Lord Ragn!" I screamed into the night, and Ragn spun just in time to knock Karst's hand away. He was fast and nimble, but Karst was big and mean, and the deck was wet, and when Lord Ragn advanced with his dagger drawn, all it took was one lunge of Karst's boots on the slippery boards for Lord Ragn to stagger back into the stacked-up barrels, hand at his side, a look of surprise brightening his whole face.

"Don't take another step." We all turned at the sound of that calm voice. Koya had soundlessly drawn her weapon once more. Karst had the knife in his hand to strike again, and Koya leveled her pistol at him, cool as moonlight. Water splashed the hull as the *Belprisa* rocked in the current, and Lord Ragn slumped hard against the barrels. Karst turned his coarse face toward us, and the look in his usually bland eyes was fiery and mad. He grabbed clumsily for Lord Ragn a second time — and Koya's pistol went off.

I saw the puff of smoke from the muzzle, heard the hiss of the fire in the damp night. Karst's knife clunked against the deck, followed by the thump of his body, and a fat, bloated splash as he tumbled into the water.

Koya's arm did not move, stayed straight and steady before her, the pistol gripped in her smooth, white hand. But her knuckles tightened and her jaw quivered once, before she lowered her arm and slipped the pistol into her belt. And then she broke forward and ran across the ship, dodging masts and rigging, to Lord Ragn.

Durrel got there first, and he knelt beside his father, one arm propping him up, his face wild with panic. In the shining moonlight it was all too easy to see the spreading stain of blood on Lord Ragn's doublet, his hand curled to his side. Koya stood frozen, white hands to her mouth, just staring, but I skidded in the wet, dropping beside Durrel, and ripped Ragn's doublet open.

Blood pooled everywhere, turning the white linen to red. I fumbled for the nearest blade and sliced away at the sodden cloth, finally, finally revealing the wound, an ugly, gaping mouth deep in the flesh of his taut flank, thick, dark blood pumping out as he breathed.

"Press *here*," I told Durrel, balling up a handful of wet shirt, and my voice sounded shrill and not my own. Durrel's hand brushed mine, but he didn't see me. He was watching his father's face, which had turned pale and ashen.

"Son —" Lord Ragn gasped as Durrel held the rags to his side.

"Don't talk," Koya said, and her voice sounded like mine. Behind us, the *Belprisa's* crew had scattered, and Vorges had climbed back aboard, dragging the second Greenman by the collar. Assisted by a fierce-looking Irin, he rounded up the few remaining crewmen, who looked on, faces unreadable.

"Celyn, what do we do?" Durrel turned desperate eyes to me.

"Can you help him?" Koya asked me urgently.

I didn't think so. I knew a little medicine — enough to tell me the black blood bubbling up from Lord Ragn's wound was very bad. I did all I could to stop the bleeding, but the pressure on the wound, the hasty bandages weren't enough. All around me in the night air were glittering particles left from Vorges's blast of light, lingering there in the murk and smoke as if waiting for someone to shape them, and I felt furiously impotent, all this magic nearby, and I could do *nothing* with it. "I'm no healer," I said helplessly.

Someone knelt beside me, and I scarcely noticed until he spoke — the short, dark Sarist from the hold. "My name is Lenos. I can heal," he said in his soft voice, and laid his small, brown hands against Lord Ragn's wound. The scattered power still hanging in the air gathered around his fingers like cloud floss, and Lenos held it against Ragn's flesh like bandages and ointment.

Lord Ragn was breathing shallowly, looking from his son to Koya. "It's no use," he said, but his voice was a faint, faint whisper. "I hear the crows."

"No, my lord — Father —" Durrel gripped his hand harder. "You're not going to die." But the look Lenos gave me then, all crushing shock and sadness and disappointment, agreed with Lord Ragn. He never stopped working, though. As Tiboran turned from half to crescent in the sky, he pushed as much magic as he could into Lord Ragn's body.

We can sometimes stay the hand of Marau, for a time. . . . Another magical healer had told me that once, and now I finally understood exactly what she had meant. As long as Lenos worked, until he exhausted himself and his magic, he could hold Lord Ragn's life in his body, keep soul intact and body breathing, though that body bled itself to nothing. But eventually, eventually he must stop, and when he did — I didn't need to see what the magic could tell me to know the truth. Even Jos's power couldn't help us now.

"Enough," I said gently, finally, my hand on Lenos's arm. He shook his head and bent lower, but Durrel watched me, a question in his eyes. Something in my chest turned to ice and cracked, but I nodded, once, as briefly as I could. Durrel took a shaky breath, looked skyward for a moment, then turned to his father. Lord Ragn's eyes fluttered faintly, opened, recognized his son.

"I'm sorry," Ragn said.

Durrel bent low, his hair brushing his father's chest. "No, no . . ."

But his words were sighs, breaths, crow feathers carried into the night. And for the first time, as Durrel held the body of his dead father, I saw that Koya was still there, as well, silently holding fast to Lord Ragn's other hand.

CHAPTER THIRTY-FOUR

That long night stretched on forever, in a slow blur of smoke, noise, and confusion. Koya smoothly took control of the scene at the *Belprisa*. Under her direction, her boatman carried the Sarists to safety at Cartouche. She coaxed Durrel to stand guard over the rounded-up Ferrymen, and I remember the set of his shoulders, the determined look on his face as he turned from her, gun in hand. The fight was over, that look said; the losses were insurmountable, but his steady calm, his *nobility* never wavered. Lord Ragn had died for the refugees, and Durrel would not waste his father's sacrifice by letting even one Ferryman escape justice too soon. Sometime during the night, Barris Ceid and the Night Watch arrived. Koya's word was enough to convince the guard to take her brother and the remaining Ferrymen into custody.

When Barris protested, the Watch captain turned to him. "Look, I don't know what all's been going on here tonight, but a lord's been murdered, and you're right in the middle of it. You're not leaving my sight until this is settled." He gave a nod to one of his men. "And bring Greenie-boy there along too. He looks like he's got something to *confess*."

They left Durrel alone, however; perhaps even they were reluctant to seize a man as his father lay dead beside him. Or they lacked the authority to arrest the new Lord of Decath.

Lenos the healer performed the sacred rites for Lord Ragn, closing his eyes and arranging his hands to call Marau's crows and let the god of the dead know where to find his soul. As the Sarists filed away, some touched Lord Ragn's fallen body reverently, giving final thanks to the man who was, at the last, their savior.

Night turned to morning, and friends appeared out of the fog to help. Cwalo looked characteristically imperturbable as he sifted through the chaos on the docks, and even Raffin made it, clad improbably in his green uniform once more, and bleeding from a new cut on his cheek. He'd gone back to the Celystra, he told us, in hopes of sneaking back inside and learning more of the fate of Karst's Sarists. But he'd run into the fighting there, and somehow helped save the temple from looters. He looked like he wasn't entirely sure how he felt about that.

What I did next, I did for Durrel. And for Lord Ragn, for Koya, for Lenos and Jos and Teina and Meri and Reynart and all the others. I didn't have to think about it; if Koya and Durrel might have had other ideas, I did not consult them. I searched the *Belprisa*'s captain's quarters, where I found enough evidence to damn all those involved in Talth's smuggling ring — should anyone ever care about the fates of exploited Sarist refugees, that is. It was the work of an afternoon to move a seal, change a date or two on the *Belprisa*'s manifest, draft an incriminating voucher . . . and by the time the moons rose again, I had all the proof of Karst's and the Ferrymen's guilt spelled out in irrefutable detail, or enough to convince the Ceid of Durrel's innocence in Talth's murder, at least.

I turned the new records over to Koya, including a letter in which "Karst" described in brutal if half-literate detail how he'd poisoned Talth Ceid with Tincture of the Moon he'd bought from a potioner in the Temple District, along with signatures attesting that this confession had been extracted by the honorable Lord Raffin Taradyce, Acolyte Guardsman, and witnessed by one Davinna Koyuz. She gripped them tightly, fingers white, but agreed to deliver them to the proper civic and royal authorities. We may have painted Karst in a dimmer light than even he deserved, but I felt no regret. What Karst *had* done, the things he had unquestionably been guilty of, went beyond anything Gersin or even Llyvrin laws were currently equipped to judge. I thought he was lucky he only had Marau's justice to contend with.

Lord Ragn had murdered Talth. There was no doubt of that, not after his admission to me. *I had married my son to a monster,* he had said, overcome with remorse for that, and he had compounded his guilt by lying and letting his son be framed for murder. That it was done in a good cause, to save innocent lives . . . In the end, Lord Ragn had redeemed himself, and his explanations, his reasons justified everything he'd done.

Didn't they?

But it still troubled me. Lord Ragn never had the chance to explain his actions to Durrel or make up for putting his son's life in danger in favor of the survival of Sarists he didn't know. All the lies and the pretense and the good he had done knotted into a tangle I was too weary to undo, and not even sure I wished to. And so I let Lord Ragn's guilt sink to the bottom of the Big Silver river with Karst's body, and I did the only thing left I could, for both of them, Durrel *and* Lord Ragn. I made a lie into the truth, and the truths into secrets no one could ever uncover.

The city changed that night. Rioting soldiers, mad with hunger and fed on rumors that had spread through their ranks like a plague, marched on Hanivard Palace to demand bread, wine, and payment, and were brutally mown down by the king's better-fed and better-armed palace guards. Their comrades, upon hearing of their brothers' fate, stormed Gerse's sealed gates from the inside, slaughtering the sentries posted there and throwing open the city to the world beyond — and Prince Wierolf's army, camped some twenty miles downriver and slowly but inevitably fighting their way toward the capital.

The Celystra fared much the same as the palace, though the force that attacked her was smaller and more mercifully set down. Greenmen calmly fended off the handful of royal troops that had broken rank, hoping to sack the temple's rich stores of grain, wine, and other treasures, and the soldiers' wrath proved no match for the temple's wall or her loyal Acolyte Guard.

I learned all this news in passing, as if watching it unfold behind a scrim of gauze; it happened, but it didn't touch me, somehow. I went back to the bakery, though the room no longer quite felt like home, and in the days that followed, as the entire city waited in the wake of the massacre at Hanivard, holding its breath to see what would happen next, I kept my distance from Durrel. Knowing everything I did, I wasn't sure what to say to him, and he was deep in the burdens of planning his father's funeral while learning how to become Lord Decath. I had done the job I'd been conscripted for — I'd solved his wife's murder, after all — and I wasn't sure where I fitted into his life anymore.

I ought to have realized he'd have thoughts of his own on the matter. Early one evening I dallied outside Grea's, halfheartedly trying to decide whether or not to go to work. From a long distance away, I watched a shape gradually resolve itself into Lord Durrel, slowly walking down Bargewater Street, glancing into arches and doorways as if I might be lurking in some shadows there, and looking altogether lost, like the world was too big for him. The sky spread out above him, the river curving huge and gray and fathomless beside him, and he looked so . . . *inconsequential* that my heart squeezed, so sharp and sudden it caught my breath.

And then he saw me, and the shadows lifted, partly, from his face, and his step hastened, and before I could prepare myself, his arms were around me and he was breathing into my hair. I let my face rest against the hollow of his throat, and for the longest moment I didn't even think of pulling away.

Finally we parted, just enough to allow the other to breathe.

"We held the funeral," he said, and just then it seemed the only possible thing to say.

"I know." Hidden on a neighboring rooftop, I had watched the procession of Lord Ragn's body from Charicaux, draped in white, his son at his shoulder. Durrel still wore his white mourning doublet, but tonight it hung open in the hot air, as if he was half afraid the Bargewater residents might recognize him for a nob. Koya had been at the funeral too, although there was no official call for her presence; she had stood beside Lady Amalle, her glittering eyes staring into the distance, as Amalle clutched her white-clad arm with thin hands like claws.

"You didn't come." There was no accusation there, just wonder.

"I —" I faltered, looked away for a moment, and told the truth. A funeral, even for a nobleman like Ragn Decath, was a family affair, not a public spectacle. "I don't know where I would have stood."

The way Durrel's fingers sought mine gave his answer to that, and I felt a surge of grief I didn't quite understand.

"I'm leaving for Favom tomorrow," he said after a long moment. "I need to settle the affairs at the farm. I want to ask you to come, but I know you'll say no. You'll tell me I have to do this on my own, and you'll be right."

"How long will you be gone?" I asked.

"It will take time," he said. "A month, maybe more? But I'll come back. Don't think I won't."

I wanted to say, *Don't go.* Or maybe, *Don't come back, stay there in Favom with the horses and the orchards and Morva and all those beautiful gardens, where everything is safe and easy,* but I couldn't find my voice.

"Why didn't he tell me, Celyn?"

"I don't know." It was one bit of the puzzle I still couldn't figure out. Why hadn't Lord Ragn included his son in his rescue operations? I couldn't imagine anyone better suited for such a job than Durrel Decath, yet his own father had either overlooked him or deliberately excluded him, neither of which made sense.

"I think —" I took a breath and looked out over the water, as if I could somehow see the spectre of Lord Ragn hovering there, judging what we said of him now. "He was trying to protect you. He risked everything to save those people — his money, his House and rank, his life. But he wasn't willing to risk *you.*" *I promised myself I would never put my son in harm's way again.* "You were everything he had, the only thing that mattered, in the end."

He looked at me helplessly, his shoulders slumped. "I never had a chance to — I don't know."

But I did. I pulled him closer, feeling his heartbeat near my face. "He knew what kind of man you are." I thought of his actions aboard the *Belprisa*, how Lord Ragn had looked on in pride as he fought beside his son. "I know he did."

Durrel held fast to me, in the heat and the setting sun, and I wondered how I could ever have imagined any part of the world thought this man didn't *matter.* He was anything but inconsequential. I bent his face to mine and held his cheeks, softly coated with new-grown beard, as our foreheads touched, and then our lips.

The next few weeks were so upside down, there was hardly time to feel his absence. The royal army had suffered mass desertions since the riots, and a hysterical Astilan had struck back at his own forces with all the violence at his disposal, ordering the heads of executed traitors set on display along the city walls and thoroughfares. It only served to further enrage the remaining troops, until — as Cwalo and Berdal and Lord Hobin had predicted, not so long, yet forever ago — the city was for all purposes undefended.

In this climate, Wierolf's army arrived, crouching just outside the western wall and offering terms for peace. He would not sack the city and burn Hanivard to the ground, if Bardolph would abdicate and Astilan surrender absolutely. The ranks of troops at his back — more cheerful, certainly, though hardly better fed than Astilan's own — were like a surging wave threatening the city, and for a few tense days Hanivard Palace sat cryptic and silent, as Prince Wierolf prowled outside Gerse and waited.

As the tension in the city tightened into a knot choking all of us, a messenger finally sent a flag of truce to Wierolf's camp, and the slow process of negotiations began. A few regiments of Sarist troops made tentative inroads in Gerse, setting up hospitals and breadlines for hungry citizens and soldiers alike; but the prince himself would not set foot inside the city until the peace was finalized, he announced. It could take weeks, months, but Wierolf was adamant. Not until Bardolph was gone and Hanivard empty of all the old king's men would he return to the city from which he'd been banished as a boy.

In the rocky, uneasy peace that followed, we all tried to get back to normal, but no one remembered what that was. Grea's bakery did its familiar thriving business, with a whole new clientele — Raffin, fully restored to his Guard duties, brought his fellow Greenmen to dine, this time without the threats of violence or seizure.

I was still not sure how I felt about him, about them. The fate of Werne and the Inquisition was one of the sticking points of the peace talks; the Celystra was not technically under the authority of the king, so there was confusion on both sides about what could or should be done about them. But Raffin told me things that filled me with disquiet — and they were not all dark secrets buried at the Greenmen's feet, not all blood and torture and fearmongering. He'd been assigned to the division releasing Inquisition prisoners as a gesture of good-will; holy sisters went to the front to pray for the dead, and sent alms to the widows of soldiers on each side. It both did and did not accord with what I knew of Werne, and left me unsettled for reasons I could not explain.

Lord Ragn's words burned in my memory — *Do not judge too harshly actions taken out of love* — until ultimately I put my hand to one last document. Five words, set on plain, coarse paper and sent back with Raffin: *I will speak with you.*

Maybe people deserved a chance to explain themselves.

I saw much of Koya too, passing along news of the refugees, now safely settled in distant lands, or with Wierolf's troops, with Meri and Reynart. I had wondered about the boy at Cartouche, and his mother and sister, and Koya assured me they had made it to family in Brionry.

"And Jos!" she told me. "You won't believe it. He's gone to Reynart to be a soldier. Or a student, at least. He wants to learn, thanks to you. They all do."

That was not all. Two of the Sarists we'd rescued had declined Koya's help and disappeared into the city, including Vorges, the man with the tattooed palm. Koya didn't know what had become of them, and I was relieved. He'd saved my life, but the Greenman he'd injured with magic had not recovered, and that was one offense even peacetime couldn't smooth over. As for Barris, there was ultimately nothing to charge him with, but his involvement with Ferrymen and the murder of his mother had sullied his reputation, at least temporarily.

"So he's sulking in Tratua," Koya said. She was as bright and ebullient as ever reporting this, but somehow it saddened me, like a shadow of her old mask again. With Lord Ragn's death and the end of the war, Koya had lost her purpose and direction. What did she have, now that there was no one for her to save?

One steamy afternoon, Raffin strolled into the bakery as Koya breezed out, and they paused briefly in the doorway together. I couldn't help but notice the way Raffin's eyes followed her as she slipped away toward her lovely boat.

"How is she?" he asked, and I knew he was remembering that night at Cartouche, and probably others, when he'd escorted her home. Even if her debauchery hadn't been entirely real, I knew her gratitude for Raffin's kindness was.

"You should go after her," I suggested. He turned to me, surprised.

"I — no. You think? She won't remember me."

"She might surprise you. You might take the chance to surprise her." I eyed him sideways. "I think she's still hoping to find a candidate to replace Durrel."

He looked startled, and I thought his face colored. "You don't mean —".

I couldn't help grinning. "It would make your father *crazy*."

The startled look turned sly, and Raffin laughed. "You might be onto something, peach. Maybe I should get to know Mistress Koyuz a little better." He kissed my hand, bowing low. "Good day, little sister." Raffin Taradyce, disreputable nob and Greenman, set off after Koya's boat. I watched him wave it down, and drop inside with all the easy grace he possessed.

More weeks went by, until one afternoon somebody slid a note across the bakery's threshold. At Grea's shout, I scooped it up, milk white paper with an amber core, *Celyn Contrare* inked out in a carefully anonymous hand. Inside was nothing but an address.

I threw open the door, but there was no one outside but the chattering neighbors. I felt a tug near my breastbone, like the call of magic, sweet and urgent.

I flagged down a boat, but the riverways were crowded with the renewed commercial traffic and giddy citizenry out celebrating on the water. After a few blocks I gave it up and scrambled off onto the shore. The feeling in my chest was like a knot loosening, and I wanted to run, impatient to get — wherever. Revelers had lit a string of firefly lanterns and strung them across the Oss, where they glowed like full moons against the hot afternoon sky. In the road below the Celystra, I pushed through a crowd of Greenmen trying their confused best to organize a crowd that had become an impromptu festival. Nobody was paying them the slightest mind. One fat merchant cheerfully grabbed his nearest Greenman and thrust a tankard of ale into his hand.

Finally, finally I reached the address on the slip of paper, a grand yellow town house not far from the Spiral, with an open gallery along the top floor and square towers fitted out with ridiculous stone frippery at every corner. I stood in the shadow of one of those towers and peered up, and saw a figure in gray perched easily in an open stone arch, a hand lifted casually in a wave.

Durrel met me at the mouth of the staircase, just inside the rooftop gallery. He grabbed me bodily and spun me round, like we were silly townspeople in the festival below. And I let him. I kind of liked it.

Finally breathless, he let me go. "What do you think?" he said, gesturing toward the empty gallery, with its mosaic tile floor and fretwork ceiling.

"What is it?" I asked, and I didn't care about the architecture. I wanted him to take my hands like he had in the Keep, and let his warm voice wash over me, telling me every detail of his weeks at Favom Court, down to the scratches in the kitchen tables and the muck in the stables.

"I've rented it." He sounded enormously proud, and I stepped back, eyeing the space.

"For what?"

"To live in. I'm not ready to stay in the country full-time. King Wierolf will need his loyal nobility close at hand for a while."

King Wierolf. We'd been hearing it for weeks now, but from Durrel's lips it gave me a funny little thrill in the pit of my stomach. "But what about Charicaux?"

Durrel grew sober. "I sold it," he said. "To cover some of Father's debts. Don't look so sad — Lady Amalle's father was happy to take it off my hands. She'll be able to stay there. It's her home."

"And Favom Court?" I asked.

"We're down a few thousand acres and a couple dozen horses, but we'll survive."

"I'm so sorry."

He gave a half smile, and his hand was still wrapped tightly around mine. "All in a good cause," he said. "I'll make a fresh start for the House of Decath in Gerse." I heard the unsaid words: *a fresh start for myself.*

"By renting an empty attic," I said lightly. "Or did you take the whole building?"

He laughed at the hope in my voice. "No, just this floor. What do you think?"

I looked around. It was lovely on a day like this, with cross breezes tempering the afternoon heat — but it would be ghastly the rest of the year. Durrel led me out to the open gallery overlooking the streets and the river. One side of the building dropped down on the roof next door. "I thought I'd make it easy for my friends to come and go," he said.

"Your *friends*?" I said. "How many are there?"

"Just one that matters." And he curved one hand around the back of my head and bent his face to mine, and all my objections were swallowed in the heat of our kiss.

It was long and low and gentle, and we spent the waning afternoon in each other's arms, curled into the gallery window, as Durrel told me all about his days at Favom Court. It turned out I was wrong about what I wanted; I thought I would *die* of impatience. Finally I could stand it no more, and I stopped his mouth. My lips on his, my fingers sought out the clasps on his doublet, and he shrugged it off, bumping me up against a pillar. I helped his hands find the laces to my bodice, but he pulled away, gasping for breath.

"Wait," he said. "Are you sure?"

I paused in my search for the points to his breeches and tilted my head upward. "Only if you are."

And he answered that by scooping me up and carrying me bodily across the gallery, to where a nest of cushions and coverlets made a makeshift bed.

Afterward, we lay there together until it was full dark, the moons rising up over the water and throwing their light through the open gallery arches. Durrel traced patterns on my back with his finger, as if memorizing my shape by touch.

"You should get some furniture," I said, watching the moonslight track a wide beam across the tile floor, like a shaft of magic.

"I don't know; I've always thought furniture was overrated." His voice was cool and dreamy, his eyes half closed.

"I like it," I said firmly, and then a treacherous thought squirmed its way upward and turned into a giggle.

"What's funny?" Durrel asked, propping himself on his elbow.

"Nothing," I said. "Except that your friend Raffin is prescient. He told me I'd be sharing your bed eventually."

"Well, I hate to gainsay a figure as honorable as Raffin Taradyce," he said solemnly, and gestured to the heap of blankets. "But strictly speaking, this is *not* a bed."

That giggle turned into a full-fledged laugh that echoed off the open stone walls. Finally I peeled myself away from Durrel and fumbled for my smock.

"You're not leaving?" he said.

I smiled. "I have to. Grea's going to be swamped tonight. But I'll come back tomorrow, unless you're busy."

"Doing what?" he asked, but tugged me backward to kiss me again.

I almost *flew* home, after that. It was later than I'd thought; nearly midnight and the roads finally clearing of festival traffic, but I noticed none of it. There was a sweet taste still on my tongue, and I was loath to breathe it away so soon. Back at the bakery I could smell the yeast of the rising loaves, and felt a twinge of guilt for not helping. *Tomorrow*, I told myself. I danced up the dark stairs, my head still lost and buzzing somewhere near the Spiral, thinking about moonlight on bare skin, glinting against a soft beard. Rat was at Hobin's, so the room was dark; he'd pulled the shutters closed before he left.

I entered into a pool of shadow and clicked the door shut behind me — and realized, a breath too late, that I wasn't alone.

A hand came out of the darkness and caught me by the throat, a thin, cool line of steel pressing into my neck. I froze, breath and heart with me, as a low voice murmured, inches from my ear, "Hello again, Mouse."

The chill of the knife at my neck went straight to my bones, but my heart was thumping wildly. I knew that voice, that hand, even in darkness, even after all this time.

"Tegen?"

LEXICON

Acolyte Guard: The Celystra's honor guard; once ceremonial, now King Bardolph's de facto secret police. Universally feared and hated. Called "Greenmen," in slang for their entirely green uniforms.

Astilan of Hanival: Prince of the realm. Commander of Royalist forces. King Bardolph's nephew; cousin to Prince Wierolf.

Bal Marse: Residence of Talth Ceid and Durrel Decath.

Bardolph of Hanival: King of Llyvraneth.

Belprisa: Ship belonging to the Ceid.

Berdal: Sarist soldier. Friend of Digger from Bryn Shaer.

Big Silver river: *Llyd Tsairn* in Llyvrin. One of two major rivers flowing through Gerse.

Briddja Nul: One of the three provinces that make up the nation of Llyvraneth. Briddja Nul occupies much of the northwest, and is home to the port city of Yeris Volbann.

Bryn Shaer: Mountain fortress in northern Llyvraneth. Home to the House of Nemair. *See StarCrossed.*

Cartouche: Private club and theater in Gerse.

Ceid, Barris: Gersin businessman. Son of Talth Ceid; brother of Koya.

Ceid, House of: Powerful gentry-class family in Gerse.

Ceid, Talth: Gersin businesswoman. Wife of Durrel Decath; mother of Barris and Koya. Deceased.

Celys: The great Mother Goddess, goddess of life and the harvest. Her symbols are the ash tree and the full moon.

Celystra: Temple complex in Gerse devoted to Celys. Seat of Celyst worship and power.

Charicaux: Decath family home in Gerse. Residence of Lord Ragn.

Claas: Gersin gentleman. Lover of Stantin Koyuz.

Confessor: An investigator for the Inquisition, trained in the arts of torture.

Contrare, Celyn: Digger's alias.

Corlesanne: Nation to Llyvraneth's east. Allied with the Sarists.

Cwalo, Eptin: Merchant from Yeris Volbann who keeps a home and business in Gerse. Friend and confidant of Digger.

Cwalo, Mirelle: Wife of Eptin.

Decath, Durrel: Young nobleman from Gerse who once saved Digger from Greenmen. Husband of Talth Ceid.

Decath, Lord Ragn: Durrel's father.

Digger: Thief from Gerse.

Eske: High Priestess of Tiboran.

Favom Court: Farm and manor house north of Gerse. Country residence of the House of Decath.

Fei: Confidence artist and sometime thief. Acquaintance of Digger.

Ferrymen: Ruthless human smugglers who typically charge exorbitant fees for their services and have a well-deserved reputation for violence.

Geirt: Former chambermaid of Talth Ceid.

Gelnir: One of the three provinces that make up the nation of Llyvraneth. A fertile region of farmland to the west and south, and home to Llyvraneth's capital city of Gerse.

Gerse: Capital city of Llyvraneth. Digger's home.

Granthin, Halcot: *See* Rat.

Grea: Baker in the Seventh Circle. Digger's landlady. Rat's aunt.

Greenmen: *See* Acolyte Guard.

Grillig: Seventh Circle fence and dealer in secondhand goods. Acquaintance of Digger.

Hanivard Palace: Royal residence in Gerse. Home to King Bardolph.

Hobin, Lord: Nobleman in Gerse. Official in the Ministry of War. Rat's lover.

Inquisition: Dedicated arm of the Celyst church charged with eradicating heresy. Led by a staff of inquisitors (specially ordained priests) under the command of the Lord High Inquisitor, Werne Nebraut. The Inquisition has wide-ranging powers and very little oversight.

Irin: Sarist refugee.

Jos: Sarist refugee.

Karst, Alech: Employee of Talth Ceid.

Keep, the: *Bryn Tsairn* in Llyvrin ("Silver Keep"). Royal prison in Gerse.

Kellespau: One of the three provinces that make up the nation of Llyvraneth. A hilly region covering the northeastern third of the island.

Koya: Gersin socialite. Properly Davinna Koyuz, estranged wife of Stantin Koyuz. Daughter of Talth Ceid; sister of Barris.

Koyuz, Stantin: Wealthy Gersin merchant. Koya's husband.

Lenos: Sarist refugee.

Light of Yraine: Ship belonging to the Ceid.

Llyvraneth: Island nation consisting of three provinces: Gelnir, Briddja Nul, and Kellespau.

Marau: God of the dead and consort to Celys. Twin brother to Sar. His symbol is the crow.

Mend-kaal: God of the hearth, the home, and of labor. Twin brother to Tiboran; son of Celys and Marau. His symbol is the hammer.

Mondeci, Evalia: Courtesan in Tratua. Acquaintance of Durrel. Deceased.

Nameless One, The: Goddess of justice and divine retribution. Daughter of Celys and Marau.

Nebraut, Werne:Lord High Inquisitor. Known as "Werne the Blood-letter." Digger's brother.

Nemair, Merista: Noblewoman and mage serving in Prince Wierolf's army. Cousin of Durrel Decath. *See StarCrossed.*

Oss, River: One of two major rivers flowing through Gerse.

Ponvi: Ship belonging to the Ceid.

Rat: Digger's roommate.

Reynart, Tnor: A Sarist mage. Commander of Prince Wierolf's magical army.

Sar: Goddess of magic and dreams. Twin sister to Marau. Her symbol is the seven-pointed star.

Sarist: Term used to denote magic users and/or worshippers of Sar. Also a supporter of Prince Wierolf's rebellion against King Bardolph. Not all Sarists are magical, but it is widely believed that everyone with magic must be a Sarist. In general, Sarists support a legalization of magic.

Seventh Circle: Poor district in Gerse. Digger's neighborhood.

Silver: *Tsairn* in Llyvrin. An elemental metal that cloaks magic.

Talanca: Nation to Llyvraneth's south.

Taradyce, Raffin: Acolyte Guardsman. Nobleman from Gerse. Best friend of Durrel Decath.

Tegen: Thief in Gerse; victim of the Inquisition. Formerly Digger's partner and lover. *See StarCrossed.*

Teina: Sarist refugee.

Temple, the: Tavern, inn, and theater serving as the center of worship for Tiboran in Gerse.

Temus: Prisoner in the Keep.

Tiboran: God of wine and theater. Twin brother to Mend-kaal. His symbol is the mask, and he has been adopted as a patron by those who must lie for a living, most notably thieves.

Tincture of the Moon of Marau: Poison used to kill Talth Ceid.

Tratua: Port city on Llyvraneth's southeast coast.

Varenzia: Nation bordering Corlesanne. Allied with Sarists.

Vorges: Sarist refugee.

Watch, the: Gerse's municipal police force. Divided into shifts (Day Watch and Night Watch).

Werne: *See* Nebraut, Werne.

Wierolf of Hanival: Prince of the realm. Commander of Sarist forces. King Bardolph's nephew; cousin to Prince Astilan.

Yeris Volbann: Port city on Llyvraneth's northwest coast.

Zet: Goddess of war and the hunt. Her symbol is the arrow. Patron of the nobility.

WARRANT OF ACKNOWLEDGMENTS

The following persons are wanted on suspicion of aiding and abetting the author in the perpetration of this novel: Chris Bunce, Erin Murphy, Cheryl Klein, Barbara Stuber, Laura Manivong, Rebecca Barnhouse, Susan Jeffers Casel, Phil Falco, Juliana Kolesova, Mike Schley, Colleen Johnston, and Jill Walker. Additional suspects have been implicated but their identities remain unconfirmed. The public is advised that the above-named conspirators are extremely crafty, cunning, and resourceful, and should only be approached with due caution.

This book was edited by Cheryl Klein and designed by Phil Falco. The text was set in Alisal, a typeface designed by Matthew Carter in 2001. The display type was set in Angelo. The book was printed and bound at R. R. Donnelley in Crawfordsville, Indiana. The production was supervised by Cheryl Weisman. The manufacturing was supervised by Adam Cruz.